Dancing Over the Hill

Cathy lives in Bath with her husband and three cats. In her spare time, she is happiest digging, planting or reading in the garden or on a walk with friends in the local countryside – usually ending in a pub. For more about Cathy, find her on Twitter @CathyHopkins1 or Facebook/CathyHopkinsAuthor or on her website www.cathyhopkins.com.

Also by Cathy Hopkins

The Kicking the Bucket List

Dancing Over the Hill

CATHY HOPKINS

HarperCollins*Publishers*

This novel is entirely a work of fiction.
The names, characters and incidents portrayed in it are
the work of the author's imagination. Any resemblance to
actual persons, living or dead, events or localities is
entirely coincidental.

HarperCollins*Publishers*
The News Building,
1 London Bridge Street,
London SE1 9GF

2

www.harpercollins.co.uk

First published by HarperCollins*Publishers* 2018

A catalogue record for this book
is available from the British Library

ISBN: 978-0-00-820209-5

Typeset in Birka by Palimpsest Book Production Ltd, Falkirk, Stirlingshire

Printed and bound by CPI Group (UK) Ltd, Croydon CR0 4YY

MIX
Paper from
responsible sources
FSC™ C007454

Grow old along with me!
The best is yet to be.

Robert Browning (1812–89)

Cait

Friday night (thirty years ago):

Our passion spent, we lay back on the grass, satiated, our limbs entwined, the sun shining down on our naked bodies. It was one of those times, I would remember and cherish forever.

After a few moments, we sat up and surveyed the valley below and fields stretching out in front of us.

Matt turned to look at me. 'Forever,' he said as he looked deeply into my eyes.

'For—waaargh! Ants!' I cried as I leapt up and began to brush the invaders off my legs.

'And . . . Cait, get dressed! *Fast*. We have to leg it *now*!' said Matt as he pointed to the bottom of the hill where two walkers could be seen advancing up the lane towards us.

'No!' I grabbed my dress from where it had been thrown over a fence and dived into it as Matt jumped up and began to scramble into his jeans. Stumbling and laughing, we ran off before the intruders spotted us and realized what we'd been up to.

*

Friday night (now):

'Fancy an early night?' I asked. I knew he'd get the subtext, we'd been married long enough not to have to spell it out; plus 'have sex' had been on my to-do list for weeks.

'We could, or . . .' Matt replied.

'Or what?'

'Glass of wine and a box set?'

'What have you got?'

'Latest series of *Game of Thrones*.'

'No brainer. I'll get the glasses, you open the bottle.'

1

A year later: Cait

- Items mislaid:
  1) Reading glasses.
  2) Book (it *was* by the bed).
  3) Bottle of Ginkgo biloba (it's supposed to improve memory but I can't remember where I put that either).
  4) Mobile phone.
- Chin hairs plucked: 4

'Matt, *Matt*. Are you OK? *Matt*.'

No response. I'd just got home from work to find Matt, stretched out and snoring softly on the sofa in the sitting room. He'd taken off his suit jacket, tie and shoes and cast them onto the nearest chair. An empty bottle of red wine and glass were on the coffee table in front of him, together with an open dictionary. Something must have happened. Matt was never here on a weekday, he was in Bristol, working, usually back on the train which got in around 8.30 p.m. He wasn't a big drinker, either.

Maybe I shouldn't wake him, I thought. Should leave him to sleep it off. But . . . he's never home in the day. What's happened? I gave him a gentle shove, then a more persistent one, but he was dead to the world. I checked he was still breathing. He'd been snoring a moment ago – of course he was.

Reassured that Matt was still in the land of the living, I tiptoed out and into the kitchen to search for my mobile to see if it offered any clues. I'd forgotten to take it out with me, so didn't know if he'd been trying to reach me. I found the phone in the fruit bowl and turned it on to see if there were any messages. There were four missed calls and one text. All from Matt. The text said: *When r u back? Need 2 talk.*

Two minutes later, the doorbell rang. I opened the door to my two closest friends, Lorna and Debs. They had said they'd drop in on their way back from a trip to the garden centre.

'Spring flowers,' said Debs, and handed me a bunch of white tulips.

'Thanks, but shh, Matt's home, asleep on the sofa,' I said as I ushered them through the hall and into the kitchen diner, where I shut the door after them. They made an odd pair. Debs, a curvaceous bohemian, forty-seven years old, with a mop of dark hair piled on top of her head and kept in place with a chopstick, was wearing a kingfisher blue silk top, green harem trousers and a big emerald amulet fit for an Egyptian high priestess. Although British born and bred, with her olive skin and brown eyes she looked Spanish, a throwback to her Andalusian great-grandmother, she'd told us. Next to her, Lorna was small and slim, in her fifties, and was in jeans and a blue shirt, rolled up at the sleeves, her silver-white hair cut neatly to her shoulders. I was the oldest of the three of us, but often felt like the youngest, a twenty year old trapped in an old body. Matt called my friends the S and S, the silly and the sensible, Debs being the first, Lorna the latter; he said that each of them represented a different side of my nature. 'There's more to me than that,' I'd told him. 'I have many sides – I'm multifaceted, like a diamond.' He'd laughed. Cheek.

'Matt? What's going on?' asked Debs, and was about to go barging in to see him but I pulled her back.

'I don't know, but he's clearly had a skinful. Best leave him for now.'

'Not like him,' said Lorna as she settled on a stool at the island.

'Why don't you wake him?' asked Debs. 'Find out?'

'I thought I'd let him sleep whatever it is off first.'

'Wise,' said Lorna and stood up. 'Should we go?'

'I . . . maybe. In case . . . I don't know, something's clearly happened and, until I know what, I don't . . . Probably best you're not here to see him in whatever state he wakes up in.'

'No clues at all?' asked Debs.

'No, apart from a dictionary on the table. He must have been working on something.' He always had his nose in a book, researching something or other for his job as a TV programme developer.

Lorna handed me a pot; in it was a wild geranium, its white flowers tinged with the faintest pink blush. 'It's a Kashmir White. If you like it, we can get more,' she said as she headed for the front door, where she pulled out a leaflet and handed it to me. 'And this lists the gardening classes on locally. We could go together, but we can talk about that another time. Come on, Debs. Call us if you need.'

'Call us anyway,' said Debs.

'I will,' I said, and saw them back out. I was sorry to see them go. I'd been looking forward to an hour catching up with them with a bottle of rosé on the decking outside in the warm May sunshine, plus Lorna had promised to help me make a start on the long overdue task of designing the garden borders. 'And thanks for the plant, Lorna. It's lovely.'

Lorna stepped forward and hugged me. 'Keep calm and carry on, as they say.'

'Ditto,' said Debs, and hugged me as well.

After they'd gone, I went back to the kitchen and put the kettle on. My mind had gone into overdrive. What'd happened? *Need 2 talk?* That wasn't like Matt. Over the years, he'd become Mr Incommunicado. He never *needed* to talk, unless it was to discuss what to get from the farmers' market for Sunday lunch, or to ensure I recorded some history or sci-fi programme for him while he was out.

I glanced at our wedding photo on the dresser. Thirty years ago. Matt, handsome in his wedding suit, was smiling at the camera, his brown hair worn longer back then. Although padded out around the middle now, with grey flecks through his hair, he looked younger than his sixty-three years. Beside him in the photo frame, I was two sizes smaller, my hair long and chestnut brown, worn straight and loose, and topped with a wreath of white gypsophila to complement a medieval-style ivory velvet dress. I'd wanted to look like one of the Pre-Raphaelite heroines; I was such a romantic back then. My bridesmaids, Angie and Eve, stood to my right. Both were in pale mint velvet: Eve, a waif with long Titian hair; Angie not much taller. She had short dark hair and looked uncomfortable in her dress, much preferring jeans and a T-shirt to anything remotely girlie. So much had changed, of course it had. My hair was now three shades of blonde and shoulder-length, and I was no longer a size ten. Angie had moved to New Zealand over twenty years ago and Eve was dead. I missed both of them sorely. And Matt and I . . . We looked so happy in the photograph: in love, full of hope for the future. It had been a great wedding, a sunny day in a picturesque church in Dorset, then sausage and mash at the local pub with close friends and family, followed by a honeymoon exploring the Cornish coast. We hadn't had the money for exotic locations – not that we minded. We'd set off in Matt's Golf convertible, top down all the way, stayed at B & B's along the route, eaten chips on windy beaches, stuffed ourselves with cream teas in roadside cafés and relished every minute of it.

At what point had we given up on each other and settled for what we had now? A relationship where we muddled along, taking each other for granted and barely communicating beyond the mundane everyday necessities of what we were going to eat, who was picking up the dry cleaning or going to plant the spring bulbs. Was it after our two boys, Sam and Jed, had left home? Or later? A slow fading-away of passion, to the comfortable stagnancy of familiarity and death of desire. Although we'd been together a long time, ridden the rollercoaster of marriage with good and bad times, more recently we'd become like lodgers sharing the same house. We had two TVs (one in the living room, one in the bedroom), we had two bathrooms, two cars, and occasionally slept in separate beds because sometimes Matt snored like a bear with a blocked nose.

I glanced at the booklet Lorna had left me. Gardening classes – they would be good, but when would I fit them in? I found a piece of paper and pen and began to outline my week to see if I could find a space.

Monday
Day: Receptionist job at the local doctor's (temporary). I am really a global, bestselling children's author (undiscovered due to the fact I haven't finished a book yet).
Evening: writing class (learning how to be global, bestselling author and how to get published).

Tuesday
Day: Writing. Yoga class.
Evening: Film club or book club (alternate weeks).

Wednesday
Day: Receptionist job again.
Evening: Choir.

Thursday
Day: Receptionist job.
Evening: Supper with friends Debs and Lorna or Zumba.

Friday
Day: Supermarket shop. Writing my bestselling children's novel. (*Hah, that's a joke,* I thought. So far I have several abandoned attempts in a drawer in the desk in my

study, and have written Chapter One of a new book on my laptop. I mean the words, Chapter One, not the actual chapter one with sentences and the beginning of a plot line and all.)

Evening: Pilates then drink with the group.

Saturday
Household chores. Walk with walking group.

Sunday
Day: Visit Dad in Chippenham.
Evening: New Age therapy course with Debs (i.e., couple of hours of clearing chakras, waving crystals and acting like a pair of lunatics).

No space for gardening classes unless I let something go, I thought. Not wanting to disturb Matt, I began to outline his week too.

Monday–Friday: Work 8 a.m.–8.30 p.m.
Evenings: Home. Occasionally has a work-related dinner; otherwise home for supper and he watches the news, history channel, sci-fi or a war film.

Saturday
Day: Chores. Sometimes watches the rugby or football.
Evening: Sometimes pub with brother Duncan.

Sunday
Reads the papers, front to back. Catches up on emails and work. Dozes in front of the TV.

Hmm. I know what anyone reading this would conclude, I thought as I compared our weeks. Here is a couple who don't spend a lot of time together. Exactly. We don't. We co-exist. Not that we don't spend some evenings with each other, of course we do. That's when we watch box sets or whatever's new on Netflix. We'd worked our way through *The West Wing*, *The Wire*, *The Sopranos*, *Orange Is the New Black*, *Boardwalk Empire*, *Mad Men* and many more. We were polite to each other, kind even, but we don't talk much beyond everyday necessities, not any more, not to each other. Who needs to talk when there's a new series of *House of Cards* to watch? Our arrangement had worked, but lately I'd been wondering: was it enough?

I'm having an existential crisis, I thought. My friends, Debs and Lorna would say: Not again, Cait. You had one of those last year, and the year before, but this is different because of a few major things that have happened.

My mum died a year ago.

My oldest and best friend, Eve, died eight months ago.

Lorna's husband, Alistair, died last year, a few weeks before Eve.

My youngest son, Jed, moved to Thailand.

My eldest son, Sam, moved to LA with his wife and my grandchildren.

All of this has made me very sad and has reminded me that no one knows what's round the next corner, so I've taken the 'seize the day' attitude. I've been trying to make the most of life by filling my days with things to do, people to see, places to go. If I keep busy, busy, busy, I don't have to think about loss and I can get by. However, the recent events have made me question many aspects of my life and my relationship.

Is this it?

Should I accept that my marriage has gone stale and carry on as we are?

What could change things?

Do I want to change things?

How would I change things?

Should I get some Wonderbrow paste to dye my grey eyebrows?

As I said, all existential stuff.

With those happy thoughts, I made tea and wondered again what Matt had to tell me. I mentally made a list of possibilities.

- An affair?
- He was ill?
- Someone had died?

I liked a list. Some women of my age are ladies who lunch. I am a lady who lists. It's just the way my brain works, it makes an inventory of everything; lists always make me feel calmer. Debs said that's because my star sign is Virgo and they like things to be ordered and in the right place. She also said I had Aquarius rising, which was at odds with the Virgo part and accounted for my slightly eccentric and split personality and tendency to surprise people by doing or saying something out of the blue.

When I was younger, my lists looked like this:

- Look for God.
- Find a way to change the world for the better and bring about world peace.

- Find my soul mate.
- Live happily ever after.

Now the lists looked like this:

- Check blood pressure.
- Buy supplement for arthritis.
- Google best anti-wrinkle cream.
- Buy over-the-counter sleep remedies.

2

Cait

After half an hour, I fetched my laptop from the top floor and went into Facebook for my daily fix of animal rescue clips. There was one of a baby orang-utan playing with a monkey. Cute. Orang-utans are my favourite animal. Now . . . what else had people posted that was essential viewing and part of life's rich tapestry? I'd just opened footage of a bunch of Yorkshire men singing 'Mi chip pan's on fire', when I heard a groan from the sitting room. I was about to close the page when I noticed a new friend request from a Tom Lewis.

'Cait, are you back?' I heard Matt call.

Tom Lewis. The *Tom Lewis? It couldn't be*, I thought, as I abandoned the laptop and went through to the sitting room. I used to know someone of that name, but it couldn't be him, surely? I hadn't heard from him in over forty years. He had been the love of my life many, many moons ago. No. Couldn't be him. Probably some random request. I got a number of those from men, mainly in the military, I didn't know. Everyone on Facebook did. Spam. Couldn't be my Tom Lewis. Either way, I'd have a proper look later.

Matt opened his eyes, usually conker brown and focused, now red and blurry. 'Ah, there you are.' He smiled at me. On the rare occasions that Matt drank too much, he was a nice drunk – affectionate and sleepy, no trouble.

'So what's happened?' I asked.

He looked over at the dictionary. 'Was looking up words.'

'Words?'

He reached over, picked up the book and read from a page. 'Redundant – no longer needed or useful, superfluous. Retirement – to recede or disappear into seclusion. I *am* sorry, Caitlin.'

Ah. So that was it. 'Seriously?' I asked.

He nodded. 'Seriously as in not funny.'

With that, he lay back, closed his eyes and nodded off again. I noticed that his left sock had a hole in it and his big toe was poking through. He was usually so perfectly turned out in his spotless shirts and well-cut suits for work, and this vulnerability endeared him to me.

I need a drink too, I thought.

I went back into the kitchen and found a bottle of Pinot Grigio in the fridge as the implications hit me. I opened the French doors and went to sit on the bench in the sunshine on the decking outside. I got out my mobile and called Lorna.

'Matt's been made redundant.'

'Shit.'

'Exactly.'

'Will he get a pay-off?'

'Maybe but it won't be much. He was there as a freelancer

though he'd been with the same company for a long time. He's still out for the count so I don't know the details yet.'

'Is it definite?'

'Think so. Hell, Lorna, how are we going to get by? We don't have savings, or any cushion money, in fact.'

'Don't panic,' said Lorna. 'At least you have your job at the surgery.'

'Only until Margaret Wilson is back from her maternity leave.'

'What about your writing?'

I laughed. Despite time spent at my laptop, my ideas were sparse. 'Nothing happening at the moment.'

'You need to get an agent.'

'I need to get a good idea first, and getting an agent is as difficult as getting a publisher.'

'Something will come.'

'Maybe. Hope so.'

'In the meantime, at least you're earning something.'

'I guess.' My job didn't pay a lot. Matt and I had an agreement. I paid for the fun stuff. I earned enough to keep us in wine, the occasional meal out, and holidays once a year – and those to Devon or Cornwall, nowhere too expensive. Matt paid for the boring stuff – gas, mortgage, electric, phone, car, insurance. In short, he was the breadwinner.

'He could always look for another job,' said Lorna.

'Maybe, but will he be able to get one at his age? It may be time to sell the house.' It had always been on the cards that we might have to sell up one day, in order to release money for our non-existent pension pot because, like so many of my generation, we didn't think we'd get old. 'Matt didn't just say redundant. He used the word retirement too.'

'Big change for you both,' said Lorna.

'Wasn't part of the plan just yet.'

'Never is. Sometimes we chart the course of our lives internally with our choices, decisions and plans for the future, and think we're in control. Sometimes change comes from unforeseen and unexpected external forces, and we realize that we're not in control at all. Sounds like today is one of those days and you have no choice but to go with it.'

I got the feeling she was talking about Alistair's short illness, as much as what had happened to Matt. Her husband had died last year of pancreatic cancer, eight weeks after he got the diagnosis. 'So what should I do?'

'Stay calm. Have a glass of wine. See how things unfold. Not all change is bad.'

'We'll see.'

'Call if you need to.'

'Will do.'

After she'd hung up, I began to think how this change might affect us. Losing his job meant Matt would probably be at home all day. How would that be?

We had our lives worked out perfectly to avoid each other, without actually admitting that was what we were doing. When he got in from work late in the evening, I gave him space and let him retreat into his cave (as advised in the book, *Men Are from Mars, Women Are from Venus*). If I wasn't out at one of my classes, I'd have a brief chat when he got home, and then I usually went up to bed to read. He came up around twelve when I was asleep and, if I wasn't, I pretended to be. He got up early and was gone by the time I rose in the morning, and so it went on until the weekend. I hardly knew what went on his head any more, nor he in mine, but this never troubled us because we were both so busy living our separate lives that we had never had to confront the fact we'd grown apart.

Will we need to sell the house if he can't find other work? I asked myself. *Probably.* I liked our home. It was a five-bedroom semi-detached Edwardian in a quiet tree-lined street in Bath, with a south-facing, level garden at the back – hard to find because so much of the city is built on hills, so most gardens are sloped or terraced. We'd moved here over fifteen years ago after a weekend trip when we'd fallen in love with the area with its Georgian architecture, crescents and houses built with honey-coloured stone. We could walk into town in five minutes and be in the countryside in ten. I looked around at the wooden floors, which were scuffed and in need of sanding, and the magnolia walls, which I noted were overdue a lick of paint. I didn't mind. It had a cosy, lived-in feel from when the boys were teenagers with a hundred interests and hobbies, hence shelves and cupboards in every room that were full of books, DVDs, games and sports equipment. I'd even found a snorkel and pair of flippers the other day, under the bed in Jed's old room.

The house was too big for just the two of us now, but I loved having the extra space, even though the whole place needed a clear-out to really take advantage of it.

Although Jed had moved out when he went to university, he had still come back from time to time, and had only gone properly when he'd moved to Thailand over a year ago. I know other mothers who mourned when their kids finally left home, empty-nesters, and I did go through some of that when they disappeared. For a while the house seemed so empty and silent, but in time I found it liberating. I'd paid my dues; had the house full of noisy boys, sleepovers, cooking endless meals, laundry, ironing, never being able to get near the TV remote, shelling out money for all sorts, not being able to sleep until I knew they were home, safe and in their beds. Of course I missed them, but not their mess and the worry when they were out late. Now I had peace and quiet, two rooms to spare for storage, food in the fridge that didn't get eaten within twenty-four hours of being bought, time for my friends, and beds down the corridor to go to if Matt was snoring. I went to my part-time job and worked on book ideas with no pressure. It hadn't mattered that I wasn't a high earner. Hadn't mattered. It would now.

A text came through from Debs. *Everything OK?*

I texted back. *Matt's lost his job. Details l8r when I get them.*

Debs texted back. *Take Star of Bethlehem flower remedy for shock, both of you. Want me to send some over?*

She had an alternative cure for all ills and, over the years, I'd been given all sorts of concoctions to apply or ingest, though I quite liked the flower remedies, probably because they came in brandy.

She texted again a moment later. *We'll sort it this evening. Will have to take a rain check. Want to see how Matt is.*

We had a supper night when we could all make it. It was our private counselling session. Debs had suggested it last year as an excuse to get together, and she'd made up rules. We took turns in choosing where to go. It had to be somewhere we hadn't been before. We put our troubles on the table and offered each other support and advice. It had been a life-saver, an evening to laugh, cry, try out a new place and air any problems. *I'm not sure I'll be able to afford supper nights for a while*, I thought as I decided to opt for Lorna's advice, poured myself a second glass of wine and wrote a list of things to do.

- Check out local house values on Rightmove.
- Check out properties for sale in areas we could afford.
- Stop worrying. It's only stuff.

Cue the mini princess from *Frozen* singing 'Let It Go, Let It Go' in my head. Cue visualization of smashing her in the face with a frying pan.

3

Cait

- Chin hairs plucked: 1
- Nose hairs trimmed: 3
- Items lost: my space

3 a.m. Bedroom. Yoda, our cat, decided he needed to declare his undying love. He's a honey-coloured Persian chinchilla, named because he resembles Yoda from the *Star Wars* movie, only furrier. He jumped on the bed, onto my chest and began kneading and purring loudly. I got out of bed and put him outside the door.

3.05 a.m. Banshee howling loud enough to wake the dead. Desperate scratching at the door. Not a spirit from beyond the grave, it was Yoda again. Got up and let him back in.

3.10 a.m. After more chest-kneading, Yoda wrapped himself around my head and fell asleep, but my mind was wide awake, thinking about our future. It had been almost ten days since Matt lost his job. What if we ran out of money? Should we sell the house? Stay? Should Matt try and find another job? What? Anything? Should I try to go back into teaching? It paid better than the temporary part-time jobs I'd been doing for the last five years.

Dad. He's lonely. Care home? Not necessary. He doesn't need care, just company. Maybe he'd consider sheltered accommodation for that. He wouldn't be alone there. Maybe he'd like Yoda.

4.07 a.m. Matt was snoring away.

I gave him a nudge and he obediently turned over, and after five minutes resumed his snoring.

Nudged him again.

Finally started drifting off to sleep when Matt did one of his spectacular snort-snores. Very loud. Almost leapt out of my skin. Nudged him and he turned over and continued snoring softly.

Debated whether to thump him in the kidneys, suffocate him with a pillow or nudge him again. Grrr.

Got up and climbed into the bed in the spare room. Peace at last, but sleep still escaped me as it has done for the past year or so.

Finally dozed off. Zzzzz.

5 a.m. Yoda found me. He patted my cheek gently with his paw. I ignored him. More gentle patting, which I ignored.

5.05 a.m. Yoda inserted a claw into my nostril and pulled. Ow! That hurt. *Wide* awake now. Where has he learnt to *do* that? Do cats come with a built-in manual of instructions on how to wake your owner? Advanced technique no. 3: locate hole in middle of human's face. Flick out claw. Insert into hole and pull.

5.10 a.m. Got out of bed, went downstairs and fed Yoda, who was now purring like an old bus. Back to bed in spare room. Can hear Matt still sleeping and snoring in our bedroom. Grrr.

6 a.m. Finally drifted off. Zzz.

8 a.m. Matt came into the room and nudged me awake. 'Cup of tea, Cait?'

I turned over and opened my eyes. 'Uh. No. I'm fine, thanks. I'll get one when I'm up.'

He put a mug on the bedside cabinet. 'Made you one anyway.'

8.05 a.m. Drifting back off to sleep, just for another half-hour . . .

Matt came back into the room. 'I've fed Yoda so you don't need to.'

'Mmm. Right. Thanks.'

'Are you getting up?'

'No. Yes. Didn't sleep too well. You were snoring.'

'Sorry. You should have nudged me.'

Kitchen. 9 a.m. 'What shall we have for breakfast?' asked Matt. He was still in his blue towelling dressing gown.

'*We?* Uh. Oh. Right. I don't usually have much in the week. I usually just grabbed something quick after you'd gone to work. A Nutribullet or something.'

'Oh. What's in that then?'

'Kale, seeds, fruit.'

Matt pulled a face. 'OK. I'll fix my own.'

He seemed miffed.

10 a.m. Top floor. Study. Stared at screen which was blank apart from two words. New ideas.

Clicked on Facebook. Watched a clip of a panda with no eyes that is befriended by a puppy. Aw.

Must start work, but I see someone's posted a clip of a

baby elephant playing in the sea for the first time. Crucial viewing I'd say.

Stared out of the window at the fields at the back of the house. It's misty out there.

Back to blank screen.

Matt, still in his dressing gown, popped his head round the door. 'Cup of coffee, Caitlin?'

'No thanks.'

'Did I hear the phone go earlier?'

'Yes.'

'Who was it?'

'Dad.'

Matt came in and settled himself on the chair opposite my desk. 'What did he have to say?'

'Nothing much.'

'He must have said something.'

'Usual stuff. How my brother's doing. How his dentist appointment went. He's lonely, I think.'

'How is your brother?'

'Fine.'

'What are you doing?'

'Trying to work.'

Matt got up. 'Sorry. I can see I'm interrupting you.'

He seemed miffed.

10.30 a.m. Sent email to my friend Lizzie, a retired literary agent in London, asking her to call.

Post arrived. I went downstairs to pick it up.

Into kitchen to open post. Matt was sitting on a stool at the island.

'What's that?' he asked.

'Post.'

He got up and hovered behind my shoulder. 'Aren't you going to open it?

'Well yes, but it's addressed to me.'

'Since when has your mail been private?'

'It's not. Junk mail,' I said as I opened the first envelope. 'See, nothing important.'

Matt looked out of the French doors to the garden. He seemed miffed.

10.45 a.m. Matt appeared at the study door.

'Anyone call for me? I thought I heard the phone go.'

'Dad again. He forgot to tell me to listen to something on the radio.'

'Oh. What was that?'

'Some programme about children's writers.'

'Anything else in the mail?'

I picked it out of the bin and handed it to him. 'Here. Only catalogues we don't really want. You can take them if you like.'

He did.

He seemed miffed.

11 a.m. Bathroom. 'Caitlin, where are you?' Matt called.

'On the loo.'

I heard footsteps in the corridor. 'Where do you keep the Sellotape?'

'Desk drawer in my study, second one down.'

'Righto.'

11.15 a.m. Hall. Matt appeared on the stairs, *still* in his dressing gown. 'Where are you going?'

'Out.'

'I can see that. Where?'

'Supermarket.'

'What are you looking for?'

'Car keys. Have you seen them?

'No. What time will you be back?'

'Not sure. I might go for coffee afterwards.'

'Oh. Who with?'

'Matt, when have you ever taken an interest in who I go for coffee with? And when are you going to get dressed?'

'No need to be prickly.'

'Sorry. Sorry. I'm going for coffee with Carol from my yoga class.'

'Do I know her?'

'No. She's new to the group.'

'What time will you be back?'

'About one.'

1 p.m. Home. Hall. 'How was the supermarket?' asked Matt. He'd dressed but not shaved.

'Same as ever.'

'Good. Good. So. What's for lunch?'

'Lunch? I . . .'

Matt sighed. 'I get it. You just grab something quick. Don't worry. I'll fix myself something.'

He seemed miffed.

2 p.m. Study. 'Who was that on the phone?' asked Matt from the corridor.

'Lizzie.'

'Anything interesting to say?'

'Not really. Just chatting over whether I'd got any new ideas. She promised she'd look over anything I write.'

'And have you got new ideas?'

'No. That's what I'm trying to do now, so that Lizzie and I have something to discuss next time I see her.'

'Right. OK. I'll let you get on.'

Back to new ideas, but first a quick look at Facebook. Oo. Someone had posted a new clip demonstrating The Art of Mongolian Flute Singing. Felt compelling need to watch all four minutes of it.

4 p.m. Study. Deleted all the rubbish I'd written after the words 'New Ideas'.

Opened new page. Wrote 'Options'.

- Write brilliant, mind-blowing and original children's book.
- Sell our house, downsize, have some money in the bank.

It's a no-brainer. Called two estate agents to come and value the house.

'Want a cup of tea?' Matt called up the stairs.

'Sure, but I'll make it. I need a break.'

I went down into the kitchen, where Matt had parked himself again, on the stool at the island, looking at his laptop. I put the kettle on. He got off the stool and came up behind me and reached into the bread bin.

I stepped back as he stepped forward.

'Oops, sorry,' we both said.

I found the teabags, then moved cups onto the island at the same time he opened the fridge door, which banged my knee. We stepped into each other again. 'Oops, sorry.'

I reached into the bread bin and got out crackers.

'Oh, what are you having?' he asked.

'Snack. Bit of cheese on a cracker.'

'Make me one, will you?'

'What do you want on it?'

He sighed. 'I'm getting in your way, aren't I?'

'No, not at all,' I lied.

5 p.m. Bathroom. I could hear shuffling outside the door. 'Where are you?' called Matt.

'Loo. What do you want?'

'What's for supper?'

'Supper? Oh, I hadn't thought about it yet. Sea bass, green beans OK?'

'We had fish last night.'

'Can we talk about this when I'm out of the bathroom?'

'Oh. Course.'

I finished what I was doing then opened the door. Matt was leaning against the wall.

'OK. Supper,' I said. 'Tell me what you want. I tended to eat light in the week when you were away. Something healthy.'

'Light? OK. No, don't bother about me then. I'll see what's there and sort myself out.'

5.45 p.m. Bathroom. 'Caitlin, are you in there again?'

'*Yes*. I'm having a shower.'

'I've just found a good website about downsizing. I'll send you the link.'

'Right. OK. Thanks.' A minute later. 'Are you still out there Matt?'

'Erm yes, just—'

'*Go* away.'

6 p.m. Bedroom. 'Cait?'

'Yes.'

'What are you doing?'

'My mindfulness exercises. Ten minutes. Just give me ten minutes.'

'Right. Just I can't find the frying pan.'

'It's where it always is. Left cupboard by the sink.'

'Right.'

And breathe in, one two three. Out one two three. Let go of tension. Stop grinding teeth.

6.10 p.m. Sitting room. *Must make an effort, it can't be easy for him*, I thought as I went and sat on the chair opposite Matt, who was stretched out on the sofa watching the TV.

'How's your day been?' I asked.

He shrugged a shoulder. 'Fine.'

'Maybe we could have a chat about what we're going to do, you know, finances; maybe do a budget.'

Matt sighed. 'Can we do it another time?'

'Sure. You OK? You know I'm here if you want to talk about what happened.'

'Happened when?'

'You lost your job.'

'Do I want to talk about it? Relive it? Let me think. No. No, I don't. Erm . . .' He glanced over at the TV. 'Just want to catch the news.'

'News. Right. Of course. OK. Good. And, just to let you know, I'll probably be going to the loo in another half-hour. Just so you know where I am.'

He gave me a puzzled look.

I felt miffed.

8.00 p.m. Opened my laptop to look for emails. None.

Quick look on Facebook to see if there are any new compelling clips that I must watch as part of my essential education on life and all its aspects.

'Want to know who you were in a past life?' *Well, yes, I think I do, Mr Facebook*. Did the questionnaire. Ah. Apparently I was a Turkish fortune-teller in the fifteenth century. Well, I never saw that coming. Must tell Debs. She'll believe it.

I was about to exit Facebook to go down to prepare supper when I remembered that I'd had a friend request from a Tom Lewis. In all the drama of Matt losing his job and me adjusting to being followed around the house, I'd forgotten about it.

I noted that whoever this Tom Lewis was, he'd also sent a private message. *Hmm, the spam requests don't usually do that*, I thought, my curiosity aroused as I clicked to see what I'd been sent.

'Hey Caitlin. Found you! Would love to see you, remember old times, plot new times and check we're both still on track re. our promise to never give in and grow old, to always seek adventure and take the road less travelled. Never forget, you were always one of the cool ones. Tom X'

I clicked his profile photo up. *Christ! It is. TOM Lewis. THE Tom Lewis.*

Cue violins, time slowing down, a flock of white doves being released into the air, rose petals falling from the sky. TOM LEWIS. I took a deep breath and reread the message, then reread it again. He'd gone abroad. I thought we'd lost each other forever, but there he was in the photo on my laptop screen, older, still handsome as hell, still got his hair though no longer black, still capable of making my post-menopausal heart skip a beat.

I remembered the first time I saw him. I was twenty years old, in my second year at university in Manchester, and he was post grad at the art college. Ours was the love and peace generation. John Lennon had released 'Imagine'. Joni Mitchell's version of 'Woodstock' played on the radio. I knew all the words by heart. The Pyramid Stage was built at Glastonbury. There was a rush of gurus to choose from: Bhagwan Shree Rajneesh, the Maharishi, Sathya Sai Baba, Sri Chinmoy, Ram Dass – to name but a handful. Friends in the know swapped their cornflakes for muesli, potatoes for brown rice; green was a buzzword. My head was full of dreams: we were going to change the world and I was going to be a part of it.

I'd heard of Tom's bad-boy reputation and the trail of broken hearts, though I'd never met him. One night, Eve and I had gone to see a band at a pub in town, a place where all the students went. I knew as soon as I saw him that it was him. In a time when the other men we encountered were about as sexy as an Old English sheepdog, with their open-toed sandals, duffel coats and pale, hairy legs, Tom stood out a mile. He was leaning against the bar, elbows back on the counter, his body turned to the room, hips slightly thrust out. He was wearing cowboy boots, Levis, a leather aviator jacket. His mane of shaggy dark hair reached to his shoulders, and those crinkly eyes, navy blue, surveyed the territory with that look he always had back then, as though he knew more than the rest of us and the whole world amused him. I was coming down the stairs and could feel him watching me. I descended slowly, my hand on the banister, trying to appear cool, not looking at him, missed the bottom step and landed in a heap. He had come over to help me to my feet, asked if I was OK. I'd nodded, said I liked to make an entrance and he laughed, so easily. I could always make him laugh.

I felt a rush as I looked at his photo on my computer screen and remembered afternoons and nights we'd spent on his mattress on the floor in his room at his digs. I even remembered the bedspread; it was from India and had a green and red paisley pattern. We'd spent a lot of time on it or under it, a whole week just after we met, locked away in a fusion of lust. There was a poster of Che Guevara on the wall, the scent of patchouli oil and sandalwood joss sticks in the air, the sound of Crosby, Stills & Nash on the record player. He used to play their track, 'Guinnevere', over and over to me, the one where they sing about her green eyes. I had green eyes. Still have them. He said they were beautiful, that I was beautiful. I was his lady with my long hair, ankle-length dresses and velvet cape.

We prided ourselves on being open-minded about other cultures and beliefs. We read Buddhist scriptures, tried transcendental meditation, did yoga, went to meetings where we chanted Hare Krishna, ate curry and rice and listened to readings from the Bhagavad Gita, then would go home, get stoned and talk about our newfound discoveries until the early hours of the morning. Some nights we'd put on 'Hot Rats' by Frank Zappa and dance like mad things before bed, love and sleep. Other nights, we would lie on the floor in Tom's room in the dark and listen to music: The Grateful Dead, Hendrix, Van Morrison, The Eagles, The Stones, The Doors, Pink Floyd, Velvet Underground, Joni Mitchell, Miles Davis. We floated around in a haze of marijuana, and the world felt full of hope and the promise of new experience. 'We must never grow old, Cait,' he'd said. 'We must stay curious. Promise me that, whatever happens, we'll always stay in touch and remind each other to always seek adventure and take the road less travelled.'

It had been a magical, mystical time that had ended just

after he'd finished his degree and Chloe Porter, a Jean Shrimpton-lookalike in a micro-skirt had arrived on the scene. She was attending her brother's degree ceremony and, two weeks later, Tom left Manchester and went to be with her in London. All I got was a note left on our bed. 'Adventure calling, Cait. I know you'll understand.' I didn't. I was gutted, heartbroken. I'd thought we were soul mates, that he was The One. He was supposed to have been my knight in shining armour but he rode off into the sunset with another lady, leaving me the damsel in distress. I threw out my Crosby, Stills & Nash LP and played 'Hey, That's No Way To Say Goodbye' by Leonard Cohen over and over again until Eve, who shared the student house where I lived, called it 'music to slash your wrists to' and threatened to smash all my records.

A month later, I'd received a letter from Tom. 'Dearest Cait. Timing. You know we were too young to have found each other when we did. There's too much experience still to have on this journey through life for both of us. But we'll meet again. You know we will, we are meant to be in each other's lives. Get out there. Have love affairs. Travel. Give your heart. I miss you but that's how it is for now. Seek adventures. Remember the promise. I will be in touch from time to time to check you haven't taken the easy option. Love always, Tom.'

What a pile of crap, I'd thought, and ripped up the letter. I'd known what he was like and cursed myself for falling for his easy charm and honeyed words for so long. I should have known better. We hadn't stayed in touch. After I'd finished university, I decided to give up on men and look for God instead, to seek a higher, unconditional love as opposed to romantic and limited. I joined the hippie trail and went to India, where I learnt to view life, its highs and lows, as a dream, a temporary illusion. I came to believe that attachment to worldly possessions and people was what caused pain. On my return from the East, I heard from an old university friend that Tom had gone to live in the States and settled in LA. I didn't take his address. No point. He hadn't bothered to let me know himself where he was going, and any thoughts of him still hurt, despite my aspiration to detachment. I wasn't going to chase him. I drifted for a few years, worked in a co-operative shop that sold organic food and vegetarian meals, did dance and drama classes and a bit of acting, sang in a band as a backing singer, but nothing that came to much. In my late twenties, I decided it was time to get real and put down some roots. I put my degree to use and got a job as an English and drama teacher. When I was thirty, I met, fell in love and married Matt and for the first time in years felt settled We set up house, Sam came along then, five years later, Jed, so I had a family to care for and no time to indulge in the youthful notion of taking the road less travelled. Bringing up two boys was enough of an adventure into uncharted territory.

And now, after all this time, Tom wants to be my friend on Facebook. Well . . .

4

Matt

Cait brought a cup of tea through to me in the sitting room. She was dressed in a summery coral dress and had done her make-up ready to go out. She was a good-looker, my missus, always was, though she never thought of herself as attractive. She'd inherited her mother's delicate features and high cheekbones and was still slim, with an open, friendly face and those cat-like green eyes I'd fallen for so many years ago.

'What are you up to today?' she asked as she glanced at the TV screen, which was showing a rerun of a *Star Trek* episode. She was trying to sound upbeat, but I knew the subtext was: 'Are you going to go out today? You've lain around for almost two weeks now. Do something useful and get out from under my feet, you good-for-nothing bastard.'

I shrugged a shoulder by way of reply, then hit the TV pause button.

Cait sighed so I sighed. There was a lot of sighing going on round here lately.

'Why not call one of your friends? Might do you good to get out.'

Hah. I knew it, I thought. 'What friends? All my friends are, or rather were, in the business, at work.' I used to have other friends, Tony, Steve and Pete, good mates from university days, but over the years we'd drifted apart as marriage, kids, work took over. Plus, as Cait would say, I'm a lazy arse when it comes to actually making contact and picking up the phone, and so are they. I had made an effort last week though, not that I told Cait. I'd gone into Bristol and met Mike from my old office. He wasn't someone I'd call a close friend, but I'd shared a building with him for the last twelve years. I'd wanted to hear what was going on there since I'd left, but he wasn't forthcoming. I had the scent of loser on me: redundant, no longer of use or need, so no longer privy to the gossip or changes. It was a short lunch – he had to get back for a meeting, which made me feel all the more pathetic, left sitting there in the restaurant with nothing urgent to do. I'd had a second glass of wine then wandered out into the late spring sunshine, not knowing where to go and not wanting to go home to The House of Sighs. *So no, Cait*, I thought, *I won't be contacting any of my 'friends' soon.* When Jed and Sam were living at home, I had no need of friends. My family was everything. The house was always full of the boys' friends and my time was taken up with giving lifts here and there; attending sports events, football or rugby matches, helping with homework and projects. It was only when they'd gone that I realized the hole that they'd left and no one to fill it.

Cait sighed again. I out-sighed her. This was a competition I could win.

'Matt, talk to me, tell me how you're feeling.'

'To be honest, bad, really bad.'

'So tell me. If I know what's going on inside you I can help.'

'Doubt it. Arsenal lost to Man United in the last game. Disaster. Not a lot you can do about that.'

'Football? We're talking *football*?'

'Yes. You asked how I was feeling.'

Cait's shoulders drooped. 'I give up.'

'Me too. If they carry on playing like this, they're going to be out before the final.'

'Matt, if you don't let me in, I—'

'Let you in to what? There's nothing to be let in to if you're not familiar with the players.'

Cait left the room. I felt bad. I knew she didn't want to hear about football, but what was there to say? Or do? Let her in to? How could I when I hadn't a clue what was going on myself. I glanced at my watch. Eight forty-five. When I'd been working, I'd look at my watch and it would be four in the afternoon and I wouldn't have known where the day had gone. Now I didn't know how to fill the long hours, the eternal minutes.

I got up, went into the kitchen and over to the dresser where I collected up my retirement cards, all sent by well-meaning friends. I sat at the table and began to flick through them.

'Retirement is not the end of the road, it's the start of the open highway. Debs.' The lyrics to the song, 'Highway to Nowhere' sprang to mind.

'Retirement means twice the husband and half the income. John and Marie.' Ouch.

'How many days in a week? Six Saturdays, one Sunday. Sue and Charles.' Thanks Sue and Charles.

'How many retirees does it take to change a light bulb? Only one, but it might take all day. Live it, love it, Duncan.' My brother. At least he'd attempted humour.

'When is a retiree's bedtime? Two hours after he falls asleep on the couch. Rosie and Anth.' Well, they got that right. Now I'm doing nothing, I do feel exhausted.

'Goodbye tension, hello pension. Love Arthur and Mary.' Well Arthur and Mary, that's all very well, but I don't have a pension and any savings were used to buy the house and subsequently into seeing Sam and Jed through university. I won't get the state pension just yet and, even when I do, it won't be enough to get by on. Our house is our pension. Cait and I agreed that property would earn us more than any savings account which is why we took the leap and bought this house. It was a stretch but we agreed: live somewhere we like while we can and downsize when we have to. Problem is, we never thought 'have to' would come around so soon. Cait's already had the estate agents in to value the place, but I don't think either of us really wants to move, so I see that as our last option and only if I can't get another job.

There was a small pile of books on the table, also sent by well-wishers – *How to Survive Retirement* manuals with cartoons depicting bald old men bent over with a walking stick. I'm not like that. I have all my hair and my teeth. I can walk unaided. Oh yes. And I still wake at seven, geared to get up and go, only there is nowhere to go to. Cait's getting irritated with me, I think; no, not think, I *know* she is and I know she's trying to help in her own way, but I wish she'd back off and give me some time and space to adjust. Losing my job, my identity, my routine had hurt. Cait had always been the leader in our private life, always coming up with suggestions which I had, in the main, gone along with. She'd research our holidays, I'd book them and take care of the travel arrangements. She'd arrange our social life, organize a dinner or lunch party, I'd go out and buy the wine, do the clearing up, be the back-up. We'd known our roles and what was expected of one another but of course all that has changed now.

Oops. Cait was back. *Look cheerful, Matt.* I knew I was bugging her. The house was her territory when I was out at work all day and I felt as if I was now in her way, but she needed to cut me some slack. What had just happened was life-changing. I needed time to adjust and, for once, didn't want to do everything her way or in her time frame.

'New lot of brochures for me to look at?' I asked as she placed a magazine on the side table. So far, she'd brought home reading material about the u3a (that's the University of the Third Age to those in the know), the rugby club – 'You can watch the matches up there with company and they do a nice lunch,' she had said, and the gym, 'Got to keep fit going into our next stage of life.' But I was not ready to venture out in my cloth cap yet. I wanted to stay home and lick my wounds for a while, least until I could make sense of what had just taken place. Lunch in my business had been a wonderfully social affair with a bottle, maybe two, of fine wine. I was not ready for a casserole and pint of beer to nurse in a corner of a club full of lonely old men.

'I'm trying to help.'

'Who said I needed help?'

'You don't seem happy – and I don't mean just about your team not winning.'

'I'm fine, Cait. I don't need you to tell me what to do.'

'Fine. I'm off then.'

'Where to?'

'Work. It's Monday. I work at the surgery. Remember?'

'Course.'

'Then I'm going to pop in to see Lorna.'

'What for?'

'I said I'd drop off a book.'

'What is it?'

'*A House Full of Daughters.*'

'What's it about?'

She looked at her watch. 'Matt, when have you ever shown any interest in what I'm reading?'

'So what was it about?'

'I'm late. I'll tell you when I get back.'

'What time will that be?'

I could see her grit her teeth. 'Not sure.'

'What's for lunch?'

I knew I was being annoying, I couldn't stop myself. You always hurt the one you love, so the saying goes, and I did love Cait, but I'd let her down and that was hard to live with. Although we'd both worked in our lives, I'd always been the main breadwinner and had been happy to be so. I'd liked being able to provide, prided myself on being someone who could be depended upon. Plus, for decades, I'd been Matt Langham, programme-maker, a man with an interesting job, somebody. Now what was I? Who was I? Matt Langham. Who was he now? What had he got to contribute? I felt as if I'd gone back to the boy I was when fifteen years old, unsure of where he wanted to go or what he wanted to be. I was rudderless. Just Matt Langham, and it scared the crap out of me.

'Fridge is full. Take your pick.'

'Just wanted to know if you'd be joining me, that's all, no need to get pissed off.'

'I'm not pissed off. I . . . oh never mind.'

'Never mind? *You* don't seem happy, Cait, never mind me. What are *you* feeling?' As if she'd like to throttle me, by the look on her face.

'I'm *feeling* I've got to get going, Matt, thanks for your concern. Er . . . don't you think you ought to get dressed?'

'Why?'

'In case someone comes to the door later.'

'Who cares? I don't. I'm retired, a free man,' I said as I indicated the pile of cards I'd put back on the dresser, 'free to choose what I want to do; least that's what they all say. So I can wear what I want when I want, and if I choose to wear my dressing gown all day then I can.'

'OK. Right. Fine. See you later.'

'Probably. I'm not going anywhere.'

'Maybe you could go and get some new paint brochures. If we're going to sell up, we'll need to bring the house into this century.'

'I wouldn't bother,' I said. 'If we do have to sell, people will only paint over in their own choices.'

Cait sighed. 'That may well be, but I wouldn't want estate agents saying "in need of modernization" on our house description. It doesn't sound good. A lick of paint will make it look more attractive – lighter, brighter. We have been meaning to do it for years. Besides, it will give you—'

'Give me what? Go on, say it – something to do, that's what you were going to say, isn't it? Well, I don't need anything to do, thank you very much.'

Cait was about to speak, but stopped herself and left. I heard the front door slam a moment later. I'd been mean, goaded her. Why? I hadn't planned to. If pushed, I could tell her I felt like a failure, but what good would that do? None, I know she thinks I'm a miserable old prick who ought to have a shave then get out and do something useful. Should I tell her how sorry I felt? No, in my business, you never admitted failure, you kept smiling through and talked it up, up up. Media work is all about good PR. Maybe Cait and I should have a huge row, let it all out, clear the air. No, best not, best we try and weather the storm, sigh a lot. *This too will pass.* So what to do? Look up nose- and ear-trimmers on Amazon?

I gathered the small pile of *How to Survive Retirement* books and went to sit back on the sofa in the sitting room to read or throw them out the window.

*

Cait

- Chin hairs plucked: 2
- Senior moments: 2
  1) Raced upstairs to fetch something before going to work. Got to bedroom. No idea what I'd gone up there to get. Stood there like an idiot. Went back downstairs.
  2) Put Savlon on my toothbrush. The tubes look so similar. Bleurgh.

- Supplements taken: fish oil for dry eyes, cataract prevention, joints and brain.

Got to my job at the surgery. I was glad to have escaped Matt and the Temple of Doom.

As soon as I walked in, Mary, the pretty blonde duty nurse, called me over. 'Susan wants to see you,' she said as she tied her dark hair back into a knot.

Susan was the practice manager. I went and knocked on her door. She was sitting behind her desk, a mousy-looking woman with thick glasses, which magnified her eyes and gave her a permanently startled look.

'Come in. Ah. Caitlin,' she said.

'You wanted to see me?'

'I did. I do. No other way to put this, but we won't be needing you any more. Margaret's maternity leave is over and she wants to come back as soon as possible.'

'Oh.'

'You've been a godsend,' Susan continued, 'and . . . you always knew it was temporary, right?'

'I did.' Margaret had been on maternity leave for a year and a half and I'd begun to think that she wouldn't be back.

'I'll let you know if anything else comes up – that is, if you're still available.'

'Right. Thanks. When is she coming back exactly?'

'Ah yes, about that. As soon as you've worked your notice. You were supposed to have been told last week but it appears that . . . well . . . bit of a mix-up. Embarrassing. One of those tasks that everyone thought someone else had done. Mary thought I'd told you, I thought she'd told you. Unforgivable.

My apologies.' She didn't look very sorry. She looked as if
she wanted me to go as soon as possible.

'Right. Got it.'

'Thanks for filling in for her, Caitlin, really, you've been
a star and, once again, so sorry not to have let you know
before.'

'No problem.'

Big problem.

*

After work, I bought a paper then went to the café opposite
for a coffee and a think. Talk about bad timing. A few weeks
ago, it wouldn't have mattered so much, but now it did. We
needed every penny that I brought in. I needed to make a
list so got out my notebook.

Options:
- Get another job, any old job. *Don't want to.*
- Go back into teaching. *Too much admin these days and
  been there, done that. I need a job, not a career.*
- Buy Scratch cards. *No. Waste of money. Will buy one
  anyway.*
- Rob a bank. *Haven't got a gun. Put 'get water pistol' on
  the shopping list. Wouldn't want to hurt anyone.*
- Go to bed and hide under the duvet. *Tempting,
  though can't remember when I last had a good night's
  sleep.*
- Research sleep remedies.
- Message Tom Lewis, have steamy hot affair. *As if.*

I went back to my notebook and wrote:
Reasons not to contact Tom Lewis.

- I am married.
- That way madness lies.
- I have bunions, occasional chin hair and senior moments. Hardly love's young dream.

It's all very well meeting up with an old lover when you're young and fit, I thought, *quite another when your body is on a fast journey south*. Tom would remember me as a young woman, long limbed and skinny, not an old bird with wrinkly knees. Forty years was a long time ago. I hadn't responded to his Facebook request so I didn't know where he was now or why he had got in touch, apart from to say hi, I'm still alive. Maybe he just wants to catch up. Fine. All the same, he may still be shocked if he saw me now. Forget him, Cait. Be sensible. Task in hand. Job. Work. Money. Put any nonsense about Tom out of your mind.

What was it Dad always said? 'Sink or swim. Those are your choices.' That was it. I don't want to sink so I'd better buck up my ideas and start swimming, I thought. Get home, get focused. I can do it. I'll find something else or make a plan, write a book. I'll think of something.

*

'How was your day?' asked Matt on hearing me come through the front door.

'I'm no longer needed.'

'At the surgery?'

'Yep. Just have to work my notice then that's it.'

'Oh.'

'I know. Oh.'

'Bad luck, Cait. I am sorry. Want a cup of tea?'

'Thanks. I'll be up in my study looking for a new job.'

'No. Come on. Relax. Go and see Lorna as you'd planned. You've had a knock. There's plenty of time to look for a job.'

'Is there? And how are the bills to be paid?'

'We have enough money for a—'

'Six months, a year if we live frugally,' I said. I knew I sounded snappy and instantly regretted it.

Matt put up his hands and backed away. 'Fine. You do it your way.'

'I will.'

I went up to my study and shut the door. I felt bad. It wasn't Matt's fault that I'd lost my job. I'd been short with him. I am a meanie as well as unemployed. I must resolve to be more patient.

I had a quick look through the paper but there were only a couple of jobs for building construction workers and one for a receptionist in a tattoo parlour. Not really my line.

I looked at my computer and reread Tom Lewis's message. 'Never forget, you were always one of the cool ones.' And look at me now, I thought. Not so cool after all, Tom. Unemployed, over the hill, and mean to my husband. I thought about deleting the message but, as my finger hovered over the button, I hesitated. Should I reply to him? No. What good could possibly come of it? Just say hi? Wish him well? No. Not today, anyway.

Lorna. I'll go and see Lorna as Matt suggested and talk

to her about it. She was my go-to friend for advice. I'd known her since I first came to Bath over twenty years ago, when Sam and Jed were in junior school. We'd met at the school gate when we waited in all weathers to pick up our kids and had clicked from the start. She was working as a GP back then and I'd liked her intelligent face, no-nonsense manner and dry sense of humour – still did – and though she was eight years younger than me, I'd always felt that she was the older sister I'd never had. Much as I loved Debs, her solution to most problems was to do the Tarot cards or howl at the sky on a full moon. Her advice was never what I expected, like the time Jed had got into trouble at school for giving cheek to a teacher. 'Good for him,' she'd said. 'Shows he's not going along with the crowd.' And the time Sam had been sacked from a summer holiday job as a waiter for dropping food all over a customer, she'd suggested that we go over to the restaurant after closing hours and write 'Shut down due to rats' on their door. I knew she meant well, but she'd always been a rule breaker and her advice and behaviour were not always appropriate. I loved spending time with Debs because she was fun, but Lorna was the one I turned to if I really needed to talk. I picked up the phone to call her but it went to message so I decided to email her.

'Hi Lorna. Lost my job today. Any ideas? Back to teaching? Library work? Stripper? There must be a call somewhere for wrinkly old ladies who can jiggle their bits. I could work old people's homes on birthdays. Pop out of a cake in my Spanx stretch-mesh bodysuit and give them a heart attack. I could be the fun alternative to Dignitas – cheaper too. And oh, guess who got in touch? Tom Lewis. I told you about him once. He contacted me through Facebook of all places.

I haven't accepted him as a friend yet. What do you think? I'm curious to know what he's been up to for the last forty years.'

No. I wasn't ready to tell her about Tom yet, so I deleted it. I'll be seeing her with Debs tomorrow, I told myself. I can talk to both of them then.

*

At seven o'clock, I went to my writing class in the village hall. The topic was 'Turning Points', and we had to do an exercise listing those times in our own life. *Easy peasy*, I thought as I wrote:

- Matt losing his job.
- Me losing my job.
- Message from Tom.
- Deaths of Mum and Eve.
- Jed and Sam leaving home.
- Discovering I can no longer get into size twelve.

Now . . . how to turn those topics into a fun children's book, there was a challenge. I spent the rest of the class thinking about Tom Lewis and remembering what we used to get up to under his Indian bedspread.

5

Cait

- Items lost:
    1) Mobile phone (again). Found it in the fridge.
    2) Reading glasses, searched everywhere, sitting room, bedroom, bathroom. Found them on top of my head.
- Supplements taken:
    1) Garlic, good for everything and keeps vampires at bay.
    2) Devil's claw for arthritis.
- Senior moments: 2.
    1) Sent birthday card, meant for my friend Annie in Manchester, to her sister Jess in Brighton. Annie's name. Jess's address. Luckily Jess let me know and forwarded it.
    2) Went out in a rush to meet Debs and Lorna for an early supper and only noticed when I got to the restaurant that I was wearing odd sneakers, one blue, one grey.

'So. What's on the agenda tonight?' asked Lorna after our waiter had taken our orders for pasta and they'd had a good laugh about my shoes.

'Debs?' I asked.

'Me finding a new man,' she replied. Her partner, Fabio, had left her six months ago. They'd been to Wales to do a Tantric sex workshop and Fabio had fallen in love with the woman running it. He was now living in the Welsh mountains and, according to Debs, was getting laid on every ley line.

'And you, Cait?'

I rolled my eyes. 'Matt and I are both unemployed.'

'But the surgery?' Debs asked.

'Not needed any more. I don't know what we're going to do. It wasn't meant to be like this at my age. We were supposed to be retired, a picture of happy contentment, sitting on rocking chairs on a veranda in the sunset without a care in the world, grandchildren and dogs at our feet.'

'Chewing tobacco and strumming a banjo,' added Debs. 'Is there a white picket fence in there somewhere too?'

'Course.'

'You'd be bored out of your mind.'

'Probably. What about you Lorna?'

She shrugged. 'Nothing in particular.' I never pushed her to talk about Alistair, because she wasn't one to air her grief in public; that wasn't her style and I'd taken my lead from her after Mum and Eve died. Lorna was a doer, not one to wallow – or tolerate other people wallowing, for that matter – but lately, I could tell by the shadows under her eyes and the weight loss she didn't need, that she still missed her late husband sorely.

'OK, back to you Cait,' said Debs as the waiter brought

a bottle of Pinot Grigio and poured three glasses. 'What exactly happened to Matt?'

'There was nothing for him to do, he was told, and not to waste the train fare.'

'That's appalling,' said Lorna.

'Yes, total crap. Didn't he see it coming?' asked Debs. 'They can't just drop him with no warning.'

'He knows that there are tribunals he could go to but I don't think he wants to go that route, losing his job was humiliation enough.'

'I must check his horoscope and yours. It will be Uranus causing trouble somewhere. Uranus is the planet that brings the unexpected. If it's badly placed, it can cause surprises like you both losing your jobs.'

Lorna rolled her eyes. Although we were both used to Debs's predilection for consulting the stars on every occasion, Lorna always had to let it be known she thought it was all nonsense.

'I can see you rolling your eyes, Lorna, and that's because you're Scorpio which means that you would scoff at astrology. Typical of the sign.'

'Sure,' said Lorna.

Debs was Gemini and a heart-on-her-sleeve type: open minded, great communicator, endlessly curious, exploring meditation techniques and alternative therapies and passing on her newfound discoveries to everyone, whether they were interested or not. Not that she always practised what she preached. She advocated healthy eating, detoxifying and regular liver cleanses, but drank like a fish, loved a takeaway and occasionally smoked roll-ups. She talked about forgiveness, taking responsibility and not blaming others, but was furious about Fabio and, so far, hadn't found a remedy to restore her equilibrium. Neither Lorna nor I had dared ask her if the break-up had been foreseen in her horoscope.

'Will he get any redundancy money?' asked Debs.

'A small amount. It's all a sore subject. Whenever I ask he says, "Just leave it, Cait, not now." It's never the right time and I haven't been able to have a proper talk about it with him.'

Debs tutted. 'He probably needs to talk.'

'Not to me apparently.'

'Maybe he can get another job,' said Lorna as our waiter brought a starter plate of toasted ciabatta with tomatoes, garlic and herbs. 'Part-time. Consultancy. Surely his experience counts for something?'

'That's what I said, but he said apparently not. It's a young person's business.'

'Another job then?' Debs suggested.

'I put that to him as well. "Doing what?" he asked. "Stacking shelves in Tesco's? No one hires sixty year olds in my business," he said. He's very down.'

'And what about you?'

'I've been looking, but there's nothing that really appeals.'

'I have a small job for Matt,' said Debs. 'I need someone to rewrite the copy for my brochures and website for the spa. He could do that, couldn't he?'

'I'm sure he could.' I knew Debs was being kind and was perfectly capable of writing her own copy. She ran a successful health centre on the outskirts of Bath where all types of alternative therapists practised. Despite some of her airy-fairy beliefs, she was a very good businesswoman.

'What are the options?' asked Lorna.

'Sell the house and downsize. I've already had the estate agent around to value the house and they're keen to start marketing, but I haven't seen anything on the property websites that remotely appeals for us to move to. For me to find another job in a few weeks, full time. Get a book contract. I've been working on some ideas, but getting an agent and then a publisher can be like winning the lottery. Finally, I could sell my body – though that's probably not an option; no one would want it.'

'Try eBay,' said Debs. 'You can sell anything on eBay.'

'Older lady, slightly batty, not quite over the hill, good at hippie dancing, talks to herself but claims it makes for long and interesting conversations. Not to be approached for fear of death in the morning.'

'If you ever decide to try Internet dating, remind me to help you with your profile,' said Debs. 'And talking of which, I need you two to help me. I need to redo my profile.'

'Anytime,' I said. 'Gorgeous goddess seeks sex god for heavenly frolics.'

Debs raised an eyebrow. 'Don't think you've quite got the hang of it, Cait.'

'Why? What's wrong with that?'

'I want more than just sex. I want a partner for walks in the countryside, good company and all that.'

'Get a dog,' said Lorna.

'Dogs don't do candlelit dinners or go to the theatre,' said Debs.

'Then put down that you want that,' I said.

'I'll bring my laptop one day and you can look at the sort of thing people write. I need something to make me stand out from the crowd,' said Debs.

'Anyone can see just by looking at you that you're different,' said Lorna. It was true, Debs did have her own unique style.

This evening she was wearing a red kaftan top, black harem trousers and chunky silver jewellery. She always wore a mix of Eastern and vintage clothes, and with her mane of fabulous hair and curvy figure, she always attracted second glances from women as well as men.

'Different? Different as in odd?'

'I meant it in a good way – you look interesting.'

'Like an exotic burlesque artist,' I added.

'Anyway, Debs, we're talking about Cait and Matt first,' said Lorna.

'Bossy cow,' said Debs.

I laughed. Lorna ignored her. 'Cait? Do you want to move house?'

'Not really. I like our house.'

'Then make your property work for you. I was thinking about your situation. You have spare rooms. Do Airbnb. I know loads of people who are doing it, and if you have a week when you don't want guests, you mark that week as booked. If nothing else, it would buy you some more time.'

'Not a bad idea. Though we'd have to redecorate.'

'You'd soon make it back. Think of it as an investment,' said Lorna. 'And you said that you have some ideas for books?'

'Yes. No. Maybe. Seeds. I need to develop them.'

'It must be nice to have Matt home,' said Debs through a mouthful of ciabatta.

I laughed. 'You're joking. He's driving me mad and it's only been two weeks. It's like living with the Spanish Inquisition. Every time I leave the house, he asks me where I'm going, who with, and what time I'll be back.'

'He's probably a bit lost at the moment,' said Debs. 'Poor guy.'

'Yes. It will be an adjustment for him,' said Lorna. 'Loss of status and routine can be tough, especially for men. They identify so closely with what they do. Cut him some slack.' She looked wistful for a moment. 'I'd give anything to have Alistair back for just one hour, even at his most annoying – and, believe me, he had his moments too.'

'Oh god, I'm sorry, Lorna. I'm the most insensitive, awful friend.'

'Hey, no, no need to apologize. Don't feel bad. Life goes on. All husbands are annoying sometimes. All I'm saying is, try to appreciate him while you've got him.'

'Yes, at least you still have a man,' said Debs.

'I know. I know. I just don't want him home twenty-four hours a day. I know marriage is for better and for worse; unfortunately this is a "for worse" bit.'

Both of them were looking at me without the slightest hint of sympathy. 'Sorry. Not serious, I'm just letting off steam. We'll get through it.'

Neither of them understood. Lorna lived alone, apart from her dogs, in a sprawling seventeenth-century manor. Debs was alone too. She had a three-bedroom ground-floor flat in the centre of Bath, which she'd shared with Fabio until he'd discovered the joys of Tantra.

'I'd sympathize if Matt was a womanizer,' Debs said.

'Or abused you,' said Lorna.

'I know, I know. He just needs something to do, to get him out of the house to cheer him up. I've tried all sorts of things to encourage him. I'm sure it would do him good to have company, something to occupy himself.'

'Early days; it's only been a couple of weeks,' said Lorna. 'Give him some space.'

'He'll find his feet,' said Debs.

'I'll put the Airbnb idea to him. Actually, Lorna, that's a great plan, because painting the house would give him something to do.'

'It has to come from him,' said Lorna. 'I'd drop the suggestions if I were you; he may feel emasculated.'

There was nothing I could say. I had a weak case. Grounds for divorce? Does he beat you? No. Does he gamble away your money? No. Is he having extramarital relations? No. So what is it, Mrs Langham? He's always there; he follows me round the house and talks to me through the door when I'm on the loo. I got the feeling that this evening wasn't the best time to tell Lorna and Debs that an ex-lover had been in touch either.

'OK. My turn,' said Debs. 'Back to my problem. Where am I going to meet a like-minded man? Men my age want a bendy babe who can do the splits, is twenty years younger and doesn't answer back. I'm forty-seven. The only ones who want a woman in her forties look like Worzel Gummidge. I need you both to help me look online and pick a man.'

'Why not just join the kind of group where like-minded men would go?' I said.

'Like what?' she asked.

'Oh. . . some kind of meditation group?' I suggested. 'Or one of your New Age weekends?'

Debs pulled a face. 'They're full of bearded men who look like tired chemistry teachers.'

'Nothing wrong with that,' I said.

'Nah. You know me. I like the bad boys, men with a bit of edge. Where am I going to find one of them?'

'Narcotics anonymous?' said Lorna.

6

Cait

I resolved to go to my computer when I got home, log in to Facebook and delete Tom's request. We hadn't even spoken yet and already he was making me anxious. I couldn't stop thinking about his message, remembering our time together and the person I was when I knew him, plus I felt bad that I hadn't told Lorna or Debs about him, and nor had I told Matt. I headed straight up to my study but, instead of going to Facebook, I called Lorna.

'Hey, what's up?' she said. 'Did you leave something at the restaurant?'

'No. Er . . . have you got a minute?'

'Course. Is something the matter?'

I hesitated.

'Hey, come on, you can tell me anything. Is it about your job coming to an end?

'Partly.'

'Could you both retire? Make that work? You are of the age.'

56

'I . . . it's not just that. I . . . thing is, Lorna, an old friend got in touch . . .'

'Old friend?'

'On Facebook. A man I used to know . . . live with many years ago – when I was at university.'

'Tim, or Tom somebody?'

'Yes. Tom Lewis.' I was surprised she'd remembered. I'd told her about him briefly, many moons ago, when we were talking about first loves. 'I haven't heard from him for oh . . . must be forty years.'

'Are you kidding? Where's he been all this time?'

'Abroad I think.'

'What does he want?'

'I don't know. He made contact on Facebook. I haven't accepted him as a friend yet.'

'And will you?'

'Not sure. I've been thinking about it.'

'Oh, Cait, you really don't need something like this in your life at the moment. I'd say tread very carefully there. He was the love of your life, if I remember rightly from what you told me. OK, probably no harm in saying hi in cyberspace, but more than that will be playing with fire. I remember you telling me what he meant to you. I'd say do *not* contact him. You don't need the complications, especially now.'

'It might be a closure of sorts and good for my soul.'

'I very much doubt it; more like opening Pandora's Box. Have you told Debs? What does she think?'

'I haven't told her and I don't want to, so please don't. He is, was, very attractive. She'd probably want to meet him, you know what she's like.'

'Yes, probably not a good idea.'

'And I can't open up to her completely, not like I can with you.'

'What can't you say to her?'

'Oh, I don't know, but it's not just Tom who's bothering me, it's also Matt, and you know Debs thinks the world of him. Things aren't good; in fact some days I'm not sure why I'm still with him.' This wouldn't be news to Lorna. I'd talked to her several times in the last few months, before he was made redundant, about my doubts over our relationship.

'You're thinking about separating? Is it really that bad?'

'It is, but thirty years of marriage is a lot of history to walk away from. The time it takes in the beginning for silences to become comfortable, adjustments made to find a way to live together in harmony and Christmases, birthdays, holidays, deaths of loved ones, my mother, his parents, the birth, early years of Sam and Jed, the madness of having teenagers in the house. So many memories, so many shared experiences, good and bad. It's a lot to let go of, and we've muddled along together so far – plus even to think about it at the moment is bad timing.'

'I agree, you can't do it when he's just been made redundant.'

'Exactly. It would be like kicking a man when he's down.'

'So what's changed, apart from him losing his job?'

'Me. I can't help asking if it's enough to muddle on.'

'And have you decided what to do about Tom?'

'Not yet. I was about to delete the request to be friends but, and I know this might sound mad, part of me likes the fact that his request is there, like an unopened, unexpected gift. As long as it remains unopened, it offers all sorts of possibilities.'

'You can't be the only woman who's had a secret fantasy, Cait. It's not as if you've done anything, and I would have thought Debs would be sympathetic if you told her. You know how open-minded she is.'

'Yes, but you heard her at the restaurant when she said I should be grateful that I at least still have a man. It's true. I should be. Matt is one of the good guys. He's dependable, hard-working, a gentleman in the true sense of the word. Maybe I'm an ungrateful old witch.'

'Don't be so hard on yourself. No marriage is perfect and you've both been through a lot lately.'

'It's not just that, Lorna. Our marriage has gone stale. On the outside, it all looks normal, but is it? Do I have unrealistic expectations? Now he's home twenty-four hours a day, I'm more aware than ever of the fact that we rarely talk about anything meaningful, never touch, not any more.'

'Oh, Cait, I am sorry, but all marriages go through bad patches . . .'

'This is a very long patch.'

'And all relationships involve a degree of compromise. I very much doubt that Mr Perfect is out there – an older Darcy, in breeches and boots, aged like a dream. He doesn't exist and for many couples, the passion wanes.'

'It certainly has for us. Our sex life? Non-existent. These days, good in bed to me is to be tucked up with a book, and the only hot stuff I experience between the sheets is a cup of tea. I don't like to ask friends how often they do it and is it worth it when they do.'

Lorna chuckled. 'Most of us swapped those kind of conversations years ago for discussions of our and everybody else's health.'

'Yes, but I get the feeling from the occasional remark made by married friends that Matt and I are the only ones who don't do it at *all* any more. I can barely remember the last time we made love. I feel I'm missing out.'

'Which is why Tom Lewis getting in touch couldn't have come at a more inopportune time?'

'I suppose. I can't help but wonder how he is, how his life has been in the last forty years. He looked good in his profile photo.'

'In a fantasy, you can imagine him as perfect, but spend a bit of time with him and you'll probably find he's as flawed as the rest of us.'

'Maybe. And not only him – me too. Sorry, I know it's a silly dream. I just wanted to talk to you about it. I know I'm older now, no longer the young girl he'd remember me being. I've changed, and not only appearance-wise.'

'Cait, you look great, always do.'

'He might be disappointed if we met up. I couldn't bear that. No. I know, better to leave the past in the past where it has the rosy glow of nostalgia, though sometimes I can't help but wonder what might have happened if Chloe Poshgirl Porter hadn't appeared.'

'Who was she?'

'The woman he left me for. Sorry. I know, it's going over old ground. What could possibly be gained by accepting his friend request but trouble? Deep inside, I do know that, but I don't know what to do to improve things with Matt. Any advice?'

'Seriously?'

'Seriously.'

'OK. Here's the ex-GP speaking. Work on your marriage.

Do what you can to improve things. Delete the request from Tom. Come over soon and we'll have a proper chat. In the meantime, stop acting like an idiot and get on with your life.'

'Advice noted,' I said. She was right, and talking to her had helped clarify my thoughts.

After our call, I was about to log into Facebook to delete Tom's request, but first got up and went to the window to pull the curtains. As I did, I noticed a man zigzagging his way up the middle of the road, clearly very drunk. He looked vaguely like Matt. *Christ, that is Matt*, I thought as he got closer. *What the hell is he doing?*

I ran downstairs, grabbed the door keys and went out into the street. 'Matt, Matt,' I called. 'Are you OK?'

He didn't hear, and continued to stumble his way up the road, then he saw me and waved.

'Harro, Cait,' he called as he managed to get on the pavement then half fell into a laurel hedge next door.

'Where have you been?' I asked as I went to pull him out and back onto his feet.

'Duncan. Drink. Cheer m'up,' he slurred and laughed. 'Bit pissed.' He stank of red wine and beer.

'Did you walk home?'

'Nhh. Think so. Not. Taxi,' he said, as he swayed back towards the bushes.

I hauled him back again. 'Why didn't you get the cab to drop you at our door?'

Matt grinned sheepishly. 'Sorry. Dunno. Dropped me at end of road . . . 'membered live near here.'

I opened our gate, put his arm round my shoulder and walked, half carrying him, to the porch, where I leant him against the wall while I put my keys in to open the front door. 'Harro, Cait, I bloody *love* you,' he said with a big smile. 'Lovely *lovely* Cait. Poor Cait. Sorry.'

He slid down onto the porch floor, then keeled over so that he was lying on the ground, where he turned on his side and curled into a sleeping position. In all the time we'd been together, I'd never seen him so drunk.

'Not yet, you can't sleep there,' I said, and tried to lift him. He was too heavy so I grabbed his wrists and, with some effort, dragged him inside.

'Wheee,' said Matt as I pulled him in over the threshold. 'Oof. Back. Mind my back.'

Once inside, I let go and caught my breath. 'Come on, Matt, let's get you to bed.'

'Okee dokee. Bed.'

'You have to get up.'

Matt looked bewildered at this request. 'Up? How?'

'Roll onto your side, push yourself onto your knees and get up.'

Matt attempted to do this but failed. 'Woo, bit wobbly,' he said as he tried again. As he floundered about, he let out a loud fart.

'Urgh, Matt,' I groaned and wafted the air.

Matt seemed to find this hilarious and lay back on the floor laughing. 'Sorry, sorry, oops.' He wrinkled his nose. 'Smell. Sorry.' He turned on his side. 'OK. Going to sleep now.'

'Fine, you do that.' I went into the sitting room and found a blanket, which I took back and threw over him.

'I bloody love you,' said Matt, then promptly fell asleep.

'Don't forget you've got a doctor's appointment in the morning,' I said.

But he was gone.

I watched him for a few moments. *And there he is, my husband, my partner, the man I have chosen*, I thought as he let out another loud fart then started snoring. 'Who said romance is dead?' I said as I stepped over him and headed upstairs. Maybe I wouldn't delete Tom's request just yet after all.

Once up in my study, I opened my laptop, found the Facebook page and the request area, where my fingers hovered over the choice whether to Confirm or Delete Tom as a friend. What harm would there be in just seeing how he was doing? Say hello, what have you been up to for the last forty years? That's all. It would be impolite to ignore his request, wouldn't it?

Confirm? Delete? Confirm? Delete? If I accepted him as a friend, Lorna might see him on my Facebook page, and she'd just advised me to delete his request. Worse still, Debs might see him, want me to hook her up. She's on Facebook every day, sometimes twice.

No, I should delete, I told myself. I have a husband and, even though he's lying downstairs in a drunken stupor, it's not something he does often; in fact, I can't remember him ever having done it to this degree before.

I was staring at the screen and suddenly realized that, although my privacy settings meant that friends only could see my page, Tom would have seen my profile picture. I groaned. It was a photograph of Debs and me, taken one evening last year at a Chinese restaurant. We'd thought it would be hilarious if we put chopsticks up our nostrils and take a selfie. Not the image I'd have wanted Tom to see after so long, but too late for that.

I scrolled down to my photos that could be seen by friends. There were lots of me acting the fool, cross-eyed in one, dressed as a nun and flashing a leg at a friend's birthday in another, at a bad angle in another in my baggy gardening clothes and waterproof hat in the rain. Thank God he hadn't seen those but, looking at mine, I was more curious than ever to look at his life now, look at any photos he'd posted.

I set about deleting the unflattering shots and downloaded a couple of me dressed up for various occasions, looking more glamorous. *And why are you doing this?* I asked myself. You're going to delete his request, aren't you? And if not, why do you even care how he sees you? Because he'd said I was one of the cool ones, that's why, and it had made my day. I was cool once. I was romantic. I was idealistic, with a head full of plans to change the world. I hadn't always dressed in comfortable clothes and shoes. I'd worn lace, velvet and silk. I was inventive. I bought colourful vintage clothes and scarves from market stalls and charity shops. I'd looked interesting, not unlike how Debs does now, in fact. I'd searched for meaning, tried different gurus, done yoga, smoked dope and Gauloises cigarettes, even though they tasted disgusting. I *had* been one of the cool ones.

No harm in cleaning up my photos, whatever I decide, I told myself.

Once I'd finished my new improved gallery, I went back to Facebook requests. Should I? Shouldn't I? What had I got to lose? And since when did I begin to always take the safe option? Tom and I had believed in seeking experience. Getting back in touch with him might put me back in touch with my younger, more adventurous self. I could find the 'me' I'd lost. What would be the harm in a few messages passed in cyberspace? When I'd been younger, I had never been afraid to take a risk, go with the flow and see where it took me. *I've become old*, I thought, *stuck in my ways.*

I glanced over at my bookshelf and my eyes went to the spine of a book given to me by Debs last year for my birthday. *Feel the Fear and Do It Anyway.* Exactly the sort of thing Tom would have said. Exactly the way I'd tried to live my life when I was younger.

I went back to the screen, found Tom's request and pressed Confirm.

There. Done it. Felt the fear and done it anyway.

A moment later, I had access to his page. His last posting had been a few days ago. He had put Majorca, LA and London as his homes. There was a shot on his timeline outside Harrods in Knightsbridge. I looked at the date on it: 23 May. Ah. So he was in the country, or had been recently. I wondered who'd taken the photo. I scrolled to his photo area where there were a few pictures of him with people I didn't recognize. He'd aged, of course he had, but he looked in good shape and still wore his hair longish, though it was mainly white now, a mane of it and swept back from his face, which was craggy and lined like a man who spent time outdoors. A silver fox. He'd weathered well, as Lorna would say, only she wouldn't say that if she saw his photo on my page. She'd say: what the hell do you think you're doing?

Sorry. Too late, Lorna.

In one photo, he was in a tropical garden, looking very chilled, wearing shades, in a casual shirt and shorts. In another with an attractive woman on a beach. Not Chloe Posh Girl Porter. *What happened to her?* I wondered. Another photo showed him with his arm around a young man who looked like him. His son? Another at a birthday party with a young woman. His daughter? Should I leave a message? *Hi. Hello. Long time, no see.* God. No. What should I say?

I took a deep breath. What was I thinking of? Madness. Tom was in the past. Matt was my present. We'd get by. We'd ridden hard times before. OK, so this was a bad patch. We'd get through. It wasn't too late. Having satisfied my curiosity, I could always unfriend Tom and that would be the end of it. Yes, I'd do that, just not quite yet . . .

7

Matt

- Cholesterol: 5.8
- Blood pressure: 155/95
- Hangover: 5 star.

Woke up on the hall floor with a blanket over me and what felt like a troupe of Irish dancers giving it the full clog-stomp in my head. No idea how I got home. Glanced at my watch. Six a.m. Crawled into the sitting room, onto the sofa and slept for another hour.

Put clothes from last night in the washing machine. As the cycle started up, I realized my mobile was still in the pocket of my trousers.

Went out to get some air, clear the cobwebs and post a letter. Only when I got home and tried to open the door with the letter did I realize that I'd posted my keys. Luckily Cait was in, though not impressed.

'Cholesterol's higher than we like. Blood pressure's a bit up as well,' said my doctor later the same morning. 'No fry-ups. Take more exercise, cut down on alcohol and eat more greens.'

Lose the will to live, said a voice in my head, which was still pounding after last night. A big fry-up was what I needed. It was too early to return home and Cait would be around. She'd given me the silent treatment and the fish eye before I'd left for the surgery this morning, but then she'd never been good first thing. I learnt in the early years of our marriage to be quiet and avoid eye contact until at least after 10 a.m. Clearly I am in the dog house; I don't think I saw Cait last night when I got home, but it must have been her who put the blanket over me at some point. I can't remember much. My brother Duncan had called round early evening and insisted that we go for a drink to 'cheer me up', and one glass had turned into a bottle, then another, and a few shots of whisky, I don't remember how many. Not something I do normally. *Never again*, I thought as a fresh wave of nausea hit me.

After seeing the doctor, for lack of anything else to do, I walked to the newsagent's and bought a paper.

Had tea in the builder's café. The aroma of fried bacon filled the air, so I ordered the full English and made a resolution to follow the doctor's advice another day. Checked watch. Told myself that I must stop looking at my watch. Read paper. A headline on page four caught my eye. Divorce rates for the over-60s reaches 40 per cent year high. Great.

What happens to drive people to separation? I wondered. One huge disagreement, or the culmination of many small ones that have built up over time? A mutual decision or one unhappy party? An old mate, Richard's wife, left him last year. He didn't see it coming. 'Men divorce when there's another woman,' he told me, 'women do so when they're unhappy.' He hadn't had a clue his wife had been planning her escape for well over a year.

Would Cait ever leave me? I asked myself. No, never, surely not, though things have been rocky lately. We don't talk like we used to. We sleep turned away from each other. We have drifted apart. Take note, Matt Langham, I told myself, and don't let things go further. Though I'm not sure what to do. Get away somewhere nice? But no, with our finances at the moment, sadly a romantic weekend away is out of the question. In the early days of our relationship, and many years after, we hadn't stopped talking: books, plans, theatre, politics, religion, our boys – there was always something to say about them and we enjoyed each other's company and opinions, which were often different. It didn't matter, it was us against the world: we were solid.

There had been rough patches before – I could see Cait in my mind just after Jed was born, staggering out of bed at 2 a.m., then again at three and four, before finally giving up and sleeping on a make-do bed on the floor beside his cot. A little bugger he was. Another night, she just lay there on her side of the bed when the crying started, each of us hoping the other would get up. She'd gently worked her feet up onto my bum and pushed until I was falling out of the bed. 'Your turn,' she said as I hit the floor, then she'd laughed, turned over and gone to sleep. We'd argued a lot too at that time; or rather bickered, we were both so tired. Sex was the last thing on our minds, sleep was all we sought, but we were open about it. I remembered suggesting it one night and Cait had replied. 'No thanks. Am already shagged out,' before conking out. It wasn't an issue, and things soon picked up again once Jed finally started sleeping.

Sam had been an easy baby; he'd slept through the night from the day we brought him home from the hospital. Jed was the opposite. A baby bouncing off the walls at 3 a.m. isn't a good recipe for any marriage, but we got through it. Later, we'd argued about how to discipline the boys, what time they should go to bed, how to punish them or not if they'd been cheeky or misbehaved – but we'd always talked things through.

If I was honest, when I was working, once I reached the office, work was all consuming and I let it be so. If there were problems in the home, or even in the world, they were soon forgotten as I got pulled into whatever the latest TV series proposal was and lost myself in research, timings, production costings. Back at home, I was sure of my role, and that Cait would always be there. I was pretty certain that I'd know if she was thinking about leaving. She'd never been good at keeping things in. I'd probably get a list, like that movie – *Ten Things I Hate about You*. It would be there on a piece of paper in her neat handwriting on the island in the kitchen. I almost think I'd prefer that to this atmosphere back at the house now. This is different to previous standoffs. We're not shouting at each other, taking out our mutual irritation or lack of sleep on each other. It feels quieter, more ominous, with silences that are loaded with the unspoken. *Is it me? Am I the problem?* Taking out my frustration on her in a passive-aggressive way, not giving her the benefit of a good air-clearing row. Maybe I should make more of an effort, starting by having a shave seeing as that seems to bother her so much.

I stared out of the window at rain splashing on the pavement. I'd been gone an hour. How much space would Cait need? *Longer than this*, I decided as I got up to order another mug of tea.

*

Home. Cait's gone out. Phew. Got out my list of my contacts. Emailed the few left that I haven't been in touch with, not that I hold out much hope. I've been emailing and phoning every day since I was let go and no one's got back to me so far. *Can they smell the scent of need in cyberspace? Has word got around? Matt Langham's out of the game.* They must know I'm out of work, been cut loose. I'd never emailed any of them when I was working. Didn't have the time. I remembered when I was headhunted, wanted, flavour of the month, the golden boy of programme ideas. Oh the fickle friend, that illusion that is success. Truth be told, my best years were back in the late 1980s, a long time ago. The industry has changed since then: more competitive, smaller budgets, a younger man's game. I'd survived, nevertheless. In the last decade, I'd worked as a producer on some contemporary documentaries, but my niche was history. I had a reputation. My programme 'The Women Who Made Cromwell' had won an award in 2000. I could deliver on a brief. I had good ideas, could oversee a project from conception to completion. Surely that must count for something?

Called Brian Fairweather.

'No one's hiring,' he said. 'Sorry, other phone's going. Let's get together for a beer next time you're in town.' I have said these very same lines in the past to people needing a job. It hurt being on the other end of it. Cait's friend Debs would probably say it's karma: what you sow, so shall you reap.

Next was Peter Smith. We'd always got on and he, at least, sounded pleased to hear from me. 'Matt Langham. Still in the programme-making business?'

'Keeping my hand in.'

'So what can I do you for?'

How do I put it without sounding desperate? I asked myself. *Deep breath, sound energized.* 'I've gone freelance—'

'I thought you always were?'

'Yes but I've made some changes and separated from my old company. Things have been a bit slow there so I've got some time on my hands and wondered if you were in the market for—'

'Ah. Sorry, mate. Nothing for you here. You know how it is, full on or nothing, feast or famine. It's a tough business, never been tougher or more competitive. If I were you, I'd enjoy the time off before the next round of deadlines hits, take up golf.' Subtext, you're past your sell-by date, *mate*.

Tried Richard Simpson then Ronnie Nash. No joy.

One more to try. Maria Briars. She'd tried to headhunt me once. I dialled her number.

'Hey, Maria.'

'Hey, Matt. How's it going?'

I couldn't be bothered with the pretence. 'Slow, to be honest. I'm looking for work.'

'*No*. God, if you'd only called last week, I was looking for someone – but then maybe it wasn't for you. Anyway, it was a done deal really. My boss insisted I take on his nephew. He started on Monday, only a kid, quite brilliant though. I am sorry.'

'No problem.' *A kid. Ouch*, I thought.

'I'll be in touch if I hear anything.'

'Thanks.'

'You OK?'

'Top of the world.'

'Chins up.'

'Chins up.'

I hung up the phone and crossed off her name. I am not putting myself through that humiliation again.

So, to my den in the garage to listen to Radio Four. I'll compile another list tomorrow. Or not. Have I had my day? Time to let the younger ones have their hour in the spotlight. In which case, what next? I could have a shave, but why? I'm not going anywhere. Not that I'm going to grow a beard, but after forty years of shaving every day, it's bliss not to have to, liberating. I know Cait doesn't like it, so I'll do it every fifth day. In the meantime, I'm having a shaving man's holiday. There have to be some perks to this retirement business.

8

Cait

Things to do:
- Unfriend Tom Lewis before he notices I've accepted his request.
- Be more understanding and nicer to Matt.
- Take Lorna's advice and work on saving marriage.
- Research ways to seduce husband and revive our love life. (Talk to Lorna and Debs about how to keep a relationship alive?)
- Think about how to be more sensual, sexual.
- Buy corn plasters.

Spent the morning filling in applications for three jobs I don't really want. Receptionist at a dentist's surgery. Receptionist in a firm of architects. Telesales.

Would it be a waste of time to send them off? I have a degree. Would they say – you're overqualified? You're too old. Move on.

I could go back to teaching, but I don't want to go back

to a career. I just want some extra money coming in to support what we might make on the Airbnb and my writing, if that ever happens.

Added to the list: look to see if I could go back into teaching.

From: Debs23@g.org.com
To: Cait@grmail.com

Help. Any chance you're free to come over?
D X

I looked at my watch. It was Saturday and I was supposed to be going for my weekly walk with the group. Fitness is important, and a session with Debs usually involved a bottle of wine and I am trying to cut down my units. However, this might be the perfect time to have an honest chat with Debs about how things were with Matt and see if she had any advice about how to move forward.

I emailed back:

From: Cait@grmail.com
To: Debs23@g.org.com

Be there around 2.
C X

I'd met Debs at a yoga retreat a year after I'd become friends with Lorna, back in the days when I could still do the Downward Dog without straining my wrists. She was in her twenties then, just back from Kerala in India, and was teaching the class. We'd bonded over sneaking out to smoke in the breaks, not that I smoked now. There were so many holier-than-thou people on the course who frowned at her roll-ups but she didn't care a hoot. I liked her for that, and for her energy, enthusiasm and slightly askew view of the world. She was from an upper-crust family, not that anyone would ever guess. Her family had lived in Holland Park and she'd gone to the best private schools but became a wild child in her teens. She was expelled for smoking dope, then decided she needed to find God. She travelled to India to find a guru, join an ashram and live a simple life. That was what first got us talking, because we'd both tried different teachers out there, the first being the Bhagwan Rajneesh. His group wasn't for me, though. I gave it a few months but I didn't feel I'd found my tribe with them, though it might have had something to do with the fact that all the followers were known as sannyasins and were given a new name. I was given the name Shital. Even though it meant 'cool', for obvious reasons I never felt comfortable with it. 'Shital, come and get your lentils and rice,' fellow followers would call, and some thought it was hilarious to abbreviate the name to Shit.

Debs had led a colourful life. As well as her travels in the East, she'd lived in a yurt in Wales, in a commune in Cornwall, then on a canal boat outside Bath. Everything changed for her when her parents died in a car crash ten years ago and suddenly, as their only child, she became wealthy with a capital W. She moved out of her canal boat and into her fabulous flat in the Circus, one of the most prestigious addresses in Bath.

Debs, Lorna and I had shared everything, the rollercoaster

ride of bringing up our children – my two sons, Sam and Jed, Lorna's three daughters Alice, Jess and Rachel, and Debs's boy Orlando, known as Ollie. We'd been through triumphs and woes and seen each other through some tough times, including their recent personal losses, which is why I'd been reticent about moaning on about my perfectly nice husband.

Debs had been devastated when Fabio left after five years together. She'd genuinely thought she was loved, but apparently not enough. After he'd first gone, she'd hidden away, smoked dope and drank to oblivion, then emerged one day and told us she was going to reinvent herself. She'd had dark hair extensions put in and wore it all piled on top of her head. She'd got a tattoo on her shoulder saying 'Carpe Diem', and had every treatment under the sun to keep looking young, not that she needed them. In the last weeks, she'd been looking into Internet dating, out to prove she was still desirable. So far, she'd had three dates and had reported back after each one, sometimes during. So far, all disasters – too old, too boring and, apparently, the last one had halitosis.

I felt for her. She was a strong woman and some men were intimidated by that. She'd used some of her inheritance to buy a run-down two-storey house on the north side of town, then spent a fortune renovating and turning it into The Lotus Health Centre, a light and elegant spa that was a heavenly place to visit.

I'd never been keen on Fabio. She'd met him on holiday in Italy and he'd swept her off her feet with his charm, plus he was great eye candy, lean and good looking with a mane of dark hair. Fabulous Fabio. They'd made a handsome pair while they were together, but I had always thought that he was an opportunist, not that I ever said that. She deserved a man to share her success who was financially independent and not after her money. Nate, her first long-term partner and Ollie's father hadn't been a good bet either. She'd met him on her travels in America, a restless artist who'd returned to the UK with her but never settled. He was last heard of running a rehab centre somewhere in the Hollywood Hills, a centre Debs had contributed to financially. She was always a sucker for a good cause. There'd been a few men in between Nate and Fabio, but no one lasting.

'What's going on?' I asked when I arrived at Debs's flat to find piles of black bin bags filling up the hall.

Her apartment was on the ground floor in a Georgian terrace, and I always felt I was entering a bohemian art gallery when I went there. The place had high ceilings, fabulous tall windows at the back looking out over a walled garden, and lovely old marble fireplaces. It was decorated in rich reds and aubergines, and she had paintings and artefacts from her Eastern travels in every room, with plush purple velvet Chesterfields in the sitting room. Even her cloakroom was an experience, with a lime green and turquoise interior, antique Victorian glass chandelier and a life-sized poster of Kali watching from the wall opposite the loo. It could be unnerving sometimes, as the Indian goddess looked fierce, her tongue out and her many arms ready to do battle.

'Fabio sent me a text yesterday,' she replied, and showed me the message left on her phone. *I'll b over 2 collect my stuff at the weekend. Can let myself in if u leave it in hall.* 'So I've been clearing out Il Bastardo's things. Should have done it months ago. You can help if you like.'

'Sure, I'd be glad to,' I said. 'Just tell me what I can do.'

'Clear him out, like in that song in *South Pacific*.' She

began to sing, "'I'm gonna wash that man right outta my hair." I've been going round the flat and I realized that Fabio's presence is everywhere – a photo in one room, an ashtray in another, a painting he'd liked in the study. Every room holds some reminder of him, and it's time to get rid.' She began to sing again. 'I'm gonna feng shui that rat right out of my lair.'

'Hasn't he been back for some of it?'

'Only to collect a small case when we first broke up. He probably doesn't need much if he's sitting bollock-naked with his legs wrapped behind his ears in a state of sexual ecstasy every day. I've gathered some of his things – shoes, books, one of his precious laptops, hairbrushes, CDs, and most are in the bin bags, but first I have some small adjustments to make to his clothes. You crack open a bottle of wine and I'll get started.'

I did as instructed, and when I took a bottle and glasses through to the sitting room, I saw that Debs was sitting on the sofa with a pair of scissors and was cutting out the crotch from Fabio's trousers. When she'd finished with those, she started on his underwear. 'Come and get these then, you arse,' she said as she made a mound of clothes near the front door.

'Seriously, Debs?' I asked. 'Is this the way? I thought you believed in letting go and moving on.'

'That's what I'm doing. I've also Super Glued all his books shut and put them in a neat pile by the door.'

I couldn't help chuckling to myself when I thought about Fabio's expression when he reached for a pair of pants. I wasn't sorry he had gone. 'Lorna still hasn't cleared out Alistair's things,' I said as I sipped wine and watched her as she went through Fabio's CDs, squeezing out a dollop of glue onto each surface then placing the CD back in its cover.

'And why should she?' said Debs. 'He was part of that house and I feel for her. Theirs was a very different relationship to mine and Fabio's. Alistair was her soul mate. She was lucky to have found him; not everyone does. I never felt that way about Fabio. I fancied him in the beginning but never thought he was my soul mate.'

'Do you really believe in soul mates?'

'Oh yes. I have no doubt that everyone has one, maybe people who have known each other in past lives; they might be back in this life somewhere, but it doesn't always work out that you meet. What if you live in Shepton Mallet and he lives in Katmandu? Bummer. Or if he was born in another time? He's in the twentieth century and you're in the twenty-first? A case of oops, bad timing. That's when the compromise has to happen and you have to make do, like I did with Fabio.'

I'd believed Tom was my soul mate when we were together. *Had I compromised with Matt, knowing that Tom had gone?* I wondered, as Debs collected more of Fabio's things. Is Matt the love of my life? I used to feel that he was once but I know I'm not happy in the way that Lorna was with Alistair. Their love was constant and anyone could see that she respected him and admired him as well. Matt's a lovely man, was attractive when he was younger – he still is when he makes an effort. It's probably me that's the problem, restless as ever. If I can let go of that, I'm sure we can work things out. Now would be the perfect time to mention Tom. Maybe Debs could tell me how to get him out of my system.

'But what if you meet your soul mate but you're already married to someone else?'

Debs stopped what she was doing. 'Why do you ask? Has that happened to you? Surely Matt's your soul mate?'

I panicked. I wasn't ready to open up to her about Tom, not yet. What would I say? I still didn't know myself how I felt about him getting in touch with me. 'I was just thinking about what you said about bad timing.'

Time to change the subject. Debs's cats, Yin and Yang, sat on the windowsill, watching with interest as she collected more of Fabio's items, including his laptop. 'Was it because of their colouring that you called your cats Yin and Yang?' I asked. Yin was a white Abyssinian and had cost Debs a fortune, Yang, a black long-haired rescue cat that'd cost a donation to the animal centre.

'Yes, because I believe in balance: two sides to everything and everyone, the light and the dark, yin and yang. Lorna says it's just a fancy excuse for having a split personality, but everyone has different facets to their personalities – apart from Fabio, he's just a plain bastard. I really tried everything to please that man. The Tantric workshop, phone sex—'

'Phone sex?'

'Yes. Don't tell me you've never called Matt when he was away on business?'

'I . . .'

'Oh, Cait, you should try it. It's liberating. You don't have to think about how you look, if your wobbly bits are showing. You're a sex goddess on the other end of the phone and your weapon of seduction is your voice. Men love it.'

'Facetime?'

'No, it's hard to get the right angles. Just keep it to audio.'

'I wouldn't know what to say.'

'Course you would.'

'What then?'

'What you'd like to do to him.'

'Slap him with a wet fish?'

Debs ignored me. 'What you'd like him to do to you.' *Stop following me round the house and questioning my every move*, I thought. 'Try it,' Debs continued. 'Men like an accent sometimes too.'

'Yorkshire or Scouser?'

'You are not taking this seriously. No, something sexy – Russian or French or Italian.'

I laughed, grateful that she hadn't pursued the soul mate conversation. 'What's next on the goodbye Fabio task?'

Debs chuckled and pointed at the laptop. 'Fabio's,' she said. 'I know all his passwords so I'm going to go to his Facebook page and change his profile photo.' I went to sit next to her and watched as she opened the MacBook Air, found Facebook, then deleted Fabio's smiling face from his page and replaced it with a photo of Jabba the Hutt.

'What do you think?' she asked.

'Creative. He'll kill you.'

'I haven't finished yet,' she said as she pulled a leather jacket from a pile by the door, laid it on the floor then painted the word 'Slimeball' on the back in white paint from a small tester pot. 'That should do it,' she said as she gathered up his things, put them in a couple of bin bags, tied them with red ribbon and put them with the others by the front door. She came back in with a couple of bundles of dried plants.

'God, Debs, what now?'

'You can help me cleanse the atmosphere of him next.'

'And how do we do that?'

'White sage sticks,' she explained. 'I bought them last week in Glastonbury.'

'What do they do?'

'Clear the house of toxins and bad spirits – at least that's what the witchy-looking girl in the shop informed me. She said they can change your environment from your current one to a mystical one. We light them, then take them from room to room waving the scent into all the corners.'

'OK, let's do it,' I said.

An afternoon spent with Debs was never normal and always made a refreshing change, but her antics reminded me that she probably wasn't the one to ask for marriage-guidance advice. I followed her instructions, lit my bundles of herbs, then went from room to room waving the sage sticks in the air, into corners, above the doorways and windows. It had a strong herbal scent that was pleasantly pungent.

'The process is called smudging,' Debs called from the corridor where she was waving her bundle with great enthusiasm. 'Goodbye Fabio, goodbye bad vibes, goodbye misery. Air, fire, water, earth, dismiss, dispel, disperse. Witchy woman told me to bury the embers of the sage once finished so, when your bundle's gone out, we'll do that.'

'Righto,' I called and went back to my task.

Ten minutes later, the bundles had burned down, so we went outside, found a spade and buried them under a lilac tree. Yin and Yang followed us out and watched as if we were mad.

'I guess they burn frankincense and myrrh for healing and to raise the spirits in churches,' I said, 'so maybe it's not so barmy to use white sage to dispel negative vibes.'

'Exactly,' said Debs. 'Though I'm glad Lorna's not with us. I don't think she'd have joined in with the same open-mindedness as you. I'm not finished yet, though. I have one last thing to do, and that's to call the locksmith to come and change the locks and then I'll be done. Fabio will have been exorcized and I have to say it's made me feel a darn sight better. OK. How about a change of scenery next? How about I put on my Bollywood movie soundtrack CD and we dance around the living room? We can pretend we're in India.'

'Excellent. I like your thinking. Lead the way, Debs,' I said, and followed her back inside the flat. *When the going gets tough, the tough act like mad old hippies*, I thought as Debs put on the music and I put my hands on my waist and began to bang the floor with my feet and bounce around the room. *Debs may be many things*, I thought when I left an hour later – *opinionated, eccentric, outspoken – but she's never boring and she can always distract me from my problems with her peculiar view on life.*

9

As I drove home, I thought about what awaited me. Matt and a house full of worries or . . . maybe I'd try the phone sex. OK, so . . . stuff to get him excited? Now let me think. Last year on the writing course, a great older lady called Lily suggested we try writing erotic fiction for a few weeks and, as part of the course, we studied what men wanted to read in contrast to women. It was interesting. We'd read a book called *Unleashing the Hound* to give us an idea of what people wrote. It appeared that men liked strong words, lots of hard thrusting, action, whereas most women liked the anticipation, the romance and build-up.

No time like the present, I thought as I stopped the car in a quiet street and got out my mobile. Now, get in the mood, Cait. Remember how it was when we were younger. I called home. I heard Matt's voice a few moments later.

'Matt?'

'Ah, Cait,' I heard him say.

'Don't say anything,' I started and went in to what I hoped was a Russian accent, 'I 'ave been thinking of you and vot I'd like to do.'

'Cait—'

'No, don't interrupt, just go vith eet. I am imagining you naked.'

He sounded surprised. 'You are?'

'I vont you to unleash the hound. I vont you to slide your hand down in between—'

'*Cait*,' Matt said urgently.

'I vill do the same. I'm sliding my hand across my breasts, my thrusting breasts—'

'No, Cait stop—'

'I cannot stop, I vont to feel—'

'No, *NO*.' My words were drowned out by the sound of Matt calling my name, louder and louder. 'CAIT. CAAAAIT.' I hadn't heard him this excited in years.

'I want to feel your body, hard—'

'CAIT—'

'You are liking vot you're hearing? Yes? No?'

'Well, yes but it's not Matt. It's Duncan.'

'Duncan?'

'Yeah.'

Noooooooo. Matt's chauvinist stoner of a brother. Same voice as Matt.

'I . . . thought you were Matt.'

'I know. You saucy minx. Who'd have thought? Though I'm not sure about the Welsh accent.' I heard him laugh. 'Matt's just popped out to get us a couple of beers. Hold on, I'm just writing down what you said so I can pass on the message. Breasts. Legs. Hound. Hard. Right, think I got most of that.'

'Fuck off, Duncan.'

I heard him laugh again then the phone clicked off.

No *way* was I going home if Duncan was still there. I turned around and headed to Lorna's.

'What have you been up to?' I asked when I arrived.

'Oh, the usual, just doing my Saturday jobs – feeding the dogs, watering the garden, cutting some herbs for supper. Come outside, I just have to finish the borders then I'll fix us a drink.'

I followed her through the house and sat on the wrought-iron veranda looking out on the garden. It had come alive since I was last here, the pergola to the right was covered with pink Clematis montana, and in the beds there were foxgloves popping up, lavender, white tulips about to fade.

It wasn't meant to be like this, I thought as I watched Lorna stride out onto the lawn with the hose, turn it on and begin watering. I recalled sitting in the same spot watching Alistair do the same thing only a year ago. It didn't seem right: Lorna, alone in her big old rambling house with no one but her golden retrievers, Otto and Angus, for company. 'No decisions for a year,' Matt had said to her after Alistair died; wise words echoed by all her children apart from her daughter, Jess, who invited Lorna to go and live with her in New Zealand. 'Get away, new scenery, new experiences,' she'd said. But Lorna had told us that she didn't want new experiences; she wanted to be home where Alistair's presence was still evident, inside and out.

After putting the hose away, Lorna made two large gin and tonics and came to join me on the rattan sofa.

'So what have you been doing?' she asked.

I told her about Debs's way of clearing Fabio out of her life, but omitted the phone-sex episode. I'd had enough humiliation for one day.

'I suppose Debs's method of doing it is one way. I've told myself every month that I'd clear Alistair's study, go through his wardrobes, give his clothes to charity, but as each month has gone by since he died, I've found I can't do it. If I cleared everything out, he'd be gone, leaving empty spaces and even emptier rooms, and I'm not ready, not yet, if ever. But the house is way too big, I know that.'

I glanced up at the back. A lovely seventeenth-century manor house with five bedrooms, Alistair's study, two reception rooms, an enormous kitchen-diner that opened out to the garden where there were three stone outbuildings. Their girls had slept and played there when they were growing up. It had been a home full of the sound of laughter, chatter, friends coming and going, always something happening and now, even with two of us here, amicably chatting, it felt silent.

'I know,' said Lorna, picking up on my thoughts. 'It's quiet here, isn't it? So quiet. For the first time in years, I'm aware of the ticking of the clock and the humming of the fridge-freezer.'

I felt for her. Her children had all been and stayed before and after the funeral, but they couldn't stay forever. Lorna knew that. Jess, her husband and two boys were first to go back, home to New Zealand. Alice and Rachel were next to leave, Alice to her job with Médecins Sans Frontières, her latest posting in Uganda. Lorna was so proud of her but I knew she worried how safe she was, not that she let Alice know that. Rachel went back to her marketing job at an advertising agency in New York, where she shared a flat with her boyfriend, Mark. Like me with Sam, and Debs with Ollie, Lorna caught up with her cyberspace family at weekends on Skype, but we often said to each other that it wasn't the same as having them here, filling the kitchen, making endless meals and cups of tea, draped on sofas with books, mobiles or laptops, the place full of life.

'When they were young, I thought we'd always be together,' said Lorna, picking up on my thoughts once more. 'I'd imagined there would be family weekends in summer, swimming by the river, walks along the canal followed by long Sunday lunches out in the garden. I'd be busy making jam or baking, preparing picnics to take to nearby fields, my grandchildren cartwheeling on the lawns, bashing balls around, playing cricket, croquet, badminton but . . . it hasn't worked out that way, and all the garden games lie in boxes in one of the outhouses, gathering cobwebs.'

Her girls were a bright bunch. They had gone off to university, met partners and carved out their careers, which is exactly what she and Alistair wanted them to do. 'No one can predict where or for how long jobs are going to present themselves,' I said, 'and there was nothing doing round here for them in the fields they'd chosen. It's great that you never held them back and encouraged each of them to follow their own path, as did Alistair.'

Lorna nodded. 'He did, but I know that he too had his dreams of an idyllic chapter as we grew older, and that they would be within driving distance. Neither of us ever imagined they'd all be so far away. They come back when they can, but travel is expensive and each visit feels too short. Then there are the inevitable goodbyes, waving them off at the gate, never showing that I'm crumbling inside.'

It wasn't meant to be like this, I thought again as I sipped on my drink and wondered what I could say to make her feel better. My two friends, both alone, though in different circumstances, both dealing with being by themselves in such opposite ways. I was glad that I'd come to see Lorna, and glad that she'd opened up to me about how she was feeling. It was a rare event, and I didn't want to spoil it by bringing up Matt, Tom or my concerns in the face of her obvious loneliness and the brave front she put on most days. Despite that courage, there was no changing the fact that she was here on her own most nights, on the veranda at the back of the house where she'd spent every evening with Alistair, the dogs at their feet, before he died.

'We'd talk for hours out here,' said Lorna, 'and while Alistair was alive, it was bearable that our family had flown to distant parts of the world. We had each other, always something to say and, you know, although he was ten years older than me, I thought he'd last at least another twenty years.'

I nodded. 'Me too. He was such a big character, the life and soul, with a hundred interests and opinions on everything, informed and stimulating ones at that.'

'And now there's just me here, an empty chair opposite where Alistair used to be, silence where there was conversation and company. Even inside, everything is as he'd left it in his study, a scribbled note on his desk reminding him to get tickets for an author event at Toppings bookshop in town, the history book he was reading on the side table by his armchair, his old cardigan hanging on the back of his desk chair. If I hold it to my face, I can still just about catch the scent of him, woody from the garden where, as you know, he spent most of his time.'

I reached out and put my hand over hers. 'Oh, Lorna. I know it must be so hard. You know you're welcome at ours any time you feel like company.'

'I know, and thanks, but the reality is, he's gone, and I'd

still have to come back and wake up here, have my evenings without him. I've been house-hunting in the last week, if only to keep my girls happy, as Jess and Rachel have been on at me again to move. I saw three houses, all perfectly nice, adequate, charming even, but I couldn't see myself in any of them. What feels right is home, my home, so it's only confirmed that I don't want to move. I told the estate agent that I'd be in touch but I won't.'

'I can't blame you for not wanting to go. It's beautiful here. So peaceful.' I knew that the house had been in Alistair's family for three generations, making it doubly hard to let go of.

'Even though it's quiet without him, I feel his presence. When I look out on the garden, I'm reminded of the endless trips to nurseries when we began to redesign the layout. It had been so neglected in his parents' old age. The bare root roses, wild geraniums, alliums, lavender, clematis, jasmine that we bought that will tumble over walls, trellises in June and July, tiny plants we nurtured that now fill the borders, they're all reminders of him. I couldn't leave them for someone else to neglect.'

'Then don't,' I said. 'It's perfect, and if it gives you comfort being here with all the reminders, then stay.' She and Alistair had done their homework in the early days and driven all over England looking at National Trust gardens, Sissinghurst, Gertrude Jekyll landscapes. There were years when I remembered they'd pored over gardening books, attended workshops at weekends until they knew exactly what they were doing, before creating the wonderful garden that was in front of us now.

I smiled and took my hand away from Lorna's. 'I can still see Alistair out there in his baggy old gardening clothes, on his knees planting or in the greenhouses watering his pride-and-joy tomatoes.'

'And inside, every room has paintings and artefacts left by his parents, and others we chose together on various holidays. Every one tells a story, to me at least. So no, I don't want to move yet. Some day. Not yet.'

Suddenly she stood up and shook herself. 'Enough of being maudlin, Lorna. I'll think of something,' she said as she went down the garden to wind a stray stem of clematis around a pergola pole. 'If Alistair going has taught me anything, it's that we must seize the day and live our lives fearlessly, Cait: life is short. Sorry. Enough of me and doom and gloom. How are things with you? How's your lovely dad? And heard any more from that Tom bloke?'

'Dad's OK though lonely I think. And no, I haven't heard from Tom.'

'Did you delete his friend request?'

'It's on my list of things to do when I get back.' I didn't need to tell her that I'd accepted Tom's request if only to satisfy my curiosity. If I unfriended him, she'd never know.

'You make sure you do it, Cait. How's Matt?'

'Same ole.'

'Same ole good or same ole bad?'

'Same ole somewhere in the middle. He keeps bringing me tea in bed. His way of making an effort.'

'I'm sure you'll get through this.'

'I know. I'll give him time.'

'And yourself, Cait. It's an adjustment for you too.'

10

Cait

To do:
- Unfriend Tom Lewis.
- Make a list of decorating tasks for Matt.
- Start clearing out rooms for Airbnb.
- Collect rubbish for the tip.
- Plant white geraniums in pots at front.
- Visit Dad.

*

Resolutions made on the drive over to see Dad in Chippenham.

- Stop saying oof and groaning when getting in or out of the car or on or off sofa.
- Stop talking out loud to myself.

I usually talk to myself at home so it's OK, short phrases like, 'Right, that's done now.' Or talking to the plants in the garden after removing bindweed – 'I think you'll feel better now.' However, I found myself doing it in the supermarket this morning when picking up a few things to take to Dad.

'Don't forget red peppers,' I said to myself as I went along the vegetable counters.

'That's another off the list,' I said as I found mushrooms.

'Good,' I said as I loaded loo paper onto the trolley. 'Now, should I get a packet of frozen peas or not?'

An elderly woman by my side gave me a curious look as she picked out potatoes.

I smiled at her and said, 'I see dead people.'

She didn't get the movie reference and backed her trolley out of there fast.

*

Dad was sitting on a bench at the front of his bungalow when I arrived and didn't see me at first. He was wearing his battered panama hat and a light summer jacket and was eating an ice cream with a spoon from a tub. He liked ice cream, and I had a flashback to days out at the seaside when my brother Mike and I were little, and he'd buy 99s for us, those cones with ice cream and a chocolate flake. Blackpool was his favourite place for a trip. He used to go there as a lad with his parents, then later as a young man when he was a ballroom dancer. He'd won prizes in competitions there back in the day, long before *Strictly*. Whatever the weather, beaches with him were always full of fun: donkey rides, ball games, squealing at the cold waves in the sea. There were always people around on those seaside trips, car-loads full of aunts, uncles, cousins, friends, all laden with sandwiches wrapped in greaseproof paper, bottles of Vimto or dandelion and burdock to drink. The journeys were noisy affairs with lots of banter and singing. The garden at home in summer was the same, with the paddling pool, tennis racquets, cricket bats all deployed. Dad was always first up to play, whatever the game – whether it was croquet, rounders, or running around with the hosepipe soaking us all. And now there he was, a frail old man with white hair, sitting on a bench, shrouded in loneliness. It was evident in the hunch of his shoulders and the slowness of his movements, and it broke my heart to see him like that.

I'd told him time and again that he could come and live with us, but he wouldn't hear of it. 'Last thing I want is to be a burden to anyone,' was his constant reply. After Mum died, he visibly shrank, incomplete without her. He'd always had double energy, a full-time job lecturing at the university, as well as the hobbies, like making wine (my brother Mike and I called it Krudo and would pour it away discreetly as soon as we could when offered a glass). Then came the making of dolls' houses, and after that barometers and coffee tables. I still had a table he'd made with a wonky leg, and wouldn't hear of having it replaced with a new one. He was never happier than when out in his shed at the old family house with a hammer and nails bashing away at something. I used to love going in there, the smell of woodchip and petrol, looking at the rows and rows of tools and screws, each neatly labelled and in its place.

When we were little, he'd read bedtime stories to Mike and me and did all the voices of the different characters. He was always a great entertainer and could sing too. Bath times were occasions to look forward to when we had to pretend we were in a soap commercial and be on our very best behaviour. He did magic tricks, pretended to swallow tooth-brushes, made dolly mixtures appear from the light fittings, traditions he continued with my two boys when they were young. He made life fun, with Friday night declared fizz and crisp night, something Matt and I carried on for many years, when one of us would arrive home with a bottle of bubbly and nibbles for us and lemonade and crisps for the boys. Dad was always in charge of the drinks. On the 24th of December, he'd set off on his bike to buy crème de menthe, Advocaat or Babycham for visitors, most of which stood untouched throughout the season, but seeing those bottles in the back room was part of our Christmas. Dad played piano, sang in the choir, was part of the local tennis club, until his knees let him down and partners aged alongside him or died off and suddenly he didn't feel it was his place.

He'd kept up exercises, though, going through an army routine every morning, with his constant companion Brandy the Labrador sitting at the door watching with interest. And now Mum had gone, Brandy too, and the bungalow they retired to has grown quiet. He told me that the days there were long. Like so many of his generation, he didn't watch TV during the day. Radio Four was permissible but not TV, despite the many box sets I'd bought him, it was only allowed after six, starting with the news. He and Mum had had their rituals: breakfast – always the same, porridge and fruit, then at eleven coffee and a biscuit, a cup of soup and crackers at twelve thirty, tea and a cake at four, supper at six. When they were younger, they'd always had a sundowner in the evening, taken with great relish, but Dad rarely drinks any more. It upsets his stomach. He could cook for himself, though it tended to be frozen meals from M & S, his once large appetite reduced to that of a bird. Despite various suggestions about sheltered accommodation, he won't move house. 'I've got my independence and I know my way round here,' he insisted. But, to me, it didn't seem right that such a happy and full life had shrunk to one where it felt like he was waiting around for his turn to die.

He was always the protector, the one we all went to in order to talk over options, always a good listening ear with sound advice to pass on. I adored him when I was a child, feared him as a teen when he became critical of skirts too short, telephone calls too long, but then came a softening as he grew older and I grew up. And now I knew he was lonely and a bit depressed, which was so unlike him. I knew he missed my mother, as did I. She had been the practical one who had run the house, he was the one who made the magic. On the rare occasions that she'd send him off to get groceries, he'd return with a puppy or a bike or a new gadget to try out. We'd always had dogs, but when Brandy died a year before Mum, Dad didn't replace him, saying it would be unfair because he wouldn't want a pup to be left behind when he died.

'Hey, Dad,' I called.

He immediately sat up, throwing off the invisible cloak that had settled around him and put on his cheerful face. 'Caitlin.'

'What you up to?'

'Oh you know, this and that.'

I waved a newspaper. 'Want a paper?'

'Already read it, cover to cover.'

I took his hand. It was like holding a large soft paw. 'Dad, you would say if you don't want to be here any longer, wouldn't you? You know you can always come and live with us.'

'Not necessary. No. This is my home. It's fine,' he said, then laughed and came out with his favourite familiar line delivered in a Scottish accent. 'I'm no long for this world.'

'You have to stop saying that. You're eighty-nine. You might live till you're a hundred.'

'Hope not.'

'Are you OK? Really?'

'Just fine, Cait. Just fine.'

I knew things could be worse regarding my parents. Although Mum's death had hit me hard, she'd gone quickly. She'd died after a fall, had five days in hospital having a hip replacement from which there were complications, and she'd never returned home. Five hellish days but, looking back, it was swift. Too swift. I'd been to visit on the Saturday then gone home thinking that she'd be out a few days later. Due to unexpected problems, she'd gone into a coma and died the next day. I'd never forgiven myself for not being there, for not having realized something like that might happen, something I found hard to come to terms with despite reassurances from Dad and my brother that there was nothing I could have done. Hard though it was, I was glad it hadn't been more drawn out. Lorna's mother has dementia, has had several strokes, and has been told she wouldn't last the night more times than I could count in the last years. In her rare lucid moments, she says she wants to go, she's tired. Lorna had grieved, let go, grieved then let go so many times that all she wanted now was release for her mother. It was the same for a few of our friends who had aged parents who had no quality of life. So hard to witness and do what could be done, but feel helpless all the same.

'So what have you been doing, Cait?'

'Planning to do up the house.' I told him about the latest plan to do Airbnb.

'You sure? Strangers in your house?'

'But that's just it. Apparently you never see them. They'll be tourists, so only want a bed for the night. All we have to do is give them breakfast.'

'If you say so, love. I couldn't be doing with strangers in my house.'

'Do you want to go out anywhere?'

'Where to? Why?'

'Change of scenery.'

'Maybe.' That meant no.

On my last few visits, he'd been reluctant to go anywhere, as if he was retreating more and more into himself.

'Let's go out for lunch. You could have a beer.'

Dad smiled. 'You're a good daughter, Caitlin. Now then, tell me all about what's happening in your life.'

I filled him in on the latest with Matt and news about the boys.

'And are you happy, Cait? How are you really?'

'I'm fine, busy, working on new book ideas, just fine.'

We are both good liars.

11

Cait

Sunday evening was time for my New Age course with Debs. Usually there were only three or four of us and we'd done all sorts of weird and whacky stuff over the year – dowsing, card readings, crystals. Matt called it my witchcraft course, Lorna pronounced it baloney, but they didn't put me off because the sessions felt like going back to kindergarten and always cheered me up, and I needed that after seeing Dad. I always came away from him feeling sad that I couldn't do more to make his last chapters happier ones.

'Excellent timing,' said Debs when she opened her door. 'I was just doing a Tarot reading. I could do yours as well. See what's in store for our future.' She was dressed in one of her fabulous long kaftans, this time a deep red one that gave her the look of a fortune-teller. In my jeans and beige top, I felt drab in comparison.

'Anyone else coming?' I asked as I followed her through to her sitting room.

'No. Just me and thee tonight so it's good to have company.'

'So what shall we do this evening?'

'As it's just us, if you don't mind, I'd like to do stage two in my post-Fabio "I'm Moving On" phase. A card reading, some visualization and maybe some Gestalt and of course, anything you'd like to work on.'

'Lead the way,' I said as I took a seat on one of the Chesterfields by the fireplace and watched as Debs shuffled the Tarot cards.

'Help yourself to wine,' she said as she indicated the bottle of Chablis in an ice bucket and two glasses on the coffee table. 'This layout is the Celtic cross,' she explained as she carefully placed cards on the table. 'First we look at the card in the position that represents what's passing out of my life. Ah. Not surprising – the Six of Swords.' The card showed a sorrowing woman being ferried across the water. 'A time of tension but she is moving away from it. Row row row the boat, gently down the stream, Fabio you stinking slime-ball, you are but a dream.' She surveyed the rest of the layout. 'The other cards reflect the same, a time of difficulty but change is coming. Hurrah.'

'Hope it's a good one,' I said.

'What's this though?' She held up a card. 'The Seven of Swords is in the place representing what's coming up next. A man looking guiltily over his shoulder. See? Hmm.' She checked her reference book. 'This card can suggest an act of dishonour. Or flight from a dishonourable act. Surely that would be Fabio, he was the cheater – so why's it in my future? Not me surely? I don't do dishonourable. Maybe it's to do with tax but I'm not asking about that. I'm asking about love. Judgement is in the place for the future. The last card shows the outcome of the reading is Death.'

'Oh no.'

'Don't worry. It isn't a bad card. It means the end of something and beginning of a new chapter. A rebirth and
transformation rather than a final end, but I'm not sure
about the man and judgement. Hey-ho. A mystery. I guess
that's what life's about. All in all, not a bad reading, apart
from the dishonourable bit. Right, let's do yours. Put all the
cards back together, then shuffle them while concentrating
hard on what you want to know about.'

'Just one thing?'

'Yes. Try and focus on one, but the readings can sometimes
pick up on other stuff as well.'

'OK.' I shuffled the cards and tried to focus just on my
work prospects, but my mind was full of questions – Matt,
marriage, Dad, my kids and Tom Lewis.

'Good,' said Debs when I indicated I'd finished, 'now split
the pile into three smaller piles to your left and place them
on the coffee table. Good. Then put them into one pile again.
Good.'

When I'd done what she asked, she picked up the cards
and, taking them from the top, she laid them in a cross
shape, similar to the one she had done earlier.

'Woah,' she said, 'lot of major stuff going on. The card
representing your present says what we already know – a
time of turbulence and change, but I see a man in your
future.' She picked up a card that said 'The Lovers' on it.
'Something you want to tell me about, Cait?'

I felt myself blush and hoped that Debs didn't notice.
'That has to be Matt right?'

Debs shook her head. 'Not necessarily. From where it's
placed, it's in your future not your past, and it denotes that
some kind of choice may have to be made.'

'Really? Something about one of my boys maybe?'

'I don't think so. And you also have a king card, so it's an older man, not a young one. The King of Pentacles.' She continued to study the layout. 'Actually, you have two kings, the King of Wands too.'

'Maybe Matt and I are going into a new phase? A more loving phase?'

'From the layout, the cards can also mean you need to get in touch with your feelings,' said Debs. She was studying me carefully. It made me feel uncomfortable.

'Stop doing Witch Woman staring at me,' I said. 'Yoda does that. Freaks me right out. So, what does it say about these lovers? Good or bad?'

Debs looked back at the card. 'You've got the Judgement card too. It's a good card to get as it signifies that things that have lain fallow will come to light, a time of new beginning. You also have the Moon card. It indicates that you may have to make a choice. It signifies uncertainty. Are you quite sure there's something you're not telling me?'

'Course not.' *Liar, liar*, said a voice in my head.

'You got the Temperance card too: that means you may have to make some compromise in marriage.'

'Well, that makes sense, and what marriage doesn't involve compromise? What's the outcome?'

Debs picked up the last card. 'The Tower. Wow. You have a lot of the major cards in your reading.'

'What does that mean?'

'A lot's going on in your life.'

I picked up the card. It showed someone falling out of a high building. 'I don't like the look of this.'

'Don't worry,' said Debs. 'Like the Death card, it's not

necessarily bad. It just means that old structures need to be broken down and left behind before new ones can emerge.'

'Looks violent to me.'

'Just change. You know the old saying – what you resist, persists. If you embrace change and aren't rigid, it needn't be painful.'

'Both Matt and I losing our jobs, it could be about that. It's a time of change. Is it looking good?'

'Yes, sure,' said Debs. I noticed she tucked a card away.

'What was that? You're hiding a card.'

Debs pulled it back out. It was the Hanged Man.

'Oh god,' I said. 'This is getting worse and worse. Burning towers, hanged men—'

'No, no, not at all. It's where they're placed that counts.'

'And?'

'All will be well, Cait,' said Debs. She wasn't convincing.

'Have you got an *I Ching*, Debs?' I asked.

'Course.'

'Get it out. I might have to throw it for clarification. We need a second opinion.'

'Quite right.' Debs laughed. 'My kind of gal.'

She went to her bookshelves and pulled out a copy of the *I Ching*.

'Can you remember how to do it?' I asked.

Debs nodded. 'We need three coins.'

I reached into my bag, pulled out my purse and handed her six twenty-piece coins.

'Three for you, three for me.'

'Good,' said Debs. 'Hold them, ask your question again, then shake them and I'll do the same.'

I did as I was told and this time I thought about Matt and Tom.

'What are you asking, Debs?'

'It's supposed to be a secret but I'm asking, will I ever meet a decent man? My soul mate?'

'OK. You go first then. Throw.'

She threw her coins, looked up the sequence and got number 29/The Abysmal. She flicked to the page in the *I Ching*. 'The book says, "If you are sincere, you have success in your heart and whatever you do succeeds." Hurrah. Now then, how many lines do I have? Six. Oo, no. That says "Means bounds with cords and ropes. Shut in between thorn-hedged prison walls." Uh? "For three years one does not find the way. Misfortune." Well, bollocks to that. I probably wasn't concentrating or it picked up on all that anger I let out when I was packing up Fabio's stuff. I'll throw the coins again in the morning and maybe again after that and see what the book tells me then. Best out of three, I always say. Now you go.'

I threw my coins and Debs looked up the sequence of lines.

'Oh dear,' she said when she consulted the book.

'What? *What?* Is it bad?'

'Separation. Secrets. Change. Cait, are you really *really* sure that there's not something you want to tell me?'

'Nope.' I wished we hadn't started on the fortune-telling. It was getting too close to the bone.

'How's Matt?'

'Same ole.'

Debs took a slug of her wine. 'OK. I've been thinking about you and I'm going to say something. Don't take this the wrong way, but with all that's happened to you both lately, have you thought of marriage counselling?'

'Not really. Matt would never agree to it.'

'We have some great therapists at the spa.'

'At the spa? No, really, things aren't that bad.' *What a good idea*, I thought. It could be just what we needed, but not at Debs's place. It was too near to home and I knew how she gossiped about some of her clients. I'd find my own. I made a mental note to check out local therapists when I got home.

*

Matt was engrossed in a movie in the sitting room when I got back, so I went up to my study to search for marriage-guidance counsellors.

I turned the computer on and had a quick look at Facebook first. There was a private message. Tom Lewis. Gulp. He'd replied. Cue violins, doves, rose petals, heart palpitations, etc.

'Caitlin, it is you! A blast from the past hey? I'd love to see you, catch up. I see you live in Bath. I'm presently in London. Are you ever up this way? Or I could come to Bath. Let's do a lunch. You might not recognize me, I'll be the old codger wearing a red carnation. I'd know you anywhere. Have posted you a song, you might recognize it. Big hug Tom X.'

I went back to my main page and scrolled down past the most recent posts. Oh lord. There it was. Unbelievable. 'Guinnevere' by Crosby, Stills & Nash. Our song. He hadn't forgotten. I felt all a-flutter, like a teenager. *Where are my smelling salts? I've come over all faint.* I realized the track was on my page, for everyone to see. Oh no. For Lorna to see, for Debs to see. For all my Facebook friends to see. When had it been left? Three thirty p.m. When I was out at Dad's. Should I delete the track? Yes. No. If I did, Tom might see that it had gone and wonder what the big deal was. It was only a music clip, wasn't it? A sweet gesture to say he remembered our time together. No one else would know what it meant to me. I'd leave it. It was innocent. A piece of music from an old friend in my past. So why was I feeling as if I was sixteen and a boy I liked had just noticed me. *Grow up*, I told myself.

I was about to close Facebook when I saw that someone had posted a questionnaire to discover if one is a good Catholic. I'm not Catholic but can't resist an online quiz. I got 100 per cent of the questions right. According to these tests, I am also a mathematical genius and, with my IQ, could be a brain surgeon.

'Cait, the *Antiques Roadshow* is on,' Matt called up the stairs.

'OK, coming.' *Such is the glamour of my life now, Tom,* I thought. You might have thought I was one of the cool ones once, but these days, the highlight of my week is the *Antiques Roadshow*, a Facebook quiz and a cup of cocoa. I am the last of the great ravers.

'And I forgot to tell you Lorna called when you were out this afternoon,' Matt added.

I bet she did, I thought as I felt a sinking feeling inside. She'd probably seen Tom's post. Had Debs seen it by now too? No doubt she'd be in touch soon as well.

I put the phone onto message and went down to watch my programme.

12

Cait

Senior moments: 2.

Came out of Co-op first thing this morning to find my car had gone. Immediately reported it as stolen to the police.

Called Matt to tell him my car had been stolen. 'And I think I might have left my mobile in it as well.'

'So how are you calling me?' he asked.

Ah.

Walked home and saw car outside the house. Uh? Ah . . . I'd forgotten I'd walked to the shop.

Must get a grip.

*

It's my writing class this evening and I haven't written anything for weeks, plus I'm meeting my friend, Lizzie, on Friday in London. I'd better have something to show her so that she can advise. I will not be defeated. Must come up with award-winning, bestselling book idea that will get snapped up by a production company and made into a film. Right then. That should be easy enough.

On the way to my study to start work, I experienced a sudden urge to clean under the sink, file my nails, dust the blinds, and then of course it was time for a cup of tea and to get ready for my job interview at the dentist's.

I opened my laptop, went to mail and saw that there was an email from Debs.

From: Debs23@g.org.com
To: Cait@grmail.com

CAIIIIT, who's the gorgeous man on your Facebook page? The Tarot cards were right. You've been holding out on me. Debs X

*

From: Cait@grmail.com
To: Debs23@g.org.com

Just someone I knew ages ago. CX

*

From: Debs23@g.org.com
To: Cait@grmail.com

Get you with your mysterious past. What's the story? Maybe he's the King of Wands we saw in the card reading?
DX

Argh. *Keep calm*, I told myself as I typed a reply.

From: Cait@grmail.com
To: Debs23@g.org.com

Ancient history. Haven't seen him in over forty years. CX

*

From: Debs23@g.org.com
To: Cait@grmail.com

Find out if he's single. Please. I like the look of him. You could introduce us? DX

I knew this would happen! *No way, Debs*, I thought, and it's insensitive of her to even ask, though of course she doesn't know what he had meant to me. I'd only ever told Lorna about him. All the same, I'm not introducing her.

From: Cait@grmail.com
To: Debs23@g.org.com

Too old for you. He could be your father.
CX

*

From: Debs23@g.org.com
To: Cait@grmail.com

Great! Bring it on. I could do with a father figure. Be a nice change from the immature idiots I've been out with.

Besides, he looks sexy. Age is all in the mind. Sixty is
the new forty and all that. Look at Goldie Hawn,
Sigourney Weaver, Susan Sarandon – and Charlottte
Rampling is in her seventies and still looks hot. You're
probably the same age as Tom? I don't think of you as
too old to be my friend. We are what we are. Plus older
men – George Clooney, Brad Pitt, Johnny Depp . . .
   DX

Nooooo. I knew it. Tom'd always had the women after him
and now he's pulling in cyberspace.

From: Cait@grmail.com
To: Debs23@g.org.com

Point taken. I'll see what I can find out.
   X

But I won't, I thought. Tom might be ancient history but he
was my ancient history.

From: Debs23@g.org.com
To: Cait@grmail.com

Great. Thanks.
   Love you Debs X

I am a bad friend, I thought as I closed the laptop and got
ready for my job interview.

*

A young blonde girl at the reception desk called my name at the dental clinic.

'Mr Johnson will see you now.'

I got up and went through to see another young thing, this time a boy with pale cheeks and a shock of ginger hair, behind a desk. 'Please take a seat,' he said. 'So, Mrs Langham. I see from your CV that you worked for a year as a doctor's receptionist and before that as a teacher, but in between I am unclear about what you were doing.'

'I worked in a library.'

'Ah. And there are a few gaps in your CV over the years. What were you doing then?'

'Bringing up my children.'

'I see. Now. What do you think you could bring to the job?'

'Enthusiasm, experience—'

'Now let me stop you there,' he said. 'That's exactly what I thought. Experience. You're clearly way overqualified for this job. My concern is that you'd get bored and move on, then we'd have to train someone else up. You do understand what I'm saying, don't you?'

'That I haven't got the job.'

'I'm not convinced from looking at your work experience that we're the ones for you,' he said. 'I'm sure you'll be able to find something else and put your skills to full use.'

I stood up. 'Well thank you for your time.'

Once home, I made it to my study and opened my laptop. Hurrah. Cheers from the crowd.

I was about to open the file where I keep my ideas but, before focusing on writing, oh no, I can't resist, it's bigger than me, I have to . . .

- See what's on at the cinema.
- Go through the online address book deleting all those who have moved or died.
- Check Facebook. Nothing from Tom, not that I was expecting there to be. The ball was in my court. My turn to reply to him. *I could always see him when I go to London on Friday*, I thought. *No. No. Bad idea. DO some writing Cait. I will, I will . . .*
- Watch a clip about a baby elephant being rescued from where he'd got stuck in a muddy hole as his mother watched. Aw.
- Google the word askew (Sam had emailed and told me to do it. V. funny. The whole page is askew. Clearly I have too much time on my hands.)

Finally I stopped messing about and wrote the word 'The'. It's a start.

Why is it a bad idea to see Tom? I asked myself. *Because it's one thing saying hi on Facebook, another thing meeting up*, I replied to myself. *But he suggested it*, my thoughts continued. *Shut up, mind, shut up. Get on with writing a bestselling, award-winning children's book.*

Stared out of the window at the row of houses opposite. New ideas? New ideas? Kids like angels. Kids like kittens.

Wrote a page about an angel kitten. Deleted it.

Wrote a page about a devil kitten. Deleted it.

Checked Facebook again. *Anything* could have happened in the last fifteen minutes. It had! Someone had posted a clip with a kitten riding about on top of a remote hoover and another of ants dragging the dead corpse of a worm. There's no end to this v. important stuff.

Someone else had posted a quiz that reveals what kind of personality you have just by the colours you choose. Did the quiz. What rubbish. It said that I was a person who likes to procrastinate.

Had a look on the Rightmove property site for houses. Nothing in our price range that looked appealing. Depressing. Debs would say don't limit yourself, expand the boundaries. I opened out the price bracket to look at the houses way out of our budget. That's more like it. Lovely. I could see myself there, just need to find two million. Looked at another fabulous manor house. That's more doable – we'd only have to find one and a half million. Must remember to do lottery.

Back to new ideas. Alien kitten? Deleted it. Vampire kitten? Butterflies? Wrote a page about a caterpillar that suffered from claustrophobia and was afraid to go into the cocoon. Deleted it.

I am writing drivel. *Maybe I should do something else and come back to it*, I thought. And not go on Facebook.

Went onto Facebook. Read a clip about how to get your very own personalized jar of Marmite. Life-changing stuff. Ordered two, one for Sam, one for Jed.

Dyed my greying eyebrows with honey-blonde dye. Left it on five minutes as instructed. Wiped it off. Perfect. *I am young again.*

Back to my study. New characters to appeal to children? Hedgehogs? Penguins? Meerkats? I like meerkats. Meerkats in underpants? No. Underpants have been done. A farting hedgehog? No, farting has been done. Bears? Done. Dragons? Done. Aliens? Done, done, done, also aliens in underpants. Fairies, elves, puppies? I'd done fairies. Unbeknown to Lorna and Debs, I'd based two characters on them. Sensible fairy and mad fairy. It had been a hit with my writing class. Maybe I should get that out to take to show Lizzie. But now what? Fat fairies. A fairy kitten, that could be cute. Probably been done. Fairies without faces. Oo, no. That's just wrong. Vampires with no teeth? No. That's it. I was out of ideas.

Managed to go to loo without Matt interrupting. Looked in mirror. Oh god! Dye must have continued working on my eyebrows, they are black. I look like Groucho Marx.

Back to work.

Creatures with dark eyebrows? Maybe I should ask Matt to brainstorm with me. He was a great ideas man.

No. I could do it myself. Dinosaurs? Been done. Dinosaurs with dark eyebrows?

Walk. I need a walk. All the creative-writing teachers say go and walk to let the unconscious mind kick in.

Put on my jogging trousers and walking shoes. Matt appeared in the hall.

'Where are you going?'

'For a walk. I need to clear my head.'

'Can you get me some shaving stuff while you're out?'

'I'm not going near the shops.'

'Oh. OK. Never mind.' He seemed miffed.

*

I took a walk down by the canal. It felt great to be out in the fresh air, looking at trees, the sky.

So. A new angle on fairies? Would that work? What kind of fairies are there? The tooth fairy? Christmas tree fairy? Water fairies? Tree fairy? Too safe? Kids like an edge these days. How could I make it up to date?

What are Matt and I going to do? What's going to happen with him? Should we move? I think we should. I don't think he's going to get a job. Our money might run out before either of us gets a job again, though we could do Airbnb as Lorna suggested. Best option, because we can't really afford to move to the kind of house we'd like. Best paint the house anyway.

What will be best for Dad? He's got too much time on his hands now that he's on his own and so many of his friends have died.

Worry. Worry.

And Jed, my lovely boy. How's he getting on in Thailand? He's working in a beach bar but will have to come back eventually. His degree is in graphic design and there aren't many jobs around. No wonder he decided to take off and see the world with his partner, Alex. Is he eating OK? Is he happy with that man of his? I'm not sure. I want him to be happy, be loved. Alex doesn't strike me as a stayer. He'd better not break Jed's heart. Jed's a sensitive soul.

Worry, worry.

And Sam. He rarely gets in touch these days, apart from to send silly messages. Boys are hopeless at staying in touch. Always were.

How many people are living in my head? I asked myself as I turned a corner and the valley opened up to my right. Seems like a cast of thousands, and each with their own concern and opinion. Is this the first sign of madness? Deep breaths, that's what I need to do. In, out, up, down, inhale, exhale.

I remembered that Debs had a list of flower remedies for different types of stress. I sent her a text. *Need some flower remedies for inner madness. Which ones?*

She texted back. *I'll bring my list next time I c u but try White Chestnut for a start. Tis gd for unwanted thoughts etc. What is going on? DX* Had another look at Tom on Facebook. He lists London as one of the places he lives. Maybe you could message him and ask when he's next in town.

I texted back – *Nothing going on, just anxiety about job ending, etc. Think Tom lives in LA.* That much was true; no way was I going to tell her that he was currently in the UK.

I stopped by the paint shop on the way home and got all the latest brochures. Had a laugh over the names. Salmon's Back. Trout's Eye. Elephant's Fart. 'Oh yes,' I could say to tourists who booked a room if we did Airbnb, 'we did the living room in Silent but Deadly. It's a subtle shade but all the rage in Bath.'

God, I need some excitement in my life. Tom. Do you spend your days looking at paint charts? Doubt it.

*

When I got home, I saw that Matt had a visitor – his brother Duncan. They didn't look alike at all, although they sounded the same. Duncan looked like a weary walrus, overweight, balding and pasty, from the many hours he spent indoors on his computer or watching sci-fi movies.

On the island in the middle of the kitchen were Rizlas, tobacco and a small lump of dope. Matt and Duncan were sitting on the floor, backs against the fridge, clearly stoned out of their minds. Matt was spooning what looked like ice cream into his mouth from a large plastic tub from the freezer.

Duncan grinned when he saw me, then winked. 'Unleashed any hounds recently, Cait?'

'Fuck off, Duncan,' I said as he and Matt started sniggering. 'And what are you eating?'

'We got the munchies,' said Matt.

'How old are you?' I asked.

'It's all relative,' Duncan replied. He'd always been a stoner, even more so now that he'd retired. He grew his own grass and always had a supply of either that or cannabis on him. Usually, Matt never partook so to see him getting high was very out of character. He was the grown-up of the two, even though Duncan was his elder by two years. 'Been there, done that,' Matt used to say.

Matt pulled a face. 'This ice cream tastes funny. What flavour is it?'

I went over to him and peered into the tub. 'Cod. It's left over from the fish pie filling that we had at the weekend.'

Matt and Duncan started to snigger again like naughty schoolboys.

Duncan offered me the joint.

'No thanks. Got things to do.'

My reply set them off sniggering again. *What is going on with Matt?* I thought. Getting drunk, getting stoned? It's not like him at all.

I left them to it to go upstairs and continue work on my bestselling, award-winning, original children's book.

'Should I go to the job centre?' I asked the photo of Mum on my bookshelf. 'At my age, should I be retiring?' Mum had retired at the age of fifty-five. I knew what she'd say. 'Do what makes you happy, love.'

*

5 p.m. Supermarket. Here I am again, the twice-weekly Kafkaesque nightmare, where I'm trapped in an air-conditioned aisle loading washing powder, coffee, tea, cheese into my trolley over and over and over again. *See, Tom, this is about the level of the adventures I have these days. Sainsbury's on a Monday afternoon*, I thought as I went out to the car and lugged my shopping into the boot.

'Done,' I said as I closed the boot. 'And now I will escape.'

A lady getting into the car next to mine gave me a strange look.

'Er . . . I'm talking to my imaginary friend,' I said. 'I never go anywhere without her.'

'Yes, I can see her. She looks very nice. Hello, dear,' she said to an empty space to my right.

I am not alone in my madness.

*

Hauled cat food out of the boot and into the hall when I got home. Unpacked it all in the kitchen.

Matt came in and inspected the purchases. 'Did you get my shaving stuff?'

'Oh no, I forgot.'

'Never mind,' he said, and sauntered out with no offer to help put things away.

Resisted urge to throw tin of cat food at the back of his head.

I am a bad friend and a bad wife.

*

I will be a good wife.

Went to chemist to get shaving foam for Matt. Went next to the newsagent to pay the paper bill. I spotted a copy of *Mojo* magazine. I bought one, took it home and gave it to my born-again teenager husband who, still bleary eyed from the dope, was now lolling on the sofa, with Yoda on his chest, watching a rerun of *Star Trek* with the subtitles on.

'Thought you might have lost this,' I said as I handed it to him.

He didn't laugh. 'Not funny. You have *no* idea how *pain*ful it is for a man to lose his job.'

'Oh, I do. And I do sympathize. I do. I'm sorry if that doesn't come across. I know you've been used to being the man everyone wanted on their team, winning awards, brainstorming over boozy lunches, at the heart of the action. I know it must be hard.'

'Mr Has Been, that's me,' he said.

'Mr Will Be Again.'

'Yeah right,' he said as I heard the phone ring. I went to pick up in the hall.

It was Lorna.

'Hi Lor—'

'Tom Lewis, Cait. Facebook. What do you think you're doing?'

'What do you mean what do I think I'm doing? I told you he sent a friend request.'

'And you accepted it. You told me you were going to delete it. He's on your list of friends now.'

'I know. It's no big deal.'

'He posted a love song on your page.'

'I know. Sweet.'

'*Sweet?* Are you out of your mind? He was the love of your life.'

'Lorna, it was forty years ago, lot of water under the bridge, and I did get over him.'

'Does Matt know?'

'What's it got to do with Matt?'

'He's your husband.'

'Matt doesn't do Facebook. I have two hundred friends. I haven't told him about any of them. Why should I tell him about Tom?'

'You know exactly why.'

'He only asked me to be friends on Facebook, we're not having an affair.' I didn't elaborate on the private message.

'Be careful, Cait. As I said, I think you'd be playing with fire if you let him back into your life.'

'I'm not going to let him back into my life. We can be friends on Facebook, that's all. I haven't even spoken to him yet, so there's nothing to be careful about. Come on, long time ago.'

'You've changed your tune. Look, I don't want to tell you how to run your life but sometimes it's easy to fantasize about the past, put a romantic slant on it.'

'I won't. He left me, remember? That pretty well burst any romantic bubble. What's the harm in staying in touch now that we're older and wiser? And anyway, I'm a long-time married woman now, not a young gullible girl.'

'Don't go and see him. Where does he live?'

'No idea.' It wasn't a complete lie. I didn't know where exactly. 'Don't worry. I won't go and see him.'

'It lists London on his page.'

'Lorna, I can cope. Don't worry. What do you take me for?'

'I . . . I'm sorry, Cait, but after our chat after supper the other week, I know you're going through a rough time.'

'We'll get through it.'

'If you need to talk, I'm here OK?'

'OK, but everything's fine. Honest.'

After I'd put the phone down, I felt deflated. She was right, of course. It was one thing to make contact with an old school friend on Friends Reunited when that was around, but an old lover? Maybe not the best idea. It was classic. A bit of a thrill, an escape from the mundane. I also felt annoyed. Why shouldn't I see him? He'd suggested lunch, not sharing his bed.

I looked on Facebook to see if there was anything more from him. Nothing. Should I reply? What should I say? Lorna's warning and Debs's request to hook her up had made me feel rebellious. I could handle Tom Lewis and why shouldn't I see him? Judging by the photos I'd seen of him, he had children, they had to have a mother, so the chances were that Tom was still married to her and his getting in touch with me was purely to catch up on old times. So what was all the fuss? Old mate getting in touch, nothing wrong with that. Anyway, Matt was out getting drunk then smoking dope, why shouldn't I have some fun?

I went to private messages and wrote: 'Would love to see you and catch up. Am up in town next Friday, meeting a friend in the morning. Could be free afterwards around lunchtime. Does that work for you? Cait X'

I deleted the X.

My finger hovered over reply. Should, shouldn't, should,

shouldn't. I pressed send. There. Done it. And what's more I don't care what you say, Lorna. I'm only curious, that's all.

*

'And do you have anything to show, Cait?' asked Fiona, my writing tutor when she got to me at the class that evening. She was a sturdy-looking lady in her late forties with long wavy hair and a smiley face.

I shook my head. 'It's just not happening,' I said.

'Don't despair, Cait. It will come,' she said. 'Even the greatest writers have times when it feels like they're getting nowhere. The thing is not to give up. Keep writing. Write anything. You can always go back and change it, but you have to get started. If you don't turn on the tap, the water can't flow and sometimes, when it starts to flow, all the gunk that's been blocking the taps comes out first. Don't be put off by that, it's part of the process. Only when the mucky water has been cleared will the pure water come through. You can edit a bad page but you can't edit a blank one.'

Well, that's me told, I thought. Good advice. Spent the rest of the class writing about a creature with six heads who gets caught in blocked drainpipe. It felt strangely familiar.

13

Matt

'Life's a rollercoaster, Cait,' I said as I munched on my cornflakes in the kitchen. 'Down we go, up we go.'

She looked at me with a puzzled expression. 'Meaning?'

'We're due for a better phase. Something will turn up. You never really liked that job at the surgery anyway and probably won't miss it when you've finished there.'

'I haven't minded it. It has paid a few bills.'

'We'll work something out. We've both been on a down slope, we're due for an up phase.'

'OK, Mr Positivity,' she said, 'and how do you propose that's going to happen?'

'Not sure yet, but it's not over till the fat lady sings.'

'What's not over?'

'Life. Work. Any of it.'

'I believe you have to make life happen. Choice not chance determines destiny.'

'I agree. Is that one of Debs's quotes?'

'Might be. Yes.'

'So what are you suggesting?'

'That you go for interviews, make contacts.'

'Right.' I felt my hackles rise. Could she really think I hadn't? I'd tried everyone I knew in the business, but what was the point of telling her that? I felt bad enough as it was, without admitting to her that I was a washed-up failure. And clearly my attempt at being positive wasn't very well received either; in fact, Cait seemed permanently annoyed with me these days. I couldn't say the right thing or be in the right place, which I suspected was out from under her feet.

'Would you like me to wash that dressing gown before I go to work?' she asked. 'You've been wearing it for weeks now.'

'I can do that, thank you. Is that what's bothering you? The fact I don't get dressed first thing?'

'No. Yes. Oh I don't know. I'm sorry. Do what you want. Or rather, maybe you could make a start on the decorating if we're to do Airbnb.'

'Oh, that's decided, is it? I don't remember having the conversation.'

'You're joking. I've mentioned it half a dozen times.'

'Yes, but I thought it was just on the table as one of our options.'

'We have bills to pay and limited savings. We have to do something. The sooner we get the house ready, the sooner we can take some shots, load them on the website and start taking paying guests.'

'Website? What website?'

'Airbnb. We have to register with the site and load some photos of the house, so people can decide if they want to come or not.'

'Right. Send me the links and I'll get on to it.' I checked my watch.

'I'll go and buy paint tomorrow,' said Cait.

'Have you chosen colours?'

'Yes. I left brochures on your desk with them marked for you to look at.'

'Right. Must have missed them.'

'And when are you seeing Debs about her website? I did tell her you'd look at it and help.'

'Don't worry, I'll go. No need to remind me.'

'Good. Great.'

I got up. *What happened to us?* I wondered as I went upstairs to dress. When did we turn in to Mr and Mrs Grumpy? We used to like each other's company, laugh a lot. We used to share everything: books, TV shows, go for long walks together discussing future plans. Now Cait has her club for discussing books, her walking group and classes for exercise, her writing group for brainstorming ideas, her friends for talking things over with. I've become redundant to her too.

Upstairs, I checked my emails on my laptop to see if, by any miracle, anyone had got in touch.

There was one offering me a penis enlargement, another offering me a Russian bride and . . . one from Maria.

From: Maria@gmail.com
To: Matt@123.org

Hi Matt
Bumped into Bruce Patterson at Soho House over the weekend. He might have something for you. Here's his

number, 01623452364. He said to give him a call.
Fingers crossed. Maria. X

I felt a flicker of hope. Bruce had his own company and I'd worked with him on a travel programme a couple of years ago. We'd always got on. Thank you, Maria. *No time like the present,* I thought as I punched in his number.

My luck was in. He picked up the phone.

'There's a gap in the market,' he said after a brief catch-up. 'We need some programme ideas.'

'Gap?'

'Silver surfers.'

'Ah.'

'Exactly. Our generation. We're not finished yet but so often depicted—'

'As old men with walking sticks and cloth caps.'

Bruce laughed. 'But the older generations have money and the retired ones have time on their hands. See what you can come up with that might be of interest to them. Factual not fiction, drama's not my department. Try and make it positive, not all heart problems, hip replacements and arthritis. We've no budget for the brainstorming, but if we like your ideas and can sell them in, you'll get a fee and the job of producer is yours.'

I can do this, I thought. 'Love to. Leave it with me.'

The rollercoaster ride had just nudged its way upwards. I decided not to mention it to Cait just yet. So often these things came to nothing, and I didn't want to get her hopes up.

14

Cait

3 a.m. Bedroom. Pushed Yoda off my head.
    I've had an idea. Got up and crept into my study to scribble it down.

Title: Fairy Freak-Out.

The tooth fairy has hit the fairy beer after a bad year. She's run out of money to leave under children's pillows when they leave a tooth there, plus she's running out of storage space for all the teeth she's collected over the centuries – there are warehouses bursting with them. She tries to get a bank loan online but it's rejected when she puts tooth fairy down as her profession on the online form – not an acceptable occupation.

She commiserates with her friend, Tinsel, the Christmas fairy, who has also had it with sitting on a pointy tree for twelve days every year and pine needles in her knickers while, beneath her, everyone's having a jolly old time. Her other friend, the Good Fairy, is also fed up with being Miss Goody Two Shoes and wants to be bad for a change.

They rebel. It's a fairy freak-out. All across the land, children are crying after leaving their teeth under their pillow and not getting any coins.

The fairy godmother gets to hear of the situation, decides to call in the big guns to restore order and brings Tinkerbell out of retirement.

However, Tinkerbell has let herself go, sits at home watching daytime TV and eating tinned rice pudding. She's blobbed out and can't get into her tiny Tinkerbell clothes any more, but the big boss fairy godmother persuades her to help so she starts a fitness campaign beginning with Zumba – for which Tinkerbell needs an oxygen cylinder.

When the new made-over Tinkerbell finally reappears, she thinks up a kick-ass campaign to make money from the mountains of teeth, save the day and get the fairies back to work. Her idea is to make the surplus teeth into jewellery, strings of teeth necklaces, earrings, bracelets. They call the brand Toothany.

The idea is a fantastic success and the tooth fairy is back in business.

While I was up, I checked to see if Tom had replied to my message. He hadn't.

4 a.m. Back to bed. Zzzzz.

9 a.m. Tweaked the fairy idea and sent it to Lizzie. Phew. At least we'd have something to discuss on Friday. I felt hopeful about it and thought it would lend itself to illustrations. I decided not to tell Matt because I don't want to get his hopes up. Last year, I'd had what I thought was a great idea about happy ghosts but it had been rejected. Matt didn't need any more rejection in his life, even if it was mine.

Today I am going to be a new me and:

- Be positive.
- Get things done. Make contacts.
- Buy Prescription H haemorrhoid cream for bags under the eyes.

Checked to see if Tom had replied. Nothing, but it was only morning and from what I remembered of him way back when, he never was an early riser.

9.30 a.m. Sent Matt links to Airbnb.

10 a.m. Job interview 2. Receptionist in firm of architects. Smart and Griffiths.

I got to the building and went up to the first floor where the company was based, but there didn't appear to be a reception area. I looked around and finally a chubby man with white hair and beard came out. He was dressed in a tweed suit and waistcoat and I thought he looked a little like the White Rabbit in *Alice in Wonderland*.

'Can I help you?'

'Hello. Yes. I'm here to see Mrs O'Rourke.'

'She doesn't work here any more. She left us last week.'

'But I had an appointment for a job. Isn't there anyone else who can interview me?'

'What was the job?'

'Receptionist. Taking calls and so on.'

'Ah. You were probably coming about replacing her, but we decided we could manage without and just use an answering service for our calls.'

'More cost effective?'

'Exactly.'

'Why didn't anyone call to tell me Mrs O'Rourke had left?'

'No one knew you were coming.'

'I'll see myself out.'

11 a.m. DIY store to buy paints, brushes, roller trays.

12 noon. Met Debs for a coffee and told her about my resolution to be positive.

'Excellent,' she said. 'You need to put The Secret into practice and put in a cosmic order. I'll do the same. Mr Perfect Man for me and a perfect new chapter for you.'

'And what is your perfect companion this week?'

Debs thought for a few moments. 'Well, your old friend looked about right.'

'In LA. Married with kids. Not an option.'

Debs sighed. 'All the good ones are taken. OK, I want a man, maybe not for marriage, but someone who will be there at the end of a fraught day with a glass of wine, someone to listen, to ask how an appointment went, to take an interest, share my life and all the minutiae in it. Someone to look outside on a sunny day and suggest, hey, why don't we go out for breakfast or a walk? Not to have to call round friends and see who's free and make a date, like I do now. A companion, as you said, I guess that's what I want; preferably one I fancy.'

'That should be doable,' I said.

'The workshops on cosmic ordering all say that it's a good idea to write down whatever it is you want, as though it's already happening. My perfect man has nice hands, a good physique, is generous, good looking but not vain, is spiritual, financially independent, kind, intelligent, open minded . . . er what else?'

'OK. Got it.'

She rummaged around in her bag and found two pieces of paper and pens. She spent the next five minutes writing while I doodled because, although I knew I wanted to be positive, I wasn't sure what I wanted. In the end, I wrote: I look ten years younger. The world is at peace.

When Debs had finished her cosmic order, she sighed. 'So what happened with Fabio? Him running off wasn't part of my cosmic ordering plan.'

'Maybe it was,' I said. 'Maybe part of you knew that you deserved better.'

'What did you order?'

'Youth and a coffee and croissant,' I replied as the waiter arrived at the table.

'Make that two,' said Debs.

'If only it was that easy.'

'Apparently it is. Ask and you shall be given. Isn't that what it says in the Bible?'

'Think it does.'

Debs went back into her bag, pulled an envelope out and put it in front of me. 'And these are for you. An early anniversary present.'

'Oh Debs, that's so kind,' I said as I ripped open the envelope. Inside were vouchers for the spa. Maybe the cosmic ordering did work after all. Six sessions of aromatherapy or facials? They could take years off me. Perfect . . . but no, when I looked closer I saw that the vouchers were to see a marriage-guidance counsellor.

'It was after our conversation the other day. As I said, we have some really good ones who use rooms at the spa.'

'I . . . thanks, Debs. We weren't expecting anything, you shouldn't have.' *Really, you shouldn't have*, I thought as I tucked them into my bag and resolved to put them in a drawer to be forgotten about.

1 p.m. Matt opened the fridge and peered inside. 'There's no food,' he said.

'Of course there's food. I only did a shop a few days ago.'

Matt went over to the coffee canister. 'And no coffee.'

I went to the cupboard where I kept supplies. He was right. All gone. Our grocery bill had tripled in the last weeks. I drank one coffee in the morning then water for the rest of the day. Matt liked six coffees or more. He wanted lunch. Snacks. I usually had a cup of soup or salad midday. I couldn't keep up. The moment the grocery bags arrived, he was in them, pulling out food, making a bacon sandwich, toast and coffee, more toast and coffee. It was like having Sam and Jed back.

'I'm sorry, Matt. I guess I haven't adjusted yet. Apart from weekends, you haven't had breakfast, lunch or dinner at home for years so I never got that much in for the week. In fact, how about, now that you're here all day, we share some of the household tasks?'

Matt looked shocked. 'What are you saying?'

'You could do some housework. We could share it. Now that you have more time on your hands, perhaps you could do the grocery shopping, for example.' As soon as I'd said it, Lorna's warning not to emasculate him replayed in my mind. Too late.

'But . . . that's always been your domain and, while we're at it, we're out of loo paper in the cloakroom.'

'So get some when you pass the Co-op.'

'Me?'

'Yes.'

And now we're discussing loo paper, I thought. I remember days, I remember nights we talked till the early hours about ideas, made plans, made love. How did it become a heated discussion over who's buying the loo roll? 'You're at home now and not going out to work. We need more groceries. We also need to sit down and talk about our finances. Maybe budget until we get the B & B up and running.'

Matt looked truly fed up. 'Budget. I'm being a nuisance by being here, aren't I?'

'Of course not. No. I wasn't saying that, but we do have to make adjustments and accept that things have changed. If you did some of the shopping, you could choose what you like and make sure we have enough of it in so,' I indicated the cupboards, 'so times like this don't happen.'

'I don't know what you like to eat in the week any more.'

'You could ask.'

'You could ask me too. Nothing too fancy.'

'Does that mean you're not going to help shop?'

He sighed wearily. 'Yes. I will. Do me a list of what you want me to do for you and I'll do it.'

'For *us*, Matt, we both live here.'

'Not my choice.'

'What do you mean *not* your choice?'

'I mean I didn't choose not to be working.'

'OK. I'll get some stuff when I'm out and we can talk about it later.' I felt bad for Matt and I didn't want to nag and make him feel worse but at the same time, I was frustrated. Our lives had changed and it seemed unfair to me that he'd expect me to carry on as before, running the house and looking after him in the way that I had when he was working full-time.

'Where are you going?'

'Town.'

'What will you be doing there?'

'Matt, stop monitoring me.'

'I'm not. Just curious. Are you going now? I could come with you.'

'In half an hour. I'm going for waxing, if you must know.'

'Ah. Waxing. Maybe I could get my legs done.' An attempt at humour. I smiled. He smiled back.

'What would you do if you were retired, Cait?'

'Not that much different to what I do now. I do a lot of classes and I have my writing to pursue. I'd fill my time. Why do you ask?'

'Just wondering.'

'I'd find a friend who was also retired. I think it helps to have a buddy to do things with.'

Matt nodded. 'Buddy? Not husband?'

I laughed. 'We spend enough time together, don't you think? I'd have thought you'd want to get away from me.'

'No. That's what you want. You want to get away from me.'

'Oh, Matt.' I felt sad he thought that although maybe there was some truth in it.

He shrugged and left the room. That went well.

*

4 p.m. My study. Checked to see if Tom had replied. No but oh, my message to him was marked as seen at 3.30.

There was an email from Lizzie. Great. Feedback about my 'Fairy Freak-Out' idea. She doesn't usually get back this quickly. It must mean she likes it.

From: Lizzie85@pgmail.com
To: Cait@grmail.com
Subject: Fairy Freak-Out.

Cait. Am on a long train ride so have had a chance to
look at your book idea. Hmm. I like the premise and the
title but it needs a lot more thought. You know if you
create something like this, you have to make it all work.
And I mean *all*. For instance:

Where were the children's teeth kept before the warehouses stored them? How did they dispose of them?
Where are the warehouses? And the fairies?

How would a fairy work a computer? Is there just one
fairy, like one Father Christmas, or is there a tooth fairy
in every country? Your fairy surely can't be responsible
for the whole world?

Where did she get the money to put under children's
pillows before she ran out of funds?

You have to create the world for these characters and
the rules within it – where they live, etc. You know this.
We'll discuss it further when we see each other on
Friday. Sorry to pour cold water on what is essentially
a nice idea but it needs thinking through more. Lizzie. X

Oh. It hurt to have someone be half-hearted about something
I'd been excited about. So, Lizzie. Nice? *Nice idea?* Needs more
work? She was right. *Grrr.* And she'd done the bloody sandwich
thing that she learnt to do when she was working as a literary
agent. 1) Make a nice comment (I like the premise); 2) Go for
the kill (your idea is basically crap); 3) End with nice comment
to soften the blow (well done you, at least you're still trying).

Of course, I should have worked out all the points she made before I sent the proposal off. I should have talked it all over with Matt. But she was right and I was lucky I had a friend with her eagle eye, annoying though she could be at times.

*

5.30 p.m. Checked to see if Tom had replied. He had. There was a private message from him. Cue violins, doves, rose petals, etc.

'This Friday. Perfect. 1.30. Chelsea Arts Club. OK for you?'

It would be perfect. I was meeting Lizzie at twelve for coffee and would probably be with her an hour. I could just about make it over to Chelsea in time. I messaged back. 'Fine. I know where it is. C u in there. Cait.'

And then came the doubt. What the hell am I doing? Should I cancel? Yes. Probably. No. Why should I? It's an innocent meeting with an old friend, OK, lover. He's probably married and just wants to meet up, that's all. What should I wear? I should cancel. He might be disappointed about how I look now. Cancel. I will. I'll cancel. I could wear that pale green OSKA outfit I wore to Jed's degree ceremony meeting. Light, quirky. Everyone said I looked good in it. Makes my eyes look greener. Better whack the Preparation H cream under my eyes.

I could tell Matt about meeting Tom then I needn't feel guilty. No, that would be a disaster with things as they are between us at the moment; the last thing Matt would need to hear about. I'll go and meet Tom and we can catch up and that will be that.

What would Sam and Jed think if they knew I was going to meet an old boyfriend? That's it. I'm going to cancel. I am. I will.

15

Cait

And there he was. Tom Lewis, leaning back against the bar, just as I remembered, his body turned towards the room; still wearing jeans, sneakers had replaced the cowboy boots. He was older, a lot older, but still oh so attractive. As soon as he saw me, his face lit up and he strode over and gave me a bear hug that almost lifted me off my feet. We were ridiculously pleased to see each other, and all my worries about him being disappointed to see how I'd aged, faded in a second. He shook his head as if in disbelief. 'Cait Mackenna. Well I never.'

'Cait Langham now.'

'Of course. You married. How long?'

'Only thirty years.'

'Same man?'

I smiled. 'Same man.'

'I think I did hear on the grapevine, but couldn't remember his surname, which is why I couldn't find you. I had looked for you before but of course you go under your married name, then last month I saw a comment of yours on John Barry's Facebook page and recognized you from your photograph.'

'Of course. We stayed in touch, John and I, if only in cyberspace. You recognized me even though I had chopsticks up my nose?'

Tom laughed. 'Yes, about that . . . Is there something you need to tell me? Some strange religion you've joined?'

'No. Just haven't properly grown up, despite the wrinkles.'

Tom studied my face. 'Not so many, you look great. Still got those beautiful eyes.' He grinned. 'So how the hell are you, Cait?'

'Good. I'm good.'

'Hardly changed a bit.'

'Hah. You were always the charmer.'

'I mean it. You've aged well. Not everyone does.'

'You? Are you well?'

'Usual stuff. Creaking bones, not as agile as I was. Come on, let's sit down, get a drink, then we can grab a bite to eat and compare our medical histories.'

'The one on the lowest medication gets a prize,' I said.

Tom ordered drinks – a beer for him, a glass of Prosecco for me – then we went to sit in the walled garden at the back.

I took a brief look at the other people there, many around my age. I knew the club was the watering hole for artists, cartoonists, writers, sculptors. Many look like they have a story to tell. Bohemians, people who've done something with their lives, I thought, had adventures. The walls were covered in paintings and the place had an air of faded grandeur. 'I like this place,' I said. 'It has a decadence about it.'

Tom nodded. 'Like the people in it. I had lunch here last

week with a table of old members, about five of them, all artists. It came to light that they had seventeen ex-wives and one driving licence between them.'

I laughed. 'Sounds about right.'

'So,' said Tom. 'Tell me everything.'

'Everything?'

'Kids? Work? What did you do . . .' He paused and looked sheepish. 'Guess we have a lot of catching up to do.'

'We do. Give me your edited highlights. What happened to Chloe Posh Girl?'

'Ah, that was an interesting time. She took off with a rich banker soon after we split up.'

'Why did you split up?'

Tom laughed. 'I couldn't even afford her dry-cleaning bills. She expected to be kept in the style she was accustomed to, not something I could begin to do back then. Last I heard she was living in a pile in Wiltshire with stables, grandchildren and regular sessions with a therapist.'

'So you stayed in touch?'

'Not really. Friends of friends. You know how it is, you hear the gossip here and there.'

'You got married too, didn't you?'

He leant back. 'I did.'

'Still married?'

He shook his head. 'Nope. I was with my first wife, Annie, for twenty years. We married too young, grew apart. I married again, more fool me. Second wife was French. High maintenance. She wanted a slave, at her beck and call. Complained I was never at home, which was fair enough. I wasn't. Big lesson that, although you've taken the "for better for worse" vows, you don't own anyone. So now I'm single.'

Single? Hmm. Get out of my head, Debs, I told myself. 'Children?'

'Two. Boy and a girl with Annie. My son, Liam is in LA working in the film business. Ariel, Ari we call her, is also in the States, in California, married with two kids. Annie lives there too. She's American; we met when I first went out there.'

'So you're a grandfather?'

'I am – makes me sound ancient, but yes. Mia and Ethan, lights of my life. You?'

'I have two grandchildren, Ben and Grace. My son Sam is also in LA. He moved out there a couple of years ago and loves it. And Jed, my youngest, has been travelling – still is. He fell in love with Thailand and stayed over there. He's not sure what he wants to do yet.'

'Good for him. He's having an adventure. Must be in the genes. And you, are you still working?'

'Recently unemployed. I'd like to write children's books. In fact, that's why I'm in London today – to see an old friend, Lizzie. I met her before coming here. She used to be a literary agent and is great for giving advice.'

'Sounds glamorous. Shouldn't you be having lunch at The Ivy with her?'

'Maybe one day, but this morning, it was a coffee in Costa.'

'Are you working on something at the moment?'

'Sort of. A work in progress.'

'And what else did you do?'

'How long have you got? I tried a number of careers before I settled.' I gave him a short history of my CV: time spent acting – he didn't need to know it was as an extra in a film shot locally; modelled for a short time, again he didn't need to know it was for a friend's maternity catalogue; time as an artist – I reckoned life-drawing classes at night school counted. He didn't need details of my other work teaching and in the library. As I talked up my life experiences, I could see that, in his eyes, I was still that girl he knew, and I'd lived a colourful and interesting life. 'And you? Do you still paint?'

'In more recent years, yes. I've taken it up again. I became a photographer so my work was all prints for decades, but hell, Cait Mackenna, I mean Langham, what are you into these days? I remember you were always a searcher, always looking for answers to the big questions. Did you ever find what you were looking for?'

You, I thought as I took in the fact that there he was, actually sitting in front of me after so many years. He had a casual elegance about him and that fabulous voice, deep and honeyed, it was one of the things that attracted me when we first met. He could have read a telephone directory and made it sound sexy. 'Not really. These days, my searching goes as far as clips on Facebook. But you're right, I was always looking for something. Restless, I guess. So much to catch up on. Where to start?'

Tom looked at me very directly. 'Are you happy? I guess that's ultimately what we were all seeking.'

'I . . . yes. Happy? What is that? Content? You know, I . . . we, that is Matt and I, Matt's my husband, we've had our ups and downs, you know – life. My mother died last year: that knocked me sideways. My father's still alive.' I felt suddenly tearful. 'And you, are you back in the country full-time now?'

'For a short while only, few months maybe. I stay at an

old friend's place in Barnes when in London. My home is LA, but I also have a house in Majorca where I go to paint or to get away from it all. I came here to sort out my mother's affairs. She died just before Christmas, so sounds like we've been through similar stuff.'

'Oh I'm sorry. And your father?'

'Three years ago. Lots of paper to go through, probate, takes forever for houses to sell. It's easier if I'm in the country.'

'I know. Awful isn't it? No one told us about ageing parents, losing parents.'

'Nobody told us nothing,' said Tom as the waiter brought our drinks. For a brief moment, I saw a glimmer of sadness in his eyes, and wondered what he was thinking, what he'd been through.

'Are you retired?'

'Retired. Me? Never. The day you retire is the day you start getting old. I wouldn't say I work full time any more, but I keep myself busy with projects of one kind or another. You said you're working on something at the moment?'

'Only just. It needs a lot of work plus, as my friend just told me, it's a tough business out there these days. Hard for beginners like me with no track history to compete with the celebrities who've decided to take to writing children's books.'

'So, just write for yourself. Write the book you want. Does it matter if you get published or not?'

'I . . . I suppose not. I hadn't really considered that.'

'Could be liberating.'

'It could be.'

'So much of our lives has been about striving – for the career, the house, the relationship. When you stop, there's a real sense of freedom.'

'And you? Have you stopped striving?'

Tom considered my question. 'I guess I have. Not that I don't have things I still want to do but, as a free man, I make my own choices these days.'

'Sounds good.'

'And your husband? What's his name again?'

'Matt. He's just retired.'

'Ah. And what does he plan to do?'

'That's the million-dollar question.'

'It can be an adjustment but, as I said, one that liberates.'

'Early days.'

'Are you happily married?'

'Wow, get you with the personal questions.'

'Sorry. Sorry . . .' he reached out and took my hand. 'Might be years since I last saw you, Cait, but feels like yesterday, know what I mean?'

'I do.' I did. I smiled back at him. Sitting, chatting to him felt so familiar, the connection there, just as it was so long ago.

'Just having two marriages behind me,' Tom continued as he let go of my hand, 'I'm curious about how those who've stayed the course have made it work.'

'Tell you what, I'll have a think about it and get back to you, though my dad always said that the secret of a good marriage is to have a night out each week, him on a Tuesday, her on a Thursday.'

Tom laughed as another waiter arrived and took our orders and we sat out amongst the roses and reminisced about old times and old friends over goat's cheese, prosciutto and green salads.

'And what about that friend of yours? Eve?'

'Sadly she died eight months ago. Breast cancer.'

'Oh I'm sorry, Cait. She was a beauty. You were good friends, weren't you?'

'The best, right till the end. Losing someone like her just after Mum made me think about a lot of things. As well as being a reminder of my own mortality, it's made me examine what's important. You know what I mean?'

Tom nodded. 'I do, and losing two people who were dear to you so close together is tough.'

I felt tears in my eyes again but didn't want to start crying, not here, not today, maybe not ever. If I ever let myself, I had a feeling I'd never stop.

'What about your friends now?'

'There's a good circle of them in Bath. I'm in a choir and a writing group, but my closest friends are Debs and Lorna. Debs is on another planet but great entertainment. Lorna's very together. She can come across as a bit stern when you first meet her but has a heart of gold.'

'Stern eh? We'd better meet up here then.'

Interesting, I thought. He's assumed we'll meet again.

All too soon, it was time to go. Tom called a cab for me and came to the front door of the Arts Club when it arrived, where he wrapped me in another bear hug. 'Really *really* good to see you, Cait. I hope we can do it again.'

'Love to,' I said. I meant it too, though I was aware that I didn't mention him coming to Bath or meeting Matt.

'Well, you know where I am. I have thought of you, many times, wondered what you made of your life and, I hope you don't mind me asking as an old friend here, are you happy?'

'Why do you ask again?'

'Something in your eyes – a hint of sadness, resignation, regret?'

'In your dreams, Lewis. There might have been regret, but that was forty years ago.'

'When we broke up?'

'We didn't break up. You left. So if I look at all sad now, which I don't feel by the way, it's probably just age. Eye bags always make people look sadder.'

Tom was studying me in that way he always used to, as if he was looking right into me. 'If you say so.'

'Don't tell me you've come over all emotionally intelligent?'

'Hah. We were big on that in LA. Sorry for intruding.'

'No offence taken and I'm fine, doing just fine.'

'What did you do after I'd gone?'

I wasn't about to tell him I'd cried for months. 'Moved on. Finished university. Went to India. Joined an ashram.'

'An ashram?'

'Part of the "looking for answers" thing. I went to India, found a guru, learned how to meditate. Ate a lot of lentils and rice.' I didn't mention I'd also got dysentery, as did half the Westerners who'd gone out there at the same time.

Tom laughed. 'Doesn't surprise me, not the lentils and rice part. And do you still meditate?'

'Sometimes.'

'And your new friends? Are they married?'

'Debs and Lorna, they're not really new friends. I've known both of them for a long time. Lorna's a widow, Debs is recently single.'

'Like me.'

'Debs is nothing like you.' I felt uncomfortable talking about her, especially as she had asked me to hook her up

146

with Tom. *Don't ask too much about her*, I thought. *Don't ruin the day.*

'But your friend Laura—'

'Lorna.'

'Lorna. Is she your age?'

'Younger, in her fifities, though seems older. An old soul. Her husband died last year. He was the love of her life, her soul mate.'

Tom looked thoughtful. 'That's tough.' He smiled. 'Soul mate, that's an expression I haven't heard for a while.' He looked directly at me again and I felt myself blush at the intensity in his eyes. I looked away. 'What's the quote? In the beginning, one soul split into two, creating soul mates. And ever the two shall wander, seeking each other. Plato, or one of that crew.'

'That's a very romantic notion. Do you believe it?'

'I think I used to,' Tom replied, not taking his eyes away from mine. 'Really it's just a connection you feel with some people, isn't it? It's only as you get older that you discover that connection is rare and precious.'

The way he was looking at me, I knew he was talking about us. And the chemistry, it was still there, standing in such close proximity, I could feel the pull between us. It would feel so natural to step closer, reach out and . . . 'My friend Debs believes in soul mates but she says you don't always get to meet them. Eve also used to believe in soul mates, though she thought we had many and, in the end, lived with her old cat Smokey. She said he was her soul mate.' I could feel myself blushing and I knew I was blabbering.

Tom laughed. 'Too many of the good ones like Eve have left the party, friends and family. We must seize the day, count our blessings and all that good stuff.' He paused then grinned. 'Look at us, Cait Langham. Forty years on and still going.'

'Still going *and* you still have all your hair.'

'And teeth.' He paused again then said, 'I'm sorry if I hurt you.'

I shrugged as if it didn't matter. 'We were young; being hurt was all part of growing up. Life's rich tapestry and all *that* good stuff.'

He nodded and lifted an imaginary glass 'To life's rich tapestry.'

*

On the train going home, I felt high as a kite. My meeting with Lizzie had gone well – better than I'd expected. We'd talked through the problems with The Fairy Freak-Out and brainstormed some other ideas, but it wasn't just that, it was seeing Tom again. It had been a long time since a man had looked at me the way he had, taken such an interest in me and what I thought, but that had always been part of why I'd loved being with him so many moons ago. We'd had a connection, almost telepathic, which is why I'd known, by watching his face when Chloe Porter had got out of the car at the degree ceremony and walked towards her brother, that I was history.

A text came through. *A tonic to c u. Let's do it again soon. Tom X.*

I stared out of the window at the houses, gardens, streets flashing by, and realized that – for the first time in years – I felt like me, the old me: desirable, dazzling even. Not a wife or a daughter or a mother, but me, just me, Caitlin Mackenna. I replayed our lunch and conversation at the Arts Club in my mind as the train sped on: Reading, Swindon, Chippenham, Bath. We'd talked, really talked, about everything, and it was true what he'd said: seeing each other again, the years had fallen away and we'd got back to that easy familiarity, as if we'd only parted yesterday.

Matt

Cait was on her way back from London and I had a Skype call booked with my boy, Sam, in LA. Even as a kid, he'd had a million ideas firing in his brain. He was just the man to talk to about programme ideas.

And there he was, his handsome, suntanned face filling my screen. I liked to think Sam took after me, and he probably did in character, but I suspected that he got his good looks from Cait.

'Hey, Dad, how's the new life going?'

I hesitated. Crap, I wanted to say, but didn't want to burden him with my troubles. 'Up and down. Different. And you?'

'Excellent. Busy as always. But life is good. Claire's fine. Kids good, starting to talk with American accents. But what about you? Mum says you're not happy.'

'Oh did she now? When did you talk to her then?'

'I called at the weekend. Did she not tell you?'

'She didn't, but then we've both been busy.'

'Busy. I thought you were supposed to be slowing down. So what's going on?'

'Readjustment, that's all. Few things in the pipeline – that's what I thought you might be able to help with.'

'Shoot.'

'I've been asked to come up with some programme ideas for the older generations, silver surfers sort of thing.'

'And what have you got so far?'

'That's it. Nothing. Nada. Nowt. First time in my life. I can't seem to find an angle.'

'Programme maker's block.'

'Something like that.'

'Have you researched the market? Seen what's been done before.'

'Course.'

'And?'

'Care homes. Programmes on what to eat to live longer. Equity release. Nothing new.'

'Never is, it's how you present it that's new. Sorry, Pa, that's your line.'

'Was. I thought I could have a shot at this but my head is a blank.'

'Not like you.'

'No.'

'What have you been doing with yourself?'

'Annoying your mother.'

Sam laughed. 'No change there then.'

'Cheek. We get on. We'll get by.'

'You going to take up any hobbies?'

'What, like golf? I'd rather cut my arm off.'

'Classes?'

'In what?'

'I don't know. What are you interested in? Surely, this period is a gift to do all the things you never had time to.'

'Or a curse. I'm not sure I'm ready. This silver surfer thing might give me a way back in to working if I can only come up with something.'

'Let me give it some thought. I'll get back to you. Maybe we could brainstorm. You know, throw it all up in the air. Something will appear – you know how it works: there's nothing, then the old unconscious mind kicks in and bingo, you have half a dozen ideas.'

'Just the one would do.'

After our call, I stared out of the window. Maybe I had lost the touch and my unconscious mind had upped and left home.

16

Cait

Matt was lying on the sofa watching the news when I got back from the train station. I went into the sitting room, leant over to kiss him hello then went and sat on the end of the sofa. He pressed the TV pause button.

'How's your day been?' I asked.

'Quiet. I got started on the painting in the boys' old rooms. You? Train crowded?'

'Packed but on time.'

'I thought you'd be back earlier to go to your Pilates class. It is on a Friday, isn't it?'

'Couldn't pass up the chance to go to Peter Jones in London. I did a bit of shopping for the spare rooms. New linen.' That much was true. I'd got the taxi to take me via the store after seeing Tom. I felt guilty not telling Matt but I hadn't lied, just not told the whole story. I sat for a few moments then asked, 'Are we OK, Matt?'

Matt immediately looked worried and sat up. 'What do you mean, are we OK?'

'I was thinking on the way home—'

Matt groaned. 'Oh no, this isn't going to be one of those "we need to talk" sessions, is it?'

'Why do you do that?'

'Do what?'

'Groan when I try to talk to you.'

Matt was about to groan again but stopped himself. 'OK. I'm listening.'

'OK, well . . . are you happy?'

'Happy? What does that even mean?'

'It means are you happy? Fulfilled?'

'God, I don't know, Cait. I don't ever think about it.' He was about to turn the TV back on.

'Are you happy with me?'

'With *you*? What kind of question is that?'

'What I asked. I was thinking, we take each other for granted a little . . . a lot. We've stopped making an effort. I mean, are you still happy being married to me?'

'Cait, of course I'm happy to be married to you. I'm here, aren't I? Have been for years. It's not something I think about. That's good surely? I think of us as solid. Forever. OK, everything else around us might be changing, but you and I, we're the base, the foundation.'

'Yes, but a lot's changed lately.'

'Like what? Apart from losing my job.'

'OK. Top of the list—'

'*List?* You have a *list for this?*'

'Yes. Finances. How long can we last? We should do the figures properly; we've both been putting it off. Will doing Airbnb be enough to keep us going?'

'Oh not now, Cait. Can't we talk about it tomorrow?'

'It's always tomorrow with you, Matt.'

'OK, just not now.'

'Why? What's more important? *Star Trek* reruns?'

'Below the belt.'

'Debs has suggested we try counselling; she's even given us some vouchers to use at her centre.'

'Marriage counselling?'

'Yes, early anniversary present.'

'What a cheek. Christ, you've been discussing our relationship with Debs?' He looked horrified.

'No, not exactly, but she's known us a long time. I think she's picked up that things aren't great with us.'

'No way, Cait. I'm not talking about private matters in front of a stranger.'

'So what do you propose I do with the vouchers?'

Matt gave me a look to suggest exactly what I could do with them. 'We're fine, Cait. We'll muddle on. We always have.'

'I think we should at least consider it.'

'Not with one of Debs's people, never. She or he would talk to Debs about it. How would you like that? I know I wouldn't.'

'I'm sure they have client confidentiality.'

Matt scoffed. 'How many times has Debs sat around our table and entertained us with tales from the spa? She's about as discreet as the *Sun* newspaper.'

'Fair point. OK. So how about we find our own therapist?'

'We live in a small place. People gossip.'

'OK, out of town then. We could go to Frome, or Bradford on Avon.'

'Or Glastonbury. That's only forty minutes away. We could go the whole hippie hog and wear beads and sandals.'

'Now you're being unreasonable. I'm trying to help us. If we carry on like we have been, we might lose each other.'

Matt looked shocked. '*Lose* each other? What do you mean by that? Cait, where's this coming from? I can't believe you'd even say such a thing.'

'If I look into finding us a therapist, will you at least consider it?'

Matt sighed wearily. 'Do I have a choice? I don't get it. Has something happened today to trigger all this? Did your meeting with Lizzie go badly?'

'No. No. It was fine – good, in fact. I just got to thinking about us on the train coming home.'

'Thinking what?'

'OK, do you remember the last time we had sex, for instance?'

Matt groaned again, then there was an awkward silence. 'I don't keep a diary,' he said finally, 'so no, I don't.'

'Months ago, and then months before that.' I didn't add, and it was disappointing, which was probably the reason neither of us had been in a rush to repeat the experience.

There was another painful silence. 'There's more to marriage than sex,' Matt said eventually. 'Companionship, that's more important.'

'Sex is important to me. I miss the intimacy that came afterwards, that feeling of us against the world, curled up in the safe, warm bubble of our bed. Now you come to bed after I've gone up and we sleep on opposite sides. I miss the closeness, the cuddling, the easy affection that came in the aftermath and I feel us growing more and more distant.'

Matt looked like a dog that had taken a kicking. He got up and headed for the door. 'Bad timing Cait,' he said, 'it's late and you've only just got home.'

'It's always bad timing,' I called after him as he left the room. 'I'll add sex to the list of things we can't talk about. Sex, money, work.' I followed him out into the hall. 'Sometimes it feels as though we don't even speak the same language, and I don't know if I can go on unless we make some major adjustments.'

'But why? We're OK, or at least we were before my redundancy.'

'But that's just it, we weren't OK. We just plastered over the cuts by keeping busy.'

'You're the one who's always busy.'

'I'm trying to make the most of life. I don't know – maybe being in my sixties, having joined the saga louts, I don't want to waste precious years when things could be better. We have to seize the day and all that.'

'Noted,' he said and headed up the stairs.

'Walking away won't help,' I called after him, but this time I didn't follow. I went and sat on the sofa in the sitting room.

Is it me? I wondered. Is it the fact I'm aware that time may be running out? My mother used to call me a divine discontent when I was younger, always questioning everything; so maybe I am the problem. Or was it having lunch with Tom Lewis? A few hours with a man who made me feel alive again. Or maybe I'm tired and I just need one good night's sleep.

I heard Matt come back down stairs. He came into the sitting room and sat down with a heavy sigh, like a boy who'd resigned himself to punishment. 'OK, say what you need to.'

'Oh god, Matt, just . . . we're not getting any younger. Who knows how long we have left? I want to live life to the full.' I paused and looked out of the window. 'Lately I have a heightened sense of my own mortality, and not because I'm morbid. Mum going, Eve soon after, Alistair – another of our oldest pals, gone.'

Matt nodded. 'I know.' His face softened. 'It's been a tough time for you, Cait. Is that what's been upsetting you? Your mum dying? Eve's death? I can understand that.'

'Partly. No doubt, their deaths were a reminder that life can be short. Everyone says it: don't waste your time, you don't know how long you've got. Like you, at sixty-three, you've already outlived your father. I think it's important to make the most of the next chapter, make the right choices, see what the golden years have to offer.'

'So what are you proposing?'

'Maybe the counselling . . .' I turned to look at him and noticed that he had his jacket on. 'Are you going out?'

'Thought I might take a walk, clear my head.'

'At this time of night? I thought you'd come back down to talk.'

'Oh. There's more?' He got up and sighed heavily. 'You're right, Cait. You're always right, and maybe we do need to talk more but, thing is, I have nothing to say.'

'That's not helpful.'

'All I can do at the moment. I'm sorry.' A few minutes later, I heard the front door close.

17

Cait

Senior moment 1: Dialled a number on my phone. Seconds later, I completely forgot who I'd called.

'Er . . . who are you?' I asked when someone picked up.

'Kara at Solis hairdressers,' came the reply. 'But you called us, who are *you*?'

*

I decided to skip my walking group again and dropped in to see Debs instead on my way back from the supermarket. 'Just popped in to say I can't make our New Age night tomorrow, so thought I'd come and see you now,' I said when she opened the door. 'Matt and I are starting the decorating.'

'No problem. Come on through, I'm in my study. I'm checking the Internet dating sites. Want to have a look?'

'Sure,' I said, and followed her into the small room at the back of the house where she had her desk. She pulled up a chair for me and then sat in front of the screen, which showed the photo of a man with a beard.

'I don't think so, Mike from Bristol,' said Debs as she clicked away from his photo then began to scroll down to show a list of different men. Mark from Trowbridge.

'Looks like an axe murderer,' I commented.

Geoffrey from Weymouth. 'Hmm. Probably a nice man but he really ought to have put some teeth in for his profile shot,' said Debs.

Eric from Kelston – he'd used a photo of George Clooney. 'Yeah right, Eric, who are you trying to kid?' I said.

Jake from Bathford. 'Looks like an extra from *Lord of the Rings*,' said Debs. 'I know looks aren't everything, but hobbits just aren't my type.'

Liam from Corston. 'Now he looks cute. Have a look at what he's said about himself. Oh. He's seeking a woman twenty to thirty years old. No way could I pass for that, even by candlelight. You're missing out on the delights of an older woman, Liam,' Debs said to the screen, 'I've done a weekend of Tantra. OK, so I managed to lose my husband on the course, but I have skills to blow your mind, just no one to practise them on.'

'Carry on,' I said. 'There has to be someone decent on here.'

Debs continued to scroll down. 'Arghhh. How am I supposed to know who to pick,' she said as we continued to look at the site. 'Dave from Saltford – nah. Jake from Barnstaple – nah. Richard from Plymouth – nah. Am I too fussy, Cait?'

'Not at all. Let me see what you've written on your profile.'

Debs found the section describing her and clicked it up

so I could see. 'Middle-aged lady,' she read from the screen. 'Does that make me sound ancient?'

'Maybe.'

'I don't feel middle aged but I'm forty-seven. Mature?'

'No. Sounds like a cheese.'

'Immature? Childish. Daft as a brush. God, this is hard. I'd put that I am curvy but would men read fat? Dark hair, brown eyes.'

'That sounds OK, and what have you written that you're looking for?'

'Someone loyal, faithful, likes walks in the country, enthusiastic about life. Surely that's not asking too much?'

'Sounds reasonable to me, Debs.' I felt a pang of guilt. Tom was in a different league to these men on the website. Debs would love him and he'd probably like her if he met her. They were both single, but I couldn't bring myself to do it.

'What about the men you've seen so far? Have any of them been in touch since you met them?'

'All disasters and no, they haven't been back in touch, and neither have I with them.'

'Why?'

'Ralph from Bath asked if I'd always been a big girl? The cheek of him. I'm only a size sixteen and he was hardly Mr Perfect, but I've learnt fast that many of the men online want a slim young babe, and for a different sort of exercise than a walk in the country.'

'What about that Arthur chap? He sounded as if he was OK.'

'The one from Rudloe? Absolutely not. We sat in silence through most of the date then he insisted we split the bill.

"I didn't have a second glass of wine," he said as he totted up every item on his calculator. "So yours is more."'

'Tight bastard.'

'Exactly. Although I believe in equal rights, I do have a romantic notion that it's nice to be paid for on a first date; in fact generosity was one of the qualities I put down that I was looking for. The man before that, Jonathan from Corsham, spent the whole evening telling me about his late wife. I was sympathetic but, after an hour, I just wanted to escape. Bereavement counsellor wasn't the role I was hoping for in a new relationship.'

'What do you really want?' I asked.

'Someone who adores me, loves me unconditionally, and whose face lights up whenever he sees me. If I put that online, men would run a mile. It sounds too needy. My horoscope in this morning's paper said that I need to broaden my horizons. Maybe that's what I should do.'

'OK. I know a site that might be the one for you. Move over, let me find it.'

Debs and I swapped places and I clicked on a few links until I found the one I wanted and scrolled down. 'Right. Try this site, and if we don't find anyone then you can give up, but maybe it's time to take a last chance.'

Debs looked at the page I had brought up and smiled. 'OK. Alfie – cute, ditto Ben,' she said as I scrolled down through the choices. 'Bruno, hmm? He looks mischievous. Fred? Says he's lively and fun. A maybe for him. But so far, so good, Cait. Go onto the next page. George.' A handsome face stared out of the screen at us. 'Hey, I like the look of him.'

'Me too,' I said as I clicked on his profile and began to

read. 'A bit older than the others. It says he's been alone for six months, since his family moved abroad.'

'I know how that feels,' said Debs. 'With Orlando in the States with his dad at the moment, I miss him so much. Although we Skype, it's no substitute for being in the same room.'

'I know. I feel like that with Sam and Jed being away and I know Lorna does with her three gone. We all miss our kids. Gone are the days when families all lived within a few streets of each other, hey?'

Debs nodded and looked back at George's face. 'He has a hint of sadness in his eyes, as if he's lost someone and been lonely too. But it couldn't work, Cait. George is a Labrador on an animal rescue site. It wouldn't be fair to take him if I can't look after him properly, and I have too many work commitments to do that at present.'

'Don't look at me like that, George,' I said as I closed down the site. 'You'll get a home soon. I'm sure you will.'

'You take him,' said Debs.

'I'd love to, but Yoda would leave home.'

'So . . . what about hooking me up with your long-lost lover?'

'Long-lost lover?' I knew exactly who she meant.

'The one on Facebook.'

'Oh him? Tom?'

'Yes.'

'I told you, he lives in LA.'

'I could fly.'

'Last thing you need is a long-distance lover. I told you, Debs, he's not the one for you. He was a player when I knew him, so not what you need after Fabio.'

She sighed. 'You're so lucky to have a man like Matt. I do hope you appreciate that.'

'I do,' I said. 'Of course I do.' Mentally, I scratched off the list any option of a heart-to-heart with Debs about the true state of my marriage.

'Did you mention the idea of counselling to him?'

'I did and, as I thought he would, he said no way.'

'Want me to talk to him?'

'You? No!'

'So who does he talk to?'

'His brother Duncan.'

'Isn't he a stoner?'

'Yes, but that doesn't mean they can't talk to each other.'

'Well, let me know if I can do anything.'

'I will,' I said. *I won't*, I thought. I needed to change the subject away from Matt, and Debs could always be distracted by my offering to indulge in one of her therapies. 'OK. How about this? We do a bit of Gestalt to get all your rage about Fabio out and see what you really want.'

'Great idea,' she said.

'Right, you know what to do, pick two cushions,' I said. 'A light one to represent your positive side, a dark one to represent your negative side. Then let it all out, Debs, the good and bad.'

'Will do.' She picked up a dark purple velvet cushion and a light silk sand one. She sat on the purple one. 'OK, so here I am, in my forties, on my own, not had sex for yonks and my partner left me. I feel like a love loser.'

'OK, now your positive side,' I said.

She moved to sit on the light cushion. 'So, Debs, you must take responsibility and move forward. What do I want? You

163

want? We want? Hmm. I want a man who is emotionally intelligent, sexy as hell, well read, generous of mind, body and spirit and . . . must have nice hands.'

She moved back over to the dark cushion. 'And no way does he exist, you stupid idiot. You're so naïve. Grow up, get in the real world. You have to compromise. Prince Charming, Mr Darcy: the perfect man does not exist except in movies.'

She went back to the light cushion. 'God, you're negative oh you, me, when on the purple cushion. Seek and you will find. Trust and it will come to you. Don't give up. Life is what you make it. Stay positive.'

Back to the dark cushion. 'Give up, Debs, you'll never find the kind of man you want. Get a cat or a dog as Lorna and Cait keep suggesting. Only they will love you unconditionally, and actually the cat won't, they are independent buggers, only dogs love totally. And you can't get a dog because you're out all day, still like to travel and any dog you owned would die of loneliness. Basically, you're fucked.'

Back to the light cushion. 'That's not nice, so you can fuck off yourself and anyway, you're only a cushion. What do you know?'

I was laughing so hard, I almost choked. 'Oh no, your light and dark sides are fighting.'

'I know. It's not going well is it? It's been a while since I've done the cushion therapy. How about a bit of primal screaming to get out all the negativity? We have to scream as loud and as long as possible, right from deep down within.'

'What about your neighbours?' I asked.

She picked up the purple cushion, put her face in it to muffle the sound and let rip. 'Warghhhhhhhhhhh.' She came up for breath then went down again. 'Warghhhhhhhhhhh.'

She indicated that I should do the same so I picked up a red cushion. *Why not?* I thought, and had a good scream into it.

It did make me feel marginally better.

'And now a cushion to represent Fabio,' said Debs. She picked a blue one this time. 'I'll say all the things I want to say to him but won't let myself to his face because I don't want to give him the pleasure of seeing how hurt I was.' She placed the cushion on the floor then stomped on it and kicked it about the room. 'Take that, you lousy slug. I hate you, you were a rubbish lover and Miss Tantric Sex is welcome to you and your small pickle of a willy. Picklewilly, that's you. God knows you'll both need all the Tantric tricks she can muster.' A few more kicks, then she'd finished. She didn't seem at all bothered that I'd been sitting laughing my head off during it all.

'Great. I feel better already. It's always better out than in,' said Debs. 'Right, what else can we try? We could realign our chakras with crystals?'

18

Cait

'Glass of wine, Cait?' Matt asked as I collapsed in front of the TV after a hard day's work.

'Sure,' I said.

We'd gone back to doing what we did so well – keeping busy and being polite yet distant. We made a good team at doing the decorating, but as we rollered over old layers of paint, I felt that it was somehow symbolic of our relationship, painting over the cracks, covering up what was out of date.

I could see Matt had been making an effort, though, trying to say he cared in the way that he knew. He'd sent out for a takeaway and offered me a glass of wine. He let me have the TV remote.

I glanced over at Matt. After supper, he had lain on the sofa and was now snoring softly. I felt a rush of affection for him. He was a good man. He had tried in his own way to make things work over the years, and I'd hurt him with my outburst on Friday that it wasn't enough. Mum always said that kindness was the key to a good marriage. Matt had been kind to me, tiptoeing around me today as though I was unwell. Maybe I was. Restless, discontent, it was a kind of sickness of the soul.

Before bed, I checked emails.

There was one from Debs.

From: Debs23@g.org.com
To: Cait@grmail.com, Lornalp@org.com

Hi Ladies,
Cait, I found another dating site after you left. I've got a date on Wednesday. This one sounds halfway decent. Nice voice, OK profile shot. Grows his own vegetables. I like a man who knows what to do with a prize-winning courgette. Lives in Devon. We've talked on the phone. Like his voice. Fingers crossed.
   Debs
   X

*

From: Cait@grmail.com
To: Debs23@g.org.com

Hi Debs
Good luck with the courgettes. You never know, he might even have a marrow.
   Cait
   X

I felt guilty as I pressed send. Debs was my friend and having a hard time finding a companion, and I could put her in touch with Tom if I could only let go of my own thoughts about him. Debs was irresistible, fun and charismatic. It might be a match made in heaven but I couldn't do it. I still hadn't replied to Tom's text after our lunch. *I should send him a message*, I thought. That's all it would be, good manners – thanks for the lunch and so on, then I could put it all behind me and try and get on with my life, my marriage, and be grateful for what I have and stop indulging in any silly fantasy that I wasn't going to play out.

I found my phone and texted: *Was great catching up, Tom. Take care, Cait. X*

That was it, polite but giving no encouragement to stay in touch. He'd get the subtext.

19

Matt

Why oh why have I got roped into this? I asked myself as I waited in reception on Monday morning for Debs to come and get me. Not that I didn't like her, but she could be full on at times, and some of her ideas about life bordered on the bizarre. As I looked around, I had to hand it to her, she'd done a great job creating a tranquil and pleasing atmosphere. Although I'd known her for years, it was my first visit to the Lotus Spa and so far I was impressed. I sat on a comfortable ivory L-shaped sofa in the corner with a glass coffee table in front with magazines – not health magazines as I'd have expected, but *Vogue*, *Harper's* and *Country Life*. From another corner came the soothing sound of water from a small fountain bubbling onto glass pebbles; in the third corner was a life-size white standing Buddha, possibly Thai, with one hand raised as if in greeting, and on the wall there was a large painted image of a lotus. On the table in front of me, a fig-scented candle burnt. Thankfully, there was no New Age music or dolphin sounds. The atmosphere was elegant, serene and chic.

The door opened and there she was, the High Priestess herself. Debs, dressed in her work clothes: an ankle-length green kaftan, silver bracelet, and one of her many amulets around her neck, this time one showing a large pale stone. She certainly looked the part of the healer goddess, if not a little bonkers.

'Matt, lovely to see you here. Come on through.'

I got up and followed her into a room at the back of the spa. On the way, we passed treatment rooms with names on the door – Nirvana, Love, Peace, Serenity – and underneath each was the Lotus logo.

'What goes on behind there?' I asked when we reached her study, which was decorated in the same style as the front and where there was another Buddha in the corner, this time seated in a cross-legged position.

'All sorts of therapies. Massage. Facials. Aromatherapy. Cranial work. Homeopathy. Acupuncture. I have a list of practitioners I can call who cover just about all the alternative therapies.'

I waited for her to add marriage counselling to the list and was grateful when she didn't. Last thing I wanted was to acknowledge that I knew she'd given Cait vouchers.

'What's your favourite?'

She laughed. 'Winotherapy. Six o'clock.'

I chuckled. In small doses, Debs could be fun. My plan was to get in, get out. If I hadn't wanted to escape from the atmosphere at home, I probably wouldn't have come at all. Cait had been in an odd mood since she'd returned from London; I felt as if I was walking on eggshells and couldn't say or do anything right. She'd asked me to come and give Debs a hand, something to do with brochures. I'd agreed if only to keep the peace and because she was one of Cait's best friends.

'Would you like something to drink? Green tea? Coconut water? Vodka and tonic?' she asked.

'Glass of water will be fine – bit early in the day for vodka. So how can I help?'

We spent the next fifteen minutes looking at old brochures for the spa. 'I need to update these,' she said. 'A fresh look. Here at the centre, we take a holistic approach, you know – look at the whole person, the body, the mind, the heart, the spirit. I want the copy to reflect more of that so it doesn't sound as if we just do massage, although we do offer that.'

'Sounds good and . . .' An idea had pinged in my head. A holistic approach? Maybe I could make that the basis of my programme for the silver surfers.

'And what?' said Debs. 'You were about to say something.'

'Oh, just some programme idea that I've been working on.'

'For TV?'

'Yes, but it's only a maybe at the moment so I'd rather you didn't mention it to Cait. I don't want to raise her hopes if it comes to nothing.'

'So what's it about?'

'That's just it. I'm not sure. My contact wants to do a factual series for the over-sixties – what to do in retirement, and coping with getting older, sort of thing.'

'Sounds like you could be just the man for the job. How *are* you coping?' She looked at me very directly while she waited for my answer and I felt myself squirm.

'Fine, Debs, thanks.'

'So what made you think of the programme just then; you were about to say something?'

'What you just said about holistic approach, mind, body, spirit. It sparked something. It might be a good way to go.'

Debs raised an eyebrow. 'Glad to be of help and, yes, I could see that working.'

'But I'm here for you. Sorry. I tell you what. Give me an hour or two and I'll have a look through your brochures and at your site and see if I can come up with anything.'

'No hurry, though. You could work on it at home.'

'I could, but actually it's nice to get out for a change and I've brought my laptop.'

Debs nodded. I guessed that Debs knew exactly why I wanted a bit of time away from home, but no way was I going to say any more.

'I think the Serenity room is free,' she said. 'You could work in there.'

An hour later, Debs tapped on the door then came in with a tray of tea and pad of paper. She sat down on a chair opposite the desk where I'd been working.

'I've been doing some thinking since our conversation,' she said, 'and I've come up with some ideas for your series. I hope you don't mind, but I do love a creative project.'

'OK.' *Probably some mad hippie shit, but keep smiling Matt*, I told myself.

'I did a bit of scribbling and thought it could start like this,' she said, and began to read from her pad of paper. 'There are many worthy books and documentaries out there that can leave one feeling depressed because what they're basically saying is what is there to look forward to? Stairlifts, arthritis and funeral costs, but hey, keep smiling and you'll get through. If you're going down that route, then this is not the series for you.'

I nodded. I'd sat in many meetings with people who had barking ideas, and I was pretty sure Debs was about to give me some. I knew exactly how to deal with them – agree to everything, praise the plans, bin them and, if asked later, say thank you very much for your help, the ideas are all in development.

'If you're retired or near it,' Debs continued, 'heading into your sixties, seventies or eighties and still feel that there's a lot of living to do, then this *is* for you. Watch on . . . that's if you have your glasses to hand.'

I smiled. Actually, so far, not too bad, and I liked her attempt at humour.

'A new generation are now in their sixties,' Debs indicated me and grinned. 'They don't feel old and aren't quite ready to settle for golf and gardening, but what to do when the alarm goes, the day begins and there's nothing you actually *have* to do? The partner who used to be up, showered, shaved and out the door by 8 a.m. is still in their dressing gown at 10:30 a.m. and hasn't much to say apart from "What are we having for lunch?" He's started wearing fleeces, she's started wearing beige and support tights. Sexy? I don't think so.'

I laughed. 'You've been talking to Cait, haven't you? The fleeces, the dressing gown part?'

'A bit, you know us women like to talk, but I know what it's like when people's perception of you starts to change when you get older,' said Debs. 'I'm only in my forties but already I can see people's reaction to me has changed.'

'Surely not?' I said.

Debs smiled. 'Believe me, some places I'm plain invisible and, at parties, suddenly I've found that I've become the middle-aged, batty aunt who hippie dances, drinks too much and says inappropriate things. That behaviour used to be seen as cool when I was younger. Not any more.'

'Too true. I was accused of Dad-dancing at a party last summer. I'd thought I had some good moves too.'

Debs laughed, and it felt good to be with someone who appeared to enjoy my company for a change.

'I reckon life is what you make it,' Debs continued, 'so I think you should stay away from the word "retirement": it sounds dull. Your message should be – make the next chapter a good one by embracing all that life still has to offer.'

'Good, I like the introductory. Then where do you propose I go?'

'Interviews with people on the street. Let people have their say – posh, poor, all sorts, and in different locations – then I suppose you can edit it?'

I nodded. 'Yes, good idea, get an overview of how people feel. I had intended to do that.'

'Then I thought you could look at various approaches that we spoke about before, bearing in mind there are different strokes for different folks.'

'Yes. Like me, I do *not* want to play golf.'

'Yes, but some people do. Show them that there are other alternatives, though. Take in the whole person – the holistic approach I was talking about. I thought you could start with the saga louts guide to keeping fit. The physical approach.'

'Saga louts. I like that. Cait uses that phrase.' Despite my earlier concerns, I was enjoying our conversation. It was only a start, but more than I'd managed to come up with to date. 'So come at it from different angles, all aimed at making the most of life and show that we're not over the hill yet. It could work, to offer something positive.' I felt the rush of adrenalin that came when ideas were starting to flow. 'So fitness.' I rubbed my stomach. 'I could probably do with some of that lark. Cait's always on about me joining a gym.'

Debs gave me a coy look. 'You look good, Matt, I wouldn't worry too much. A bit of padding can be attractive on a man.'

Was I imagining it, or was Debs flirting with me? No. Ridiculous. I'd known her as long as I'd known Cait. Debs was one of those larger-than-life people who loves everyone; probably flirts with them all too.

'So, fitness. You could look at what works, what doesn't. Do some research then do an A–Z of options that people could download afterwards, aerobics through to Zumba. In fact, you could have a pile of stuff ready to download, maybe even do a book to accompany the series. And you could grade the results to show which has most benefit. For example, I read somewhere that dance and walking are the best form of exercise for older people.'

'A book? Not a bad idea. How to survive retirement without killing your partner,' I said.

Debs was quiet a moment. 'Are things not going well with Cait?'

I coughed. 'I was joking. Things are great with Cait. Fine, but I bet a lot of couples struggle.'

'I bet they do. You could address that too.' Once again she gave me that direct gaze of hers. I looked away. 'There isn't a whole lot of material out there that hasn't got cartoons of aged people with Zimmer frames. We're not all like that.'

'No, you're certainly not.' Debs was thoughtful for a

moment. 'You know, Matt, you can always come and talk to me anytime if you need. I'm a good listener and I can appreciate what a huge adjustment you've had to make in the last months.'

'Sorry, no, wrong end of stick. I'm fine. Yes it's been a change, but I'm taking it in my stride. We both are. Seriously, we're good, but I think we should address the problems that can arise for the newly retired at some point in the series. Loss of identity when there's no longer a job to go to, losing space, that sort of thing.'

'Essential, I'd say.' She was looking at me at little too closely for my liking again. I felt torn. Debs was easy to talk to and appeared to be sympathetic, but she was Cait's friend, not mine. 'So what else? Let's brainstorm.'

'How to look good for longer could come under the physical programme. Make-up and hair tips for the ladies, get a style expert in, what to wear, what not to wear,' said Debs.

'Cait tells me there are rules to one's appearance after a certain age; less is more or something.'

Debs indicated her flamboyant outfit. 'There can be exceptions.'

'True, but what you wear looks good on you. Not everyone can carry that kind of style and it fits with what you do here.' Debs smiled. Lord, was I flirting with her now? Christ. What was going on? 'Erm . . . Clothing tips for the men. Dos and don'ts. Cait tells me I can no longer wear shirts tucked in.'

'She's right. Not a good look unless you're lean. Oh. Not that I'm saying you're not – oh, you know what I mean.' Now it was Debs's turn to squirm. I laughed and she grinned back at me.

'So what else?'

'Nutrition,' she said. 'We do a lot of that here at the centre. What are the best supplements? Devil's claw for arthritis, diet, that sort of thing. Cranberry for urinary problems.'

'Fish oils. Blargh. I take them for my dodgy knees. They repeat on me. Sorry. Too much information.'

'But they are effective and you could add a section on how to lower blood pressure and cholesterol naturally, what are the best treatments around for aches and twinges that come with ageing. We find here that most clients would prefer to take the natural route before submitting to tablets for the rest of their lives, so many of which have side effects.'

'I'm sure a lot of people would be interested in that.'

'That could fill a whole programme,' Debs continued. 'And you could also look at beds, chairs – all the items that can make life easier.'

I chuckled. 'Stairlifts?'

'Why not? After that you could go on to the other angles. So many are dealing with losing friends, ageing parents, and so inevitably having to face our own mortality.'

I nodded. 'It can be depressing; sobering at the least.'

'So important to keep talking, not bottle it all up.'

'Fear of ageing and all that comes with it,' I said. 'Losing hair and finding it growing in places you don't want it.'

Debs laughed. 'Nose, ear, chin. We have a therapist here who specializes in just that. Very popular with the over-sixties. Also . . . maybe have a section on sex for the over-sixties too; what you need, etc.'

'An oxygen cylinder,' I said, and Debs laughed again. I was beginning to see her in a new light. Her ideas were good, not off the wall, plus it had been a long time since I'd had the attention of an attractive, younger woman, and had to admit that, despite myself, I felt flattered.

'And maybe have one programme dedicated to attitude. The importance of staying engaged with others and stimulated—'

'Wahey,' she said, 'KY jelly. Sorry. I know what you mean, mentally stimulated and not just Sudoku and crosswords. The importance of learning new things.' She pointed at the Buddha. 'And you can't leave the spiritual side out. In ancient society, older people were respected for their wisdom – not so now. The word "crone" used to be a term of great respect for an old wise woman; now people associate it with sad, bent, wrinkly old folk.'

'We could look at that, I guess. In the East, this phase in life is for peace and contemplation, the family brought up, the job done. The last section of life is for meditation.'

'That's right, Matt. I didn't know you were into Eastern philosophy.'

'I've read a bit but, back in the real world, it would also be worth doing a programme on finances. So many of my generation thought we'd never grow old and aren't prepared for it, so maybe some advice from the experts on how to make the most of it. Savings, pensions, budget. Get one of those money-market experts in.'

'Excellent idea.'

'Thanks, Debs, you've been so helpful, when it was supposed to be me helping you.'

'Not really. I just jotted down the different approaches. It's talking to you that's made it all come to life.'

'We could make a good team.'

She raised an eyebrow. 'We could.' *Woah*, I thought, was

I imagining it again, or was that look she gave me loaded? There was definitely a frisson of something there.

'But aren't I taking up your time?'

'Hell, no. I love doing stuff like this.'

We spent the next half-hour writing down ideas and brainstorming more and, by the time we'd finished, we had the makings of the type of series that might just be a winner.

'Debs, you've been a marvel,' I said, 'I'll write all this up and tinker with it when I get home.'

'Do send me a copy, I can see if I can add anything else.' She reached out and put her hand on my arm. 'I've really enjoyed it.'

'Me too. I can't thank you enough.'

'My pleasure, Matt.'

'And, hope it's not too much to ask again but . . . would you mind not mentioning this to Cait?'

'Of course not. I understand, but my philosophy has always been it's best to have no secrets between couples, especially after what happened with Fabio and me.'

'And usually I'd agree, but it won't be for long. I just don't want to give her false hope. I've had enough experience in the world of media to know that the best ideas can get buried sometimes.'

'I understand.'

'Thanks, Debs, you're a star. Now. Do you want to look over the copy I've done for some of your brochures? I feel bad that we've ended up working on my stuff more than yours.'

Debs took my notes for her website, glanced down them and nodded. 'Perfect. It seems we really are on the same wavelength. And of course I want to pay you for your time.

When you've finished, could you let me know how many hours you've spent and what your rate is.'

'Absolutely not. Especially after what you've just contributed to me. No. You're a friend and I don't charge friends. It's been a pleasure, an absolute pleasure.' I also got the feeling that she'd only offered me the work in the first place to help with our finances. Having just had our ideas session, it was clear that Debs would have been more than capable of updating her brochures herself. She hadn't needed me at all.

'Then at least let me set you up for a massage session with one of our therapists. I know these past weeks must have been a strain on you, and you could probably do with some real relaxation. We have some very good masseurs here and I could set you up with one of the best. Also our secret. On the house. I insist. I wouldn't feel comfortable otherwise.'

In the end I agreed. It had been years since I'd had a massage and she was right, the last weeks had been a strain.

I left the spa feeling on top of the world, buzzing with ideas and renewed energy and couldn't wait to get home to my computer to write them all down. *Thank you, Debs. You're not so bad after all.*

20

Cait

I sat in a room on Tuesday morning with a group of young folk who looked like university graduates, all busy on their phones while we waited to be seen. The job we were lining up for was in telesales. My heart wasn't in it, but my head kept telling me that I must be serious and at least try and earn something. After a few minutes checking each other out in between texts, we were led into a room, handed sheets of paper and pens and a questionnaire.

I knew I wasn't in with a chance. I was at least forty years older than the other applicants so decided to have some fun with my form.

1) What is your motivation for getting the job? *I need to get out of the house. My husband's driving me barmy.*
2) What do you feel you could bring to the job? *My handbag and my lunch.*
3) Do you use Twitter and Facebook? If so, what would you post on there? *Photos of my bare bottom.*

4) Do you prefer to be liked or to be right? *Both. This is the right answer.*
5) Do you drive through amber lights? *Yep. Don't we all?*
6) Describe yourself in three words? *Too old for this job. That's five words. Soz.*
7) What are your strengths? *I do a great impersonation of Marilyn Monroe singing 'Happy Birthday, Mr President'.*
8) What are your weaknesses? *Chips.*
9) If I were talking to your best friend, what would they say you need to work on? *My upper arms because they are a bit flabby.*
10) If you could be any superhero, which would it be and why? *Superman so I could wear underpants over my jeans.*
11) What's in your fridge? *The head of my dead husband.*
12) If you were written about in the paper, what would the headline be? *Elderly lady flashes her bits in Waitrose.*
13) What might you not like about the job? *Dealing with people.*
14) Worst moment of life? *This.*
15) Why do you think this is the job for you? *My horoscope said so.*
16) Would you say you are a tolerant person? *What a stupid question, you idiot. Of course I am.*
17) What do you do at weekends? *Anger management courses.*
18) What are your assets? *Have a bike.*
19) How would you demonstrate leadership skills? *Arm wrestling.*
20) When can you start? *I'll have to ask my mum.*
21) Have you ever done anything you regret? *Possibly filling in this questionnaire.*

I left my questionnaire on the desk with the others on the way out. I knew they wouldn't contact me because I'd put Mrs Anne Droid as my name and Cloud Cuckoo Land, Planet Earth, The Universe as my address.

It felt good to be juvenile sometimes.

I got home to a quiet house and a heap of bills. I felt deflated after my burst of rebellion earlier as I sifted through the pile. It was all very well acting like a fifteen year old, but the harsh reality of life soon caught up as shown by the invoices in front of me reminding me that we had to find a way to get by somehow or other. *When the going gets tough, the tough look on Facebook*, I thought as I switched on my laptop.

There was a private message from Tom. It said: Please call ASAP and text me your mobile number. Mine is 077733320.

I called his number and he picked up immediately. 'Cait. I'm so glad you called.'

'What's the urgency?'

'I need to see you.'

'See me? Why?'

'I'll tell you when I see you.'

'But—'

'I'm on my way to Bath now. Can you get away?'

'Tom, you're scaring me. Has something happened?'

'Yes. No. Nothing bad. I'll be there in . . . about an hour. I can wait if you can't get away for a while or even stay a night if you can't see me today.'

'No. I could. I'm not doing anything that can't wait.' I searched my mind for somewhere to meet him. Somewhere we wouldn't be seen. 'I'll meet you in the botanical gardens in Victoria Park. They're near the centre of town and you can park.'

'OK. See you about 5.15. And keep your phone on in case I get lost or am held up.'

Matt was out so I was able to change and put on some make-up without being questioned. First I put on a smart navy dress. Blargh. No. I looked like a bank clerk. *I'm meeting him in a park, for heaven's sake,* I told myself. Put on something casual. I put on an Eastern-looking top. No. It was too evening dress. In the end I settled for my coral dress and some ballet-style slip-ons. I was intrigued. *What could he possibly want?* I wondered as I drove down to the gardens, parked, then found a secluded bench where I hoped that we wouldn't be seen. I texted Tom to tell him where I was.

I wished I'd taken a book because it felt like eternity sitting there. It was a beautiful afternoon and there were lots of people about enjoying the late afternoon sun. Some glanced over. I twiddled my thumbs and felt oh so conspicuous, like there was a sign over my head saying, 'Waiting for a lover, shouldn't really be here.'

Tom arrived after half an hour, slightly breathless as though he'd been running. I got up to greet him as he came towards me and he grinned and swept me into one of his bear hugs. It was heady stuff having such an attractive man be clearly so pleased to see me. Even in jeans and white shirt, he looked charismatic, and I couldn't help but grin back at him.

'Sorry, sorry, couldn't find a parking place. Have you been waiting long?'

'Just got here,' I lied.

'So what's going on?' I asked when he let me go and we sat on the bench, turned towards each other.

He took one of my hands in his and took a deep breath.

'Your text. It seemed to be giving me, us, the old heave-ho. So, I'll be blunt. Seeing you again stirred up a lot inside of me and since then, I've been doing a lot of thinking. In fact, I haven't been able to get you out of my mind. I know it's been forty years but . . . you know the real thing at our age. We were so young when we were together, and yes, it was all there then, the connection, the ease we have, but in my ignorance, my naïvety, my utter stupidity, I thought that was how it would be with other women, that bond, that unspoken understanding we have with each other – more than that, the recognition of having met someone exceptional. When I was with you, I took that for granted, imagining it would be there with so many others along the way, but I was wrong. It's rare and precious. I didn't know that at the time. Anyway, it's taken me the past forty years we've been apart to realize that no, it isn't like that with others. What we had was special, *is* special. I know you feel it too. You do, don't you?'

'Er . . .'

'I should have known it back in our twenties but then . . . maybe not. I may have spent a lifetime wondering what else, who else lay out there and been as restless as you might have been with me, so maybe it was for the best that we both played the field, had experiences. Not that I didn't love my wives, I did, and not that I haven't had lovers, I have, but what we had is extraordinary. I know that now. You mentioned soul mates last time we met. I believe you were, are, mine, and I owe it to myself, and to you, to say so. Are you OK, Cait? You look pale.'

'Christ, Tom, that's quite a speech. I . . . I hardly know what to say. Unexpected is a word that comes to mind.' *Overwhelmed is another*, I thought. It's unreal. One minute

I'm wondering how to pay a gas bill, the next I'm sitting in a park with a handsome older man who is claiming I'm his soul mate.

He grinned. 'I know. Mad, isn't it? And at our time of life? Who knew something like this could happen? But, oh Cait, I can't begin to express how seeing you again has made me feel. Like I've come alive again, woken up. You do feel the same, don't you?'

'Tom, I'm married. I did feel that you were my soul mate once, you know I did, but that was many moons ago. Why are you here? What do you want?'

'Remember our promise to each other? To always seek adventure? To never grow old. Well, I have a proposal. Something I want to put to you.'

'Oh god.' I got up and took a deep breath, and he stood up next to me, then he pulled me towards him. He put his hand on my chest, not in a sexual way but as though putting his hand over my heart. 'What's going on in there, Cait? I mean, really? I sensed something in you that's restless, discontent. I felt it when we met in London. Not so much by what you said but by what you didn't. Are you happy in your marriage?'

I could feel his breath on my skin, the warmth, weight and pressure of his body touching mine. Parts of me that had long been buried were stirring, awakening, firing a surge of desire through me. Tom leant towards me and grazed my bottom lip with his. My whole being wanted to respond but I panicked and tried to pull away. I glanced around. 'Anyone could see us here,' I said.

He smiled and there was that look I remembered so well – as if the whole world was for his amusement, me included.

'Let them. I *know* you feel it. We could have a lot of fun, you and I, Cait Langham.' He pulled me close again, and though part of me wanted to give in, to lie down on the grass there and then, feel his lips, his body on mine, in me, possessing me, filling me, I was also aware of where we were, of people milling about in the distance.

I took a gulp of air. 'Let go. I can't think or breathe. I can't do this. Not here. I mean, not that I'd do it anywhere else. I'm *married*. I can't just go snogging in the park like a teen-ager.'

He groaned with frustration but he let go and stepped back. He pulled me to sit on the bench again, took my hand, held it then put it to his lips and bit it.

'Ow,' I cried though it wasn't a painful bite, not physically. I understood the gesture. He wasn't the only one who was feeling the intensity of desire and not being able to act on it.

'Sorry but you're driving me crazy.' He rubbed my hand. 'I didn't mean to hurt you.'

'You didn't, not really. It was just unexpected.'

'You haven't really answered my question about your marriage. Are you satisfied?'

'I . . . Sometimes. OK. Not lately but—'

'I thought not. I could always read you. I felt something held back in you.'

'It's a phase. We'll get through. All relationships have their rough patches.'

'Get through? Is that enough? Life is short. It's up to us to make the most of it. Surely there is more than making do, living with only being moderately satisfied?'

It felt spooky to hear him vocalize my private thoughts.

Is it enough? That was exactly what I'd been asking myself these past months. I felt a rush of anger. 'Christ, Tom, who are you to ask me these things? I don't feel comfortable talking about my marriage with you after all this time. You can't swan down here and ask me things like that.'

He nodded. 'I understand. Sorry. I didn't mean to pressure you, but if these last few years have taught me anything, it's that you have to embrace the moment, take the risks. Cait, remember what I wrote to you after I'd left – that meeting when we were young was bad timing. A lot of water's gone under the bridge since then, but now . . .? We're older, maybe not much wiser but maybe a little. We know what we want and what we don't. I think we owe it to ourselves to find out if we do belong together.'

'Together as in *together* together? A couple?'

He nodded. 'That's what I'm proposing.'

'Are you *out* of your mind, Tom? We hardly know each other any more. Forty years is a long time. I'm not the same person you knew back then. I have knobbly knees now.'

Tom laughed. 'Me too. I've changed too but I'm still Tom and you're still Cait. And I remember the sex we had, don't you?'

I did and tried to push away all thoughts of it. 'We were twenty, Tom. I doubt if we could even get into some of the positions we used to.'

He thought for a while then smiled. 'We could try.'

'You'd be disappointed. I mean, how do you still do it at your age?'

His eyes twinkled. 'Very slowly,' he said in a way that was loaded and I felt myself blush.

'Get behind me, Satan,' I said. 'Stop it,'

Tom laughed again. 'If that's how you like it, I'm sure that could be arranged. Look, bottom line is, I still feel a connection to you. What have we got to lose? You've had recent losses, me too, and they do make you think, don't they? Is this it? We can either settle for a life of familiarity or take a gamble and take what we have, grab on to it, hold on to it. Maybe it's not all over for us yet. Maybe I'm out of my mind, but hooking up with you again could be the mother of all adventures, an adventure to end all adventures. We know time is limited. Life isn't a rehearsal: you only get one shot at it. We all make mistakes, and surely one of them would be not to pursue something through fear or caution. At the end of our lives, we don't want to look back with regret for what we were afraid of, do we? Maybe one of my biggest mistakes was letting you go. The loss of our loved ones has been a cruel reminder that we're only passing through on this journey of life and no one gets out of here alive. I believe that now, more than ever, we have to seize the day, be prepared to take a risk and embrace what opportunities come to make the most of what's left of our lives. We could at least try.'

'Try? How?'

'You. Me. See where it goes.'

'I keep reminding you I'm married, Tom, or have you forgotten that?'

'Do you feel like this with him?'

I thought back to the night Matt had come home drunk and slumped down on the floor. *Not fair*, I told myself, *he's rarely like that*. I also thought back to the last time Matt and I had made love, and what a flat experience it had been.

'Oh god, I don't know what I feel. I'm not sure what to

say or think. I'm in shock.' *Things like this don't happen to women like me*, I thought.

'Sorry, it must be a lot to take in,' said Tom. 'Think about it. Are you willing to take a risk? Throw everything that's safe and familiar up in the air to have an adventure with an old rogue who always loved you.'

'But you didn't always love me. You left me.'

'I did love you. I do love you. I know that now.'

'I need a stiff drink or two or three and I think I must go and buy some fags.'

'I didn't know you smoked.'

'I don't. See what you're doing to me. I'm ruined. One more meeting and I'll be on the hard drugs.'

Tom laughed. 'Can we get a drink together? Good idea.'

'*No*. This is where I live. What if someone saw us? Someone who knows Matt? Or me? Tom, you mustn't come to Bath again.'

'Are you saying you won't consider my proposal?'

'You mean an affair?'

'I mean explore what we have and see where it takes us.'

'I . . .'

Tom stood up. 'I'll go. You probably need time to take all this in but, before I do, I must say, this is not the kind of thing I do regularly—'

'Regularly?' I felt a shadow of doubt creeping in. Did Tom regularly have affairs?

'Bad choice of word, not regularly, I mean this is not the kind of thing I do at all. I don't make a habit of pursuing married women but I know what we had. I can feel what we could have and life is short. You have to grasp it by the short and curlies.'

'No need to be rude.'

He laughed again. 'When you're ready, let me know. I have a house in Majorca up in the hills near Deia. You could come there. It's beautiful. I'll be going back and forth over the next two months. Or we could meet here in the UK. Your call, and if you decided to stay with me, you wouldn't need to work. I have money, you could write or paint, whatever you wanted.'

'You're insane.'

'Part of my charm.'

'The devil sent you.'

Tom laughed again. 'Yes, to tempt you into evil ways.'

'Our situations are very different. As I keep telling you, I'm still married. You're not.'

'True. It's up to you whether you wish to explore whether you want to remain in that marriage. Your choice. When can I see you next?'

'I . . . I'm not sure, Tom. I need to think about this. Pinch myself. Make sure I haven't dreamt you up. First of all, I need to get to know you again. How do I know I could trust you?' I was shocked to hear myself even saying the words, as if what he was proposing was an option.

'What do you want to know?'

'Everything. Tell me about your life, your family, favourite food, everything.'

'My favourite food is seafood paella, a dish that I cook rather well, even though I say so myself and the rest, well, I can tell you next time.'

I glanced at my watch. 'I have to go.'

'Go? Where?'

'Home then my yoga class. I have a life, you know.' Actually

I had plenty of time before the class but I needed to get away, think about what was happening.

'OK, and I know I might have seemed impetuous driving down here today, but I wanted to say what I did in person, not in cyberspace, on Facebook or by email. Take your time to think it over. Did you drive here?'

I nodded.

'I'll walk you to your car,' he said.

We got up and he put his arm around my shoulder as we walked towards the park exit. 'Relax, Cait. I won't push you into anything you don't want to do but I had to state my case.'

Ahead in the distance, I spotted a woman entering the park. She had a dog with her and turned away, for a moment, fussing with the dog's lead. I knew that figure. It was Claire, the woman who led the Saturday walking group that I sometimes went to, and her Irish terrier, Rufus. She lived in Lorna's village.

'Get down now!' I said. I pushed Tom's arm away from my shoulder as if it was burning and almost knocked him over.

He looked startled. 'Down?'

'On the grass,' I said, and dived behind a tree. He looked around, puzzled, and followed me.

'What on earth are you doing?'

'Hiding. Christ, I knew this would happen. Someone I know is coming.'

'So introduce us.'

'No way. Get over there. Lie on the grass.'

Tom burst out laughing but did as he was told. 'For a minute there, I thought you were making me an offer; either that or you'd come over all dominatrix.'

192

'I'm serious, Tom. On the ground. Now! Close your eyes. Quick.'

Tom did as he was told and lay on the grass on his front. 'Why am I on the ground?' he called. 'She doesn't know me.'

'Best be safe,' I called back.

He didn't look out of place. All over the park, people were snoozing in the sun. I stayed behind the tree and peeked out along the path. I could see Claire approaching and, thankfully, she didn't seem to be looking our way. As she got nearer, I shuffled around the tree away from her so I couldn't see her but I could hear her footsteps, hear her talking to her dog.

'No, no, come away,' I heard her say. 'So sorry. He's only being curious. He won't bite.'

'No problem,' I heard Tom say. 'I like dogs.'

What? I didn't dare look around this time. She was too close.

I heard Claire laugh. A girlie, flirty laugh. This time, I did dare to peer round. Hell. The dog was sniffing at Tom and Claire was flicking her hair and sticking out her chest in the way that some women do when they fancy a man. 'And where's home?'

'London presently,' said Tom.

'Oh, so you're visiting here?' asked Claire.

'I am. Visiting a friend.'

'Oh, and just having a break in the park?'

'That's right,' said Tom. 'Fancied some fresh air and a bit of green space.'

He needs some space, Claire, you nosey cow, get it? Get the message? Clear off.

'I know how it is. OK. I'll leave you to your snooze and your fresh air. Sorry about Rufus.'

'No problem.'

'Might see you on the way back.'

'Bye Rufus,' called Tom.

She walked on. *Phew*. As I heard her footsteps recede, I shuffled back round the tree. I looked around in the hope that no one had spotted me but most people seemed to be going about their business, apart from a man in the distance who appeared to be watching me. I rubbed the tree bark as if I was interested in it. Hopefully, he'd think I was some kind of tree maintenance person.

'Coast is clear,' Tom called after a few minutes, so I moved from the tree to behind a shrub.

'Are you sure?' I asked as I peeked out from the leaves.

'Sure.' Tom was sitting up on the ground, clearly very amused by it all. 'What was all that for?'

'She might have seen us together.'

'We could have walked separately. She wouldn't know me, wouldn't know we'd been meeting. I could have been a stranger in the park, walking behind you. We weren't doing anything.'

'Sorry. Panicked. Haven't ever done anything like this. See. I'd be hopeless at having an affair. I think you need to go and find a more sophisticated woman.'

'I'd rather have you. More fun,' he said as he stood up and came over to remove a leaf from my hair.

'I'm not sure it's fun. We went from *Brief Encounter* to a *Carry On* film in the space of half an hour. I live a quiet life normally.'

He took a step closer. I took one back and pointed towards the gate to our right. 'Go. Now.'

'But you'll let me know?'

'I'll think about it. That's all I can promise at the moment.'

'I'll go then, but reluctantly. Might even have a look around Bath while I'm here. Call me soon.'

He walked off in the opposite direction and I began to make my way back to my car.

After a few moments, I was approached by a park warden. 'Just a moment, madam.'

I stopped and glanced around to make sure Claire was nowhere near. 'Yes, can I help you?'

It was the man who'd been watching me when I was behind the tree. 'I couldn't help but notice your behaviour back there. Behind the tree? Is there anything you need help with?'

'Me? Oh god no,' I said in a high voice. 'I . . .'

'Yes?'

'I . . . I'm interested in photography. Tree barks. Textures in nature. They're fascinating, aren't they? All so different.'

'So where's your camera?'

'In my bag, on my phone. I was just looking at that tree. Very interesting markings. I'll come back and photograph it when I've got my good camera.'

The warden looked at me closely. 'OK. On your way then.'

I shot off as fast as I could to the safety of my car. *What the hell was that?* I thought as I drove home.

When I got back, I went straight upstairs to call Lorna, but her phone was on message so I went to Facebook and looked at Tom's page. 'You *are* the devil,' I said to his profile picture. There were no longer violins at the sight of him, no doves, no rose petals falling from the sky, just an almighty bucket of cold water poured over me, shocking me back to reality. Of course it was ridiculous to even consider his proposal, but it felt like some force had called my bluff. Life had turned right round and said, OK Cait, so you're dissatisfied? Well here's your chance to do something about that. Take it or leave it. But I could never walk away from my life and all that was familiar to take a chance on a man I hardly knew any more, could I?

What's the alternative? I asked myself. Years of silence with Matt as we get older, the distance between us growing larger? The *Antiques Roadshow* on TV? Weekly Sainsbury's shops, supper nights with my friends? I was too old to throw up all that I knew. Wasn't I?

I pulled out my mobile again and texted Lorna. *Need to talk. Urgent.*

I pulled a muscle at yoga doing the Cobra, but did manage the Dead Dog, a new position I have created myself which involves lying on my back with my legs and arms hanging in the air.

When I got home, I checked my phone to see if Lorna had got my message. No reply.

21

Cait

I was awoken by my mobile pinging that I had a message.
Matt was still asleep so I got up and crept into the bathroom.

Am up. What's so urgent? Lorna.

I texted back. *Will Skype you.*

Checking that Matt was still out for the count, I got my
laptop from my study, took it downstairs, went to Skype and
called. Lorna was there at her kitchen table, still in her PJs.

She looked sleepy. 'Has something happened? Is it one of
the boys? Matt? Are you OK?'

'God no, nothing like that. Sorry if it sounded so urgent
but . . . it is in a way.'

'OK. Spill.'

'Tom Lewis has been in touch.'

'Ah.'

'I went to see him in London then he came to see me.'

'He came to Bath?'

'Yes.'

Lorna didn't look fazed but she sighed. 'I did wonder if you'd see him after you'd accepted him as a friend on Facebook.'

'He's in London presently. His mother died and he's sorting out the family house, probate, that sort of thing.'

'And?'

'And . . . oh, I loved seeing him, Lorna, I felt like I'd come alive again—'

'The connection was still there?'

'Oh yes.'

'Oh dear.'

'Nothing's happened.'

'But it could.'

'Yes. No. Maybe. I've never felt so confused in my life. His philosophy was always seize the day, always seek the adventure. Well, he wants me to do just that. He said he still felt something between us and he wasn't wrong. He's proposed that we get to know each other again, see where it takes us.'

'Oh.'

'I know. Oh.'

'Cait, you're not seriously considering this are you?'

'That's just it. I didn't think I would but I am. I can't help it. Like my head says no, be sensible, and some other part of me says why not? Life is short. That's why I wanted to talk to you.'

'Does Matt have any inkling of this? Does he know you've seen Tom?'

'No to both questions. He has no idea, but you know that we haven't been happy for a long time, not really.'

Lorna looked concerned. 'Matt's a good man.'

'I know.'

'How do you think he'd feel?'

'Hurt, shocked even.' I felt guilty as I said the words.

'Oh dear. Cait, take this very slowly. It's come so out of the blue and has found you at a particularly vulnerable time.'

'What do you mean? Vulnerable?'

'It's only a year since you lost your mother and Eve. I know everyone advised me not to make any major decisions after Alistair died. Grief is different for everyone and has no time limit.'

'Grief?'

'Yes. Don't underestimate how it's affected you.'

'I don't think it's had anything to do with Matt and me growing apart, or Tom reappearing.'

'Maybe not but—'

'I don't want to say no to Tom then spend the rest of my life regretting it and resenting Matt.'

'OK, so what if you had an affair with Tom and it didn't work out? There'd be no going back. Once the trust has gone, it's very hard to get it back, and divorce is a very messy business.'

'I know. I don't know what's come over me lately. I seem to be dissatisfied with everything.'

'Don't be too hard on yourself, Cait. Losing people you love throws everything up in the air. You start questioning what it's all about, what you're doing, as well as have a heightened sense of your own mortality which is probably exactly why Tom's "seize the day, let's have an adventure" take on life appeals to you.'

I nodded. 'He said that with the death of both of his parents, he's been reminded of his own mortality.'

'Yes, but no need to go off the deep end. Please, Cait,

don't do anything you'll regret. You have to be a hundred per cent sure. Think about your boys. Separation could bring up a lot of anger and resentment on their part, even though they've left home. They love their dad. Take it very *very* slowly. Don't make any decisions, not just yet. It's far too soon. If Tom's really serious, he'll wait for you.'

'Do you think I am a terrible person for even considering this?'

'Cait, whatever you decide, I'll support you the best I can.'

'I knew you'd understand.'

'Well, I do and I don't. I agree, we must seize the day. People do outgrow each other. Relationships do change but—'

'I know. Thirty years shared history is a lot to throw away.'

'It is.'

'Will you talk to Debs about it?'

'Maybe.'

'I'd let her in if I were you. She's your friend too. Look, let me think about this and I'll get back to you; in the meantime, don't do anything in a hurry.'

'Thanks and sorry it's all been me, me, me. How are you? What's happening?'

'I'm fine. I'm meeting with some builders today. I have plans! I'll tell you all about them next time I see you. Speak soon, coffee beckons.' She waved goodbye and clicked off.

I closed my laptop. This morning not even watching Facebook clips of dog rescues or finding my Celtic legend name held any lure. I went up to check if Matt was still asleep. He was, so I went back to the kitchen, made a cup of tea and sat down to make a list of things to do.

Goals for the week:
- Make final touches to spare rooms. Advertise on website. Prepare to receive paying guests. If we could remove some of the financial pressure on us, that would definitely help things along.
- Continue work on bestselling, award-winning, original, brilliant and unique book and not worry about getting it published.
- Buy gorgeous new underwear fit for a steamy affair. No. *No.* I didn't think that. Oh god, I did, didn't I?
- Try not to go mad.

At midday, I went up to my study and saw that there was an email from Lorna.

From: Lornaalp@org.com
To: Cait@grmail.com

My dear Cait
I've given your situation a lot of thought this morning and this is my advice. Give Matt a chance. Give your marriage a chance. Really work on it. While you think about this proposal of Tom's, pull out all the stops to get your marriage back on track and, if at the end of the period of time you give yourselves, if you still feel it's not working, then, and only then, see where things go with Tom. You mentioned that Tom is around in the UK for about three months, so take that time, or however long you need – see it as a challenge and rise to it and in that way you will also be giving you and Matt a chance, but don't drag it out because indecision can be unsettling and exhausting.

Another point to consider. I am going to be the voice
of reason for a moment, not of romance. None of us is
getting any younger. Is Tom the kind of man who would
look after you as you sail into your seventies and
eighties? Who knows what's around the corner for any of
us? (Cheerful!) What if you were ill? God forbid, but I
know Matt would care for you. Would Tom? I know that's
no reason to stay with someone, to have a carer but just
saying . . . Does Tom just want 'young' Cait who was full
of life, fit and healthy?

And what about the other way round? Would you be
prepared to care for Tom if anything happened to him?
Dribbly Tom? Toothless Tom? Incontinent Tom? Arthritic
Tom? Or do you want young, fit and healthy Tom? Sorry,
getting carried away, but you get what I'm saying? I
know, not exactly the stuff of romance, but worth thinking
about. Once the first frisson fades and it's down to the
joys of a real life together – the picking up of unwashed
socks and laundry, seeing each other first thing in the
morning again and again . . . feelings can change. Desire
changes into familiarity, both of which we crave but are
polar opposites and often one can wipe out the other.

And now, the voice of romance – better to have loved
and lost than never to have loved at all. I know many
who have said they would prefer to have a few years of
the joy of a heightened love affair than many years of
stagnation. The exceptional versus the mundane. I had
the exceptional with Alistair, and if you really believe you
have the same with Tom and not Matt, then I would
never stand in your way. So either make it work with
Matt or move on. I remember when I first met you and

how happy you were with Matt. He grounded you, gave you security, and in that you flourished. Could Tom offer the same, or would there always be that fear that he might drift off for another adventure if he got bored?

I don't envy you this choice!

Make one of your lists about how you're going to revive your marriage. Start from there. I'll contribute if I can.

Love always,

Lorna X

Good advice as always, and I liked what she had said. A challenge. Give Matt a chance. It was only fair. I took a deep breath and composed a private message to send to Tom via Facebook. 'Dear old friend and devil incarnate. I am very flattered by your proposal and, much as it is tempting, I'm not ready. Please give me time. A few months with no pressure. How does that sound? Cait. X'

I was about to close the laptop when a message arrived back from Tom. 'Cait?'

'I'm here,' I typed in response.

He typed. 'Can I call you?'

I typed back. 'Not at the moment.'

'OK. You OK? Realized I sprang a lot onto you yesterday.'

'Understatement. Are you back in London now?'

'I am. Got your message. You want time?'

'Yep.'

'How much? An hour?'

'Funny. No, longer, weeks, maybe months, three months.'

'Months? Oh. Can't say that I'm not disappointed but I understand. Take as much time as you need.'

'Thanks. Good.'

'Will I see you?'

'Maybe. Not for an affair but to get to know you again.'

'Fair enough.'

'I . . .' Part of me was saying, end this *now*, it's insane to give it even another moment's thought, but there was another part saying, give Tom a chance; but, as Lorna had said, it was only fair to also give Matt a chance.

'Cait?'

'Still here.'

'I'll be in touch. XXXX'

I closed off my screen and inhaled deeply. I had a lot to think about. A challenge to get Matt and me out of the rut we'd fallen into. It felt the right thing to do but I couldn't deny a sense of regret that a life or even affair with Tom might not be on the cards if I succeeded. I went back to my list of goals for the week and added: Make list of how to resurrect marriage.

Downstairs, I heard Matt moving about in the kitchen. Three months. Poor man. He didn't know what he was in for.

*

'You seem agitated, Cait. Are you OK?' asked Matt after we'd finished supper that evening.

'Yes. Top of the world,' I said.

'Isn't it your choir night?'

'Teacher is away,' I lied. I just wasn't in the mood for singing 'The Circle of Life' from *The Lion King*.

22

Cait

*O*K. *Let the challenge begin*, I thought. *Three months to save a marriage.* After I'd showered, I went to the list started last night and added:

Things to tackle with Matt.
- Sex. Lack of it.
- Communication. Lack of it.
- Money. Lack of it.
- Plan our future. If there's to be a future for Matt and me.
- Retirement. What it might mean for Matt and me. What we both want from it.

So, number one. Sex, and how to get Matt and me back in the groove. My thoughts went straight to Tom. Sex with Tom. I felt a stab of desire. *Stop this now, Cait*, I told myself. *Matt not Tom.* Lovemaking with Tom had always been amazing which was part of the reason that it made no sense to me when he left, but then, as Lorna had so rightly pointed out, Tom and I had never got to the stage of familiarity that comes with being with someone for a long time. It had been good with Matt once, though different to being with Tom, I'd felt more secure. Maybe that was the key – the sense of safety that was wanted on the one hand was what killed excitement on the other. With Tom, there was always a sense of the unknown, but with it was a worry that he might disappear at any moment – which he did. He says he's changed, that he now knows what we had, but if I chose him, could I ever trust him not to leave me again? Possibly not.

But I'm going to try really hard not to think about Tom for the time being, I am going to attempt to reawaken the dead, seduce Matt and revive my marriage. Debs was always saying that life is what you make it, so if I am to stay with Matt, it will be what I have chosen, so I can either accept a life of celibacy or take positive action and I choose the latter. I can't blame Matt for his lack of enthusiasm in the bedroom. It takes two to tango, and it's not as if I've been Fifi the French maid of late – not that I ever was; in fact the only fantasy figure I'd come near to recently was a Zombie queen of the dead. Not exactly a turn-on.

So. How does one seduce one's husband? I asked myself as I got a cup of tea, went up to my study and turned on my laptop. I'd never really thought about it consciously before. In the early days, sex had been spontaneous with Matt and flowed naturally. We hadn't needed to think about what to do or where or in what position – it had been intuitive. Then came the years when the boys were small and we were both too exhausted and craved sleep more than sex. Over time, when we did do it again, it became routine, a task on the list – Thursday put the rubbish out, Friday supermarket shop, Saturday sex. Pleasant, but not much more than that, and if nothing else, it kept us connected. We knew exactly how we liked it and how to touch each other, but it became a dance that was too familiar; and slowly, with nothing really being said, it had faded altogether. When in need, go to Google, I thought as I wrote 'seduction' in the search area.

A site came up with not just seduction tips but *sizzling* seduction tips. OK. I will sizzle, like a sausage. No, probably not like a sausage.

'First you have to get him to notice you as a sexual being,' I read. *Fair point*, I thought. Although I took care of my appearance, I had stopped making any effort to look sexy long ago. My shoes were bought for comfort, as was my underwear; my clothes, although stylish, were hardly seductive. So, sex tips for seduction. I got out my pen and made another list.

- Wear red. *Seriously?*
- Relax and be playful, devil-may-care even. Bring an element of surprise into your relationship – like a beach trip in the middle of the night. *Two hours' drive in the dark. No way.*
- Invest in some see-through clothing. *I have a see-through shower cap, does that count?*
- Wear no underwear and let him know. *Hmm. Might be a bit chilly round the nether regions, and when should one let him know? In the supermarket by the veg counter? By the way, lover, I've gone commando. Take me now over the aubergines.*
- Spice up your love life with a sex toy or two. *Sex toys?*

- Get into the shower with him. *Why? When we have two showers?*
- Drape yourself over him while he's watching TV. *Why squash up when we have adequate seating to stretch out comfortably? Hmm. I am clearly not getting into the spirit of this so must make an effort not to be so sensible. Sensible is not sexy. Comfort is not conducive to passion.*
- Whisper something naughty in his ear. *Like what? Would you like a cream bun? No. Not that kind of naughty, but I am out of practice at the other kind. Clearly more googling is needed.*

I felt doubtful. If I followed these tips, it would feel forced and not true to myself. *Maybe this stuff would work when younger, but at our age?* I asked myself. Immediately, I could hear Debs's voice in my head. 'Age is a state of mind and attitude. Don't put limits on what you can or can't do or you'll get old before your time.' I decided that I would give the seduction advice a try. One tip a day, because I didn't want to give Matt a heart attack, plus it would be best to have a slow build-up of getting back into being sexual. Rome wasn't built in a day, neither will be the resurrection of our love life.

Had a look on Facebook. A quiz to find out what kind of princess I am. Couldn't resist that. Result – a medieval one. In other words, ancient. Can't argue with that.

*

Tip number 1. Wear something red.

I went through my wardrobe looking for red clothing. I had three red items: a fleece, a bobble hat and thermal hiking socks. Possibly not what the website intended, though could be interesting if worn with nothing else but a red rose up the bum crack. No. *Must get in the zone*, I told myself. What I needed was a lovely red dress or some red underwear.

Texted Lorna and Debs to ask if they'd come shopping with me. Luckily both were available for an early lunch and agreed to meet in town, though I called Lorna on my way and asked her not to mention Tom to Debs, nor the three-month 'save my marriage' challenge.

*

'You want to go in where?' Lorna asked when we'd finished bowls of soup at a café near the bus station.

'The sex shop.' Lorna gave me a knowing look. She knew the challenge had begun.

'What for?' asked Debs.

'A pound of butter. You've seen *Last Tango in Paris* haven't you?'

'Yes, but you can get butter at the Co-op,' said Debs.

'Joking. I want to go in for a look for something sexy. I don't want to go in on my own. I know. I'm a wuss but—'

'Have you made contact with Tom? Your Facebook old lover?' Debs asked. 'Is that what this is about?'

I didn't dare look at Lorna. 'No. *No*. Stop being Facebook police. It's for Matt. I want to revive our sex life and don't want to end up dressed like an old tart in drag, which is why I need you two along to give me an honest opinion of what I should get.' I pointed in the direction of the shop. 'Plus I'm curious.'

'I didn't know your love life needed reviving,' said Debs.

'I know things aren't great with Matt but you never said anything about your sex life.'

'I know. Not really something to throw into conversation, is it?'

'Yes. Absolutely it is. You can tell us anything,' said Debs.

'I was embarrassed. No one seems to talk about that stuff any more.'

Debs pointed at herself and Lorna. 'Only because we haven't got anyone to do "that stuff" with but, even when you have, every relationship goes through patches when the libido is low. That's why Fabio and I went to Wales to the Tantric weekend.' She laughed. 'Just, it didn't go quite the way I expected. But you can always talk to us, that's what friends are for – to help you through.'

Lorna gave me a meaningful look, which I ignored. 'I know how much you like Matt,' I said, 'and thought you wouldn't want to hear me going on about him when—'

'When we haven't got partners,' Deb finished for me. 'Well, you know what I think, and that is you should try counselling.'

'I might just do that, but I'm going to try my own way first. Besides, a trip to a sex shop might be enlightening for all of us.'

'OK, but no way am I going home with one of those monstrous rabbit vibrating things,' said Lorna.

'They have smaller ones,' said Debs. 'Come on, ladies, let's go and check out what's on offer.'

*

After coffees, we made our way into the pink and red interior of the sex shop, which was opposite the café. We browsed the displays and saw that there were vibrators in every colour and size in pink, black, silver, green, purple, gold, and they were made in small, medium and large, some with wiggly bits on the end. All offered slow, medium or powerful vibrations.

'They're enormous,' I said as I looked at a huge purple plastic vibrator on display, complete with wrinkly balls. It looked like a candle that had burnt down and the wax gathered around the base. Not sexy.

'Is this the sort of thing Matt is into?' asked Lorna as we surveyed the variety of merchandise on sale.

'We've never tried one, but it might be worth a try to get things going. The website I looked at this morning said that you have to get your partner to notice you as a sexual being.'

'And you thought you might find something in *here?*' asked Lorna. I could tell it wasn't her sort of place.

'Makes sense,' said Debs. 'Doesn't have to be a vibrator, but you could get some sexy underwear, get out your high heels, show your cleavage . . .'

'Oh I don't know,' said Lorna. 'I don't think you have to put on clothes you don't normally wear to attract your partner. If he finds you sexy, you could be wearing an old shirt.'

'That's because you look sexy in an old shirt,' I said. 'The rest of us need a makeover.'

'Just don't overdo it,' said Lorna. 'Don't be anyone you're not.'

'What, like a naughty nurse?' I asked as I looked at the fancy-dress outfits on sale and flicked through the rail. 'Hmm, what do you think? Dominatrix, police officer, school girl, cheerleader or sailor?'

'None,' said Lorna. 'I think that if he had a fetish to see you dressed as a cheerleader, you'd have heard about it by now.'

'Lorna, you've come over all headmistressy.'

'It's one of my personas,' she said. 'I have the complete outfit at home, along with a long list of detention punishments.'

'It might be fun to do a bit of role play,' I said. 'We've never tried that, and I want to remind Matt that I have other sides to me as well as washer-upper, grocery shopper, laundry lady, social secretary and so on. There's nothing vaguely sexual there, so I need to change that perception.'

'Good for you,' said Debs as she picked up a box. 'Oh look, pink fur handcuffs.'

'And here,' said Lorna as she picked up another box. 'Latex vaginas. Ew.'

'Why ew?' asked Debs. 'If women use vibrators, I guess it's only fair that men have something too.'

'God, I don't know where to start,' I said as I looked at a set of tickling sticks. 'And those ticklers look like the sort of thing I buy for Yoda at the pet store.' As I continued looking, there were all sorts of things on sale that I'd never heard of – lubricants, fetish toys, prostate massagers.

'Or the things Ken Dodd's Diddy Men had,' said Lorna. 'They had tickling sticks.'

'Perhaps they have a Diddy Man outfit on a rail in here,' I said.

'Yeah, and that's bound to work on Matt,' said Lorna. 'Can you imagine?'

'What about this?' Debs asked and pointed to a box on the display. 'A starter kit, maybe that's what you need.'

'What's in it?'

Debs turned the box over and started to read. 'A small vibrator, a tickler for new sensations, a solid dong for vaginal or anal play, a cock ring to keep him harder, jiggle balls for better orgasms, Thai beads and a butt plug for either him or her.'

I started to get the giggles. 'Butt plug? I think Matt would run a mile if I got one of those out when I take him his bedtime drink. Butt plug to go with your cocoa, sir? And a solid dong? What the hell is that?'

'I think it's a type of vibrator,' said Debs as she scrutinized the packaging.

'Now I know what's missing in my life. I don't know how I've survived this long without one. Actually, it would make a great name for a band and their backing singers, Solid Dong and the Raspberry Lubes. We could be the lubes if we could sing.'

'Which we can't,' said Debs.

Lorna was laughing as well; she picked up a box and handed it to me. 'No, no, I think what's been missing is an enlarging cock pump. You could get it out when you next have guests over for dinner to break the ice and get everyone talking.'

Debs picked up a pair of cat ears on a band and put them on. 'What do you think?'

'OK for a fancy-dress party, but how is wearing that supposed to turn a man on? I mean, honestly. Matt would laugh his head off if I appeared one night wearing that.'

Debs and Lorna started sniggering like schoolgirls, causing the young male assistant at the counter to glance over.

'Behave or we'll get thrown out,' I said.

'Great,' said Lorna. 'That would be one for the grandchildren – the day I got thrown out of the sex shop.'

'Have you seen anything you might like to buy?' asked Debs.

I shook my head. 'Not really. Maybe we should go. Oh, but I like these,' I said as I spotted a pair of diamanté handcuffs on the way out. 'I could handcuff Matt to the bed then leave him there while I watch something I want on TV.'

I noticed that the shop assistant was coming over. 'Can I help? Oh! Mrs Langham, is that you?' he asked. I turned to see Mark Janson, a lad who had been in one of my English classes many moons ago when I was a teacher. He looked amused to see me. No doubt news of my shopping would be on social media and round my ex-pupils before you could say 'cock ring'.

'Have you seen anything you'd like to buy, or should I demonstrate?' he asked with a smirk.

'You'll get a butt plug up your jacksie if you don't stop smirking, Janson,' I said, and he laughed but I felt I ought to buy something. 'I . . . I'm looking for a present for a friend really. Maybe some raspberry lube. Tell you what, I'll have a think about it and maybe come back later.'

Behind him, I could see that Debs and Lorna were still sniggering.

'What is so funny about sex toys?' I asked when we got outside and I cracked up laughing with them.

'I don't know,' said Lorna. 'Maybe we're just so repressed and British that we have to laugh, but you have to admit, some of those things are funny.'

'And some are scary looking. I don't feel I've got very far in my mission to get something to seduce Matt.'

'And those vibrators are missing something,' said Debs. 'They need vocals.'

'Vocals?' Lorna and I chorused.

'Yes. Using a vibrator can be a lonely business. It's only vocabulary is *bzzz*. They need an app that would talk dirty, or flatter, or whatever.'

'Better still, one that gave directions,' I said. 'Men notoriously never ask for them. Imagine an app that works like a sat nav or google maps. Up a bit, go left, go left, *left!* No. Wrong hole, you idiot! Back up, back up. OK. Continue straight ahead now.'

Lorna laughed. 'When Alistair was alive, he hated our sat nav. I don't think he liked taking directions from a woman. But you could be on to something Debs. Sex should be fun.'

'It should,' said Debs. 'Once Fabio brought a glow-in-the-dark condom back from a trip to Amsterdam; that was a laugh, especially if you turned all the lights off. But apps on the vibrators would be great – a running commentary to help things along.'

'And one especially for the weary wife,' I added. 'Is it over yet? Fancy a cup of tea? Oo, the ceiling needs dusting. And they should do a singing one too. It could sing, I ain't got no-o-body.'

'Juvenile,' said Lorna but she laughed. 'I think you should forget about sex toys and apps for you and Matt and just buy a bottle of good wine, a scented candle and relax. All this stuff is too much like hard work and not really you at all, Cait.'

'OK, good, in that case, can we go to M and S? I can buy the things you suggested, plus I need to get some support tights.'

*

At home later, I escaped to my study and opened my laptop to do rewrites on the 'Fairy Freak-Out'.

I went to Facebook instead. Watched fascinating and essential clip about a cat who adopts a squirrel monkey. Three minutes. Very moving. Then another clip of a cat helping a puppy out of a ditch. Also very moving.

I spent half an hour looking at further seduction tips on various websites, and made a note to try them as soon as possible.

There was nothing from Tom. I felt disappointed. But then what was I expecting? I'd told him I needed time. *I won't think about him*, I told myself. I'm married to Matt and going to make that work.

I googled sex toys and found a site that sold the same as the shop in town and more. Ow. Some of the prostate massagers looked like medieval torture implements. 'The male G-spot is in the anus so these toys can help orgasm,' I read. *Well, I never knew that*, I thought, and made a note to pass on my newfound information to Debs and Lorna. I'd enjoyed our time together today. Somehow my and Matt's lack of sex life hadn't seemed so much of a problem when having a laugh in the shop; more like a temporary hiccup that neither of them seemed overly concerned about.

I spent the next twenty minutes familiarizing myself with the Bondage for Beginners pages on the website. When I got to the electro- and medical fetish section and read about a G-spot intimate part spreader, I decided it might be time to call it a day.

'Cup of tea, Cait?' Matt called up the stairs.

'Yes please. And make it quick or you will be beaten,' my inner dominatrix called back.

'Pardon? Didn't catch the last bit.'

'And see if there's any cake that hasn't been eaten,' replied my inner wuss, who had shoved the dominatrix aside.

'OK. Will do.'

The site did, however, have some lovely lingerie, and I ordered a lace chemise with a halterneck while Matt made us tea with not a clue that I was turning into a love beast who devoured websites selling nipple clips and leather restraints. *No, no, not for us*, I thought as I stopped at the Clean Stream douche kit which appeared to be . . . 'It's a hot-water bottle,' I said to the screen. A bit further down were pictures of candles, but they were being sold as bondage candles. Someone, somewhere, was making a lot of money peddling ordinary household things in adult packaging.

'Who were you talking to?' asked Matt when he brought my tea.

'Laptop,' I said as I shut down the site. 'Er, just checking out strap-on dildos.'

Matt laughed. 'Right-oh,' he said, and ruffled my hair as if I was a five year old. 'And why would you want one of those?'

'To wear on my forehead and pretend I am a Dalek in *Doctor Who*. Why do you think?'

Matt laughed again and went back down the stairs. Clearly he didn't think I was serious. He was right. I'd done my research into sex toys. Nothing really appealed, and I realized it wasn't anything like that I wanted. What I wanted was to be desired and to desire him, to feel close to Matt, and no way was a pair of cat's ears and a vibrating monster dong going to do that.

Must do some writing work, I thought. Back to my story. Stared at blank page . . .

Ten minutes later: Still staring at a blank page.

Ping. Had an idea. Began to type. Fairy really does freak out. She goes on the rampage with a killer-driller vibrator and a splat gun that fires pineapple-flavoured lube. She ties up all the other characters with pink furry handcuffs, then sticks butt plugs up their noses and stuffs jiggle balls in their mouths. They can't breathe. They can't fly. There's super silk lube everywhere. Soon they are dead. It's a fairy freak-out. Fairy realizes with horror that she has lost her marbles so she turns the monster vibrator on herself. She dies with a smile on her face but, oh dear, with her death, it means that there are no more characters. No more story.

Hmm. Should I rewrite? My story is definitely not appropriate for kids. In fact, maybe I am not meant to be a writer after all.

Time for another look on Facebook to see if there are any new clips of animals that have been adopted or rescued in the last half-hour.

There was nothing interesting on Facebook but there was an email from Tom.

From: tomptl@hotorg.com
To: Cait@grmail.com

Dear Cait
Have made a list of what I have to offer.
• House in Majorca with stunning views. Has an artist's studio. Photos attached.

I took a quick look. Oh my god, it was perfect. A high-ceilinged sitting room, with bleached wood floors and pale blue sofas, that opened onto a terrace looking out over a valley. *Stunning*. A huge bed in a white shuttered room with more views to die for.

- Am a great cook. Know my wines.
- Have all my own teeth. OK. Most of them. OK, one wisdom tooth gone.
- Have all my own hair.

I wrote back.

From: Cait@grmail.com
To: tomptl@hotorg.com

Dear Tom,
Please send a list of all your faults, medical complaints and any medication you are on.
   Cait.
   X
   PS: I am not on any medication but think I may need some soon due to increasing sense of insanity.

'I reckon that they're ready to photograph,' said Matt as we surveyed the finished spare rooms later that day. They'd both been transformed from scruffy boys' bedrooms into light elegant spaces that I felt proud of. Sam's old room was painted in dove grey and white and I'd found a pale silver silk bedspread that went perfectly. Jed's room was painted in ivory and had a duck egg bedspread and curtains.

'I agree,' I said. 'We just need to tidy up the bathrooms a bit, get some posh products in there, then hopefully we'll have paying guests in the next few weeks.'

'Excellent. Well done, Cait,' said Matt from the doorway to Jed's old room. 'This was a good idea.'

'And well done to you,' I replied, and went to pass him while brushing myself up against him (seduction tip number 8 from the LoversLateinLife site). As I did so, he stepped back up against the doorframe to let me through, so I moved forward towards him again. He tried to move back further.

'Christ, Cait. What are you trying to do? Squash me?'

I held him with my gaze, looking directly into his eyes (seduction tip number 9 from the SexatSixty site).

He looked alarmed. 'What? Why are you looking at me like that? Have I done something?'

I tried to transmit sexual energy up and through my eyes, so continued to hold his gaze. He looked away and made a run for it down the stairs. 'Sometimes you can be scary,' he called back.

It appears that I haven't got the hang of sizzling seduction yet. Maybe it can't be forced. I thought back to when I'd seen Tom. He'd stared into my eyes directly and it had tugged deliciously, deep inside. I'd looked back at him. The magnetic pull had just been there, hadn't had to be evoked or forced. Maybe the fire between Matt and me had simply gone, the passion petered out, the battery gone flat.

I went back to my study and opened a new file for book ideas. Closed it and went to Facebook and watched clip of Kenyan Karate Mammas. Three minutes. Fascinating.

*

'Forward, back, jump, shout Zumba,' cried my teacher later at the class in the local church hall. I got some Kenyan Karate Mamma moves in. The rest of the class were very impressed.

23

Cait

Seduction tip for the day. Get in the shower with your partner.

I took a shower but Matt was still asleep, despite me having taken him a cup of tea and poked him several times. Maybe I should have bought a monster vibrator. I could have used it as a novelty alarm clock.

Matt was at the island in our kitchen having breakfast, in his dressing gown.

'Did you want something?' he asked.

'No. Why?'

'You're hovering with that look on your face.'

'What look?'

'Like you're waiting for me to do something.'

'No. No, not at all. Um, are you going to take a shower?'

Matt sniffed his armpits. 'Probably. Why? Do I need to?'

He was on the defensive. Not a good start but, five minutes later, he went up to the bathroom. I followed him up and

221

waited outside the door. Once I heard the water turned on, I went in. I could see him soaping himself behind the shower screen. My plan had been to slip in beside him and join in the soaping, but I remembered that one of the sites on seduction had also advised being unpredictable and devil-may-care. This was the perfect opportunity, plus the imagery from that famous scene in movie history had given me an idea. I picked up the electric toothbrush and began slashing the shower curtain while making a rhythmic screaming sound.

Matt yelped and leapt back. 'What the hell? Cait! What are you doing?'

'Norman Bates in *Psycho*.'

'I got the reference but *why?*' He held his hand to his chest and took a deep breath. 'You almost gave me a heart attack.'

'Sorry. Sorry.'

'Hand me a towel. Christ.'

'Sorry. Thought it might be funny,' I said as I sloped out of the bathroom.

Clearly acting like a psychopath didn't qualify as risqué or fun. Fair point.

*

Seduction tip number 4 from the sexforbeginners website. Drape your body over him while he's watching TV.

Matt had taken a coffee into the sitting room to watch the midday news, so I went in to join him. He was stretched out on the sofa so I sat at the other end, then slowly slid down and began to edge up until my back was lined up with his torso.

'Cait, if you want the sofa, just say so,' he said as he peered over me in an attempt to see the TV screen. 'You don't need to muscle your way in.'

He clearly wasn't getting the message, so I pushed myself back against him in the hope that he'd pick up the signals. He didn't. He saw it as a challenge to determine who got the sofa. He shoved me forward, which took me by surprise, and I rolled off and landed with a thud on the rug in front of the coffee table.

'Oh. Sorry, Cait. I didn't mean to—'

I sat up and was about to turn and be cross but he was laughing. 'Sorry, sorry. What were you trying to do?'

'Snuggle. It's ages since we did.'

He moved back on the sofa to make room for me. 'Come on then. Sorry. Didn't mean to laugh.'

Too late, I said and got up, put my nose in the air and left the room. Whoever wrote the seduction techniques ought to add one – do not attempt to distract partner if he is watching the lunchtime news.

*

Seduction tip number 11 from the sexforthesexless website. Whisper something dirty in his ear. This can be very arousing.

Yes but when? I asked myself. Why aren't these sites specific? When he's brushing his teeth? Having a cup of tea? Plus, I couldn't think of what to whisper – Don't forget it's rubbish collection day tomorrow? I'm going to be doing a white wash later? Put your dirty T-shirts in the basket? No, not that kind of dirt. Even I know that. It has to be more – hello, big boy, I want to fondle your hunky, hairy body. No. If I came out with something like that, Matt would laugh his head off.

Clearly I need to go to my laptop and google 'how to talk dirty for beginners'. So. Back to the site for suggestions. Oh. Right. There are loads of sites, even on how to talk dirty in Spanish. *Hola.*

I began to read the suggestions and made notes as I scrolled down:

- I am not wearing any underwear. *Hmm. If I whispered that, Matt would think it was the onset of dementia and I'd forgot to put any on.*
- I woke up wet this morning. *Matt would think we had a leak in the ceiling.*
- You're such a sex machine. *Cue hysterical laughter from Matt.*
- Ride me like a cowboy. *Uh?*
- Fuck me like I'm a farm animal. *What? Which farm animal? Chicken? Pig? Cow? Horse? Sheep? Or should one go exotic and think alpaca?*
- Deeper, deeper, bang me hard you bad, bad boy.

Cripes almighty, I can't come out with any of that. Ride me like a cowboy? It's just not my style. In fact, just reading the examples made me want to laugh. I decided to opt for some of the tamer lines and I went down to find Matt. He was on the sofa in his den, looking at his laptop so I sat down and slid towards him. This time, he didn't attempt to push me off but he did look wary.

'I'm not wearing any underwear,' I said huskily.

He pointed at the ceiling. 'I did a wash yesterday. I put all the clean stuff upstairs in the drawers in our bedroom.'

I *knew* it. *Knew* he wouldn't get what I was trying to do. Maybe I need to lower my voice, be more husky.

'No, I mean . . . I woke up so hot this morning.'

This got his attention.

'Really. Hot flush? But surely you went through the menopause years ago, Cait? Maybe you should see a doctor – night sweats might be a symptom of something serious. Or maybe it's a cold coming on, you do sound a bit throaty.'

One last try – what was it? Ride me like a farm animal, or was it a cowboy? OK. Here goes. 'I want you to ride me like a horse.'

Matt burst out laughing. '*What?*'

'Farm animal. Cowboy. I'm talking . . . Actually, you know what? Never mind.'

Matt's expression went from amusement to confusion. 'What? Have I upset you again? Oh god, what have I done now?'

'Nothing. It's me. Just . . .'

I am a failure at dirty talking, just as I was at phone sex. I shall look to see if they do classes in it at the adult further education college. Under languages – French, Spanish, Filth.

Texted Lorna and Debs. *Did you ever try talking dirty? If so, how?*

Lorna texted back. *Not really, though loved it when Alistair spoke Italian.*

Debs texted back. *All the time. I told you, I tried it all – phone sex, Tantric sex, dirty talking. He still left me.*

Back to Google, but first I saw an email from Tom:

From: tomptl@hotorg.com
To: cait@grmail.com

Faults. Have been trying to remember what my ex-wives said.
- Works too hard (no longer an issue as I come and go as I please regarding my work which is now more of a hobby).
- Snores sometimes. I know. Sorry. Ear plugs?
- Impatient, though in my defence, I would say, don't suffer fools.
- Medical conditions: am on no medication. Healthy and hearty.

I didn't reply. I was on a mission so had a look at further tips on the sextipsforthedesperate site.

- Wear nice underwear.
- Create a romantic atmosphere.
- Prepare a meal with food with aphrodisiac properties.

It was only day one in the challenge, and no way was I going to give up after a few disastrous attempts at getting Matt's attention. I would do something more our style, I'd decided; would go all out and combine several of the seduction tips, as well as take Lorna's advice and cook a nice meal to go with a good bottle of wine. Simple pleasures.

It had been years since I'd cooked 'a romantic meal', and lately we'd taken to eating our supper on our knees while watching the news. We even have those lap-safe trays. Next stop will be a huge fleece onesie and one giant slipper to share.

Matt had gone to check out a gym early evening, so I had time to prepare. Everything would be ready by the time he got back.

List of things to do:
- Bathe in unguents from the Orient.
- Dress in flattering clothes with special attention to underwear.
- Make room look romantic: scented candles.
- Prepare meal with aphrodisiacs.
- Open wine to breathe.

I bathed in perfumed bath oil, then applied body lotion to every part of my body, even the under-soles of my feet, so I am silky smooth – too silky smooth. I slipped on bathroom tiles, hit head, might be concussed.

I went to the chest of drawers to look out some sexy underwear. Oh dear. There must be something in there somewhere, I thought as I rummaged through. But no. Nothing apart from a pile of white cotton knickers.

'Over my shoulder goes one pair,' I sang as I threw them out one after the other. There was nothing vaguely lacy or silk. My bras weren't any better, and I'd got rid of suspender belts and stockings several decades ago. Maybe if I could get Matt in the mood, I could strip off and he wouldn't have to look at my underwear. Or, better still, I could entertain him by doing the Dance of the Seven Veils with the set of tea towels we got on a day trip to Weymouth last autumn.

I got undressed and surveyed myself in the long mirror. Hmm. The line, 'Very nice but needs ironing,' came to mind.

Candlelight in the bedroom later would definitely be a good idea – that is if we got that far.

Or, if all went as planned, we could move on to advanced seduction tips and 'have sex in unusual places'. I wasn't sure what they meant by unusual – in a wardrobe? Under the coffee table? On top of the spin dryer? Who knew where we'd end up if the mood so took us. We might even end up in the garden shed and do it over the lawn mower.

Now. What to wear for a Friday-night supper that won't look over the top but will look attractive. I chose my 'going out for dinner' outfit, a pale green dress, and applied a little make-up so that it didn't look as though something was going on, then went downstairs to cook. As I went about the preparations, I felt optimistic that it was going to be a good evening and that things could change for the better. Matt and I had been through many phases in our marriage: good, happy, indifferent, busy, sad, irritated, so there was no reason we couldn't have yet another phase – one that we determined together.

I'd been to the shops to buy the list of aphrodisiacs and managed to get them all apart from oysters. I laid the ingredients out on the island in the kitchen, ready to start preparing, but first I looked out the decent china, crystal and cutlery. *It's a shame this never gets used*, I thought as I pulled it out from the back of the dresser. While I washed and polished, I remembered something Eve had said before she died, and a wave of regret rose and caught in my throat. 'Promise me that you'll live every day as if it's a special occasion – because it is. Every day is to be celebrated. You never know what's around the next corner and how many more days you'll have. So wear your best clothes. Burn the candles put away for Christmas. Use your good perfume. Eat off your best china. Drink from the crystal stacked at the back of the cupboard. Use all that stuff you put away, and make every day a special occasion.' I'd promised her that I would, then life had taken over and I'd completely forgotten. Until now. 'I will, Eve. I'll use all my best.'

I lit candles in the dining room and laid the table. The room looked soft and romantic. *We had stopped making an effort for each other*, I thought, *that's probably been part of the problem*. I remembered our early years, before the boys were born. One night I'd lit the ground floor with candles and strewn the floor with flower petals. OK, so I almost sent the place up in flames due to one of the candles being too close to a curtain, and the floor had looked as if it needed a good hoovering, but the thought was there. I used to regularly buy Matt's favourite wine, cook him a special meal. He'd bring back the occasional bottle of champagne, buy me unexpected gifts – books he knew I wanted or a CD. After supper, we'd sit and talk, and then came the boys and dinner à deux became endless cooking for four, and when they left came takeaways and the box sets . . .

The list of ingredients that had aphrodisiac properties was an odd one, so it took a while to find a recipe that would work. I finally settled on a spicy Caribbean dish.

I put on a red apron (found at the back of the cupboard – wear red, seduction tip number 1 from sextipsforthedemented site) and set about frying garlic. I was going to cook white fish with chilli peppers, garlic, mushrooms, sesame seeds, celery to be served in a salad with almonds, aniseed, asparagus, avocado, fennel, pine nuts, with a honey mustard and ginger dressing to be followed with a fruit salad of bananas, pineapple, mango, figs with vanilla ice cream and then chocolate and coffee. Plus a bottle of good Malbec, the one I knew Matt liked.

I looked through CDs in our ancient collection, chose a Sting compilation and put that on.

As I heard Matt come through the front door, I sprayed fig-scented room spray into the air.

'Wow, smells like a brothel in here,' he said as he came through and looked around. 'What's the occasion? Oh shit. No. Is it our anniversary? It's not, is it?'

'Relax, Matt. No, it's not our anniversary. It's Friday night,' I said as I poured a glass of wine and handed it to him. 'We've both had a bit of a rough time lately, so I thought I'd make a special dinner to celebrate.'

'Celebrate what?'

'We've got the spare rooms ready and it's looking fabulous. We're ready to take guests.'

Matt nodded. 'I guess that is an achievement of sorts. Especially after them both looking such a mess for so long.'

'Exactly.'

Matt looked touched and came over and put his arm around me. 'What a nice idea, Cait. So, what are you cooking?'

'New recipe. I thought I'd be adventurous. How was the gym?'

'Good.'

'Are you going to join?'

'I think I will. There are loads of classes on offer, as well as the machines to work out on Hey, you look nice. Do I need to change?'

'Only if you want to. No need.'

He went over to the CD player and turned the music down. 'Sorry. Can't stand Sting, and you really ought to upload your CDs onto your phone or laptop.'

I decided to give the 'hold eye contact' seduction tip number 7 one more go. I stared into his eyes meaningfully but, once again, instead of returning my gaze, he looked worried.

'Oh god, you're giving me that look again? Sorry. You like Sting and your CDs, don't you? I'll put it back on. Or is there something I should have done? Laid the table?'

I stopped looking at him. Clearly my come-hither look needed practice. 'No. Just relax. Drink your wine.'

'OK. I'll just go and freshen up,' he said.

'OK, take your wine with you.'

While he was gone, I went to the mirror to examine my 'hold the gaze' look. It was a bit intense – more Hannibal Lecter than Mata Hari. I crinkled my eyes. That's what was needed, to look softer, more smiley, less *Silence of the Lambs*. 'Here's your supper, Matt,' I said to my reflection in my best creepy voice, 'a lump of raw liver with baked beans served with a nice Chianti.' Or was it fava beans? I did the hissing, sucking-in sound, 'thuh, thuh, thuh', that Anthony Hopkins did so well in the movie, just as Matt popped his head round the door.

'Are you OK, Cait?'

'Oh yes, just had something caught in my teeth.'

Matt gave me a puzzled look. 'OK. Just going to take a quick shower if I have time.'

'Go ahead, Officer Starling.'

Matt shook his head and went back upstairs. He returned after fifteen minutes and I saw that he'd made an effort and shaved. 'Smells great in here, garlic and spices,' he said. 'Anything I can do?'

'Nope, just relax.' *So far, so good*, I thought, as I poured him another glass of wine. Here we are, being nice, making an effort for each other.

I served dinner and sat opposite Matt.

'This is really thoughtful,' he said as he took a bite.

I tried to eat slowly and seductively (sex tip no 3,007 from sextipsforpeoplewho'velosttheplot site) as I looked directly at him again.

He put his hand up to his mouth. 'What? Have I got spinach on my teeth?'

'No.'

'Are you OK, Cait? Something gone down the wrong way? You look uncomfortable.'

'No. I'm fine,' I said in a low husky voice.

He put down his knife and fork and looked directly back at me. At *last*, he was getting the hang of it. 'Cait. Is something wrong?'

'Wrong? No. Why?'

Matt indicated the room. 'This. It's very nice and I appreciate the effort, I really do but . . . is there something you're not telling me? Is this leading up to something?'

'Like what?'

'No idea. You're ill? Leaving me? Decided to have a gay relationship?'

'No. Just because I've cooked up a nice supper, why would it mean that there's a problem?'

'Because you've been acting weird all day. You haven't been yourself at all.'

'I'm fine. Honestly. Just eat while it's still hot.'

He glanced at the CD player. 'Do you really want music on while we eat?'

'Yes. It helps with the atmosphere, but turn it off if it's annoying you.' Of course, I knew Matt didn't like music when he was eating. He always complained in restaurants and asked waiters to turn it down.

He took another forkful of the meal.

'What do you think?' I asked.

'It's different,' he said as his face grew red, his eyes began to water and he began to splutter. 'Actually . . . hell, Cait, what have you put in this?' He downed a glass of water in one.

'Chilli. To spice things up a bit.'

'You've certainly succeeded at that. It's . . . fiery.'

I took another bite myself, and in a few seconds my mouth was on fire too. 'God. Sorry. Overdone it. Try the salad. Cucumber.'

The salad was edible but a strange combination, and neither Matt nor I ate very much.

Matt smiled. 'Fancy a takeaway?'

I smiled back at him. 'Actually I do. '

'Pizza or Indian?'

'Pizza. We could share.'

'Perfect,' said Matt. 'Now. Are you going to tell me what's going on? I've been worried about you.'

'Honestly?'

Matt nodded. 'I can take it.'

'OK. Well, I thought I'd try to revive our love life, so I've been trying out some seduction techniques.'

'Seduction techniques?' He thought for a moment, then I could see he was struggling not to laugh. 'Is that what you were doing in the shower and snuggling up to me, giving me meaningful looks?'

'You might laugh, but I've realized that actually I haven't a clue any more. I've grown rusty. What turns you on, Matt?'

'Er . . . when you're not being weird? I don't know. What's the right answer? Is this one of those – *does my bum look big in this* type of questions? Can't win.'

'You can. Just give me a clue. Or have you completely given up on us?'

Matt moved his chair close to mine, leant over and kissed me. We both leapt back. We had chilli on our lips and it burnt.

'Woah. Hot.'

Matt burst out laughing again. 'You don't need to do anything, Cait. Just be yourself. I know things have been strained of late and I apologize, but no need for special seduction techniques. I love you just the way you are. Always have. Always will.'

I moved over beside him and we kissed again. I stroked down his arm, his torso, then . . . the doorbell rang.

'Who the hell could that be at this time of night?' I asked.

Matt got up. 'I'll tell them to go away.'

I followed him out into the hall and peered through the small frosted window at the side of the front door. I could just about make out two shapes. Whoever it was knocked and rang the bell again.

'Mum, *Mum*, is that you?' asked a familiar voice.

'*Jed?* Matt, I think it's Jed,' I called as Matt opened the door and we saw two very suntanned, dark-haired young men standing in our porch.

Jed came forward to give Matt a bear hug. 'Surprise,' he said and, on seeing me, did the same to me.

'But I thought you were in Thailand?' I said.

'I was,' he turned to acknowledge his friend, 'we both were, and now we're here.'

'Come in, come in,' said Matt and ushered them inside. 'But why didn't you call?'

'I . . . that is we . . . wanted to surprise you.'

I looked over to the man standing behind Jed. 'And this is?'

'Oh sorry, course, this is Martin.'

'Hi, Mr and Mrs Langham,' he said.

'Cait, Matt, please,' I said.

'Is it OK? Can we stay a while?' asked Jed as he dumped his rucksack and bag onto the floor.

'Yes. Of course,' I said.

'Great,' said Jed, as Martin put his stuff next to Jed's. 'We can have my old room right?'

I glanced at Matt and he half laughed, half nodded.

'OK,' I said, 'but we've decorated. I'll explain later. What happened? I thought you had a job and place to stay?'

Jed shrugged and looked at Martin. 'Time for a change. We thought we'd come back to the UK and see what the job situation is here. If we could use this place as a base, we can check out what's happening. God, Mum, I'm starving. What've you got to eat? Something smells good in here. Where's Yoda?'

'Yoda's gone for his evening walk and there's plenty of food in the kitchen, come on through. You too, Martin, then I'll show you where you can put your things for the time being.'

'And I'm dying for a proper cup of tea,' said Jed. 'Been dreaming of it all the way here.'

I ushered Martin into the kitchen, where Jed opened the fridge and helped himself to a carton of apple juice as though he'd never been away. He took a long swig, handed it to Martin then looked around. 'God, it's good to be home,' he said. 'Let's have a bit of grub then bed. We're both cream-crackered. We can have a proper catch-up in the morning.'

I made mounds of cheese on toast, mugs of tea, and Jed filled us in on his last weeks in Thailand.

'Alex and I parted months ago,' he told us when Martin went to the loo. 'Just wasn't working out. Alex had the roving eye, he was never ready for steady. Martin's different. He knows who he is and what he wants and he wants me.'

'So Martin's your new boyfriend?' asked Matt.

'Oh yeah. Didn't I say that?' Jed replied through a mouthful of toast, on to which he'd ladled mounds of the chilli dish I'd made earlier. He took a bite. 'Wow, this food is hot, Mum. What were you trying to do? Kill Dad?'

'Hope not,' said Matt, 'though I wouldn't put it past her lately.'

*

I finished clearing up after the boys around midnight. Matt was already in bed. I could hear the sounds of three people snoring as I went up the stairs to my study where I had a quick look on Facebook on my laptop to see if Tom had been in touch again. All quiet. Couldn't resist quick quiz to determine which is my weakest chakra. I knew I wouldn't be able to sleep without knowing. Hmm. Apparently it's the throat chakra, which signifies a difficulty in communicating. Rubbish.

So much for my first day of sizzling seduction. *Maybe I should just jump on Matt*, I thought as I went through to the bedroom and got into bed. No. I'd scared him enough for the time being, so I lay beside him and curled away from him as he was from me. Best-laid plans, I reflected as I realized we wouldn't be doing Airbnb in Jed's room for a while. So, our spare-room guests weren't the ones we'd expected, but that was life and it was wonderful to see Jed.

Clearly, how to seduce one's partner would have to be a subject for next time I saw Lorna and Debs. Hopefully they'd have more to offer than me and my friend Google.

24

Cait

I looked into Jed's room to see an unmade bed, clothes strewn everywhere and somehow one of the new curtains had come off its rings and now hung precariously at the window. It stank of dirty socks and that stale biscuit boy smell that was only too familiar.

In the bathroom, there was a strong scent of apple body wash and wet towels all over the floor. *Welcome home, Jed*, I thought as I set about making the bed, putting the curtain back on its rail then cleaning the bathroom.

*

Matt

Three men sitting on stools at the island in the kitchen. Martin and I were in dressing gowns, Jed in his boxers.

Cait came in, took one look at us and burst out laughing.

'What's so funny, Mum?' Jed asked.

'I was thinking of that saying "what you resist, persists."'

'And what are you resisting?' asked Jed.

'Men in dressing gowns,' she replied, and started washing up mugs at the sink.

Jed looked over to me as if for explanation but I just shrugged.

'Women are one of life's biggest mysteries,' I said.

Jed got up and went and put his arm around her. 'Hey, Mum, do us the full English, will you? Bacon, eggs, mushrooms, tomatoes and baked beans. Dad, Martin, you in?'

'Yeah. Fab,' said Martin.

I knew she would. She was always a soft touch when it came to spoiling Jed.

'Sure, the full English,' she said, 'but not for me thanks. Matt?'

'Yes, I'd love some. It is Saturday, after all.'

'No, I meant – could you make it? Please?'

'*Make it?* Oh. Yes. Course I will.'

'Thank you.' She came over and touched me gently on the back. 'You're a hero.'

I wasn't sure what had come over Cait of late, but whatever it was, I thought it best to just go along with what she wanted, though most of the time, I hadn't a clue what that was. She'd been in a strange mood all week, one minute distant and quiet, another acting as psycho-woman and a bit scary; other times, there was the old loving Cait, and then all that talk of seduction last night before the boys arrived. I was glad when they turned up. Saved by the bell. It's not that I don't love Cait – I do, and I still fancy her, but sex just hadn't seemed to figure in my mind or to be high on my list of priorities lately. Not that I wanted anyone else either but – what is it they say that women want? A man to open the bedroom door for her like a gentleman, then throw her on the bed like a sex-starved ruffian. I needed to be feeling better about myself, about us, before I could be the man in charge in the bedroom. With Cait, I hadn't seemed able to do or say anything right recently, and it was not conducive to making me feel like making love, in case I got that all wrong too. We needed to make the peace first. But an idea had flashed into my mind last night as I was falling asleep. Cait had said she wondered if we even spoke the same language any more, so I was going to show her that we did and that I understood her unique way of expressing herself. Her language was that of lists, so I intended to speak to her through them. I was going to write a book for Cait. In it would be lists about her, about me, about how to make the most of the next stage of our lives as discussed with Debs – the physical approach, mental attitude, emotional, spiritual. Next time she asked what plans I had for the future, I would present it to her, and I hoped that when she saw the pages written in her language, she would know that I had been listening all along.

'And we've a pile of washing,' said Jed. 'We've been on the road for days. Should I bring it down, Mum?'

'Don't worry,' said Cait. 'I looked in your room and your laundry's already standing up. I am sure it will walk to the utility room by itself.'

'Hah. Funny, Mum.'

I laughed. It would be nice having Jed home for a while. It would remove some of the pressure from me.

*

Cait

Jed and Martin went into town leaving the kitchen looking as though a bomb had hit it. I was about to start clearing up the breakfast things but stopped myself. Why should it always be me? Matt was in his den so I went through.

'Matt, would you mind tidying the kitchen?' I asked.

'Don't I always?'

'No, I usually do.'

'Is this a complaint?'

'Not at all. A request. I do most things about the house—'

Matt sighed. 'I didn't realize we were keeping scores. What happened to the loving Cait of yesterday evening?'

'She died in the night.'

'Did you not sleep well again?'

'Nope, so just have a tidy up, will you?'

'I got it first time,' said Matt.

This wasn't going well. Maybe I'd just make him a list of things to do and shove it under his nose, then I wouldn't have to actually ask him to do stuff around the house, but if we couldn't even have a normal conversation about the chores, we really did need help.

'Have you thought any more about counselling?'

'Can't say it's been top of my agenda.'

'I can understand you not wanting to use the vouchers Debs gave us, but how about we find our own therapist?'

'Is it really necessary?'

'We've nothing to lose; we could agree only to go if we can find someone we both feel comfortable with.'

Matt sighed. 'If we must.'

So . . . back to the drawing board. I didn't want to ignore

my mission to get our relationship back on track now that
Jed had returned. Maybe the seduction idea and pineapple
lubricants were too much, too soon. We needed to work on
other stuff first – like how to feel close to each other again,
get talking, work out a way to be now we were both at home,
and with Jed and Martin.

Number two on the list of how to save my marriage was
communication and, judging by my failure to even ask Matt
to do a simple task without getting prickly, I had to admit
that we could probably benefit from some professional help.

No time like the present, I thought as I went up to my
study to my laptop and googled 'marriage-guidance therapists'. I found a few that sounded promising in the area and
made a note to call them. In the meantime, I looked up 'how
to communicate with your husband'.

Hmm. Interesting stuff. More doable than the seduction
tips. *I should have started here*, I thought.

As always, I made a list as I scrolled through the websites
I found.

- Say please and thank you. *Good advice. I should have
  said, Matt, please tidy the kitchen. Thank you.*
- Lead by example. *Nah. Tried that years ago with all the
  men in my house. Waste of time. They just thought, hurrah,
  Mum will do everything.*
- Don't attack your partner, it will only make them defensive. For example, don't start conversations with 'you
  should . . .' 'why don't you . . .' 'you ought to . . .'
  Instead say, 'it's hard for me when . . .' 'I feel . . .' *Again,
  good advice. I will make a special note of that one.*
- Reward good behaviour. *This always worked when my*

boys were little. Also, years ago, when we had Dave, our dog. Must apply the same to Matt, though maybe not by giving him dog treats.

- Timing. Best to talk when your partner is relaxed, not when he or she has just walked through the door. Go for a drive, a walk, a meal. *Good idea for a drive, lock the doors, then he can't get out of the car.*
- Don't expect your partner to read your mind. *A romantic notion, of course, but I always felt that Tom could read mine.*
- Listen as well as talk. *Yes.*
- Mirror each other in body and in speech. For example, ask your partner to say what they need, then repeat it back and ask, 'I am hearing . . . Is that right?' *OK.*
- Compliment each other. *God, yes. I don't do it enough.*
- Questions to ask – what are you worried about? If you could change anything about our relationship, what would it be? When are you happiest? What can I do to support you? What would improve our lives? Express interest. *Must practise interested face.*
- Put yourself in your partner's shoes. *Bit big for me. Oh. I see what you mean.*
- Don't exaggerate to make a point. *Aw, that takes all the fun out of it.*
- Listen non-defensively. Many couples don't listen to their partner because they are too busy planning what they're going to say in their heads. *God, this is a long list!*
- Do something nice for each other once a day. *Will do.*
- Don't yell. *I WON'T.*
- Take responsibility for your part in it all and let go of having to be right. *But I am always right, aren't I???*

- Pray together. *Hmm. God grant me the serenity to accept the things I cannot change, courage to change the things I can, and the wisdom to know the difference etc.*

I went through to find Matt in his den. I sat opposite him. He was sitting on the sofa with his legs crossed so I crossed mine and mirrored his posture.

'You're looking good today.'

Matt looked surprised. 'I am?'

'Yes. I don't often say it, but I often think that you look good for a man your age.'

'What do you want, Cait?'

'Nothing.'

'OK,' said Matt. He crossed his legs the other way, so I did the same.

'How are you feeling these days?'

Matt shrugged so I mirrored his shrug. 'Fine. OK.'

'I'm hearing that you're fine. Is that what you're saying?'

Matt laughed and crossed his arms. I did the same. 'Yes. That is what I am saying, Cait.'

'Good. That's marvellous.'

'So what is it you want to say?'

'To ask how we can improve things in our relationship? Practical things.'

Matt shifted so I shifted too.

'Well, you can stop copying everything I do for a start,' he said. 'It's spooky.'

'It's supposed to make you feel that I empathize with you.'

'I think you're supposed to do it subtly, so that the person you're mirroring doesn't notice.'

'So you know all about it?'

'It's the sort of thing they teach on weekend team-building workshops but I'm not sure about it. I think it can be manipulative if it's not natural. However, if you take notice, you will see that people do it naturally and without thinking when they're getting on.'

'That was how I was trying to make you feel.'

Matt laughed again. 'OK, but maybe don't be so obvious. The way you were going about it made me feel uncomfortable.' He shifted again. I was about to do the same but stopped myself. 'What has got into you lately, Cait?'

'I'm trying to make things better and I thought a good place to start was with talking.'

'Last night you said it was by being seductive.'

'I changed my mind. Thought that might be too much, too soon. I've found some therapists we could try.'

Matt's face fell. 'How did we get here, Cait?'

'I don't know.'

We sat in silence for a few moments while I tried to remember some of the tips I'd just read for better communication. 'Take some of the responsibility' was one of them. 'Not easy, is it?'

'What's not easy?' Matt asked.

'Being married. Keeping it all alive. I know I'm partly to blame.'

'Are you?'

'I must be. Tell me what you'd like to change.'

'I can't think of anything. I think we muddle along quite well really.'

'Muddle? But is that enough? Muddling?'

'I think so. OK. Is there anything you'd like to change?'

I began to think of a list of things. 'OK. Er . . . share household tasks more.'

Matt sighed. 'Just let me know what you want me to do.'

'I think it would be good if we both knew what the other was responsible for – like who does the shopping, who does the cleaning. Please. Thank you.'

'Fine. I will do my share of the chores. And try to communicate more . . . in fact, how are *you* feeling lately, Cait?'

I felt sudden tears fill my eyes and brushed them away.

'Oh. Sorry. I didn't mean to upset you.'

'It's OK just . . . I can't ever remember you ever really asking before, or at least in a caring way. You've asked what's got into me, but in an accusatory way that makes me feel defensive, like I've done something wrong.'

'Surely not. Well I'm asking now. Are you OK? How are you? Really?'

'Mixed up, I guess. Sorry, that doesn't help much, does it? As I've said, I feel like something needs to change. Maybe us. Maybe just me. I do know that I haven't felt happy lately.'

'I know. I do know that even if I don't say,' said Matt. 'I've lived with you long enough to know when you're unhappy. Is there anything particular going on that I should know about? Anything you're not telling me?'

I shook my head. I felt confused and unsure about what I wanted any more. I could see Matt was trying, though, and remembered the tip about rewarding good behaviour. 'Well done. Ten out of ten for effort.'

Matt's concerned expression changed to puzzlement. 'Are you being sarcastic?'

'No. No. Sorry. Not at all.'

Matt sighed. 'As I said to Jed earlier, women are one of

life's great mysteries. You have to remember, Cait, us men are simple folk. We're not psychic. You have to spell things out very clearly to us or we just don't get it. Any other top tips? You've obviously been looking into this.'

'Nope.'

I felt hopeless. I'd pushed for better communication then hadn't known what to say. It threw me a little and made me think that maybe I needed some help in opening up too.

I went back to my study, looked at the list of marriage counsellors and picked up the phone.

*

'No need to laugh quite so heartily,' I said after I'd filled Lorna and Debs in on my night of seduction when we met up in our local café for a light lunch. 'What is love? Here we are, mature women with a lifetime's experience, but I still don't think I know.'

'That's the million-dollar question,' said Debs. 'All those soft-focused pictures you see of a woman's head on a pillow, a soft smile in the light of the morning, all that imagery. It's not like that, is it?'

'Matt says I am like Medusa in the morning,' I said. 'He keeps out of my way.'

'That's love, being considerate of each other and each other's moods,' said Lorna. 'You learn your way around each other and he knows when to keep his distance. I think love is practical stuff exactly like that, like looking after each other when you're ill; small acts of kindness.'

'It used to turn into a competition with Fabio when one of us was ill,' said Debs. 'Who could out-ill the other. Fabio always won, especially when he had man flu. He was like that cartoon of the man lying in bed, looking pale and wan and his wife hoovering around him and he says, never mind your hysterectomy, where's my Lemsip?'

Lorna and I laughed.

'Love is blind,' Debs continued. 'The blind leading the blind.'

'Not always. My brother said he fell in love with his wife because she gave him his first proper look at a naked woman with the lights on,' said Lorna.

'What about passion?' I asked.

'That never lasts,' said Debs.

'I disagree,' said Lorna, 'but you have to work on it.'

'How?' Debs and I chorused.

'Dates out together, doing something you both enjoy, whether that be theatre, eating out, travelling or learning something new together. Time away from the familiarity of the domestic scene. You need times when you can remember why you both fell in love in the first place.'

'How's your search going?' I asked Debs.

'I'm starting to lose faith in online dating.'

'So why do it?' asked Lorna.

'Companionship, but I'm not sure I can be bothered any more.'

'I know I couldn't be bothered,' said Lorna. 'All that stuff to go through before you get to the living-in-harmony part. It can take a long time to discover who someone really is and that he leaves his socks on the floor, top of the toothpaste off, loo seat up, gets grumpy in the mornings. Then there are the arguments over décor. He likes minimal, you like country clutter. He's unsociable, you love a house full of friends. It worked with Alistair but it took time. I'm not sure I could go through that again.'

'Our compromise was – my money so I made all the decisions about what to buy, he got to appreciate everything I bought,' said Debs.

'Maybe that was part of the problem,' said Lorna. 'Maybe he needed to have more say. Men do like to feel included and be heard.'

'Unless it's about who shops, who does the cleaning, who does the admin,' I said.

'Who does that in your house, Cait?' Debs asked.

'Mainly me because Matt was always working, but we're working on changing that.'

'Fabio used to believe there was a fairy in our house, one who mysteriously replaced the loo paper and the tea bags,' said Debs.

'How are you working on changing things, Cait?' Lorna asked.

'Early days, but I've asked if we can share the chores now that he's at home.'

'Only fair,' said Debs. 'And I might not know what love is, but I do have some tips for the perfect marriage. A cleaner if you can afford one, two bathrooms and two televisions, so he can watch sport and you can watch whatever you want.'

'Fair point,' I said, 'but we can't afford a cleaner.'

'Then it's a good idea to ask Matt to do more,' said Lorna. 'He must have time now, and get those boys to help out too, now that they're back for a while. They can't just move in and expect an unpaid servant.'

'And what are you going to do about reviving your love life after last night?' asked Debs.

'No idea. When I say Matt is good in bed now, I mean not too restless, doesn't snore or wriggle. I don't know if Matt even finds me attractive any more.'

'I'm sure he does,' said Lorna. 'You look great, years younger than your age.'

'Do you still find him attractive?' asked Debs.

I hesitated. 'Yes, but more in the way of a comfortable old friend with some annoying habits.'

'Often what attracted you in the first place is what drives you mad after years together – decades, in your case,' said Lorna. 'In the beginning, you love how reliable and sensible he is, and that ends up being what drives you mad – you find him boring.'

'Exactly.'

'You find Matt boring?' asked Debs.

'Er . . . no, not exactly but I used to love how reliable he was in the beginning, but I often wish now that he'd do something spontaneous, exciting, I don't know, be a bit wilder, be more adventurous.'

Debs shook her head. 'I'd give anything for a man like Matt, someone loyal and dependable, but I get what you were saying, Lorna. With Fabio, I loved his childlike spirit then ended up wishing he'd grow up. I loved his independence, then would get mad when he was never at home; loved the fact he was open to new experiences, then off he went with Tantric Tracy. So, it can work both ways. If Matt was wilder, you'd probably be wishing he was more reliable.'

'Overfamiliarity can be a killer,' said Lorna. 'You need distance sometimes.'

'Yes, but that can have negatives, like with Matt and me. Over the years, we both created lives that were separate from each other. His whole social life was his work and his colleagues.'

'He must miss that,' said Debs.

'I guess he does but the friendships were all based around work and sadly none of them seem to have lasted beyond that. Maybe I need to appreciate and acknowledge him more.'

'Can't do any harm,' said Debs. 'Men like to be admired. We all do.'

'And maybe I need to take care of my appearance more. Spruce up a bit.'

Debs nodded. 'True. Men like to feel proud of their partner and vice versa, but you always look good, Cait.'

'Thank you, but not sexy.'

'So give yourself a makeover. Buy some new clothes. Get your make-up done,' said Lorna. 'It has to start with you. If you feel more attractive, people around you see that too.'

I sighed. 'Maybe, but maybe some people just grow apart.'

'I think what you're going through is just a phase,' said Lorna. 'Lack of romance can be caused by worry, boredom, bad health, lack of exercise, pressure, stress, overfamiliarity, alcohol. All sorts of reasons.'

'That's what I've tried telling myself.'

'Take it a day at a time. Instead of "I'll be loving you always", try for "I'll be loving you Tuesdays",' said Lorna.

I laughed. 'Thanks, and sorry to go on.'

Lorna put a hand over mine. 'You can always talk to us and I'm glad you have.'

*

'Where's Matt gone?' I asked Jed when I got home.

'Said something about going for a walk?'

'Your dad? What kind of walk?'

'A walk walk.'

'Did he say where he was going to walk?'

'No. He just put on his walking shoes and off he went. He's probably having an affair.'

'Very funny.'

It was puzzling, though. Years ago, Matt used to go off hiking but more recently, although we'd occasionally go for a walk together or with friends, he never went on his own.

25

Matt

An attractive, slim woman in her thirties came into the reception area of the gym then over to where I was sitting. She had blonde hair tied back from a glowing face and was dressed in hot pink Lycra. She exuded energy and I felt pale and stodgy beside her.

'Hi. I'm Chrissie,' she said, and gave me a handshake so strong it made me wince. 'You must be Matt. I believe you wanted to talk about keeping fit?'

'I do. I'm researching methods for living well for the over-fifties and -sixties and when I came in last week, the girl on reception said you're the person to talk to.'

'I am.' She gave me a quick glance up and down. 'Not for you?'

'Well . . . I'm sure I could benefit, but it's mainly for a TV programme idea that I'm working on.'

She beckoned me to get up and follow her. 'I work with a lot of older people and not only the retired. I'm glad you came.' She led me through to a small white study at the back of the gym where she indicated that I should sit on one of the plastic chairs by a desk. 'We can talk in here. So how can I help exactly?'

'If you could outline the essentials to keeping well in later years, that would help. Any tips.'

Chrissie sat behind her desk. 'I work as a lifestyle coach. Every case is individual, so I like to devise a programme that works for that person.'

'Ah. Anything generally?'

'I can give you some fitness tips, but what a person eats can also contribute immensely to their wellbeing.'

'Sounds great. Sounds just what I need too.'

'You're not that old,' she said, and I laughed to myself. Not that old? Cheek. 'But I can't emphasize enough the importance of keeping up your fitness levels, whatever your age. Fitness can mean either an active old age or a restricted one, but anyone can take control of that by getting moving on a regular basis. Not only will this improve quality of life, but also the ability to deal with the ageing process and any potential illness. It's a fact that the fitness level of people of any age can deteriorate if they are inactive.'

Too true, I thought. With just a few weeks of sitting at home on my computer, I'm starting to feel like an old man.

'But you need to find an exercise regime that you enjoy or you won't keep it up,' Chrissie continued. 'You don't have to join a gym. Walking or dancing can be just as effective.'

I got out my notepad. 'Mind if I write this down?

'Go ahead.'

'You need to invest time,' said Chrissie. 'Short daily sessions to build strength. Longer weekly sessions twice or three times a week to build stamina.'

'Build stamina? How?'

'Do something that makes you slightly breathless. Staying active can also reduce blood pressure, help maintain a healthy weight, assist regular bowel movements and stimulate poor appetite.'

I need to do that too, I thought. I'd huffed and puffed on my way to the meeting. 'And to build strength?'

'Lifting weights can help. Alternatively, yoga and Pilates are good for increasing strength and for flexibility, which can of course affect movement getting in and out of cars, getting dressed and so on.'

Oh god, she's talking about me, I thought. I did the involuntary groan when getting into the car and have lately had to sit down to put my socks on. 'My wife does yoga and Pilates and walks with a group.'

'Good for her, but it has to be what *you* enjoy. If you're not one for joining classes, then find out what works for you.'

'Hiking,' I said. 'I used to hike many years ago but haven't done for a long time.'

'Perfect. It's never too late to start again, even just using the stairs when you can instead of a lift. It all helps. Also regular housework.'

'My wife would like that.'

Chrissie laughed. 'I advise people to see it as an activity to help prolong their life rather than a chore.'

'So strength, stamina, flexibility.'

Chrissie nodded. 'The big three, but I'd add exercises to improve balance as well.'

As she talked, I realized that what she was saying was more than relevant for me. I creaked when I got out of bed,

I groaned when I got up from the sofa and I was aware I got breathless if I had to run even the shortest distance. *I ought to start doing this stuff myself*, I thought. Never mind *ought* to, I *will*.

I patted my belly. 'And what about diet?'

'I prefer to call it healthy eating, as diet sounds like deprivation. I advise five a day and the Mediterranean programme, which is rich in vegetables, nuts, grains, olive oil, fish, and only moderate red meat. If you eat well, you'll feel so much better than when you eat junk, and by controlling your body weight, you can reduce the need for blood-pressure tablets and the risk of diabetes and arthritis.'

'Sounds good. I've been told to try and reduce my blood pressure or to take tablets.'

Chrissie gave me a quick up-and-down look. 'Shift ten pounds and get moving and you might find that you don't need medication.'

'Any vitamins or minerals older folk should take?'

'Again, that depends on what they're eating. If they're eating a good healthy diet then they should be getting all they need from their food. But many older people are deficient in B12, so it's not a bad idea to get checked for that. Vitamin D deficiency can be responsible for a number of illnesses, too, but as I said, I'm a great believer in that if you eat right, you won't need supplements.'

'And what about ailments that affect the older generation?'

'So many, but there are all sorts of things that can help, like devil's claw for arthritis and Siberian pine-nut oil for acid reflux. Again it's individual, but a good nutritionist will be savvy about what's around and can be used as a preventative measure, if not a cure in some cases. Of course, sometimes the New Age supplements aren't enough, but they can work hand in hand with Western medicine and are often preferred to taking the kind of medication that comes with a long list of side effects.'

We talked for about half an hour and by the time I was finished, I had pages of notes, including one to myself at the bottom of the page and that said, 'This is for you too, Matt Langham, you fat old bastard.'

*

After my meeting with Chrissie, I went to get a coffee in the local café and write up the pages I'd scribbled. The smell of bacon filled the air and I was tempted but, no, I was going to take Chrissie's advice. She'd inspired me. I needed to change, get out of the rut I'd been in since I lost my job. I used to love hiking, especially with a couple of friends. Fresh air, stunning views, great locations, good company. It used to be one of the joys of my life. Why had I let it go? Work, that was why. I made a resolution to get out regularly and get walking, ready for a long hike, maybe drag Duncan out. He was turning into a lazy old arse too. I might look up a couple of college friends, get them out there like in the good old days.

And while I was at it, I would shift a bit of weight. No harm. Start having those Nutribullet things that Cait had. You never know, she might start fancying me again. I'd start in the morning. Monday is always a good day to start a new regime. While I waited for my coffee to arrive, I took a look at the notice board. It was crammed with leaflets, cards and advertisements for classes on everything from cake-making to

Zumba. I took a few of them to take home. Perhaps Cait and I could do some classes together, share things again, and in doing so rediscover what we once had. I went back to my table and began to make my notes for my booklet of lists for Cait.

Notes for Dancing Over the Hill
Dedicated to:
- My wife
- My best friend
- My lover
- My companion
- Mother of my children
- Favourite person on the planet

Cait

Things to do:
- Shop for Dad. Take supplies over to him.
- Be jolly when I get there.

I filled up on easy-to-prepare meals at the supermarket, threw in a couple of treats and set off to see Dad.

On the way, I sang songs from the musicals in the hope that it would shift my mood from apprehensive to cheerful.

When I'd arrived and he'd let me in, I saw that there was a suitcase in the hall behind him.

'You going somewhere, Dad?'

'Maybe. Yes. Come and sit down, Cait. I have something to tell you.'

Immediately my mind flooded with images. I found it hard to breathe.

Dad off to the hospital? An illness he hadn't told me about?

Or he'd met an old dear and was off on a cruise with her? No. That wasn't ever going to happen, though I'd be pleased if it did.

Or, oh no, he'd booked himself into Dignitas in Switzerland.

I followed him through to the kitchen and watched as he put on the kettle. 'So what is it? Is everything all right?'

'I have a plan, Cait.'

'OK.' I sat down and braced myself for bad news.

'You know I said I didn't want to be a burden to anyone?'

'Yes, but oh god no, Dad, not Dignitas. That's for people with terminal illnesses.'

Dad chuckled. 'We've all got one of those, love. It's called life. Believe me, no one gets out of here alive.'

'Cheerful.'

'I'm not going to Dignitas.'

'No? Thank God for that.'

'No, it's even worse.'

'Worse?'

'Yes. I thought I'd come and live with you.' He laughed. Dad had a strange sense of humour – probably where I got it from.

'Me?'

Dad nodded. 'Going to live with your brother in Edinburgh is out of the question so it has to be with you. That Airbnb you were telling me about? I'll be your first guest. Paying guest, mind. I won't have it any other way. You need the money. I need the company. How about it?'

'I'd love it, but really, you don't have to pay us.'

'I pay or I'm not coming. I have the money. That's the deal. Take it or leave it.'

'I'll take it.'

'I know I said I didn't want to leave the house, but being here on my own is ridiculous. It's too quiet without your mother and it's driving me mad. So, how about I come and stay with you and Matt? See how it feels? It might not work, but I don't like it here and don't want to stay a moment longer. I can get by in the day, but it's the nights when I feel it the most. I need to know there's some company around somewhere. What do you say?'

'I say great, Dad, I'm really pleased.' I was. It was an excellent solution.

'So, let's have a cup of tea and get on the road. We can get the rest of my stuff later. First I want to see my room and catch up with that grandson and son-in-law of mine.'

I hadn't seen Dad look so happy or enthusiastic about anything for a long time, and felt a sense of relief flood through me. He had a great relationship with Jed. I'd been concerned how my parents would react when he'd told us that he was gay, but Jed had insisted on telling them himself. I've no idea what was said between them, apart from them both saying that they'd welcome whoever he chose to spend his life with as long as the man was kind. I loved them for that. So now, OK, we'd have a house full, but better with people we knew than strangers every week. It appeared that life was taking a turn for the better, even though not in exactly the way Matt and I had planned.

26

Cait

There are three men and a cat at the island in the kitchen. Martin and Jed in their dressing gowns on stools, eating toast; Dad, dressed and shaved, standing and leaning on the surface, and Yoda licking the remains of Jed's bowl of cereal.

'Ah, there she is,' said Dad when I came in. 'Make us a cup of tea, love.'

I picked up Yoda and placed him on the floor, put the kettle on and surveyed the scene. Jed glanced at the mess then me and shrugged.

'Where's your dad?' I asked him.

'Said he was going shopping for food,' said Jed.

'Food? But the car's still outside?'

'He said he was going to walk.' *What is Matt up to?* I wondered. Maybe he had taken it on board and was making an effort to share the chores. Good for him – but out walking for a second time in two days? What was that about? I'd ask him later. In the meantime, I had a list in my hand. I waved my piece of paper at the assembled crew.

'OK, lads, some ground rules,' I said. 'I've made a list.'

Jed laughed. 'Mum likes a list,' he said to Martin. 'When we were kids, she used to make them for us before we went to school; we had to check off the items before we went. Lunch – tick. Gym stuff – tick. School books – tick.'

'Sounds very sensible, Mrs Langham,' said Martin.

'Call me Cait. Now. Here's the list. I'll read it and pin it on the fridge so you can all see it. OK? You tidy up after yourself, even if you've only had a snack. Make your own beds. Change your own sheets. You keep the bathroom clean, put wet towels in the laundry. You do your own laundry. You don't put empty cartons or jars back in the fridge. You help with the household chores, and those include cooking and cleaning.'

'It's like having your mother back,' said Dad.

'This doesn't apply to you, Dad. You're a paying guest. This is for Matt, Jed and Martin.'

'We'll contribute,' said Jed. 'So, if we're paying guests, does that mean we're let off doing the chores?'

'Maybe when you *do* start to contribute, but you can't do that if you haven't got jobs, can you?'

'Fair point,' said Jed. 'OK, hand me the rubber gloves.'

I pulled a pair of Marigolds out from under the sink and handed them to him. He immediately blew one up, held it over his head and made clucking noises like a chicken. Dad and Martin cracked up then, one by one, they sloped off to their rooms, leaving the kitchen surfaces covered in plates, cups, knives and breadcrumbs. I stuck my list to the fridge door anyway.

Matt returned a few moments later looking breathless. He dumped a carrier bag full of food on the counter. 'Supplies,' he said. 'I went to the farmers' market. We need to up our vegetables to five a day. And I'd like to try the Mediterranean diet.' He patted his stomach. 'This has to go. I got us some Vitamin D as well. It's good for keeping bones strong.' He pulled out some leaflets which he handed me. They showed lists of classes available locally. 'And I'm thinking of joining a t'ai chi class.'

'T'ai chi?'

'Yes. I got the leaflets at the café the other day. They have all sorts of good stuff up there. Pilates and yoga, but lots of other activities as well. I thought I'd go for t'ai chi because it's good for flexibility and balance.' Matt stood taller. 'I thought I might do a few sessions of Alexander technique as well to improve my posture. Apparently, you have to imagine you have a helium balloon coming out of the top of your head and a lead weight pulling on the bottom of your spine. Something like that but, see, it makes you stand taller. Try it.'

Matt started putting the shopping away, then picked out two cans of beans from the cupboard, which he used as weights for an arm exercise.

'Are you having an affair, Matt?'

He laughed. 'As if. Just want to get fitter, that's all. I thought you'd be pleased.' He went over to the fridge and saw the list. 'Ah, chores, excellent.'

'Yes. Now we have a house full. Er . . . did you just say excellent?'

'Yes. All good for keeping you moving.' Matt studied the list for a moment. 'Put me down for the most active. I'll do the hoovering, window cleaning, bed changing—'

'Are you on drugs, Matt?'

'Nope. I just want to pull my weight, that's all.'

'And you haven't forgotten we're seeing a counsellor at two.'

Matt grimaced. 'Not forgotten.

*

We drove in silence to Bradford on Avon where the first counsellor on the list had a room in a health clinic. The place had good reviews on the Internet and I was surprised that I'd managed to get an appointment so swiftly. However, now that we were on our way, I couldn't help feeling apprehensive.

'We don't have to go again if it doesn't feel right,' said Matt once we'd found a parking space near the clinic.

'Agreed,' I said. 'Like hairdressers, you have to find the right one.'

'Or builders. Always get three quotes.'

'Exactly. I've lined up two more sessions with different counsellors over the next ten days and if we don't like any of them then we can rethink the plan.'

'Agreed,' said Matt.

On entering the clinic, we were told to take a seat in reception until we were called. As we waited, I looked at the other therapies on offer that were advertised on a notice board – acupuncture, homeopathy, aromatherapy. It was a place similar to Debs's centre but the plain décor gave it the look of a doctor's surgery, unlike the elegant and scented sanctuary that Debs offered, but the plus was that it was far enough away from home to not bump into nosey neighbours.

Matt read his newspaper as we waited and I closed my eyes and tried to do a calming breathing exercise. Breathe in, breathe out. Oh god, what have we got ourselves into? What if the therapist can mind-read? What if she gets me to reveal something I don't want to? Breathe in, out.

I opened my eyes when a cry of pain came from the other side of a door marked Acupuncture.

'Are there acupuncture points for marriage problems?' Matt whispered. 'Might be less painful than having to talk to a counsellor. We could still make a run for it.'

Too late, I thought, as the stern-looking lady behind reception peered over her glasses and called our names. 'You can go up now,' she said. 'First floor. Room two.'

We made our way up and into a light room with three plastic chairs set out and a coffee table on which was a box of tissues.

Our therapist's name was Lucinda Hartley. *Nice name*, I thought as I took a seat and told myself to be open-minded and hopeful that at last we were taking positive steps.

A pale, skinny young girl with a nose ring and long henna'd hair came in. She looked about sixteen and was dressed in a black T-shirt and skirt that needed ironing. *Probably got either a drug problem or an eating disorder*, I thought as she took the third chair.

'I'm sorry but this room is already booked. We have a session here,' I said.

'With Lucinda Hartley?' she asked.

I nodded.

She smiled brightly at us. 'That's me. You must be Matt and Cait.'

'Er . . . yes, we are.' I felt my heart sink and didn't dare look at Matt. The girl was young enough to be our grandchild.

She leant forward and looked at us earnestly. 'I'm very

happy you've made the brave decision to come and take a step towards greater closeness. Well done. Before we start, have you any questions?'

Where's the way out? I thought, as Lucinda continued to smile at us.

Matt cleared his throat. 'I have a question. Could you tell us a bit about your methods?'

Lucinda nodded. 'I take my lead from my clients in the first session to try and feel out what the best approach is, then I use a variety of methods, some hypnotherapy, some visualization, some goal-setting.'

'OK,' I said. 'So what do you feel might be a good approach?'

Lucinda leant over, clasped both my hands, closed her eyes and breathed deeply. A minute later, she did the same to Matt. He looked over at me and crossed his eyes and I had to suppress the urge to burst out laughing. Lucinda sat back, closed her eyes again and began to sway a little. I glanced over at Matt. He rolled his eyes and shrugged his shoulders.

After a short time, Lucinda opened her eyes. 'OK, I think I'm getting a feeling for what's going on here.'

'You are? Really?' Matt asked.

Lucinda nodded. 'Yes. I sense discord. I sense an absence.' She looked sad at this.

Well, that much is true, I thought. 'So what do you suggest?'

'Love,' said Lucinda. 'If you're to get anywhere, you have to learn to love yourselves; only then can you love others.'

'Fascinating,' said Matt. 'And how do you propose we do that?'

'You could start by acknowledging your best points individually then as a couple. Remember your best times together and try and acknowledge the positive. Today is just a get-to-know-you session, but what I would urge you to do is to write down five good things about your day every evening before you go to bed. You'd be surprised how much better you'll feel by the end of the week.'

'Good things?' I asked. 'Like something we've enjoyed? Or do you mean something good about ourselves?'

Lucinda looked confused for a moment. 'Er . . . both,' she said. 'The two are sometimes inseparable. If you feel good, you tend to be more loving and also attract more love.'

'That sounds like a tremendous idea,' said Matt. 'But first, Lucinda, a bit about you? This is a get-to-know-you session for us too. How long have you been practising?'

'Oh, about four weeks.'

'Have you had many clients?' Matt persisted.

'I've just started and a few friends have let me practise with them, but you're my first real clients.'

Ah, so that's why I got an appointment so easily, I thought.

'And when did you finish your training?' Matt continued.

'About this time last year, but I took a break to go travelling before I settled into work.'

'Ah,' said Matt. 'Like a gap year?' Lucinda nodded. 'Good for you. And was it hard to find a job?'

'Not really,' said Lucinda. 'My aunt owns the clinic here so let me have the room.'

'Ah, your aunt,' said Matt. 'That's marvellous.'

'And are you married?' I asked.

'No,' said Lucinda. 'But I did eight case histories of people who are when I was on my course.'

'Eight?' said Matt. 'And what did you learn?'

'About how important communication is,' said Lucinda.

Matt continued to grill her and ask how she felt about what she'd learnt. She didn't seem to get that he'd turned the tables. She was a sweet kid with her heart in the right place, but no way was I going to open up to her about my relationship with Matt. The session was a waste of our time and we burst out of there forty minutes later like two teenagers bunking off school.

'I am sorry,' I said when we were on our way home.

'No need,' Matt replied. 'You weren't to know. So, five things you feel good about?'

'One, we're out of there. Two, we're on our way home, er . . .'

'Three, in a peculiar way, it was bonding because we both totally agreed that she wasn't the one,' said Matt. 'Four we're still speaking after our first session and five . . . er . . . it gave me a good laugh.'

*

I got home to find an email from Lorna.

From: Lornaalp@org.com
To: Cait@grmail.com

How's the 'revive your marriage challenge'? Any progress?
    Any word from Tom?
    LX

*

From: Cait@grmail.com
To: Lornaalp@org.com

Had our first counselling session. Therapist was a child
so no progress really, though Matt is behaving very
strangely. Disappearing out for walks, says he's going to
join the gym, do t'ai chi, go on a diet.

    Jed plus boyfriend is back. Dad's moved in with us.

    Tom sent photos of his house and studio in Majorca
and invite to spend a couple of days out there.

    CX

*

From: Lornaalp@org.com
To: Cait@grmail.com

Good for Matt. Sounds like progress to me. Men work in
mysterious ways but sounds like he is changing or
attempting to. Re. Tom. So, he's got a fancy house? So
what? You could go and stay somewhere fabulous with
Matt as part of your save-your-marriage challenge.

    Lorna. Killjoy and the voice of reason.
Sorry.

    X

*

From: Debs23@g.org.com
To: Cait@grmail.com, Lornaalp@org.com

Thought you might like to know how my last date went
last week. Sorry, long email but you've both been out all

day and not picking up your phone messages and I need to write to GET IT OUT of my system.

Met Colin the Courgette King for lunch in the farm shop out at Winsley.

Glorious day, good mood, tra-la-la. I arrived ten mins late so not to appear too keen. Dressed in jeans and red silk top, hair loose – I know you like a visual.

Colin was already there. He stood up as I reached the table. *Un point for good manners*, I thought as I sat down, but I could tell in an instant that he wasn't my type. He had the look of a weasel plus he was shorter than he'd said in his profile. Being five foot nine, I like a man to be at least my height, if not taller. *Ah well, best get on and get it over with*, I thought.

This is how it went.

'Hello, Colin, I'm Debs.'

'Well *hello*, Debs. How are you today?' he said and ogled my cleavage.

'Good thanks. Er . . . shall we get a drink?'

'Good idea, I like your style,' he said, and summoned the waitress. 'In fact, let's get a bottle, start as we mean to continue.'

After ordering drinks, we sat in silence for a few moments.

'So, tell me all about your vegetables,' I said in an effort to get the conversation going. For ten minutes, I was subjected to my own personal talk on soil prepara-tion, the right kind of compost and importance of mulching. Fascinating.

'May I say how lovely you're looking today, Debs, though not what I was expecting.'

'Who or what were you expecting?'

'I don't know, but not someone like you.'

'In a good or a bad way?'

'Oh good, you're hot.'

And you're not, I thought as I looked around and wondered how long I would have to continue before I could escape.

'Why don't you tell me a bit about yourself? How long have you been single?' I asked.

'Few months.'

'Had many dates?'

'Oh lots.'

'Not worked out then?'

'I think I must have been waiting for you. So, tell me about yourself.'

'I'm recently separated. I live in Bath, run a health centre offering alternative therapies—'

'Alternative to what?'

'Homeopathy, aromatherapy, reflexology, massage—'

Colin's eyes lit up at the word 'massage'. 'I can see we're going to really get on.'

'What star sign are you, Colin?'

'Star sign. What's that then?'

'Astrology. When's your birthday?'

'January the fifth. Don't tell me you believe that crap they put in the magazines.'

'It's not all crap. If astrology is done properly, it's very precise.'

'If you say so. Load of baloney as far as I'm concerned.'

Well, this is going well, I thought.

'So what's Debs short for?'

'Penelope.'

'Penelope?'

'No, I was joking. It's short for Deborah. So what are you looking for in a partner?'

'Er . . . someone fit, to have a bit of fun with, if you get my meaning.'

'I'm beginning to.'

A waiter came over to take our orders, but I didn't want to delay the agony by having lunch. 'Just the glass of wine for me, thanks. I'm not that hungry.'

'You not eating? Dieting eh? Good for you, girl. I like a girl who doesn't give in to getting fat. So yes, let's not waste time on lunch . . . what are you doing afterwards?'

'I have to go back to work.'

Colin got out a key and held it up. 'Sure you can't bunk off for a few hours? I've got a room booked just down the road. I like to be prepared. You look like a girl who might be open to an adventure.'

I burst out laughing. 'You're very sure of yourself.'

'Have to seize the day at our age.'

'I couldn't agree more,' I said. *I wonder if there's a window in the bathroom, I could escape through?*

'I got you a present,' said Colin, and handed me a carrier bag.

I took a peek inside. Stockings and suspenders.

'And what am I supposed to do with those?'

Colin winked. "Wear them. For me.'

'Er . . . would you excuse me for a moment?'

'Little girl's room?'

I nodded. He flicked a finger at me as I got up. 'Missing you already. Are you going to put on the stockings?'

He can't be real, I thought as I made my way to the cloakroom where, thank god, there was a window. I opened it as wide as it would go, hoiked myself up onto the ledge and began to clamber out. Halfway up, one leg on the sill, I felt mean. *I'd hate it if someone did something like this to me*, I thought; one of my mottos is to 'do unto others as I'd have them do to me.' I'm not a coward. I climbed down off the ledge, went back to the table and sat down.

'So lovely lady, are you ready for some afternoon delight?' Colin asked.

'I am, Colin, sadly not with you. I always feel it best to be honest and . . . well, I don't feel the connection.'

A flash of anger crossed his face. 'But I've paid for the room and . . . your gift.'

'A tad presumptuous on your part and you can have your gift back.'

He shrugged. 'Your loss, doll,' he said, and made a grab for the carrier bag.

'I'm sure it is.' I got out my purse and put down five pounds. 'To cover my drink, and now I really do have to get going. Good luck, Colin, with your next date.'

He was barely listening. He was looking on his phone, probably for his next date. I was no longer of interest.

As I drove away, I thought, *that's it. No more Internet dating. I am giving up. It's not working.* Am I doing something wrong? Am I unlovable?

Love Debs

I felt bad for Debs. She was trying so hard to meet a man. She was a great woman and friend and I'd been holding out on her, not introducing her to a man who I know she'd like, and keeping secrets from her by not telling her I'd been to see him. However, despite my guilt, I still couldn't – wouldn't – introduce her to Tom.

From: Cait@grmail.com
To: Debs23@g.org.com, Lornaalp@org.com

Don't give up. Mr Right is out there somewhere. It's not you. Colin just wasn't the one for you.
C
X

*

From: Lornaalp@org.com
To: Debs23@g.org.com, Cait@grmail.com

Ditto what Cait said. Don't give up, Debs.
    I have some news too. I've had the builders in re. putting in a kitchen on the west side of my house and walling part of it off with a view to renting a third of the house. Plan is to find some nice professional or couple to take it. Good solution all round. I think my kids will be happy about the compromise. I get to keep the family home; they won't have to worry about me being alone.
    Lorna
    X

*

From: Cait@grmail.com
To: Lornaalp@org.com, Debs23@g.org.com

Excellent idea, Lorna.

Debs. Mr Right will come along when you least expect him. You never know, he might just walk into the spa tomorrow.

CX

27

Matt

I sat in the waiting room and read a magazine while I waited for my masseur. Oriel. Debs had said she was one of the best. I felt nervous and wished I'd asked for a bloke but then, didn't want to seem like a prude. It was a long time since I'd taken my clothes off in front of anyone apart from Cait and a male masseur in Egypt when we were on holiday about ten years ago. We'd had one of those treatments for two in the same room. Cait paid for the treatments as a birthday present to me. Her therapist was a young woman and my chap looked like a professional wrestler. Not the most relaxing hour I've spent, but hearing me groan in agony made Cait, and her masseuse, laugh. 'Try not to kill customer,' Cait's woman called to my man, a phrase Cait adopted for the rest of the holiday.

An inner door opened and Debs came out to greet me. 'All ready for you,' she said, 'come this way.'

I got up and followed her into the room named Nirvana. It had been painted in shades of pink; with the low lighting and candle burning it had a womb-like quality. In the centre was a massage couch and towels.

'Strip off and lie on the couch, face down,' said Debs.

'What? Everything?'

'Whatever makes you feel most comfortable. Keep your boxers on if you like.' She left me alone so I stripped down to my underwear, lay down as instructed and waited for Oriel. A minute later, there was a gentle tap on the door. 'Ready?'

'Yes,' I said. I turned my head ready to greet Oriel, but it was Debs who'd come back in.

She opened a bottle of oil and began to put it on her hands.

'But I . . . I thought Oriel was going to do it?'

'She's got a bug. I offered to step in. It's not a problem is it? Don't worry. I've had all the training she had and more.'

'No. No problem,' I said. *Yes, yes, a problem*, I thought as I lay back down. I didn't feel at all comfortable.

'Good. Now relax and put all thoughts out of your mind.'

I immediately tensed up. *Shit*, I thought. If Cait ever gets to hear about this, I . . . Debs began to run her hands along my back. I tensed even further. 'How's the pressure? I can go deeper or softer, whichever you prefer.'

'Fine. It's good. Er . . . so how are you, Debs?'

'I'm fine, Matt, but there's no need to talk. You'll get more out of the session if you just lie there and surrender.' She continued to move her hands up my back and began to knead a knot in my shoulder blade. 'God, you are very tense.'

I know, I thought, *because you're my wife's best friend and this feels really weird.*

'Take some deep breaths,' urged Debs. 'In . . . out . . . In . . . out . . . That's it. Let it all go.'

For ten minutes, I felt myself resisting and couldn't relax, then the scent of the room and the warmth of Debs's touch began to work its magic. She had good hands and seemed to go right to the spots that needed it and I felt myself letting go. After fifteen minutes, it felt fantastic and I was drifting, feeling months of anxiety start to ease away. After half an hour, I was floating with the fairies.

'Turn on to your back,' said Debs, bringing me back into the room. She held the towel so I could turn over discreetly, though I still felt the need to pull in my stomach muscles. Once on my back, she re-laid the towels, I closed my eyes again and Debs began to massage my feet. Once again, I felt the floating sensation. *Why don't I do this more often?* I asked myself. In fact, it would probably do both Cait and me good to have regular sessions. I felt Debs's hands move up from my feet onto my legs. Her palms felt warm, healing. The combination of the scent, the warmth and the touch was working its sensuous magic. I opened my eyes briefly and Debs looked down on me and smiled. 'Nice?'

I nodded and closed my eyes again. It had been a long time since I'd been touched by anyone other than Cait and it felt good, really good; helped, I had to admit, by the fact that Debs was an attractive woman. Her hands went up my inner thigh and I felt myself melting, melting . . . Then there was a stirring and I felt myself tense. *No, oh shit no, I'm going to get an erection, oh Christ I have got an erection. Down, boy, down. Oh bugger and blast.* I lifted my head to see the towel around my groin resembled a mini tent with a very stiff pole.

Debs smiled over at me. 'Well hello sailor.'

'Oh god, I'm so sorry,' I blustered.

'No need. Lie back. It happens all the time.'

But it was too late. Sailor boy was standing to attention whether I liked it or not. I thought of gas bills, mortgage payments, my overdraft, and the tent pole did finally subside, but I couldn't relax back into that lovely state I'd been in ten minutes earlier. I felt guilty. For months, sex with Cait hadn't been on the agenda, and now, half an hour with her friend, and it was hey ho and away we go. Willies really do have minds of their own. I remembered agonizing times as a young adolescent when mine would arise to salute the world at the most inappropriate times, especially on the bus when the warm interior and rhythmic motion would set me off. Other lads confessed that a girl in a tight T-shirt, a glimpse of thigh or cleavage would arouse them. For me, it was the back seat on a red double-decker bus and I worried I was some kind of pervert. As teenage boys, Duncan and I had been obsessed with our penises and how big they were. He'd come back one day having heard somewhere that if you use toothpaste, it enlarges the appendage. We'd both dutifully tried it that night but overlooked the fact that our toothpaste was menthol. It had stung like hell and neither of us could sit down for a few hours.

'What are you thinking about?' asked Debs.

I laughed. 'Toothpaste.'

'OK. Fair enough, but you've tensed up, Matt. Take a few deep breaths and try and relax again.'

I did as I was told but I knew there was no way I would let go again. I just wanted to get up and get out of there.

Although Debs tried to do her best to get me to relax again, it wasn't going to happen.

Finally the hour was up and Debs finished then left me to get dressed. I was up, in my clothes in a shot and went out to find her.

'That was quick, Matt.'

'I remembered that I have a few things to do.'

'OK, but try and relax when you get home and drink plenty of water.'

'Will do and . . . er, Debs, about before . . .' I held a finger up.

Debs laughed. She had a great laugh, a throaty chuckle. 'Hey, it's forgotten. As I said, happens all the time. It was a good sign you were relaxed.'

'I . . . would you mind not mentioning it to Cait?' I was aware that this was the second time I'd said this when with her.

Debs smiled and put her hand on my arm. 'Our secret. Besides, there's client confidentiality. I never talk about what goes on in these rooms.'

Liar, I thought as I left. Cait had often reported back on hilarious clients Debs had talked about. I just prayed I wouldn't be one of them.

28

Cait

I woke early. I'd hardly slept a wink. I'd tried counting sheep but when I started giving them names – Rambo, Shep, Jet, Babah – and individual hairstyles, I knew it was a lost cause. Tom Lewis. Tom Lewis. Tom Lewis. I can't stop thinking about him. How it felt when he pulled me to him. The weight of his body close to mine. Must watch *Fatal Attraction* to remind myself what can go wrong. I know Tom isn't Glenn Close and unlikely to be a bunny boiler but . . . Tom and I in Majorca in that big bed in the photo, looking out over the mountains. I drifted back to sleep and dreamt I was with Tom in a field in the sun. We were alone apart from twenty or more rabbits that were beginning to look fierce.

I was awoken by Matt prodding me in the back. 'Are you OK, Cait?'

'Yes. Course. Why?'

'You were groaning in your sleep.'

'Bad dream.'

Betrayed by my own subconscious.

*

'We have only just enough money to get by with what Dad's paying,' I said as I sipped the tea that Matt had brought me in bed.

Matt sat on the end of the bed. I noticed he was dressed in his sports gear. 'I don't suppose we can ask the boys to contribute.'

'I'm sure they would if they had work, but so far I don't think either of them even know where they want to be. They've got no money. They need to get jobs and then, if they want to get their own place, they'll need to save for a deposit.'

'Has Jed talked over his plans with you?' Matt asked.

'Only that they won't be leaving any time soon. They're not even sure where they want to live – London, Bristol, here, or go travelling again.'

'Well, this is his home I suppose.'

'And Dad seems happier which makes me feel a lot better too. He wants to see how it feels here for a month or so before burning his bridges. He said if he likes the set-up with us, he'll put his house on the market and then he'll split the proceeds between Mike and me, but I told him that was premature and he might need the money for care.'

'Sensible advice. He could live for many more years, but if he does settle here, it might be an idea to sell his place. But even then, if he got a buyer straight away, it would still take three months or more for a sale to go through.'

We were both quiet for a moment. 'Are you thinking what I'm thinking?' asked Matt.

Doubt it, I thought. Tom Lewis, Tom Lewis, Tom Lewis. 'I might be. What are you thinking?'

'That the boys might appreciate some independence. They're young. It's probably cramping their style a bit being here.'

I nodded. 'If Dad was open to it, they could go and live in his house. In fact, better to have someone living in what would otherwise be an empty property.'

'Let's see what he says. I think it would be a good idea, and then we could do Airbnb in Jed's room and at least have some income.'

'But Dad wouldn't like that. It's one thing having people he knows in the room across the corridor, quite another bumping into strangers on your way to the bathroom. We won't mind but Dad would.'

'Would he like to go back to his home with Jed and Martin? He'd have company, which is what he wanted.'

'But they might take off any day, which would leave him there on his own again. Better he stays here and feels settled. I'll make a list.'

I found some paper in the bedside cabinet and wrote:

Options:
- Ask Jed and Martin to move in as caretakers to Dad's old house. *Good idea, space and independence for them.*
- Do B & B in Jed's old room. *Not a good idea. Dad snores, you can hear him on the other side of the house, and he splashes everywhere in the bathroom which guests won't like.*

- Sell house, downsize. *Where would Dad go?*
- Move Dad back into his house with Jed and Martin? *But don't want to move him twice if they take off again.*
- Matt and I get jobs and all stay where we are.
- I run away with Tom and leave them all to it.

I went down to feed Yoda. I put his favourite food in bowl. I'd bought loads of it. He took one sniff, looked at me as if to say 'and you expect me to eat *that*?' Walked away.

In the kitchen, there were four men in dressing gowns.

'Do you have porridge, Cait?' Dad asked.

'Where's the jam, Mum?' asked Jed. 'And I think we need more bread.'

'Don't worry,' said Matt. 'I'll see to the breakfasts then I'm going out for my walk then to my t'ai chi class. Anyone want to come? Now, Cait, can I get you anything while I'm out? And before I go, is there anything you'd like me to do around the house?'

Uh?

'You need a magnetic cat flap, Mum,' said Jed. 'The neighbour's cat has been in eating all Yoda's food.'

'Matt? Could you get one while you're out and see if they sell dressing gowns for cats. Yoda might as well join in. In the meantime, I'm going to email Sam to see if he and the family might be moving back in as well.'

Jed laughed. 'Do you by any chance need some space, Mum?'

'No, no, not at all, didn't sleep well, that's all. I'll be in my study if you need me.'

Dad went off to watch the morning news, turned up loud so he could hear. Jed tuned the radio in the kitchen onto some noisy pop channel. I escaped upstairs to find a text from Tom on my phone.

Am in Bristol for the day. My meeting has ended early. I know it's short notice but it's only twelve minutes on the train to Bath. Any chance you could meet up about 12?

I texted back. *Sure. But I'll come to Bristol. Only got a short time. Meet you in the café on Platform 3.*

He texted: *Love it. Very* Brief Encounter.

I replied, *Utter madness (to be read in best BBC voice).*

I was glad of an excuse to get out of the mayhem and noise in the house. I walked over to the station, hopped onto a train, did my make-up in the loo and was in the café to meet Tom just over an hour after he'd texted. I had it in mind to tell him that nothing could ever happen between us, that I would stay with Matt. I wouldn't, couldn't abandon Matt or Dad or my boys, even though the house felt crowded. It really was madness to have even considered it, but then he walked in, his face lit up when he saw me and anything seemed possible again.

'So, Cait. How goes it?' he asked once we'd bought coffees and settled on a leather sofa at the back of the café.

'Interesting. My dad and son have just moved back in, not to mention all the neighbourhood cats.'

Tom laughed. 'Ah. Just when you thought you were free.'

'And had space. First Matt home all day, then Jed and his boyfriend, now Dad. I'm wondering who's going to be next.'

'You can always escape and come and see me. Could you? Get away for a few days?'

'I'm not sure that would be a good idea.'

'Why ever not? Come over to Majorca or to London.'

I shook my head. 'I might get to like it.'

He laughed. 'That's the plan.'

'It's tempting, but really Tom, it has been wonderful seeing you again but my life is with my family. You can't just re-appear in my life and expect me to drop everything.'

'Why not? There are no rules.'

'What if it was you? Still married and one of your children just moved back in?'

Tom sighed. 'I understand, but they're all adults and each responsible for themselves as you are. OK, don't decide just yet. Your son being home is a temporary measure, isn't it?'

'I think so.'

'And your father?'

'Probably more permanent, and no way I could leave him with Matt. That would be unfair and I wouldn't do it to either of them. I spent the last year worrying about Dad and it's a big relief to know he's OK after all that time. I couldn't abandon him again. You see, I come with baggage and compli-cations. It's different for you. You're a free man.'

'We don't have to decide anything yet.' Tom reached over, took my hand and stroked it. I didn't resist so he shifted over, put his arm around me and pulled me to him.

'Not fair, Tom,' I said and pulled away.

'What am I supposed to do, Cait? Come on, I know you feel it too. Let go a little. OK, no to Majorca for now, so let's go and book into a hotel and spend the rest of the afternoon together.'

I laughed. 'What?'

'I'm serious.' He grinned and raised an eyebrow sugges-tively. 'You know it would be fun.'

'I can't do that.'

'Why not? Come on, let's go and make love.'

I felt panicked. This was way beyond a nice fantasy to escape to when my life at home got tough or dull. 'Too soon, Tom. I've never been unfaithful to Matt. It's not something I'd do lightly.'

Tom grimaced. 'Cait, you're doing my head in, but can you blame me for trying? I understand that it's a huge thing to think of leaving your husband, so I'm offering you a sort of halfway alternative.'

'You mean like try the goods before buying?'

'Exactly, though it's not as if we haven't ever done it before.'

'Forty years ago, Tom. I'm a lot older, more wrinkly.'

'Is that what's holding you back?'

'Partly.'

'Hey, we've both got older.'

'You were never shy.'

'Neither were you. We'll close the curtains, buy some candles on the way to the hotel.' He started to get up. I pulled him back.

'I am *not* going to a hotel with you this afternoon.'

He sat back down. 'OK. No hotel. Back of the car? It's in the car park.' He laughed, but I got a feeling that if I'd agreed, we'd be on our way out there.

'Yeah, right. Sorry, but a gear stick in the groin is not my idea of romance.'

'I'm not going to give up, Cait, and we did do it once in the back of a car. Remember? Back of that old Volkswagen I had.'

'I do, I had a crick in my neck for days.'

'Was worth it, though. Come on, stop being so sensible. Let's live a little.'

'You are doing *my* head in, Tom.' I motioned to a very

attractive brunette in her thirties who had just walked into the café. 'Why not go for someone younger?'

'I don't want younger. I've had younger. I want you, Cait, wrinkles and all, though as I said when we first met up in London, you've aged well.' He took my hand again. 'Is that what you're worried about? That you're not twenty any more?'

'Amongst other things.'

'I want a woman I have a connection with, someone I can talk to, can laugh with, and I can do that with you. I don't care about smooth skin, pert breasts. It's the spirit, the soul of a woman that makes her really attractive.'

'You're a silver-tongued old devil. Stop it, stop it now.'

'So what is this meeting up about? To sip tea and chat like a pair of old-age pensioners? I don't think so. You might not admit it to yourself yet, but I know that's not what you want either.'

The expression 'play with fire and you get burnt' went through my head. 'But you know nothing about me any more, not really.'

'OK, but if we're going to get to know each other again, we need to do exactly that: spend time, get naked, get to know each other again.'

'This is only the third time we've met up, Tom.'

'I seem to remember you succumbed to my charms on our second date.'

'I haven't forgotten. I was clearly a slut back then.'

'You were acting on what you felt. Why can't you do that now?'

'Because, as I keep telling you, our situations are different. My father and Matt, he has no idea where I am right now. It's not fair to him.' I was saying the right words, but when

I looked at Tom, there was no denying the tug of desire. I wanted Tom as much as he wanted me. I felt torn. I remembered Lorna's advice about how it would be with Tom as we got older and more familiar. I wondered if I would ever feel safe with Tom.

'Do you think there's any way to unite the two elements, desire and familiarity?' I asked. 'We haven't seen each other in a long time. Seeing each other now is forbidden, the thrill of secrecy, anticipation, and so all the more inviting. We haven't been through the day-in, day-out routine of living together, getting to know every habit, thought, action. Say I did cast caution to the wind and we did have an affair, then we tried living together; you might grow bored, irritated even. For instance, I'm rubbish in the mornings.'

'Ah. Changing the subject, Cait. Don't think I don't see what you're doing here. OK. So you're crap in the morning? I'd go out until you're ready for company. Truth be told, I'm not great in the morning either. Oscar Wilde said that only dull people are brilliant in the morning.'

'I knew I liked him.'

'We could make a pact not to talk until at least ten a.m.'

'Sounds about right.'

'People work these things out, Cait.'

'Do they? Or do they just get bored with each other's annoying habits.'

'Is that what's happened with you and Matt?'

I wanted to keep Matt out of it. It was one thing having a moan to girlfriends, but it felt like a betrayal to talk about him to Tom. 'At the moment, I'm out of your reach and maybe that's why you're here. How do I know you'd stay if I wasn't unattainable?'

Tom looked around the café. 'There's only one way to find out. I'd be taking a risk too. You'd be just as likely to tire of me. You were always a restless soul.'

I squeezed his hand. 'I might have been, but I've stayed with the same man for over thirty years.'

Tom sighed. 'So how do we leave this?'

'I go home. You go back to London.'

'Doesn't feel right. Have a think about coming to Majorca or even to London for a night. I won't push it, just let me know when you're ready.'

We sat holding hands in silence for a few minutes and Tom gently caressed my thumb and fingers in a way that felt as intimate as making love.

I pulled my hand away. 'Stop with the hand sex. I know what you're doing. I have to go.'

Tom leant into my neck and inhaled. 'Irresistible, that's what you are,' he crooned softly.

I stood up. 'You're an old rogue.'

Tom stood up. 'Will we meet again soon?'

'Not sure. I have some serious thinking to do.'

'Don't be too serious. Let the other side of you have a say too. I remember how spontaneous you could be.'

'You were the spontaneous one. I followed where you led then, when it was too late, you spontaneously disappeared.'

'You have to forgive me for that.'

'Oh I have, sort of, but I have to protect myself, and in doing that remind myself of what you did and that you might do it again. I have a lot at stake here.'

Tom nodded. 'Message understood.'

'Good, so now I'm going to get on the train and you can do the Trevor Howard part.'

Tom smiled. 'I need a tweed hat, don't I?'

I smiled back at him but suddenly felt overwhelmingly sad.

'I wonder how it would have been if we'd stayed together?' asked Tom, voicing my thoughts.

'Too late for that,' I said.

'But still not too late for us.'

We walked out to the platform, where Tom hugged me, kissed my cheek, then we went our separate ways. *I ought to end this*, I thought as I stared out of the window of the train, and tried to push thoughts of what it might have been like if I'd said yes and gone with Tom to a hotel room for the afternoon. *Must end this.* Texted Debs: *Please bring Bach flower remedies to restaurant tomorrow.*

*

In the evening, a few of us from the book club met up for a midsummer get-together. Someone had chosen *The Prince* by Machiavelli as the book for us all to read. I hadn't had a chance so I cribbed some notes from the reviews on Amazon and tried to repeat them. Was caught out but congratulated for being Machiavellian.

29

Cait

12.30 p.m. Office doing admin.

'Caitlin, what's for lunch?' asked Dad.

2 p.m. Caitlin, where are you?' called Dad.

'On the loo.'

3 p.m. 'Caitlin, where are you going?' asked Dad as I put my jacket on to go out.

'Just popping out to the post office.'

'Get me some Nytol while you're at it, will you?'

'Sure, but there's some in the bathroom cabinet.'

Jed appeared behind him. 'And could you get me some shampoo?'

'Sure.'

4 p.m. Home.

'Caitlin love, where are you?' called Dad.

'Loo again.' *Where I am going to stay for a very long time. I liked having Dad with us, I really did and I knew he was happier but I felt I had less personal space than ever.*

'Where are the biscuits kept?'

'Tin in the cupboard above the sink. Ask Matt.'

'He's busy.'

'Doing what?'

'Labelling jars in the kitchen.'

'Right. So he's in the kitchen?'

'He doesn't know where the biscuits are. Have you hidden them? Your mother used to do that.'

'No.'

'So when will you be down?'

'Soon.'

*

4.15 p.m. Matt was sitting in the kitchen reading a recipe book. In front of him were jars of herbs and spices.

'What are you doing?' I asked.

'I'm going to learn how to cook. About time, don't you think?'

'Great.'

'And I've signed up for a cookery class on Saturday mornings at the deli.'

'Wow.'

'In the meantime, I've bought some ingredients. The cupboard's a right mess. I don't know how you find anything in there, so I've pulled everything out and am labelling it all.'

'Matt, are you on drugs?'

'I thought you'd be pleased.'

'I am. At least I think I am. And I see you've shaved.'

Matt stroked his chin. 'I have. I was starting to look like an old tramp.'

'No comment.'

*

8.10 p.m. 'So how did your last supper go, Debs?' I asked as we settled at our table in a Greek restaurant in town. I knew that she'd had another date since Colin the Courgette man.

Debs pulled a face. 'This one didn't grow his own vegetables, he looked like one. He had a face like a potato, large and lumpy.'

Lorna laughed. 'Not your type then.'

Debs shook her head. 'He was a nice man. Nice. Divorced. Not an ounce of chemistry between us and he spent the whole time talking about not seeing his kids enough. I felt sorry for him. But, Cait, you said you wanted a remedy? What's going on?'

'Million-dollar question. What do the remedies cover?'

'All sorts of emotions. Dr Bach believed that all illnesses start with *dis*-ease in the mind or spirit, so it's always best to treat whatever you're not at ease with.'

'Got it. So what do you think?'

'I could advise but . . .' She pulled a sheet of paper out of her bag. 'I'll read the list and you tell me when one resonates with how you're feeling. You too, Lorna.'

'OK. Shoot,' I said. Lorna stared at her drink. She didn't hold much faith in the remedies.

'Agrimony – mental torture behind a cheerful face.'

'Yes, put me down for that one.'

'Aspen – fear of unknown things.'

'Yes, especially since Mum and Eve died, like my safe bubble was pierced and it felt anything could happen.'

Debs reached across and squeezed my hand. 'That can

happen after the death of a loved one.' She gave Lorna a meaningful look.

'Next,' said Lorna.

'Beech for intolerance,' continued Debs.

'And don't either of you dare give me one of your looks again,' said Lorna. 'Different strokes for different folks. A G and T is my remedy and I'm going to stick with it.'

'No to beech. I reckon I'm pretty easy-going,' I said, then I remembered my reaction when I'd found Duncan in the kitchen getting Matt stoned, Matt in his dressing gown mid-morning. 'Actually, thinking about it, yes to that one too.'

'Centaury – the inability to say no.'

'Clearly another yes,' said Lorna, 'if your replies to this list are anything to go by.'

'Cerato – lack of trust in one's own decisions.'

'Yeeeees for her,' said Lorna.

'Cherry plum – fear of the mind giving way.'

'Definitely.'

'Chestnut bud – failure to learn from mistakes.'

'Yes. How many are there?'

'Thirty-eight.'

'Sounds like I need them all. Tell you what, let me glance down them and have a think.'

Debs handed over her list. 'It's not usual to take all of them. A blend of seven at most.'

I glanced down the paper. 'I think I need them all, Debs.'

'Tell you what, we'll dowse.'

'Dowse?' asked Lorna.

Debs pulled out a crystal on a chain from her bag. 'This little beauty will tell you what you need. Where were you up to?'

'Heather,' I said, 'and what will a crystal do?'

'I hold it over the list and it will swing round to indicate "yes" and back and forth to indicate "no".'

'"When shall we three meet again, in winter, summer, or in snow?"' said Lorna in an old woman's voice.

'Shut up, Lorna,' said Debs. 'It doesn't do to be cynical, and the second line is "In thunder, lightning, or in rain", not what you said.' She held her crystal over the list and the crystal began to swing around.

'You moved your hand,' said Lorna. 'You're moving it.'

'Did not.'

'Did.'

'Not.'

'I tell you what, Debs,' I said, 'how about we do this another time?'

'Good idea,' she said as she looked directly at Lorna. 'The vibe's not right here.'

Lorna held up two fingers in the love and peace sign. 'You know I love you, Debs.'

Debs stuck her tongue out.

'How old are you two?' I asked.

'Old as you feel,' said Lorna.

'So that would make me about nineteen,' said Debs. 'Why do you feel the need to take thirty-eight remedies, Cait? How are things at home?'

'Fine.'

'Liar,' said Debs. 'I can always tell when you're lying because you don't make eye contact.'

'What is this? The Spanish Inquisition?'

'You said you needed remedies,' said Debs, 'so clearly something isn't right. Has something happened? Something you're not telling me about?' She glanced at Lorna then at me. 'Whatever it is, let us help.'

I took a deep breath. It was now or never. 'OK, I'll tell you, but you can't repeat what I am about to say to anyone and I mean, anyone.'

'Sounds serious,' said Debs.

'I've seen Tom.'

Lorna looked surprised that I'd come out with it in front of Debs, but I'd decided, Debs was one of my oldest friends and I wanted her input as well.

'The silver fox?' Debs asked. 'So he's in the UK?'

I nodded.

Debs looked shocked. 'Wow. And?'

'I've never been so confused in my life which is why I need your support.'

Debs shook her head, as if finding it hard to take in what I'd said. 'But you have Matt. Why would you jeopardize that?'

'I know, but things haven't been right with us for a very long time. We don't communicate. Our sex life is non-existent. We co-exist in the same house.'

'So what happened when you saw Tom? What does he want?' asked Debs.

'An affair.'

Debs let out a low whistle. 'Did you know, Lorna?'

Lorna looked over at me for confirmation. I nodded. 'I told her when I first met up with him and I know what you're thinking, why did I tell her and not you, and I'm sorry, it was just . . . after Fabio having gone, I wasn't sure you'd understand, I hardly did myself, and how could I even consider such a thing anyway but . . . life is short. I'm in

my sixties. Eve has already gone. I don't know how long I
have left. Why not have one last adventure? Tom was the
love of my life and we still have an amazing connection. I
feel different when I'm with him, more alive, like the world
has suddenly opened up and is full of possibility.'

'But what about your father? And the boys?' Debs asked.

'I know. I've thought about them, but Jed will leave again
at some point. Dad, I'm not so sure, but Tom said we could
work these things out.'

'Wow, you really *are* serious,' said Debs. 'Matt has no
idea?'

'None. As I said, we barely talk about anything these days
apart from household issues.'

'What do you think, Lorna?' asked Debs.

'I've already told her – don't do anything in a hurry and
do everything to make things with Matt work first. It's a
really big decision, but all my alarm bells are ringing.'

'Mine too,' I said. 'At first I dismissed the idea as crazy
and I'm well aware of how it sounds but—'

'You're in love with this guy,' said Debs. 'No wonder you
wanted the remedies. How many times have you seen him?'

'Three.'

'You told me he lived abroad when I asked about him,'
said Debs.

'He does. He's in London at the moment, sorting out
probate on his mother's estate.'

'So you lied when I asked you?'

Oh god, I thought. *This was a big mistake. I wish I'd kept
my mouth shut.* 'Yes and no. Please don't judge me. I couldn't
bear it. I *knew* you'd disapprove, and you do.'

'I . . . it's a lot to take in, Cait. I feel an idiot for having pressed you to hook me up with him. I had no idea he meant so much to you. And Matt? I guess no one ever really knows what goes on behind closed doors in a marriage, but I had no idea that things were so bad.'

'Not bad as much as flat.'

'Whatever we think, we're your friends, and here to help and support you in making the right choice. Right, Debs?' said Lorna.

Debs nodded, but I sensed a hesitation before she said, 'Course.'

Opening up to Debs was a really bad idea, I thought as I took a gulp of wine. 'Look, let's change the subject. I'm sorry. Let's talk about your love life, Debs. It's always much more entertaining.'

'Not at the moment,' she said as she studied my face in a way that made me feel uncomfortable. 'I might look at more dating sites and need your help because so far, I seem to have picked the wrong men, and wonder if I'm sending out the wrong message. Plus I'm looking for a completely different type of man now – no more bad boys like Fabio, I want someone dependable, fatherly even. I don't mind if he's older than me. I want a man who likes the simple things in life, doesn't stray, and likes being at home.'

'Sounds like Matt,' I said.

Debs nodded and stared over at me. 'Exactly. I'd *love* to find a man like Matt.'

'I'm not sure you would,' I said. 'His type might not be exciting enough for you. You might get bored.'

'I'm done with excitement, I really am. I want reliable. Someone who won't let me down.'

'Forget about the websites for a while,' said Lorna. 'I believe if love is meant to be, you'll find each other. It could be somewhere really mundane – in the street, at the library.'

Debs shook her head. 'Maybe once upon a time, but I think you have to make your life happen, or at least take steps to show the universe that you mean business and are actively looking.'

'But how can you tell online?' asked Lorna. 'What about the connection, the magic, the chemistry? Surely you can't get that from a photo.'

'No, but you can see pretty quickly if it's there or not on the first date,' said Debs.

I was grateful for the change of topic away from Matt and Tom. 'You can probably tell in the first minute,' I said.

'Five seconds with most men,' said Debs. 'That's why I want your help, so I don't waste time. It's awful when you know straight away that it's not going to work but still have to sit there and be polite.'

'What about joining one of those exclusive sites,' I suggested, 'where you pay a fee? They sift through for you and try to match you with someone like-minded.'

'They probably do but to tell the truth, I'm losing heart. It's hard to find a decent man.' She turned to look at me. 'That's why I can't understand why you'd give up on a man like Matt.'

'I think it would be a good idea to look at the more elite sites,' I said in an attempt to keep the conversation away from Matt. 'What is it you want exactly, Debs? Do you want a companion or do you want a husband?'

'I don't want to get married. No. I like being independent.'

'And what about you, Lorna? What's happening with you and builders?'

She grinned. 'It was talking to you about Airbnb that gave me the idea. I don't want to move. I don't want to be alone. Solution – convert my house into two. I've been busy. I've checked with the council and they reckon I could get planning permission, so all I have to do is submit drawings, get the necessary go-ahead and I'll be off. I've already met with an architect and it's all doable, not a lot more than building some partition walls and putting a kitchen into the second sitting room that Alistair used to use as a den. I can stay at home, my girls will still have their home to come back to.'

'So you'll be doing Airbnb as well?' Debs asked.

Lorna shook her head. 'No, I want lodgers or a lodger on a more permanent basis so that there'll be someone in the other part of the house all the time. I might advertise at the university for a young professional or someone like that.'

'I think it's a great idea, Lorna,' I said.

'Maybe you could move in there, Cait,' said Debs.

Lorna shook her head. 'I doubt it will be big enough for you, Cait. It will only have one bedroom – a large one, yes, but I guess you'd want rooms for the family when they come back, and a study.'

'That's right. We need space.'

'That's if you stay with Matt,' said Debs.

'I've already booked my builders,' said Lorna quickly, and I was grateful that she was trying to steer the conversation away from Matt as well. 'I wanted to get them on board before anything else. For the first time in months, I feel optimistic. I have a project that could work.'

'Good . . . but back to you, Cait,' said Debs, and I felt my heart sink. 'What are you going to do about this Tom bloke?'

'Nothing,' I said. 'I'm doing everything I can to make things work with Matt.'

'Hmm,' said Debs as she looked at me thoughtfully.

I went home later feeling troubled.

30

Cait

From: Lornaalp@org.com
To: Cait@grmail.com

Hi Cait
I've been researching marriage-guidance tips. One
advised kindness so I'm passing that on to you. Give
it a try, not that I think you're not kind, you are but
maybe a bit extra? Also, suggest you don't discuss Tom
or Matt any further with Debs. Lorna X

*

From: Cait@grmail.com
To: Lornaalp@org.com

Point taken. Be extra kind. I will buy him a Toblerone
when at the shops. See, I am kindness personified. Yes,

wish hadn't mentioned Tom to Debs, feel it was a
mistake. Anyway, upwards and onwards. CX

Matt

Our meeting with the second counsellor on our list was
scheduled in Chippenham late morning. A man this time.
Richard Lees. I'd checked his age online before we set off.
He was fifty-five, looked a friendly chap, and had been
practising as a therapist for over twenty years. *That's more
like it*, I thought as we set out.

We parked the car by the station and made our way along
a street of terraced houses to number 24.

Cait knocked on the door, which was opened by a tall,
pale, thin man dressed in beige. He looked like a weary
banana with the weight of the world on his shoulders. The
photo I'd seen online must have been taken on a day he was
feeling more cheerful.

'Puddleglum the Marshwiggle,' Cait whispered as we
followed him inside.

'Pardon? Did you say something?' asked Richard.

He might look weary, I thought, *but his ears work OK*.

He ushered us into a cosy-looking room at the back of
his house, where there was a comfortable-looking cream sofa
and leather chair. We went in and sat on the sofa while
Richard got himself a notepad and sat opposite.

'So,' he said. 'How can I help?'

'We were wondering if you could tell us how you could
help us,' said Cait. 'What do you do? I mean, what are your
methods?'

'That depends on why you've come,' said Richard.

Cait glanced over at me. 'We've come for marriage coun-selling, or at least to find out about it.'

'I do that,' said Richard. 'I work with many married and unmarried couples. Can you tell me a bit about why you think you might like to do couples therapy?'

Cait looked over at me again. Cue me to say something. 'Well, er . . . Cait thinks our marriage has gone stale, that we don't talk any more.'

'OK. Good. Cait, is that right?'

Cait shrugged. 'Sort of.'

'Would you like to clarify?' Richard asked.

'I feel we live like lodgers in the same house and don't really share anything anymore or talk. So much is unspoken.'

'OK. Good. So you're here today to air your unspoken feelings. Matt would you like to start?'

'Not really. It wasn't my idea to come.'

Richard turned to me. 'So, Cait, I take it that it was yours. Would you like to start?'

'No. That's just it. I feel I take the initiative with everything. I found the therapists.'

'Therapists?' Richard asked. 'You're seeing more than me?' He didn't appear to like this.

'No. Yes. Sort of. Not at the same time,' said Cait. 'We've never done anything like this before and wanted to make sure we got the right person.'

'OK. Good,' said Richard, though he looked pretty pissed off. 'And I am number?'

'Number two,' I said, then had to suppress a juvenile urge to laugh.

'And how many are you seeing?'

'One more to go.'

'OK. Good. Interesting. So – let's address your unspoken feelings.'

I felt like saying, maybe we should address your unspoken feelings. He was clearly annoyed that we were seeing other counsellors. We sat in an awkward silence for what felt like an eternity.

Finally Richard sighed. 'Do either of you want to say anything yet?'

I looked at Cait. 'You?'

She shook her head and asked, 'You?'

I shook my head. We both turned to Richard.

'Sometimes in a partnership, one is the leader, the other the follower,' he said. 'Were you saying that Cait is the leader in your relationship?'

'Yes,' I said.

'As I just said, not by choice,' she said.

'OK.' Richard looked at his watch. 'So what are *you* saying, Cait?'

'It was never my choice to be the leader but, if I didn't lead, a lot of things wouldn't get done. Things have changed lately, though. My husband has recently been made redundant. We have to make a plan about how we're to survive. Rethink how we live, in fact.'

'And how do you feel about that, Matt?' asked Richard.

'It's early days.'

'And how do you feel about that, Cait?'

'Frustrated. Early days. What does that mean? He doesn't talk to me. Won't discuss plans.'

'And what would you say to that, Matt?'

I shrugged.

'See,' said Cait. 'That's what I get.'

'And how do you feel about that, Cait?' Richard asked.

'I just told you. Frustrated.'

'And how do you feel about Cait being frustrated, Matt?'

I laughed. 'Frustrated too. Not much I can do about it though, is there?'

'Hmm,' said Richard. 'Are you hearing what Matt said, Cait?'

'Yes. He just said there's nothing he can do about the situation.'

'Is that what you meant, Matt?'

'Yes.'

'Hmm. And how do you feel about that, Matt?'

Like I'd like to hit someone, I thought. *Preferably you, Richard, then ask how you felt about that.*

'I *feel* like we're not getting very far,' I replied.

'Cait. Would you like to chip in now?'

'Not really,' said Cait.

We continued in this vein for the rest of the hour. Going round and round in circles, with Richard nodding and asking how we felt and asking us to repeat back to each other what we'd said. It was very annoying.

*

'Cross him off the list?' I said as we got back into the car after the session.

'Definitely.'

'OK good. And how do you feel about that, Cait?'

She laughed. 'Like I'd like to throttle you, no, him actually.'

'OK. Good. See, we do agree on something. Let's go to the pub on the way back. I need a drink after that, but first let me ask, how do you feel about that?'

'I feel that you should lead the way and make mine a double,' said Cait.

Maybe this therapy lark does have something going for it, after all, I thought as I started up the car. *You feel liberated when you get out.*

*

Cait

'Let's have a blitz,' said Matt when we got home to an empty house and a note from Dad saying that he had gone over to Lorna's to walk her dogs. I was pleased to hear that because they'd met on many occasions over the years and always got on well, particularly when Alistair was alive. He and Dad had always loved to put the world to rights. 'Clean the place up.'

'Excellent,' I said.

We were interrupted mid-hoover by Duncan arriving, so coffee was made and, as he often did, he pulled out a joint.

'Got some new stuff,' he said. 'Want to try it?'

'No thanks,' I said, and gave Matt a look to say 'and neither do you.' Sadly he didn't appear to be telepathic because he took the joint and inhaled deeply. He immediately went white and almost keeled over.

'Woa. Feel sick,' he said as he steadied himself on the island, then staggered his way to the cloakroom.

Two minutes later, we heard moaning. I ran to the cloak-room to find Matt on the floor. I bent over to help him up but he groaned in pain and refused to move.

'What happened?'

'I slipped, felt I was going to pass out,' he said. 'I must have twisted as I went down so I wouldn't bang my head on the sink. Hurt my back.'

Duncan came through and, between us, we managed to get him into the sitting room, where he lay on the sofa, clearly still in pain and very pale.

'Have you broken anything?' I asked.

'Don't think so,' he said as he attempted to change position. 'Arghhhhhh.'

Duncan sat on the arm of the sofa. 'He's had a whitie.'

'A whitie? What's that?'

'Like a whiteout – when you almost pass out.'

'*What* was in that stuff?'

Duncan shrugged and laughed. 'Not sure. Skunk is quite strong. Same thing happened to me last year.'

'Not funny, Duncan. Skunk? Matt's not used to that stuff.'

'Sorry. Painkillers will do the trick for his back. Ibuprofen. Got any? He might have torn a muscle.'

'I'll get some, and it might be an idea if you left before I punch you.'

Duncan grinned. 'He'll live.' Thankfully, he made a swift exit, and I was left with Matt, who looked slightly bewildered; his pupils were dilated and he had come out in a sweat.

'Still feel sick. Need to get up to bed before everyone gets back,' said Matt. 'So sorry.'

'Can you walk?'

'I'll try. Oh . . .' He made an effort to lift himself but yelped and lay back, where he writhed in pain.

'Am in agony but need to pee. Can you help me?'

'You need me to help you pee?'

I try to lift him but he could barely stand. I managed to get him, groaning loudly, back to the downstairs cloakroom.

'I can manage,' he said, and steadied himself with one hand on the wall.

I left him to it and stood outside the door.

'You OK?' I asked after a few minutes.

'I can't get my trousers back up.'

'I'll help.'

I went in and knelt down in front of him to pull his trousers back up. At that moment, we heard someone come through the front door.

Dad came into the hall, took one look in the cloakroom at Matt's bare bottom and me kneeling on the floor and took a step back. 'Oh lord, sorry. Disturbed your private time.'

'No, *no*, Dad. It's fine, we weren't, we were . . . just Matt . . .' What could I say? Your sixty-three-year-old son-in-law has been smoking skunk and almost passed out.

Dad had hotfooted it up the stairs and I heard his bedroom door close a few moments later.

Matt attempted to bend and pull his trousers up but still couldn't. 'Please help me,' he said, and groaned in agony again as we heard the front door open once more.

This time it was Jed and Martin. They took a look in the cloakroom, where Matt was still moaning and I was still kneeling

'Urgh, Mum,' said Jed and put his hand across his eyes. 'Do you have to?'

'Your dad's hurt himself,' I said,' he's groaning in *pain*.'

'If that's your story,' said Jed, and he and Martin headed

up the stairs, sniggering. I heard Jed saying, 'shouldn't have used her teeth', which led to more sniggering. Their bedroom door closed a few moments later.

Matt looked very sheepish. 'So sorry, Cait.'

'Best get you into bed so you can sleep it off.'

'I don't think I can,' he said. I pulled his trousers up and helped him hobble back to the sofa. I could see there was no way he was going to make it up the stairs, so I stripped off his clothes then raced up to the bathroom to get his dressing gown and comfy pyjama bottoms. Getting him into them was a difficult process. I managed to pull his trousers off, but his back went into spasm again, causing him to cry out. He really did look in a bad way. I was just bending over trying to get the pyjamas up Matt's legs, and was nose to nose with Matt's groin when, unfortunately, Dad decided to venture down again.

He took one look in the sitting room, turned on his heel and fled. 'Oh. Whoops. Sorry. Not finished. Was just going to make myself a cup of tea,' he called behind him.

'No. Dad, come back. I'm just getting Matt comfy,' I called back.

I looked at Matt lying helplessly on the sofa, stark naked from the waist down, his pyjamas round his knees, his face as white as a sheet and his hair all mussed up. 'I think I've really hurt myself. I can't move.'

'I'll call 111,' I said.

A lovely man at the other end of the phone recommended an ice pack for Matt's back, that I ask the doctor for pain-killers, then suggested a hot-water bottle be applied tomorrow. I had to suppress the urge to sing, 'I believe in miracles, where you from? You sexy thing', as I rummaged in the freezer then took a pack of frozen peas through to the sex god on the sofa.

*

'Cait, please can you collect my prescription?' Matt asked later the same day. Cue a lot of groaning in case I hadn't realized how hurt he was.

'Is there any of that Toblerone left? I've got the munchies,' he called five minutes later.

'Cait, please could I have a cup of tea, that chocolate's made my mouth dry.' More groaning.

'Cait, please could you put some more cushions behind my back.' More groaning.

'Cait, I forgot to post a letter to the accountant. Could you . . .' More groaning.

'Cait, have we got any of that anti-inflammatory gel? No. Please could you get some? Sainsbury's is probably still open.' More groaning, which I decided to join in with. A duet. Sadly, Matt wasn't amused.

I'd have felt more sympathetic if he'd fallen or slipped by accident, but no, it was due to him being a first-class eejit. Of course I didn't like to see Matt in pain, but I'd also have liked to slap him and say, grow up, you're not in your twenties any more, the rock-and-roll days are over. I was finding it hard to maintain my kindness resolution, plus any thoughts of resurrecting the romance seemed impossible in the light of seeing my husband, hair standing up like Marge Simpson's, in pain, dignity flown to the wind, bollocks akimbo.

Some are born kind, some achieve kindness, and some have kindness thrust upon them. That is me today. I have had kindness thrust upon me. Of course I will get the pain-relief gel, serve the tea, bolster the cushions. I am not a monster, but it is not the same as choosing to do it from the goodness of my presently withered heart.

In the meantime, Dad was avoiding eye contact and Jed couldn't look at me without sniggering.

I skipped my Zumba class and went upstairs to look at photos of Tom's house in Majorca. I sent him a text asking – do you smoke dope? He texted back, no, don't do drugs. Why? What are you suggesting?

*

Matt

I am in agony and God, I've done it again, let Cait down. I'm back in the doghouse. So much for my keep-fit programme too – that's scuppered now. Why oh why did I take a toke of that joint? And just after things were feeling marginally better between Cait and me. I really must shape up and stop acting like an idiot. Smoking dope was never my thing, not even back in the Seventies but I've felt a bit reckless since losing my job, at sea with who I am and where I'm going which is why I want to try new experiences but that's no excuse for my stupid behaviour. Lately, I'd felt that I was finding my way again . . . until this. So, no more. Once I'm mobile again, I am going to change, show Cait that I haven't taken a dive into drugs, depression and depravity. I shall resume my work on the TV series, do what I can to support Cait, act like a man again and sort our present situation out. In the meantime . . .

'Cait, I need some more painkillers,' I called, 'and please could you pass me the TV remote, I can't reach it.'

She came in a few moments later and I could tell she was finding it hard being kind. She'd never have made a nurse or doctor. She was good for a few rounds of tea and toast then she turned into Harold Shipman.

31

Cait

Our wedding anniversary.

Presents received.
- An M & S voucher from Dad. *Nice.*
- A landscape watercolour of a beach in Thailand from Jed, by Jed. *Fabulous. I shall treasure it.*
- Bottle of bubbly sent from Sam. *Appreciated.*
- White roses from Lorna. *Thoughtful.*
- A Post-it note from Matt saying 'Duncan's giving me a lift to the chiropractor. Will get some more gel for inflammation while I'm out. C U l8r.' *It's the thought that counts, isn't it?*

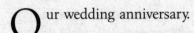

Items lost:
- My waistline.
- My willpower.

- Jaw line. Pulled cheek skin up and back to see how I'd look if I had a facelift. Hmm. Fish face comes to mind. I wonder how much it would cost? I read about a procedure where they put a metal hook under your ears and a thread under the chin then sew it up to the hook so tightening a slack jaw. Argh. Think I'd rather be wrinkly. Must stop looking in mirror. Of all the things you wear, your expression is the most important, so smile. I smiled at my reflection. It didn't make me look any younger.

*

I've decided to start the 5:2 diet. Everyone's doing it. Five hundred calories a day for two days a week. I could do that. I must do that.

Why are you doing it? asked an inner voice that sounded distinctly like Lorna. I wasn't overweight but it wouldn't hurt to shed half a stone.

In case I decide to run away with Tom Lewis, said another inner voice.

No it isn't.

Yes it is.

So why not tell Matt about him? the inner dialogue continued.

Matt had gone by the time I got downstairs in the morning, but he never forgets the date. He always sent a card and arranged for flowers to be delivered. We did keep up some traditions. I'd bought him a couple of history books, plus a bottle of Armagnac and another Toblerone. I wrapped them and left them on the desk in his den, ready for when he got back.

Late morning, I spent an hour filling the boot and back seats of the car with rubbish from Sam and Jed's room ready to go to the tip. It had been stashed in the garage, along with all the stuff that had accumulated in the garden shed. It was surprising what was in there – piles of plastic plant pots, paint cans and roller trays, stacks of old papers and magazines, old curtains, damp and mouldy cushions and bed linen. It would be good to get rid of it all and a clear-out always made me feel better.

'What a glamorous place to go on a wedding anniversary,' said Lorna, who had agreed to go with me, as we sat in the car waiting for a slot.

'I know. I go to all the best places.'

'Let's put on the radio,' said Lorna as she looked at the queue, 'it looks like it's going to be a long wait.'

I turned on the radio and tuned to Radio Four. There was a programme on about life coaching, and I half listened as I stared out at the sudden downpour of rain.

'So much for a flaming June,' said Lorna as she gazed out of the window.

'In essence, you have to see prospects and potential everywhere. Reach out and grasp them,' said the life coach on the radio, 'don't just expect opportunities to come knocking at your door. You have to go out and find them, but not only that, more importantly, you have to be ready to recognize them when they appear, because sometimes the most remarkable breaks in life aren't glaringly obvious, nor do they always come in the guise we expect. The ability to recognize them is often what marks out the successful from the unsuccessful. Be ready. Be open. Be amazed.'

'Be gone,' I said as I switched off. 'She sounded like Debs.

She's always coming out with "seize the day", "reach for the stars" type sayings. Sometimes I want to throttle her.'

Lorna laughed. 'And not much chance of being amazed at the tip,' she said as we looked at the dismal grey buildings ahead of us and the queue began to nudge forward.

When a place finally came up, I drove in, switched off my engine, and Lorna and I began to unload the back, then looked around to see what went where.

'First time?' asked a voice to my right. I looked over to see an attractive man with white hair, a beard and a friendly face. He was addressing Lorna.

'Yes, I'm a tip novice,' Lorna replied.

'It takes a bit of getting used to,' the man said as he took a quick look at our pile then pointed to a corner. 'Wood is that way, plastics over there, paint cans next to that.'

'Thanks,' said Lorna.

'Would you like a hand?' he asked, and indicated his car, which was empty apart from a large chestnut-coloured dog, which was watching us from the open window of the passenger seat. 'I've done mine so could show you where it all goes.'

'That's very kind of you, if you're sure you have time,' said Lorna, and she went over to stroke the dog, which began to wag his tail at the attention.

'What's his name?' she asked.

'Geoffrey,' said the man.

'A very handsome fellow,' said Lorna.

As is his owner, I thought, as I took in his tall, lean frame. Although dressed in old jeans and a sweatshirt, he had an air of sophistication about him.

'He is. He's a Labradoodle – more Labrador than poodle.'

He held out his hand to shake Lorna's then withdrew it. 'Sorry, filthy hands. I'm Patrick.'

I noticed that he was wearing a wedding ring. Shame, I thought, but then as Debs is always saying, all the good ones are taken. And shame Lorna has got her old togs on and no make-up because that man likes her.

'I'm Lorna,' she said. 'Pleased to meet you. So – d'you come here often, Patrick?'

He laughed. 'I do, particularly in the gardening season.'

'Are you a gardener?'

'Not professional, but I do like to work in my own, especially now I'm retired. My wife always used to be the gardener but now . . .' He trailed off and looked away.

Ah. So he was either a widower or divorced. 'You been having a clear-out then?' I asked.

'Some. It's frightening how fast stuff accumulates. But it feels good to get rid of it, doesn't it?' he said as he picked up a pile of papers and began to stride over to an area with huge closed bins.

'Actually it does,' said Lorna as she picked up another pile and followed him. 'My husband always used to do regular tip visits when he was alive, but since he died, I'm afraid I've let it all mount up.'

Well get her, I thought.

With his help, it took about fifteen minutes and we were done.

'Thank you so much,' I said. 'Much appreciated.'

'Glad to be of service.' He turned and was about to get into his car, then he stopped and approached Lorna. 'I . . . er . . . Don't suppose you fancy a coffee? There's a nice place round the corner.'

Maybe he'd been listening to the same radio programme with the life coach, I thought. But no way would she agree. I knew Lorna. She didn't want another man.

'Love to. Is that OK, Cait?'

'Sure,' I said.

As I drove off, leaving my friend behind, I laughed at the ridiculousness of the situation. *Just wait till Debs hears about this*, I thought. All those Internet dates and Lorna pulls at the recycling centre.

On the way back, I went to the pet shop to buy a different kind of food for Yoda and a magnetic collar and cat flap so the neighbour's cats couldn't get in.

When I got home, Dad helped me to fit it to the door, then I attached the new magnetic collar to Yoda. He was not happy about it, so I put new, expensive luxury cat food down to appease him. He went straight to it. Yum. Purr. However, his tin cat-food bowl leapt up and attached itself to the magnetic chip on his collar. He freaked out. There was cat food everywhere as he tried to run away with the bowl still stuck to his collar. I chased after him and detached the bowl. He ran into the utility room and thwang, got sucked onto the washing machine. *The magnets must be very strong*, I thought as I tried not to laugh. Poor Yoda. *Such is the glamour of my life, Tom Lewis*, I thought as I grabbed hold of Yoda and removed the collar. He ran out through the cat flap, but not before giving me one of his most evil, accusing looks.

For lunch, I prepared slices of cucumber, then Jed came back from town laden with local cheeses, chutney and fresh olive bread from the deli on Walcot Street. Will start 5:2 again tomorrow.

*

Matt called early afternoon. He sounded upbeat.

'Where are you?' I asked.

'Library. Had a lunch out with Duncan after my session, then signed up for piano lessons, then came here.'

'Piano lessons?'

'Yes. I've always wanted to play.'

'But we don't have a piano.'

'Duncan can get me one on the cheap.'

'Do you know what day it is?'

'Friday.'

'Our wedding anniversary. Thirty-one years.'

'Shit.'

'Not all of them,' I said.

Silence. 'Sorry, Cait. I didn't forget. I just forgot the date. I'll make it up to you,' he said as I spied Yoda crying to come in through the French doors.

I opened the doors. Yoda stared at me then looked away, bored. I closed the door, only to hear heartbreaking meowing. I opened the door. Yoda looked at me again, put his nose in the air then walked away. I closed the door, only to hear more crying from outside. I ignored it. It became louder. I opened the door.

'I can't go on like this all day,' I said.

Yoda started to come in, then stopped about six inches from the door, as if to say, I might come in, I might not, but if I do, it will be in my own time.

I picked him up and shoved him through the door just as Jed came into the kitchen. He ran over, picked up Yoda and cuddled him. 'You're mean to that cat, Mum,' he said as Yoda nuzzled in and gave me a smug look.

Matt appeared back from town an hour later with a large

silver envelope. He was in a good mood and looked pleased with himself. I knew he'd come up with something for our anniversary. He'd never forgotten before. For our first Valentine's together, he'd lined a box with white silk and filled it with Liquorice Allsorts (my favourites back then, before I started the thirty-year-long diet). Another year, he gave me a life-size rubber lizard with a piece of paper rolled up on its tongue that said, 'I think you're rubbery.' Who needed two dozen red roses when you could have your very own fake amphibian? It had made me laugh. Matt used to make me laugh a lot in our early years. For our twenty-fifth anniversary, he bought me twenty-five silver presents, thoughtfully chosen, all wrapped in silver paper. He was a man that could make an effort.

'I thought about this one long and hard when I was out,' he said. 'I wanted to get you something special, something you'd really like.'

I gave him a hug and took the envelope. *What this time?* I wondered as I ripped it open. I remembered tickets to Paris on our fifth anniversary. Vouchers for a spa break in the Cotswolds for our tenth. A weekend in a romantic hotel in Venice for our twentieth.

Inside the envelope, there was a photo of a baby orang-utan. I looked to Matt for explanation.

'I know. Isn't it great?' he said as he limped over to the fridge then poured himself a glass of juice.

'His name is Pichu. I've adopted him for you.'

'Adopted?'

He grinned. 'He's not going to come and live with us. He's in a sanctuary in Malaysia. While I was at the library, I registered online to pay an amount every month to keep him safe. I remembered you saying once that orang-utans are your favourite animal. I'll have the photo framed so you can put it somewhere you can see it.'

It's true, orang-utans are my favourite animal. *Can't fault him there*, I thought, and made a note to store the framed picture in the loft with the rubber lizard.

He pulled a package out of his case. 'I also bought this, though it's for both of us.'

Ah. I should have known he'd have got something else as well, I thought, until I opened it and saw it was a blood-pressure machine.

'At our time of life, best to keep an eye on it,' he said.

So romantic, I reflected as I watched him take it out of its box and put it onto his arm to take a reading. '146 over 87,' he said a few moments later. 'That's just about OK, isn't it? You want a go?'

I sat at the table and dutifully took my blood pressure. 'Oh, the larks we have in this house. Endless fun to be had with this,' I said. 'No one could ever accuse us of letting the romance fade.'

'No need to be sarcastic,' said Matt.

The blood-pressure machine was a big hit. Dad took his, Jed and Martin took theirs.

'Mine's 128 over 85,' said Jed to Matt as they compared results.

'I can better my result, get a lower score,' said Matt. 'I'll do it again.' He put the armband on again, took a few deep breaths and switched the machine on.

'It's not a competition, Dad,' said Jed. 'Hey, let's do Yoda's.'

Yoda took one look at them and was gone.

*

Now time to relax, I thought after clearing up the supper dishes. I went to the bedroom to watch TV to find that Jed and Martin were sprawled on our bed. 'You don't mind, do you, Mum? It's the latest series of *Twin Peaks*. We missed it when it first came out. It's awesome.'

'Why don't you watch downstairs?'

'We can't get near the remote since Granddad moved in. He totally monopolizes that TV.'

I went back downstairs to find Matt in his den. 'Our house has been taken over,' I said.

He nodded. 'Tell me about it.'

'Fancy a glass of wine? It is our anniversary after all.'

Matt hesitated. 'I would but . . .' he patted his stomach, 'I'm off the booze for a few months. I could get you a glass, though.'

'No. It's fine. I'll go and check my emails.'

Once upstairs, I had a look to see if there was anything from Tom. Nothing. However, there was an email offering free terminal illness cover and insurance to meet funeral costs. Cheerful. All in all, an anniversary to remember.

32

Cait

To do:
- Start 5:2 diet again. Plan out meals.
  Breakfast: Boiled egg. Stick of celery. Black coffee.
  Lunch: Cup of miso soup.
  Supper: Steamed white fish and one floret of broccoli.
- Items lost: will to live.

When I got up, I saw that the shared bathroom was full of wet towels and splashes all over the mirrors. The beds in Dad's room and Jed and Martin's were unmade.

Downstairs, the kitchen looked as though a bomb had hit it, with dishes and glasses left from Martin and Jed's post-TV, late-night snacks. The breadboard was covered in crumbs, and the butter had been left out so it had gone soft. The utility room was full of un-ironed T-shirts, jeans, sheets and shirts, apart from the clean pile I had ironed yesterday. Although Dad had managed perfectly well on his own for a year, since he'd moved in, he'd assumed I would take the role of my late mother and do his laundry, cooking and cleaning. The whole house needed hoovering, and although Matt had promised to help, his back was still troubling him so no joy there.

I went through to the sitting room to find that it was occupied by four men in dressing gowns. Plates of toast and half-drunk cups of tea littered every surface. All, including Yoda, were watching a *Star Trek* rerun with the sound turned up loud so that Dad could hear.

'Clearly no one's taken any notice of my list,' I said.

'Chill, Mum,' said Jed. 'It's Saturday. Come and watch with us.'

I glanced over at Matt. He looked sheepish and kept his eyes firmly locked on the TV.

'Got stuff to do,' I said, and escaped into my office. In my fantasy, Tom's house in Majorca is spotless and smells of mountain breezes, there are vases of fresh flowers on tables, bowls of exotic fruits in the kitchen. I had a quick look on his Facebook page. He'd been tagged into a few photos. A wedding. He hadn't mentioned that he was going to one, but then I realized I had no idea how he spent his time or who with. The photo showed him smiling in the middle of a group of women. Harrumph. And another photo on a terrace with a blonde woman, also smiling. He had his arm around her. Huh. Who was she then? I felt a stab of jealousy. Should I ask him? Had he propositioned her as well? Hmm. I didn't like the feelings the photos brought out in me.

A text arrived from Debs asking me to meet up for coffee. I texted back that I would, though had a slight sinking feeling that she might want to confront me about Tom.

Did a quiz on Facebook to see which song was written about me. Who could resist that? I got 'Wild Thing' by the

Troggs. One learns so much about oneself with these online questionnaires. I am wild, a wild thing; I do outrageous things like go for coffee in town.

I texted Tom. *Realized I have no idea of what you do every day, what your life is like, who you see. Please send days in the life of Tom Lewis so I can get a picture. Cait. X*

*

Matt

I am shaved and dressed, not in my dressing gown any more. Cait came into the kitchen but didn't even look at me so probably didn't notice my appearance. She had a jacket on.

'Wher—' I checked myself in time. I knew it bugged her when I asked where she was going. Free spirit, my Cait.

'Have a good time,' I called as I heard her go out of the front door. She didn't reply. No matter. I had my own projects to be getting on with.

I spent a happy day in cyberspace researching various sites for the TV series. I wanted to do one programme about people who had achieved great things after fifty, so spent a few hours reading about people who had started late in life: writers, artists, politicians, entertainers, sportspeople. The lists were endless and inspiring. People who hadn't let their age define them, who had dreams and aspirations and they'd made them happen. If the series went ahead, it would be an interesting programme to make, plus could be a good section in my book of lists for Cait.

Cait's father, Louis, appeared at the door. 'Got a minute, Matt?' he asked.

'Sure, come in.'

Louis came in and sat on the chair opposite my desk.

'Did you need something?'

Louis shrugged. 'Not really, just wanted a chat.'

I turned off my computer and gave him my full attention. 'All ears.'

'I don't mean to be ungrateful, but I don't think living here is working for me,' he said.

'OK. You mean you want to go back to your house?'

'No. I'm going to let Jed and Martin have that. I'm going to stay and then live permanently at Lorna's.'

'Lorna's? OK. Er . . . does Cait know?'

'Not yet. That's just it. I don't know how to tell her. I know she worries about me, and what it means to have me here, but I need my independence. Lorna's doing work on her house, splitting it into two. Perfect for me – an ex-GP next door, a fantastic garden, and two dogs that remind me of my old Brandy. I can walk them when I want. So I'd have company if I chose but time alone too. Being here has made me realize, I have my own way of doing things, my own routines.'

'Sounds ideal, Louis. So what's the problem?'

'I don't want to upset Cait. Don't mention it just yet.'

'I won't.'

'And you? How are you getting along?'

'Actually OK. I was a bit lost to begin with—'

'Understandable.'

'But I'm starting to see things differently and view this next chapter not as a void but an opportunity.'

Louis nodded. 'I remember when I first retired. I didn't know what to do with myself, but after a while, you see it as liberating. All my life was about obligations, and suddenly I was free of them. You make sure you enjoy it all. Have a good think about what you'd like to do and make sure you do it.'

'I will. I'm starting to see things that way already. No more having to wear the suit, adhere to fixed times – as you say, liberating.'

*

Cait

In town, I popped into the abbey to say a prayer. I noticed other women dotted about on other pews and wondered if they were asking for guidance as to whether they should run off with their ex-lover.

I came out feeling peaceful. In the square next to the abbey, a skinny opera singer with an out of tune voice was singing 'House of the Rising Sun' by The Animals. I had to resist the urge to go and put a bag over her head and then push her over. Anything to get her to shut up.

So much for my recently found peace. I went and put a few coins in her hat. Didn't push her over.

*

'So how's it going?' asked Debs, once we'd ordered coffees and croissants in the café in the square by the Pump Rooms. 'I was very concerned about you after what you told us at our supper the other night.'

'All good.'

'OK,' Debs said, though she didn't look convinced. 'And how's your fairy book coming on?'

I pulled a face. 'Not so good. I killed them off with turbo-vibrators.'

'Forever?'

'Maybe. Probably. The story needs work and I'm not sure I even want to do it any more. By the way, you didn't mention that I'd been working on anything to Matt when he came to help you with your brochures, did you, Debs?'

'No, of course not – but maybe you should.'

'Why?'

'Sounds like you have a lot of secrets from each other at the moment. How is he?'

'A lot happier lately. He'd actually had a shave and had got out of his dressing gown by the time I left this morning.'

'And have you heard any more from Tom?'

'No. It was just a brief catch-up really. I won't see him again. He was my past, Matt is my present.' I was aware that this was probably the first time I'd lied to Debs. 'Seeing him again was just curiosity, really.'

'What's he like now?' I felt myself blush and prayed that Debs wouldn't notice.

'He's lived an interesting life, doing photography, painting. He'll be going back to LA soon.'

'But didn't you say that there was still something between you?'

I laughed, probably a bit too quickly. 'We always got on and it was nice to see him, but really we're very different people now to when we were in our twenties.' I decided to try and change the subject. 'What about you? Had any more dates?'

Debs rolled her eyes. 'I went on one last night. Almost enough to send me back on the hippie trail. He didn't look at all like his photo and was really boring. We both knew it was a non-starter, that's partly why I wanted to meet up with you today. I know how hard it is to find a decent man, and after what you said the other night, I feel very worried that you might lose Matt.'

'Why would you think that?'

'Because you blush when you talk about Tom, so I know there's something going on, and because you told us things aren't going well with Matt.'

'We'll get through it.'

'Matt is a good man; don't lose him because of a bad patch or do anything you'll regret. Retirement for a man is a huge period of adjustment.'

'Lorna made it work when Alistair retired, and so will Matt and I.'

'They retired with pensions and savings, that must have made things easier. No offence, but I know you and Matt don't have their resources, and that must put an added strain on you.'

'We'll get by.'

'Well, if there's anything I can do, just let me know. In the meantime, I think you should tell Matt about seeing Tom.'

'I think that's a terrible idea. The last thing he needs is to feel threatened by an old lover of mine.'

'But you just said it was innocent. If it really is, then why not mention it to Matt? It would take the secrecy out of it and maintain the trust.'

I sighed. 'You're probably right. Let me think about it. I'd have to pick my moment, though.'

'I just don't want you to make a mistake you'll regret. If you tell Matt, he could never accuse you of betraying him.'

I nodded. She was right. If it had been anyone else who'd got in touch, I probably would have mentioned it to Matt. Maybe I would, one day, but not this week.

*

Matt

Time for a heart-to-heart, manly discussion, I thought on my way to meet my brother in town early evening.

'Cait and I have been looking for a counsellor,' I said when I'd got to the pub and Duncan had bought us two beers at the bar.

'What for?'

'That's what I said.'

'Counselling you say?'

'Yeah. Marriage guidance.'

'You going to do it?'

'Don't think I have much choice. We've seen a couple but didn't feel they were right, one more to go.'

'Ah. I get what you're doing. Going along with it. Good tactic. Agree to everything, say you're sorry a lot even if you're not quite sure what you've done. Women seem to like that.'

'Well, not exactly. I am prepared to give it a go if we can find the right therapist.'

'Nah. You either get on or you don't. Did you see the game last night?'

'I did.'

'Gregson played a blinder.'

'He did. Did you ever try it?' I asked.

'Try what?'

'*Counselling* – with your ex?'

'Me. Nah. Load of bollocks. When it's over it's over, no need to pay to have a slanging match with some bearded hippie acting as referee. Is it over with you and Cait?'

'I don't think so, but she's not happy.'

'Women never are. Probably hormones. If they're not premenstrual, they're postmenstrual or menopausal. Buy her some flowers.'

I should have known it would be useless to try and talk to Duncan. He had two failed relationships behind him and now lived alone in a flat on the edge of town.

'Right. Thanks.' *Hopeless*, I thought. *No wonder he's single*. Time to contact my old mates.

*

On the way back from the pub, I bumped into Debs coming out of a wine bar. She looked pleased to see me and a little drunk.

'Hey, Matt, how's the project coming along?' she asked.

'Good. In need of work still but it's progressing.'

'You off home?'

'I am.'

'How about a nightcap before you head back? We could talk about the series a bit more.'

'I . . .' I was about to say no but thought, why not? Debs was so helpful before. I had nothing to lose. 'Sure, why not?'

Debs grinned and pointed back to the wine bar she'd come out of. 'Come on then, first round's on me.' She linked her arm through mine and led me into the bar where we found a quiet corner.

'So, how's it going?' Debs asked after we'd ordered a bottle of wine.

'Fine. I'm thinking of doing one programme on people who have had success late in life. Could be inspiring.'

Debs put her hand on my arm and looked deep into my eyes. 'I meant with Cait.'

'Why? Has she said something?'

Debs hesitated. 'No, course not – well, a little, but I know that every relationship needs a bit of work sometimes. That's why I gave her the counselling session vouchers. Did she tell you about them?'

'Ah yes, she did mention them.'

'It must be a big adjustment being home full time after being out at work for so many years.'

I nodded. 'We'll get by.' I wondered if Cait had mentioned our two futile attempts to find our own therapist. It didn't sound as though she had, so I decided not to say anything either.

'I also thought having sessions might give you some insight into the emotional side of your retirement journey for your TV series,' Debs continued.

'Really? How?'

'Many couples stop really talking, take each other for granted. If you went along, you could see it as research and maybe at the same time get something out of it yourself.'

'Yes, good idea.' *But not if you'd met the two therapists we've seen so far*, I thought.

'Have you got anyone you can talk to?'

I laughed. 'Duncan, my brother, though he's a fat lot of good – about as much emotional intelligence as a potato.'

'Haven't you got a close friend to confide in?'

'I . . .' I thought about my old freinds. I used to be able to really talk to Tony, my mate from university. 'Actually no, Debs, not at the moment.'

'It only takes one.'

'You're so right.' I'd get in touch with Tony first thing in the morning. 'One friend can get you through anything.'

Debs was looking at me with an intense expression that made me feel slightly uncomfortable. Oh Christ. I hope she didn't think I meant her. *Backtrack, Matt, backtrack*. 'Enough about me. What about you Debs? How's things in your life?'

Debs grimaced. 'Hasn't Cait mentioned my long list of date disasters?'

I shook my head. 'Disasters?'

'Dates. They're either too old, too short or too boring.'

'I would have thought you'd have a queue of men lining up for you.' I indicated the crowded bar. 'I've seen a few men check you out already.'

'Really?'

'Yes. You're a great-looking woman. Who wouldn't be interested?'

'Not the ones I want,' she said, and gave me that intense look of hers again. 'And to tell you the truth, Fabio leaving me knocked my confidence.'

'His loss. He was an idiot.'

Debs looked pleased at my reaction. 'That's kind of you, Matt, but let's not ruin the night by talking about Fabio.' She raised her glass. 'A toast to the future and new possibilities.'

'To new possibilities,' I said as I raised my glass. I had to admit, it felt good to be sitting in a bar with an attractive companion who appeared to be enjoying herself every bit as much as I was.

33

Cait

'Who's next on the tour?' Matt asked as we set off for our third marriage-guidance meeting.

'Gina Marshall. Older lady. Maybe our age.' She had good reviews on the Internet, but after our last two encounters I didn't hold out much hope.

'Still can't relate to my age,' said Matt.

'Me neither.'

'What if we don't like this one either?'

'We take to drink and drugs.'

'Sounds like a plan to me.'

'Good, because I can think of more enjoyable things to do on a beautiful June morning,' said Matt as he looked up at the cloudless sky.

We got to a village on the outskirts of Warminster and found the address we'd been given. It was a twee-looking place, with white cladding and a garden planted country-style with delphiniums, lupins and foxgloves at the front.

A woman came to the door, along with a Jack Russell that

began to hump Matt's leg. *Great start*, I thought as she pulled the dog off.

'Hi, I'm Gina. Sorry. This is Bertie. He's a bit over-friendly, as you can see.' She had frizzy white hair, round brown eyes, a chubby small frame and was dressed in a stylish, navy smock dress. She exuded warmth. She led us inside and into a room at the front of the cottage where she indicated that we should sit on a sofa covered with a crocheted patchwork throw and turquoise cushions. The room smelt of a recent log fire, had one wall lined with shelves that were crammed with books. On others hung what looked like Aboriginal paintings; a stone Buddha sat on a low table by the window. The place had a cosy feel and I immediately felt at home.

'I know you told me a little on the phone about how you want to work on your relationship, but how are you feeling about being here?' Gina asked after she'd settled herself in a chair opposite. 'Let's start with you, Matt.'

I heard him groan. I knew he was thinking, not another 'how do you feel' session.

'Apprehensive, if I'm honest.'

Gina turned to me. 'And you, Cait?'

'Also apprehensive. I don't really know what to expect.'

Gina nodded. 'Understandable. Embarking on something like this can be daunting. How about first I tell you a bit about how I work? I like to think of myself more as a life coach than a therapist, so rather than analysing feelings, I work more with making goals and thinking about what you'd like to change in your life, why and how. We might look a little at what's been holding you back from achieving what you want, but I aim to help people move forward from where they are, not spend too much time reliving and picking over the past.'

'Sounds good,' I said and glanced at Matt. He nodded.

Gina laughed. 'But I *am* going to ask a bit about your past so I can get to know you. How about we start at the beginning with when you two met. What first attracted you to each other? Matt?'

Matt thought for a few moments. He smiled. 'We met at a friend's party in London. Cait'd recently returned from India. She was brown, glowing and beautiful, with long hair down her back.' He laughed. 'She wore ankle bracelets and toe rings.'

'An old hippie,' I said.

Matt nodded. 'Nothing wrong with that. She seemed different from other women I knew at that time. Interesting. We had a good conversation about her time away. She was fired up with ideas on how to change the world.'

'Is that when you got together?' asked Gina.

'Oh no. It was some time after that. Years, in fact, when we met again, purely by chance, remember?'

I nodded.

'It was in a park in North London. A Saturday. I think you'd started teaching by then, hadn't you?'

I nodded.

'I took her for supper at an Ethiopian place. We got on well. I liked her view on life; she made me laugh as well as think. We began dating after that.'

'Cait?'

'As Matt said, we met at a party. That's right, I'd just come back from India. I was drifting, not sure where to go and live, what to do. I liked him but, at that time, I wasn't looking for a relationship; in fact, I didn't know what I wanted. Later, though, when we met up in the park, Matt made an impression. He seemed safe, solid.'

'That makes me sound boring,' said Matt.

'No. Not at all. You seemed dependable, yes, but not boring. You knew where you were going, were so full of energy and ambition. I liked that. It was a nice contrast to the men I'd met on my travels, many of whom had been drifting as I was. I think you'd just started working in TV, had a ton of ideas and confidence.'

Matt sighed. 'What happened to that man?'

Gina turned to Matt. 'Has something happened to that man?'

'Age,' said Matt. 'No work. How long have you got?'

Gina looked at her watch. 'About forty-five minutes, or more if you choose to come back.' Matt laughed. I could tell he liked her. I did too. 'We'll get back to that either today, Matt, or in another session. But back to you, Cait. Go on about when you first met.'

'At first, on my return to the UK, I didn't want a relationship—'

'Why was that?' asked Gina.

'Oh . . . disillusioned by men.'

'And why was that?'

I felt myself blush. If I carried on I'd be telling her all about Tom. 'I guess my head was full of romantic notions back then and the men just didn't measure up.' I laughed. 'I blame the Brontës and Jane Austen. Maybe I was looking for a Darcy or a Heathcliff.'

Gina nodded. 'Darcy OK, but Heathcliff was a head-case.' She was watching me very closely and I blushed again then cursed myself. She'd know there was something I wasn't saying and I prayed she wouldn't keep digging.

'I know, but he and Cathy in the book had such a passion.'

'Ah . . . passion, soul mates,' said Gina. 'Is that what you wanted?'

I shrugged. 'I thought I did but . . . well, it wasn't happening. By the time I met Matt again, I'd changed my mind about having a relationship, and maybe I didn't have such romantic expectations.'

'That sounds as if you made do, compromised,' said Matt. He didn't look happy. 'You lowered your expectations and settled for me. A compromise.'

'No. Sorry. I didn't mean it to sound like that. No, I *wanted* someone like you. Someone I could trust who wouldn't let me down.'

'Had someone let you down, Cait?' Gina asked, and I noticed that Matt was also watching me closely.

'Uh . . . sort of. I was in my twenties and most of the men were immature; their idea of commitment was to stay the night.'

'So no one special?'

'No. No, in fact in India I was in an ashram and we were all celibate.'

'Really?' said Gina. 'Had something happened to make you go and live in an ashram?'

Inside I was squirming, but determined not to talk about Tom, despite Gina's digging. 'It was the time of love and peace. We were all looking for God.'

'Woodstock and all that,' said Gina and smiled. 'I loved that song by—'

'Joni Mitchell,' I said. 'Or Crosby, Stills and Nash. By the time I met Matt again, I'd been re-evaluating everything and I was ready to settle down. Bumping into him was good timing, and it wasn't a compromise, Matt, you mustn't think that. I just didn't know what I wanted before then.'

He inclined his head slightly, as if to say he'd heard what I'd said but he didn't look convinced.

'And what do you hope to get out of the counselling?' asked Gina. 'What's brought you here?'

I looked over at Matt. He gestured with his hand that I should answer. I took a deep breath. This was hard. Talking to friends about our problems was bad enough, but it was worse coming out with things in front of a complete worse. 'We . . . I . . . we seem to have grown apart lately.'

'Lately being months or years?' asked Gina.

'Months,' said Matt at the same time as I said, 'Years.'

'Which?' Gina asked.

Matt shrugged. 'I'd say a year. Since your mum and Eve died. Wouldn't you, Cait?' He looked at Gina. 'It's Cait who's unhappy.'

'Really?' I said. 'You're perfectly happy?'

'Well, of course I'm not,' said Matt, 'not when I can see that you're unhappy. What I was trying to say is that I am, was, happy with the relationship, with you.'

'When did your mother die, Cait?' Gina asked.

'Over a year ago, and then my best friend Eve.'

'Oh, I am so sorry, that must have been very hard for you,' said Gina. She looked at me with such kindness, I felt myself well up. 'Still raw is it?'

'I . . .' I was surprised that my grief was so close to the surface. I thought I'd dealt with it by shutting it away and didn't want to break down in front of her and Matt. I sat up and took a deep breath. 'I'm coping.'

'Have you given yourself time to grieve?'

'I . . . Sort of.'

'I meant have you let it out?'

I shook my head. 'Not really. There didn't seem any point, it wouldn't bring them back and it was too painful to even think about either of them, so I decided to get on with life, fill my days and distract myself.'

'Block it out?' Gina asked gently.

'I suppose so. I didn't know what else to do. It felt too devastating to dwell on what had happened, so I decided to get on, keep busy.'

Gina nodded. 'It can be scary and overwhelming. Also when a parent dies, friends and family always ask how the remaining parent is and quite right too but as a daughter, the loss of a mother is also great.'

I felt myself well up again. What she'd said was true but no one had expressed it before. All the enquiries after Mum had died, had been 'how's your dad doing?' and I'd chosen to put my grief aside and be strong and cheerful for him.

'People also have different timescales on grief. Some shut themselves away and howl from day one, others not for months or sometimes even years. You'll know when you're ready.'

'If ever,' I said.

Gina nodded. 'Yes, but it can take a tremendous amount of energy to maintain the wall needed to keep that level of emotion inside. When you're ready, I'd encourage you to let some of it out.' She smiled kindly at me. 'Whose idea was it to come to counselling?'

'Mine, though it was a friend who suggested it initially,' I replied. 'It felt that we had nothing to lose. You see, we don't talk any more, not really.'

'What do you want to talk about, Cait?' asked Gina.

It felt as if she was directing all the questioning to me. I thought: *Matt's the problem, isn't he? He's the one who doesn't communicate. Why doesn't she interrogate him a bit more?*

'Oh I don't know. Everything.'

'Have you talked to Matt about the loss of your mother and friend?'

'I . . . No. Not really. He knew what was happening and there was nothing he or I could do about it. He couldn't bring Mum or Eve back.'

'Do you think you might have blamed him for not being able to fix it?'

'Blame him? Heavens no. Why would you say that?'

'As you said, your attraction to him was because he was dependable, a man who could be relied upon, but he let you down this time.'

I shook my head. 'No, of course not. I didn't think that at all.' *At least I don't think I did*, I thought.

'And what specifically do you want to talk to him about now?'

'Why we've grown apart.'

'OK. How does this manifest?' asked Gina. 'This feeling that you've grown apart.'

'Oh . . . we're just not close any more. Even before Matt lost his job, we lived separate lives—'

'You just lost your job, Matt?' Gina remarked.

'A few months ago.'

'Sorry, you were saying, Cait, you lived separate lives?' said Gina.

I nodded. 'We had done for years. Polite but separate, and if we did spend time together, it was watching a new box set.'

Gina smiled knowingly. 'You and a million other couples, but go on.'

'And now, Matt's home but he never lets me in. I've no idea what's going on in his head. He doesn't tell me when he's feeling down, but I know he is; like lately, I know he hasn't found it easy not going out to work.'

'Talk to Matt,' said Gina.

I turned to Matt. He looked uncomfortable. 'I remember when we first met, we had so much to say to each other: plans, goals, shared aspirations. Our two boys came along and of course that was a shared responsibility, so much to plan for, schools, futures and so on, and you were a good father, still are. Those years were great, but since they've gone, it feels like we don't share a goal any more. For years, you were in Bristol working, home at weekends, both of us busy-busy. It felt like we were sharing a house but not a life any more, and then it all changed, now you're home all the time. I have no idea what your plans are but I can see you're not happy. You don't talk.'

Matt looked thoughtful as he listened to me. 'Cait, has it ever occurred to you that you don't talk to me either? Gina's right, you never really opened up to me about the death of your mum or Eve. You never want to spend time with me, and when we are together, I feel I'm in your way. You don't talk to me, apart from to tell me what I should be doing or to criticize something I'm doing or wearing. The only feelings you communicate are those of disappointment or dissatis-faction.'

What he'd said came as a shock. 'I—'

'And yes, I may have been uncommunicative of late, but I don't talk to you about other stuff that's going on because I don't know what's happening myself, still don't. I don't know what to say. It's been a strange and uncertain time and I didn't want to burden you with any of my concerns.'

'Sticking your head in the sand didn't help.'

'Go back a minute, Cait,' said Gina. 'Have you really told Matt how it's been for *you* since he retired? Or have you swept it all under the carpet too? Or, as you say, stuck *your* head in the sand?'

'I think I've told him pretty clearly how I feel.'

'Did you hear that Cait was so unhappy, Matt?'

'Oh yes. I know she doesn't like me being at home all day, in her space, and before that, I thought we were doing OK – muddling along, a phase. Marriage goes through many phases, that's the contract – for better or worse, isn't it? I guess we have different approaches. When I'm unhappy, I go quiet, but Cait says she wants to talk it out, presses me into doing the same but I don't think she gives a lot away either; for example, what's behind her dissatisfaction. But when I see she's unhappy, I don't press her. I think she'll talk when she's ready. Plus her way of dealing with a bad time, like after her mother died, was to fill it with things to do, to keep so busy that she didn't have space to think about it – joining book clubs, the choir, a walking group, out with friends. I've tried to respect that. On the other hand, when I'm faced with a rough patch, like after losing my job, I wanted to retreat, to think things over. Recently, I became aware of how empty my life is outside of work, and that's been confronting and something I need to look at but I didn't want to rush into anything. I needed time to acclimatize. Still do.'

I hadn't heard Matt say so much for a long time, and it made sense. We had different ways of dealing with things. And he was right, I had kept him out. I thought about Tom, my attempts to write, the hole left by Mum and Eve's death, sadness at seeing Dad age and concern for his happiness, fear about getting older, life being short and wasting it. I'd kept all of that to myself. I was as guilty of not communicating as he was.

'Cait, have you tried to say how you really feel?'

'I . . . I thought I had, but OK, maybe not, not until recent weeks. But when I have tried, I've met a brick wall. He's refused to discuss anything.'

'Because I feel like I'm continually under attack,' said Matt. 'All you ever say is that we don't talk, that we need help, our marriage has gone stale. How am I supposed to react to that? You haven't really let me into your head. You put up a wall, too, after your mum died. Your wall of being busy. You're always hiding up in your study or off out somewhere.'

'That's not unusual,' said Gina. 'After the death of a loved one, people often try to lose themselves, distract themselves from the pain of grief by finding a different self or rediscovering an old one. Some try to numb themselves with alcohol or drugs, some have affairs; others fill their time with work or keeping busy – anything to avoid what's happening inside.'

What Gina said rang true and I hoped that I wasn't blushing.

'That makes sense,' said Matt. 'And you lost two people you loved, Cait.'

'My attitude was to try and move on, live the life they would have wanted me to.'

'But somehow shut me out,' said Matt.

'You had your own life, work, plus you were never at home.'

'That was then. I am home now.'

'And did Matt agree to come here, or did you pressurize him?' asked Gina.

'I agreed to come,' said Matt. 'Cait wanted to come so yes, that was partly it. I wanted to see if it would help, but listening to what she's been saying and hearing it all again here, I'm beginning to wonder if she's right and it *is* too late for us. We've been living separate lives for so long, maybe we would be happier apart; it sounds as if she certainly would be.'

I was surprised by Matt's outburst. I'd been pushing him to open up for so long and, now that he had, what he had to say was totally unexpected.

'Do you want to say anything in response, Cait?' Gina asked. 'Do you want to break up or heal the rift? Get beyond the walls that both of you say the other has created?'

I felt confused. I had always felt that I was the restless one who would choose to leave or not, and yet he'd just said that maybe we'd be better off apart. 'I don't know. We've been together a long time, I don't want to throw that away, but I'm also aware I'm getting older, we both are, and I don't want to drift into some boring existence.'

'Me neither,' said Matt. 'I want to be appreciated, not always seen as lacking and letting Cait down. I think we all want to be wanted and loved, to get home and see our partner's face light up. I can't remember the last time I saw that; all I see is annoyance or exasperation and, to be honest, I'm not sure I deserve that.'

'You say you're both home every day,' Gina said. 'Do you ever go out together?'

'Out? Er . . .' I said.

'When did you last go for a meal or walk with each other?' She directed the question to Matt.

'I can't remember, can you, Cait? Ages ago. Never. As I said, Cait has a busy life; there's not a lot of room for me in it, apart from to be a scapegoat for her dissatisfaction.'

'You sound angry, Matt,' said Gina.

'I guess I am. I hadn't realized before, but our house is my home too. It's my space too, and I often feel unwelcome there.'

'And what do you do when Cait's out?'

Matt laughed weakly. 'I've been looking for work. As Cait said, I've recently lost my job and not sure where I'm going from here. I'm not quite retired but not employed either.'

'How are you finding that, Matt?'

'Not easy. It's a young man's game and there aren't many opportunities for anyone my age. It's been tough. I feel I've lost my purpose as well as my identity. I'm used to routine, knowing exactly what's expected of me; now I feel I've been cut loose. I'm drifting, but unsure in which direction, and it isn't helping that my wife doesn't want me around.'

'Where's all this coming from, Matt?' I asked.

'I'm not sure. I didn't even realize I was feeling this way myself until I said it, but maybe you've been right all along, Cait. Maybe it is over and you've seen what I hadn't.'

Gina made some notes. 'It can't be easy for either of you, and no need to decide anything major so soon. How about

I have a think about how we can progress from here? It's a big life-change when one or both of a couple stop working. You need to redefine the boundaries, your living contract, who does what and so on. I think we could have our next session on that – what's expected in the home. Cait, when you were at home and Matt away, I'd imagine you took care of the running of the household?'

I nodded.

'It might be helpful to redraw the plan on that, then. Is that acceptable to you both?'

'It is to me,' said Matt. 'We did make a start of sharing the chores, then I did my back in so I feel like a spare part. I'd like to help more but, so far, it's felt as if I just get in the way or do it wrong. Cait has her way of doing things, but I live there too. I have my way of doing things as well, just not always her way.'

'OK, we'll look into that. Cait, maybe you could write a list of everything that needs doing – shopping, laundry, cleaning, etc., and we can divide it up next time you're here.'

I laughed. She made it sound so simple.

'Then after that,' Gina continued, 'we'll look into what your goals and aspirations are.'

'OK,' I said, and Matt nodded.

'Had either of you made plans for retirement?'

'No,' we chorused.

'Then I suggest a session on that too. Rather than just drifting towards it, have a think about what you'd like. How you see yourself in five years' time, and what you'd like to be doing. That way, you direct the course rather than just letting it happen to you.'

'Sounds good,' said Matt.

'May I ask how are your sexual relations?' Gina asked.

Neither of us answered.

'Difficult question?' asked Gina.

We sat in an awkward silence with neither of us wanting to admit the truth.

'Uncomfortable,' I said finally; 'an uncomfortable question because we don't have sexual relations, haven't had for months.'

Matt looked as though he wanted the floor to open up and swallow him.

'We can work on that,' said Gina, 'if you're both willing.'

Matt looked at me and made a helpless gesture with his hands.

'OK with you, Matt?' asked Gina.

Matt nodded. He didn't look happy.

'I always suggest four to six sessions at least, if you're willing to commit to those, then we can look again. It can take a while to make any lasting difference, so maybe we'll leave the session on intimacy until towards the end so that we have time to get more comfortable with each other. In the meantime, I'd like you to do some homework. Don't worry. Nothing too serious. I want you to spend more time with each other.'

I laughed. 'Not possible and now that my job has come to an end too, we're together twenty-four hours a day.'

'Possibly, but being in the same house doesn't mean together. I want you to go on a date together. Go out, take a walk, have a meal, go to a concert, spend some quality time with each other, but first you're going to spend a little time identifying what would be an enjoyable date. Do you think you could do that?'

Matt and I looked at each other. 'I guess so,' I said.

'Yes,' said Matt. 'Definitely.'

Gina smiled. 'Just because you're partners and have lived together a long time, doesn't mean you can read each other's minds, so be specific. Make sure you let each other know what you'd like to do, so it really is a mutually agreed outing that you can both look forward to. Often one can plan the kind of time you would want for yourself, not your partner. So find out what you both want. Make it a pleasure, not a chore. Maybe make plans over a glass of wine; get the local magazines that tell you what's on in town, then write down your idea of the perfect romantic day or evening. Keep plans in the realms of possibility. Put in lots of details. Make a list, because I hope it won't be a single event. It's important that couples keep dating and doing things together outside of the home.'

Make a list. I was beginning to like Gina even more. She was talking my language.

'When you've chosen what you're going to do, get ready in the same way that you probably used to when you first met. Remember, the long soak in the bath, choosing the outfit—'

'Making an effort,' I said.

'That's it,' said Gina. 'Book a taxi so neither of you has to drive. And you could make the same kind of plan for a perfect weekend, perfect birthday and anniversary.'

What Gina had suggested sounded positive and pleasurable and I could see that Matt had visibly relaxed since the beginning of the session.

As we were leaving, Gina handed us a sheet of paper. 'A little more homework. It's a "let's get to know each other" questionnaire. No need to look at it now, you can do that when you get home over the next week. It will only take ten minutes or so.'

'Do you want us to bring it back?' Matt asked.

'No,' replied Gina. 'It's for you. Have fun with it.'

*

'Wow. She was amazing. What did you think?' Matt asked as we got into the car.

'Confrontational. She comes on pretty strong and doesn't miss a thing.' I felt disturbed and anxious. Gina's probing about Mum and Eve had stirred up some deeply buried part of me that I didn't want unearthed.

'I liked that. I liked her. Which part felt particularly confrontational?'

'Oh . . . all of it I guess.' I didn't want to elaborate. I was also still in shock from hearing what Matt had said. He'd done a complete turnaround and I needed time to think about the fact he'd agreed it might be an idea if we went our separate ways.

Matt seemed buoyed up. 'It's true, we haven't had a night out, just us, in years. What would you like to do? A movie?'

'But then we couldn't talk. How about a meal out somewhere?'

'Yes, but could be expensive. We need to watch our finances.'

'Needn't be. OK. A walk in the country.'

'Then a pub lunch. How does that sound?' said Matt.

'OK but not very romantic.'

'I think romance is a state of mind,' said Matt. 'It doesn't have to be love hearts and candlelight. If you're with the right person, anywhere is romantic. In our early days, just being with you was enough to make a place romantic. It never mattered where.'

'That's the nicest thing you've said to me in years, but in our early days?' I sighed. 'What changed?'

'I guess we have. I'm sorry, Cait, I realized back there that I hadn't been listening to you. No wonder you've been angry and frustrated. But in the session, I began to get what you've been saying recently. Things have changed. We've changed. We're not the same people we were when we met. Thing is, do we have a future together? I always thought yes, never questioned it, but you've made me do that, and now that I feel I've finally heard how strongly you have been feeling, I will consider separating as an option if that's what you want. You're right. We are going into a new chapter. Who knows how long either of us has left. Ten years? Twenty? Muddling along, as I've always been OK with, probably isn't enough. It would be a half-hearted way of living the rest of our lives. We have to make the right choices and make the most of the time we have left, and whether that's together or apart, we must decide.'

'You've changed your tune.'

'Only through finally listening to you. I'm sorry I haven't before.'

Bluff called. Mine, I thought as we drove home.

*

There was a private message from Tom on Facebook when I got home.

'In answer to your question about how I spend my days. Every day is different. As you know, I am in between countries at the moment. This week, spent time with solicitors (boring). The sale of Mum's property is almost through. Lot of paperwork. Final clearing of her house (sad). I spent too much time looking at old photos. Other days, I eat out with friends. I do some photography for relief from endless admin. Some days I go looking at exhibitions to see what's new. I spend a lot of time having fantasies about what I'd like to do with you, to you, have you do to me (nice).'

Hmm. What friends? I wondered.

'Too general,' I wrote back. 'Who are the friends? What do they do?' I restrained myself from asking, are these friends female? Even though I'd been out of the dating game for decades, I still knew not to be too inquisitive about other women.

34

Cait

Matt woke me. He was up and dressed and had brought me a cup of tea. He had a sheet of paper in his hand. He went round to his side of the bed and sat down. 'I thought we could do the questionnaire before I go,' he said.

'What, *now*?' I asked. He'd made plans to meet up with a couple of old friends from his university days and was off hiking for the weekend in Cornwall.

'Well, our next session is on Monday evening and I'm not sure what time I'll get back.'

'She's a counsellor, not a headmistress. She's not going to tell us off if we don't do it.'

Matt looked puzzled. 'It was you who wanted to do this counselling, Cait, and now you're resisting.'

I sat up. 'OK. Let's have a look then.' I took the paper and glanced down. 'Favourite colour?'

'Blue,' said Matt. 'You?'

'Same. Favourite flower. Mine's a rose.'

'I like . . . oh god, I don't know the names of flowers – those tall things your mother used to grow.'

'Delphiniums. Favourite restaurant. Rustico. Yours?'

'Same. OK. What annoys you about your partner?'

'Nagging.'

'I do not nag.'

Matt laughed. 'OK. What annoys you about me?'

'When you wake me up with a questionnaire first thing in the morning.' Matt laughed again. He was being very jolly. 'People who are in a good mood before ten a.m.,' I added.

'Oh dear, still not sleeping well?'

'No.'

'Might be worth mentioning to Gina. She may be able to help. Anything else annoy you?'

'The way you twitch your foot when watching TV.'

'I do not twitch my feet.'

'You do.'

'OK, moving swiftly on,' Matt said as I sipped tea. 'What makes you happy?'

'I'd say our family being together. For both of us.'

'It's true, I do love those times,' said Matt. 'You can't beat the bubble of family, but I also like seeing the boys separately, quality time with each of them; otherwise all the old competitiveness comes out when they're together and it can end up like a battleground.'

'Really? Like when?'

'Last Christmas when Sam was over and we played Twister. I swear the boys almost came to blows. I think Jed feels that Sam has outshone him and he needs to prove himself.'

'OK. What else?'

'How do you like to be kissed?' I continued.

'You go first.'

'I like tender and passionate, anything but those cold dry kisses you give sometimes.'

'Cold dry kisses? That's harsh, Cait.'

'Sometimes you kiss me goodbye in the same way you'd kiss an old aunt.'

'I do not.'

'You do. Like it's an obligation rather than there being any real feeling.'

'Really? I had no idea you felt like that, or that I did that.' He looked upset.

'Well, as you said, if we're to move forward we need to be honest. What would you say?'

'I've never really thought about it until now. Er . . . tenderly, deeply, it depends on where we are, you know – in the sitting room or in bed.'

I glanced back at the questions. 'What turns you off sexually? I'd like to know. My answer would be a lack of feeling desired.'

'Feeling desired?'

'Yes. That's a big turn-on for most women – to know, or rather feel and see, that they turn their partner on. I see nothing in you but disinterest. No fire in the eye.'

'Oh, Cait, we've been together thirty years. Fire in the eye is for when you first get together.'

'Is it?'

'Yes. What we have is deeper and I think you're being hostile.'

'No I'm not, I'm just answering honestly. What are your three most important qualities in a good relationship? I'd say communication, trust, nurturing for you.'

'I can answer for myself, but nurturing? That doesn't sound very sexy.'

'It isn't, but it's what I think you want these days – looking after.'

'Meaning?'

'Someone to cook, shop for you, do your laundry.'

'Hey, come on. I'm doing what I can, especially now my back's better. We've agreed that can change. The house was your territory—'

'Which needs go unmet in your relationship? I'd say acknowledgement, appreciation, desire.'

Matt let out a deep sigh. 'I seem to remember that Gina said to have fun with this.'

'I know. She must be mad. What could we do to improve our relationship?'

'Stop doing questionnaires like this,' said Matt.

'You're the one who insisted we do it.'

'Only because Gina asked us to and we made a commitment to try and work with her.'

'OK. Next question. What would you like to change about your relationship?'

Matt turned and looked at me and sighed wearily. 'To go back to the days when we didn't have to do stuff like this. Sorry, it was a bad idea, and especially first thing in the day. I am trying, you know I am but . . . I wish we could go back to the time when we didn't have to *work* on our relationship.'

I nodded. 'I know what you mean. Let's leave it for now. Maybe we can talk about it all more when we're with Gina.'

'I agree. I am sorry, Cait.'

'What for?'

'Everything. That we've come to this. That we're not working.'

'No, no, don't be. You know I'm grouchy in the morning. And what's the alternative? To go back to those silences when neither of us knows what the other is thinking?'

'I guess not. I don't know.' He sighed. 'I think you've been right about so many things, one of them being that both of us had started taking each other for granted.'

An hour later, he was gone. He'd been planning the trip for a while and I couldn't help but feel slightly miffed that he hadn't considered a weekend away with me, not for a moment, especially as it was so close to our wedding anniversary. *But then, why would he?* I told myself. He probably needs time away from old misery me; it would probably do him good.

*

I went downstairs to find bags and rucksacks in the hall and Jed and Martin finishing off toast and tea in the kitchen.

'What's happening?' I asked. 'Are you going somewhere?'

Jed came and put his arm around me. 'We are! Grandpa's offered us his house so we're heading over there today.'

'Today? Why didn't you tell me?'

'I just did.'

'It's a bit sudden.' Matt and I had discussed it but I didn't think anyone else had.

'Not really. We've been chatting about it for weeks and then last night thought, why hang about? See, we need our space, Mum,' Jed said, 'and I can see we're cramping your style here.' He glanced over at Martin and sniggered. No doubt a reference to the day they found me with my head in Matt's groin. 'It's the perfect solution until we get sorted.'

'Sorted how?'

'Decide if we want to carry on travelling or settle down. While we do, Grandpa's house is standing empty, and he's more than happy that we'll be there for a while or until it sells.'

'Sells?'

'Yes. He's putting it on the market.'

'He is? So, he's decided to stay with us?' I said.

Martin and Jed exchanged glances. 'Er . . . best let him fill you in on his plans. But isn't it great? Everyone's happy. We won't be getting in your way, messing up your kitchen, Grandpa will have peace of mind knowing his house is occupied, and we'll have our very own home for a bit. A win-win all round eh?'

'Makes sense I guess.'

An hour later, they were gone.

*

When I came down to make lunch I saw that there was a suitcase in the hall. I went through to the kitchen and found Dad sitting at the island.

'What's going on?' I asked.

'Ah yes, Cait. I've been meaning to have a word, but you're always out at one of your classes or away with your friends.'

'Are you going somewhere?'

Dad smiled happily. 'I am.'

'Back to your house with the boys? But they've just left.'

'Lord no. Now, don't take this the wrong way, love, but – thing is – I need my own space and a bit of quiet, and Lorna has come up with a solution. She's offered me part of her house. I've seen the plans and it looks perfect and it will save her looking for lodgers or having strangers there when the time comes.'

'Oh but . . . yes, I knew of her plans, but haven't you been happy here?'

'Yes. No. Thing is, love, I didn't realize how much I'd got used to living on my own. I need my own kitchen, my own sitting room and, more than that, my independence. Not that I haven't appreciated being here. I have, and it's made me realize that I like a bit of company now and then, but not full time. I like it over at Lorna's. She'll be around in the background and I think she'd like to know someone's nearby too, which I will be. Plus, there are her dogs. Walking Otto and Angus has reminded me what a joy dogs are, the perfect company. I don't want the responsibility of owning my own, not at my age. I wouldn't want them to end up in a rescue centre if I pop my clogs, but Lorna said I can borrow hers any time I like, and I do like. Same breed as my old Brandy.'

'But the building work hasn't been done yet.'

'I know. Plan is, I'll stay on her side while the building on my side is completed. Shouldn't be long now, and you know that place, the house is huge, she'll hardly know I'm there. Lorna and I have a lot in common. We've both lost our partners and she doesn't want to replace Alistair. Plus, there's her beautiful garden to spend time in and I could help her with a bit of pruning. She also said I can have one of the old sheds out there, do a bit of hammering when I fancy. And you're not far away. What do you think?'

I smiled at him. 'I guess it makes sense, Dad, and you were always happiest pottering in your shed with a dog getting in your way. I think it will be great, really.' I meant it too. I could just envisage him there and the image made me glad.

Dad looked at me tenderly. 'But how about you, Cait?'

'What about me?'

'You seem restless. I've only been here a short time, but long enough to see when my daughter's struggling with something. I don't think I've seen you relax once since I've been here.'

I shrugged. 'I'm OK. Just not sure what to do with myself any more.'

'Cait, love, at your time of life you have to stop running and take stock. Recognize that you *can* stop. We spend so much of our lives striving. It starts straight after college – striving for the perfect job, to find the right partner, build a family, find the house and where you want to be in life. All that time on the treadmill, going somewhere, with something to achieve, but if you stop and look, I think you may find you're where you wanted to be and you've got a lot of what you were aiming for. You've had your career, had your family, you've got your home. You don't need to strive any more, so why not appreciate what you've got; enjoy your achievements. Maybe it's that time for you. What more do you want?'

I recalled that Tom had said something similar when we'd first met up. 'That's just it, Dad, I don't know.'

'How about you give yourself some time out? You don't always have to be doing things. Why not sit back and smell the roses for a change?'

'I'd have to grow some first.'

'I remember when I was about your age, one phase of my life had ended and the next not quite begun. Reaching sixty is a turning point for many. See it as a gift that you don't have to prove anything any more; you don't, nor does Matt. Rearrange a few things and start to enjoy your life with Matt now that the boys have grown and gone.'

'I have a fear that it's all over.'

'Not over, just beginning a chapter at a different kind of pace, but you have to let go and embrace that this is actually a new phase. Life is what you make it, Cait. Think about it, then create a different kind of existence, a bit slower maybe, but it can be just as fulfilling if you give it some thought.'

'You mean retirement?'

'I do. It doesn't have to mean the end, there are all sorts of things you can still do, but just stop for a bit and you might realize that there's no place to go because you're already where you were aiming to be. You can get off the treadmill. Learn to be, to be a human being instead of a human doing.'

'Food for thought, Dad.'

He kissed the top of my head.

An hour later, Lorna came to collect him and he was gone.

I noticed Yoda heading for the back door. 'Don't tell me that you're moving out too?'

Yoda looked at me with disdain, blinked his eyes and walked away. A moment later, I heard him go out through the cat flap.

*

After lunch, I joined my walking group on the canal in the rain and tried to take in everything that was happening. Everyone gone. That awful questionnaire. I wished I'd made my responses kinder. Matt considering going. Me thinking about Tom. I knew the ball was in my court with him. He'd made his proposal; I'd told him I wasn't ready. I thought about what Dad had said. Time for a new chapter. Would Tom be in it? Maybe it was time to go and find out. *I could do it this weekend*, I thought, *while Matt's away. Is it too late to invite him to meet up somewhere?* I wondered as the group trudged on, anorak hoods down, jeans splattered with mud.

When I got home, I took a deep breath and texted Tom. *Am alone for the weekend. Want to meet up? Cait.*

In the meantime, I cleaned. The kitchen is immaculate. The bathrooms are sparkling. The sitting room is tidy. The beds are made. The house is silent. Time for a list.

- Send Tom the 'get to know each other' questionnaire I was supposed to do with Matt.
- Write the list for Gina of all the household chores plus the admin that needs doing.
- Make up my mind who I want to be with for the rest of my life.

I checked to see if Matt had sent a text to say he'd arrived and met up with his friends. He hadn't.

I texted Jed to see if he'd settled in. No reply.

I called Lorna's to speak to Dad and check he'd got everything he needed. No reply.

I checked to see if Tom had replied. He hadn't.

What was it Churchill said once? I asked myself as I took a bottle of wine out of the fridge. Bugger the lot of them, that was it. *Yeah, I'm right with you, Winston.*

35

Cait

The next day, I was in a taxi on my way to meet Tom in London. He'd replied late last night, delighted that I'd decided to go and see him. I was feeling very apprehensive as the cab drove through the streets towards Barnes, partly because of the fact that I'd got no sleep due to the butterflies in my stomach, and partly because I'd got up early to buff, wax and oil every inch of me, just in case . . . I felt like a teenager about to have sex for the first time. How would it be? Although there was a time I knew every inch of Tom's body and how he liked to be touched, that was a long time ago. Matt was the only man I'd had sex with in over thirty years and we'd given up on each other. I was out of practice. Would Tom still find me attractive when he saw me naked? Would I remember what went where? Of course I would. *Breathe, Cait, relax.* I reminded myself that it wasn't just about sex, though I had no doubt that was on the agenda today, it was about chemistry and connection and Tom and I had that and more. All the same, I felt tense, caught between anticipation of what could be wonderful and anxiety about taking the plunge into something I might not be able to return from.

'I've brought us a lunch from the deli,' Tom said when he opened the door and ushered me through to a beautiful sitting room with high ceilings and a tall bay window overlooking a courtyard garden full of pots of red geraniums.

'Very elegant,' I said as I looked around at the tasteful pale grey and ivory furnishings in the room.

'It suits my purpose for now.'

'Where's your friend?'

'Out of town visiting his kids,' he said as he went over to an ice bucket where there was a bottle of champagne on ice. He popped the cork and poured two glasses. 'To celebrate you being here.'

I drank the glass in seconds to quell my nerves and immediately felt tipsy. Tom set out the food – cheeses, artichokes, sun-dried tomatoes and olives – but when he'd filled our plates and we'd sat down, neither of us ate much. The air felt charged with sexual tension. We both knew why I was there.

'I got your questionnaire,' Tom said as he topped up my glass. 'Where did you find that?'

'Online,' I lied. 'I thought it would give us a good opportunity to get to know each other better.'

Tom smiled. 'I can think of more pleasurable ways,' he said, but he got up from the table and went to fetch his laptop while I gulped down another slug of champagne at the insinuation.

Tom sat back at the table and began to read from the screen of his computer. 'OK. Let's go. What's your favourite colour? The colour of your eyes.' I groaned. 'I know. Sorry. Corny. Next. What's your favourite flower? You. You are my favourite English rose.'

'You're on a roll of cheesiness here,' I said, but I was glad for the questionnaire because it broke the ice and put us more at ease with each other.

'Favourite restaurant?' Tom continued. 'So many. A fish place on the shores of Lake Como. A beach café in Thailand at sunset. I'm trying to make this as romantic as possible. Favourite food? Again too many. Where would you like to go on holiday? I would like to take you to my favourite place in Bali. A quiet and heavenly hideaway with views that will blow your mind. We had a few holidays when we were together, remember?'

I did. We'd hitch-hiked around the lakes once and, another time, we'd gone to the south of France with a bunch of Tom's friends. I remembered I'd wanted to go to Greece, just the two of us. Another time we'd gone to stay in Rye, with his friends again. I'd wanted to go to a festival on the Isle of Wight with Eve but, back in those days, Tom led, and I followed without question.

'What annoys me?' Tom continued. 'Fascists. Politicians. Narrow-mindedness. Queues! Don't get me started. What makes me happy? So many things. Being with the people I love. Having a project. Watching a sunset/sunrise with someone I love. Happiness is a state of mind though, isn't it? Can it be manufactured? Hearing from you makes me happy. Ah, now, this a good one. How do I like to be kissed? Tenderly, passionately, teasingly, erotically, softly, deeply. And where do you like to be kissed? Neck. All over, and again some. Are you listening, Cait? You look far away?'

'Just remembering the past,' I said. As I sat there with Tom, so many memories were flooding back, memories I'd conveniently forgotten until now. We'd always eaten where he felt like eating, gone to the exhibitions he'd elected to see, spent time with his friends; always done what he'd wanted to do. He had been Mr Cool, and whatever or whoever he deemed worthy of attention had immediately become cool too. In fact, he had been utterly selfish, his wants and needs always first, but I'd never let myself acknowledge that because, along with everything else that he'd desired, he'd selected me and that had given me credibility.

'What might make me happier? If you shared my life, Cait. Possibilities make me happy. Anticipation.' He reached out and took my hand and stroked my thumb as he continued reading the questions. 'What turns you on sexually?' He looked straight at me. 'I challenge you to find out.'

I laughed, probably a tad hysterically. I was beginning to doubt why I'd come. Had he changed from the selfish charmer who always got his way? Does a leopard ever change its spots? He'd appeared back in my life and made his proposal with no thought for the disruption he'd cause, the hurt he'd cause to Matt. My husband was just an obstacle in his way to be brushed aside as he took what he wanted. It also occurred to me that he'd answered the questions, but not appeared in the slightest bit interested in what my replies might have been, assuming that either he already knew the answers or that my replies were insignificant, just as they had been so long ago. Tom clicked his fingers, people jumped around him. Was I prepared to do that for the rest of my life, all for a few sessions of steamy sex?

'Not hungry?' Tom asked as he looked at my plate of barely touched food.

'Not really.' I stood and began to help clear, but he took the dishes and placed them back on the table. He pulled me to him so that I could feel his body against me. 'So why are you here, Cait Langham?' He looked deep into my eyes; as I felt the sweet stab of desire, any doubts receded. *Tom Lewis was and is addictive and irresistible stuff*, I thought as he led me over to the sofa.

We sat, then he gently pushed me back and moved to lie alongside me. I felt consumed with longing for him. I wanted him as much as he wanted me. I wanted to touch him, have him caress me, possess me, put his mouth on mine and to lose myself in him. He began to stroke my neck, shoulders, the curve of my hips, my thighs, all the time staring into my eyes. It felt deliciously erotic and oh so familiar; I was back, twenty years old, vulnerable, helpless to refuse him. I put my hand up and traced his cheek, his jaw line and, in doing so, caught sight of my wedding ring. I suddenly froze. I wasn't that twenty year old any more, free, single: I was married to Matt.

'What is it?' Tom asked as I abruptly sat up.

'I'm sorry, I can't do this. We have to stop before we go further.'

Tom groaned in frustration. 'Nooooo. Cait, then why have you come?'

'I . . .' I couldn't explain. 'I don't know.'

Tom sat up next to me. 'I can't go on like this. Either we see this through or we don't.'

I took a deep breath. 'I . . . I need to think.' We were so close, hands almost touching, thigh next to thigh. It would be so easy to lie back and lose myself in what we'd started, but to continue would come at a price and I was beginning to feel that it wasn't one I was prepared to pay. Tom said he had feelings for me, but how long would they last? There would never be any certainty with him. He'd texted, then appeared in Bath and just assumed I would meet him – and I had. Then there was the call from Bristol: he'd summoned me, I had gone. I could suddenly envisage a life with him. He'd play the tune, I would dance, but is that what I really wanted? And would he tire of me if a better offer came along? He'd always craved experience and adventure and, as he'd said, us being together could be the mother of adventures, but what if another quest or challenge came along, beckoned, promised more than I could give? I had to leave. I had too much to lose if I stayed.

Tom reached over, took my hand and looked at me, trying to gauge what was happening.

'I'm so sorry, Tom.' The white doves had gone, the violins were silent, there were no more rose petals falling from the sky. It was time to say goodbye.

'You're going to tell me that you're staying with Matt, aren't you?'

'I am.'

'So why come? Put me through this?'

'I wasn't sure. It hasn't been easy for me either.'

Tom sighed heavily. 'Is there nothing I can say that will persuade you?'

'There isn't. I've been flattered by the offer you made me, truly, but it was never going to happen. I realize that now.'

'Will you tell Matt about me or have you already?'

'When the time is right, I might tell him I met up with an old friend, and we could stay in touch maybe.'

'We could,' he said.

'Liar.' I got up to go. 'I wish you well, Tom, I really do, and I hope you find a companion who you can go sailing into a merry old age with, preferably one who's not married.'

He smiled, but the look in his eyes was sad.

When he called me a cab, he didn't come down to the street to see me off, just gave me one last hug at his door. 'If you ever change your mind, you know where I am,' he said.

'I do,' I said.

When I boarded the train at Paddington and found a seat, I felt an enormous sense of relief and closure. In my life, my relationship history, Tom had always been the one who got away, but this time, it was me who'd left. I had no regrets.

36

Cait

M att came through the front door on Monday around midday looking tanned and glowing with health. He strode into the kitchen and gave me a big hug, which I returned; I was genuinely pleased to see him.

'So it went well?'

'Brilliant,' he replied. 'So good to catch up with the lads and be out there in the open air. We all agreed we should keep it up – maybe the Lake District next time. How was your weekend?'

'Oh good, fine,' I said, and hoped he wouldn't press me. He didn't. He got out his phone to show photos he'd taken along the way. I was relieved that he was so fired up from the trip that he didn't notice the sackcloth I was wearing, nor the neon sign that I was sure was over my head saying: your wife's been off with another man.

'And tonight's our date night, isn't it?'

'It is.'

'I'm looking forward to it. Right. Off for a shower,' he

said, and disappeared upstairs with his rucksack. I heard him singing in the bathroom, a sound I hadn't heard for many a year.

Well, there it is, I thought. *Normal life resumed.*

*

We opted for a meal out for our date and I decided to take Gina's advice and spend more time than usual getting ready. I bathed, applied Chanel No. 5 and dressed in a simple white summer dress. I felt optimistic about our evening, more determined than ever to get our relationship back on course

'Wow. You look lovely,' said Matt when I came down the stairs. I'd chosen to wear a pair of shoes with a small kitten heel that I'd hardly worn. They pinched a bit, but it wouldn't matter because we planned to park near the restaurant.

I could see Matt had made an effort too, and was wearing a smart jacket. He looked great after his weekend away and I could see that his efforts to lose weight were paying off.

'So do you,' I said.

He looked pleased. 'Change from the dressing gown. I'll drive.'

We set off in a good mood, and already I was mentally thanking Gina for her advice. This was just what we needed. A night out together away from the house. 'Park near the sports centre. There's always space there.'

'OK,' said Matt, and set off in the direction I'd instructed. When we got to the turn-off to take us to the car park, we saw that there were No Entry signs all over the road.

'Oh no. We can't get through.'

'No matter,' said Matt. 'I'll drive round to Laura Place.'

When we got to Laura Place, there wasn't one free space. Ten minutes later, we were still driving around.

'What about the cricket ground?'

'Good idea,' said Matt, and we headed there and into the car park, but again there was no room. Matt rolled his window down to speak to a man walking away from his car. 'Is there something on this evening?'

The man nodded. 'Rugby. Home game.'

'No wonder,' I said. 'We should have checked.'

'We could try Widcombe and walk through the station,' Matt said as we drove away from the cricket ground. 'We'll never get a space in town.'

'I don't think we have any choice. We should have taken Gina's advice and got a taxi.'

We drove up to Widcombe; luckily a car was just driving away from the tiny car park there, so we drove in swiftly.

We walked down to the restaurant, but there was a 'Closed For a Private Function' notice on the door.

'Oh *no*,' I said. 'It's booked.'

'*No*. Never mind,' said Matt. 'Come on. We can go to that French place at the top of town.'

'Good idea.'

We made our way up to the other end of town, by which time my feet were beginning to hurt in my new shoes. When we got there, we found it was no longer a French place. It was a pizza place.

'I'm not in the mood for pizza. We could have that at home.'

'Lebanese?' Matt said. 'There's a place down in Southgate.'

We turned around and headed back the way we'd just come. By this time, I was beginning to feel hungry and my feet were killing me.

When we got there, a young man with a beard, his hair coiled into a bun at the back of his head, came forward to greet us. 'Do you have a booking?'

'On a Monday night?' Matt asked. 'I wouldn't have thought we'd need one.'

The man gestured to the restaurant full of happy diners, not one empty table in sight. 'We have a new chef and special offer on this week. We're booked solid every night.'

'When is your first available table?'

'Next Tuesday.'

'Don't you do two sittings?' Matt persisted.

The man shook his head. 'I'm very sorry.'

Back out on the pavement, I looked around. 'What do you suggest?'

'There are hundreds of places in Bath. Rustico? They do great food.'

'But that's at the top of town where we've just come from. I'm not walking all the way back up there again – my feet are killing me. We really ought to have checked or booked.'

'I thought you would. You do usually.'

'Or you could have. Why would you assume I would do it?'

'Because you always do,' Matt replied. 'Look, let's not argue. What do you want to do?'

'Go somewhere back up near the car; there are a couple of pubs up there that do food. My feet are hurting.'

At that moment, the skies opened and it started to pour. Neither of us had an umbrella so we darted into the nearest shop entrance to shelter.

'So how's it going for you so far?' I asked.

He rolled his eyes. 'Had better nights. Let's just get in

somewhere dry. Shall we make a run for it? Or wait till it's dry?'

'Wait till it's dry.'

We waited a few minutes, then a few more. 'I think we're going to have to go,' I said after another five. 'It looks like this rain is in for the night.'

We set off into the night and were back at the car in ten minutes. Both of us were soaked through to the skin.

'Takeaway?' Matt asked once we'd got into the car.

'Can't say I'm in the mood any more.' My hair was flattened against my head, with rivulets of water dripping down my nose and chin. 'And what's that on the window?'

'I don't believe it!' said Matt. 'A parking ticket. At this time of night? We were only five minutes over, then it's the free time.'

'That's when the wardens get people,' I said.

Matt let out a heavy sigh. 'All in all, a night to remember.'

'For all the wrong reasons. I am sorry, Matt.'

'I'm sorry too. I feel I've let you down.'

I reached for his hand. 'It doesn't matter. Don't blame yourself, it takes two.'

Matt looked surprised that I was making light of it, but I wasn't going to let one failed date get in the way of making things work again.

'Guess we're a bit out of practice,' said Matt. 'I'll make it up to you. I promise.'

I smiled. 'I'll hold you to that.'

We drove home in our wet clothes, then had poached eggs on toast and a cup of tea.

'Romantic huh?' said Matt before he retired to watch the news.

'As you said at Gina's, as long as we're together, any place is romantic.'

'Yes, indeed,' Matt said, but he looked puzzled.

I went up to my study and laptop and watched a fascinating clip about a man interviewing a guinea pig who appeared to be able to talk back. Next was a quiz with fifty questions about books to discover if I was a literary genius. Turned out I was. Did the quiz again and purposely answered the questions wrongly. Turned out I was still a literary genius. Then I did one last questionnaire to find out what kind of music will be played at my funeral. I got 'Stairway to Heaven'. It's amazing what you can discover on Facebook.

37

Cait

Catalogues received in the post:
- Hotter shoes for comfortable feet.
- Easy Living: with stairlifts, mobility scooters and incontinence pads.

OK. Who sent this? What a cheek, I thought, *although . . . oh, there's some great stuff in here. Where's my credit card?*

Items purchased:
- Automatic tweezers for chin hair.
- Insulated gel shoes to relieve the pain of corns and calluses.
- Magnetic bracelet for arthritis.
- Eye cream for puffy eyes.
- Bicarbonate of soda ear drops to remove ear wax.

And that just about sums up my age, I thought as I looked at the list of what I'd bought. *In thirty years, I've gone from leg warmers for keep fit to toe spreaders for bunions.*

*

'So how did the date go last week?' Gina asked us once we were seated and her dog had humped Matt's leg in greeting. It was our second session with her and I felt slightly apprehensive. Would she notice anything different about me? Would she be able to see through me with her razor-sharp vision? Would she expose me for my betrayal with Tom?

Matt looked sheepish. 'Not great,' he said, and filled her in on the evening.

She burst out laughing which took me by surprise. I thought she would ask, 'And how did you both feel about that?'

'I hope that hasn't put you off,' she said. 'You're just a bit out of practice. Have you got another evening arranged?'

'No I—' I began.

'Don't let one disaster put you off. Don't give up before you've even got started. Maybe factor in that one of you looks into the reservations, etc. The other books a taxi. It was meant to be a night off for both of you.'

Matt nodded. 'We got that.'

'And the lists of chores?'

I handed it over to her. She glanced down the list. 'OK, twenty-two things listed. That's eleven each. OK?'

'OK,' we chorused back.

'If you find you are rubbish at one task, say so. Like one of you is a lousy ironer, you don't just drop it, you swap for something you can do better. Now, how did the questionnaire go?'

'Not much better than the date,' I said. 'We did it before Matt went off hiking.'

'You went hiking?' Gina asked.

'I did. It was fantastic, reminded me of how much I used to enjoy it.'

'Good, and what did you do, Cait?'

I felt myself blush. 'I was home alone, so caught up on a few jobs.'

'And was that OK?' asked Eagle Eyes.

'Yes, but I was glad when Matt came back and, er, wished we'd done the questionnaire when we had more time. I felt we rushed through it and we didn't seem to get the answers right.' I hoped that she didn't notice I was attempting to change the subject away from what I did at the weekend.

'Right?'

'The same.'

'And I felt Cait was hostile, as if she was using the questions as an opportunity to make me feel bad.'

'And did you feel bad, Matt?'

'Yes, yes I did.'

'Cait, did you feel hostile?'

'I . . . Maybe but I . . .'

'Is being right an important factor for both of you in your relationship?'

'Possibly,' said Matt, 'but I feel increasingly unable to do anything right in Cait's eyes and aware just how far we've grown apart, like we no longer know what the other one wants or needs or how they like to be kissed.'

I cursed myself for not having considered the answers more at the time. I wanted to say, no, hey, I've come to my senses. I know I want to stay with Matt now. I want to make it work, but I knew I couldn't without exposing exactly what had given me a change of heart.

'We can deal with that more later,' said Gina. 'In the

meantime, let's talk about what you like or don't like about each other, from the trivial to the deeper. Let's get it all out: good, bad, small complaints through to the bigger issues. I like her eyebrows, for example, or I like the way she cares for our children.'

'Right,' said Matt.

'Matt, why don't you start?'

'I liked Cait because she stood out in a crowd. I was drawn to her, and not just because she looked great. It felt right, meant to be, and when we got together, I felt like I became my best person when I was with her.'

'Really?' I said. 'That's nice.'

'But as I said last time, I don't like how she seems angry with me most of the time these days. I don't like the way she has shut me out of her life. I don't like how I see myself when she's around. I didn't like how she got upset when I wasn't dressed first thing in the morning – it's not like I had to go anywhere. I don't like the way she puts the milk in before the tea—'

'You never said. Why didn't you say?'

'Cait, let him finish,' said Gina.

'I don't like the way she turns away from me in bed and almost seems repelled by me being close to her. That's about it.'

'And is any of this rectifiable, Matt?'

He smiled. 'Milk in the tea would be easy enough. Tea first, milk after.'

Gina smiled back at him. 'Anything else?'

'I don't know. Only she can tell you that.'

'You seem to be putting a lot onto Cait's behaviour towards you, Matt. Do you think there's any reason she feels irritated with you?'

'Lots of reasons. I've let her down. She prefers the company of her friends. I know I haven't been a lot of fun lately, but I have been taking steps to change that.'

'Cait? Would you like to say anything now?'

'I'm not irritated with you all of the time. I guess I let petty resentments build up, but I think we're addressing that.'

'Resentment can happen when things aren't expressed,' said Gina. 'And it can also happen when there's been a loss. When someone can't deal with the intensity of grief, it is common for the psyche to choose an emotion it does understand and can deal with and, in your case, that could be irritation or even hostility, and it can sometimes, often, be directed to those near and dear to you.'

'So are you saying I'm irritated with Matt because I haven't grieved about losing Mum and Eve? Surely it can't be that simple?'

Gina reached out and put her hand on my arm. 'That might have felt safer than dealing with deeper feelings that you're not ready to address. Grief is a sensitive, prickly and complex area. I'm saying it's a possibility that, in not having dealt with it, you may have taken things out on Matt, he being the closest person to you. Only you will be able to tell when you're ready to deal with these feelings, and I don't want to press you but . . . maybe have a think about it, and when you're ready, think about the people you've lost if you feel able. For now, let's concentrate on what's happening between you and Matt. You were saying?'

'I don't know where he goes any more or what he's working on.' I turned to Matt. 'You used to tell me in the early days, share it all.'

'I didn't think you were interested in my work any more,'

said Matt, 'and lately, I didn't want to get your hopes up when nothing's definite.'

'So you are working on something?' I asked.

Matt looked at Gina. 'I think it's important to say if you are,' she said.

'*You* never discuss what you're working on with me,' Matt said.

'Only because it's not gone well and I didn't think you needed more bad news. To tell the truth, I'm not even sure I want to write any more, or can, and if I don't do that, what else can I do?'

'I could help,' Matt said. 'You always used to come to me to discuss ideas.'

'So you're both working on things that the other knows nothing about?' asked Gina.

'Yes,' said Matt.

'Not any more,' I said. 'I've given up.'

'Well, it sounds as if you'll have lots to talk about on your next date. In fact, I'm going to ask that you leave that until then. Let's go back to your list of likes, Matt?'

'I like the way she looks. I like her sense of humour, though it's been somewhat absent lately. I love her kindness and tender heart. I like her company when she's in a good mood. I like her loyalty to our sons and me. I like her cooking, in the main.'

I inwardly winced at the word loyalty.

'You like my cooking, *in the main*?' I asked.

'You always do scrambled eggs too dry.'

'So you make them.'

'I intend to now I have time,' Matt replied.

'OK, how about you, Cait?'

'Well, as I said in our first session, what I first liked about Matt was that he seemed so together in a time when a lot of us were drifting. He was attractive, but it was more than that: he had purpose, plans, goals. I wanted to be with him and part of that. What I don't like is that he seems to have lost that and seems at sea.'

'That's because I am, but that's changing, and you might have noticed that I do get dressed in the morning now.'

'Can you acknowledge that, Cait?'

'Yes, I can. I had noticed. And I think the dressing-gown issue was symbolic of what I don't like, as if it typifies how he'd given up.'

'But you just said it was you who'd given up,' said Gina.

'I . . .' God, she was right. I felt myself squirming. 'Are you saying what's happened to Matt and me is all my fault?'

'Not at all, Cait,' said Gina. 'In any relationship, each person plays their part in the dynamic, and it's often unspoken but mutually agreed. Anything else, Cait? No matter how trivial.'

'I don't like it when you nick the duvet.'

'I don . . . sorry . . . Your turn,' said Matt.

'I don't like it when you don't communicate with me. I don't like what's become of us, and that maybe you've given up on the possibility of us being happier.'

'Have you given up on that, Matt?' Gina asked.

'Not completely,' he replied.

'And what else do you like about Matt?' asked Gina.

I turned to him. 'Your kind heart, the fact you're a gentleman, that I can trust you; you used to make me laugh; your hard work over the years looking after all of us.' I suddenly felt tearful. Matt was a good man. It was unfair to have even considered leaving him, or to have blamed him for my unhappiness.

'What is it, Cait? Can you say?' Gina asked.

'I was just thinking what a decent man Matt is. Maybe it's me. My restlessness causing him to suffer.'

Matt looked at me tenderly. 'As Gina said, it takes two. Don't blame yourself. I'm here, aren't I? Trying to make things work, and yes, it was you pushing for counselling, but I recognize my part in what you call our stale marriage too.'

'See, and now you're being decent again.' I thought about Tom, the fact I'd seen him behind Matt's back, trying to recapture someone I no longer was. 'There's a lot I like about you, Matt. I just . . .'

Matt finished my sentence. '. . . wonder if it's too late and we've outgrown each other.'

'In a lifetime,' said Gina, 'a person can have many marriages, all while married to the same person. A good marriage, a passionate marriage, a stale marriage, a turbulent marriage, a marriage of minds and friendship, marriage when you're together, a marriage when you're apart; it can all go on over a long period of time within the same relationship. It keeps changing and it doesn't necessarily mean that you've outgrown each other, just gone into a different phase.'

'But what if the phases are mismatched and you don't want to be in the phase your partner's in?' I asked.

'That's where communication comes in. If you can reconnect with what's behind all the changes, find that thing that never changes, then you can decide if you're going to stay with each other.'

'And what is that thing that never changes?' asked Matt.

'Love,' said Gina. 'That's what it comes down to in the

end. Do you still love each other? Because if you do, you can ride any passing storm or stale phase.'

Matt and I looked at each other. The expression in his eyes was so deeply sad, it made my heart twist. *Do I still love you?* I asked myself. I cared. I was fond of him, and loved him in a way that had changed over the years. Was I *in* love with him? That was a different question altogether. Although I'd decided not to have an affair with Tom, it hadn't magically made everything right with Matt. We still had a long way to go to get back to the familiar ease we once had.

'Is there anything rectifiable?' asked Gina. 'Apart from how you make the tea and scrambled eggs?'

'I hope so,' I replied. 'If we start talking, I mean really talking and listening to each other about how we feel, I think it would help.'

'Good,' said Gina. 'So – a second date, and this time fill each other in on what you've both been working on.'

38

Cait

The following evening, the restaurant was booked. We got a cab.

We went back to the Lebanese place and inside was buzzing with people.

After we'd given our orders for a mezze to share and got a glass of wine, I sat back. 'So – do you want to go first or should I?'

'Let's toss for it,' Matt replied. We tossed a coin, I won.

'Over to you.'

'OK. An old colleague, Bruce Patterson, asked if I could come up with some ideas for a programme series for people our age. A look at how to make the most of the next chapter, how to embrace life and not give in to a dull old age.'

'But, Matt, that sounds wonderful. Why didn't you tell me?'

Matt shrugged. 'Because it's one of those "maybe" projects. If Bruce likes what I come up with, he'd still have to pitch it, and you know how hard it is to get anything made these days. I didn't want to raise your hopes then let you down again.'

I reached out and took his hand. 'I'm tougher than you think. So what have you come up with?'

'To approach the subject from different angles: the physical, nutritional, mental, emotional and even spiritual.'

'What Debs would call a holistic approach,' I said.

'Exactly.'

'I love it. I'd watch it. Where are you up to so far?'

'I've been working on the programme to do with the physical approach and all that entails. Keeping fit is so important at any age, but particularly in later life.'

'Ah, so that explains your newfound interest in the gym and disappearing off for walks instead of taking the car.'

'And getting back into hiking. Partly research, partly I realized I could do with getting fit myself. Now what about you?'

'Zilch. I had a mad idea to write a book about a fairy who'd lost her way. A tooth fairy who'd run out of money to put under the kids' pillows, so she turned to drink.'

Matt laughed. 'Sounds good, could be funny.'

'It's not, it's rubbish. The last version I wrote was an adult-only version and the fairy annihilates everyone including herself. I don't think I am a writer after all. I get to chapter three and want to kill my characters.'

Matt laughed again. 'Finding it tough?'

'I just don't know what's me any more. I think the writing appealed as a way to escape into other worlds, but maybe, as Gina said, that was a reaction to Mum and Eve dying.'

'How so?"

'Create a new self, Cait the writer who lives in another

world. Anything to avoid living in the real one and an excuse to hide away upstairs.'

'Is it so bad?'

I shrugged. 'I don't know what I really want to do. I mean, it's the same for you. Time to retire? But what does that mean?'

'I'm finding out. When I first lost my job, it felt like my life was over, the end, but lately, I'm starting to see that it could be the beginning of something.'

'Dad said something interesting to me before he moved out. He said if I stopped, I might realize that there's no place to go because I'm already where I was aiming to be. It's not that life is over, but maybe one part of my life is and, as yet, I don't have a clue what's next.'

'I feel exactly the same,' he said. 'Maybe we could find out together.'

'I'd like that, Matt.' I meant it too.

Matt looked touched. 'We could research this retirement business together, partly for the TV series but also, partly for us. We could be the guinea pigs – look at what's on offer, then we can decide if that's what we want. Travel, learn new skills, but without the pressure of having to make money from them.'

'Great idea. I could help. We could do all the things you suggested. And I'm sorry I've been a pain lately and made you feel like you couldn't do anything right.'

'I'm sorry too, that I've been so grumpy and shut down.'

'Onwards,' I said. 'I have a feeling the worst is over.'

'Me too,' said Matt and looked at me tenderly. 'I really would like to make things work.'

'Me too. We will. So . . . what's next after the physical approach?'

'Just starting to look at the emotional. The importance of staying connected, not becoming a recluse or giving up and hiding away, watching daytime TV.' He grinned sheepishly. 'The importance of talking.'

'Is that why you agreed to therapy?'

'No, not really, but it may help. It's for us too, but maybe we could bring looking at retirement into it – in fact Gina said as much.'

Cait nodded. 'I think a lot of people would like to hear that there's more that awaits you than old age—'

'And golf.'

'And mobility scooters. What you have sounds good, really good. I could make some lists for you.'

'You could.'

We spent the rest of the evening making plans. I could see that Matt was fired up by the idea and it felt good to share it with him.

'And perhaps an extra one looking at what's on offer in terms of accessories.'

'Ah, so you sent for the catalogues that arrived in the post?'

'I want to look at all the things that can aid old age.'

'Thank god for that. I thought maybe some cosmic force somewhere had picked up on the idea that we needed all that stuff.'

Matt laughed. 'No, it's all for research. How about Monday to Thursday we could work on the first four areas – not all day but for a few hours – and Friday we could look at alternative things to do.'

'A shared project, sounds like it could be fun. Dad might have something to contribute too.'

'And perhaps we should start advertising on the Airbnb site, now that your father and the boys have gone.'

'I agree.'

It was great to see Matt like this again, taking charge, motivated, more like the man I'd first met. We spent the rest of the evening chatting over plans and he appeared to value my input.

'Hey, that was fun,' I said as we left the restaurant.

Matt nodded. 'It was. Let's do it again soon.'

39

Cait

The change in Matt continued. He was up and dressed before me in the morning, doing more than his fair share of household tasks, out for walks, down the gym, researching various classes and courses, and telling me all about them with great enthusiasm. Curiously, the more he signed up for things, the more I found I was less and less inclined to go to my classes; in fact, I had a strange urge to put on my dressing gown and to stay in with my feet up, watching telly, instead of dashing out to Zumba or yoga or choir.

Matt and I had agreed to travel separately to the third session with Gina, because I'd been visiting Jed, and Matt had been down at the gym doing a t'ai chi class. However, my car broke down on the way over to Warminster and I had to wait for the road recovery men. When I texted Matt to let him know, he'd just arrived at Gina's, so he decided to have a session with her on his own.

He got home around the same time that I did, and got out of his car looking subdued. He let out a deep breath.

'You OK?' I asked. 'Has something happened?'

He nodded and let out a deep sigh. 'I had an *amazing* realization.'

'You did? Come inside then and tell me.'

We went in and sat in the kitchen.

'So what is it?'

Matt took another deep breath. He really did look over-come by some deep emotion, and I wondered what trauma Gina had unearthed. 'I realized that you're not Rex,' he said as he sat on a stool at the island. Rex had been his dog and constant companion from childhood until he left for college.

OK, I thought. *Not quite what I expected.* 'I'm not your dog?'

Matt seemed genuinely moved and close to tears. He always got that way when he talked about Rex. 'Yes. Remember I told you about him? I had him from when he was a puppy. He was my constant companion, went with me everywhere, slept at the end of my bed and always knew what I was thinking, if I was sad or happy.'

'OK. And how does that relate to me exactly?'

'Rex instinctively knew what I was thinking and feeling. I realized that I actually have to voice my thoughts to you; you're not telepathic in the way that he was.'

I had to try hard to resist the urge to laugh. I knew that would be the worst possible reaction and that Matt was having a sincere moment.

'Oh . . . OK. So does that mean you'll be talking to me more now?'

Matt nodded. 'Yes, absolutely, and I'm sorry that I expected you to just know what I was thinking and feeling.'

'As long as you don't get me a lead or call me for a walk, that's fine.'

Matt laughed. 'But it got me thinking, how about we get a dog again?'

'Oh, Matt, we can't, not at the moment. Animals cost money – vets' fees, food, kennels if we go away. There's too much uncertainty in our lives at the moment.'

Matt looked so disappointed that I almost changed my mind, but then he nodded. 'You're right as always. It's not a good time to make a commitment like that.'

'I am sorry, Matt.'

'Maybe later, when we're settled again.'

'Sure.'

'Oh, and Gina's given us some homework.'

'Another questionnaire?'

'No.'

'Another date?'

'Nope. We have to give each other a non-sexual massage. Twenty minutes each. It's to get us used to touching each other again.'

'Homework?'

'She wants us to get comfortable with each other physically.'

'I'm hopeless at massage.'

'Me too. She said to use our hands to explore and stroke each other, to trace each other's faces, necks, frames, right down to the tip of our toes with our fingers, but not the breasts or genital areas. We can stroke, rub, squeeze, but that's all. You up for that?'

'Guess so. How often?' I asked.

'Two or three times a week. Does that sound OK?'

'Can't do any harm.'

'We could try it tonight if you're not doing anything, and she said to try not to see it as a chore.'

'Gina was the one who used the word homework.'

'Fair point,' said Matt.

*

In the evening, Matt dimmed the lights in the bedroom and we stood there looking at each other. It felt odd and awkward.

'Who goes first?' I asked.

'I will,' said Matt. He stripped off and lay on the bed on his front. I climbed up next to him and ran my hands up his back.

'How's that?'

'Like you're tickling me. Needs more pressure.'

I pressed harder. 'Like that?'

'Hmm. Not really. Maybe try my shoulders.'

I attempted to knead in the way that masseurs did, but I was on my knees and leaning over him felt uncomfortable. 'We need a massage couch that we can get round if we're going to do this. This is clumsy. Maybe we should do it on the floor. How does it feel?'

'Like you're pinching me. Try gliding up with the palms of your hands.'

'OK but maybe we need oil,' I said as I tried using my palms then felt the right side of my back pull. 'Owwwwww.'

'What is it?' Matt asked and turned to look. 'Arghhhhh.'

'What is it?' I asked.

'I've cricked my neck.'

'And I've pulled my back.'

He turned over and lay on his back, and I lay back next to him and both of us started laughing.

'You OK?' I asked.

'Yeah. You?'

'Yes, but how about we do each other's feet to start with. Remember? You used to massage my feet when the kids were young. You were good at it.'

'I do, and you used to do mine. Let's go and watch telly and do that.'

We hobbled off the bed like a pair of geriatrics and made our way downstairs, where we put on the TV to watch the latest series of *House of Cards* on Netflix.

'Subtitles on or off?' Matt asked.

'On.'

Matt settled at one end of the sofa and I sat at the other and we took turns massaging each other's feet. It felt good, comfortable and familiar. *Maybe this is what love is*, I thought, *not the fireworks or intensity of passion, but something softer and safer.*

'It's a start,' Matt said when we'd finished.

'Not very arousing, though.'

'No, but it wasn't supposed to be, was it? It was just to get us back touching each other.'

'Job done. You still want to leave me?'

Matt squeezed my foot. 'Never, Cait. Relationships change, don't they? We can make it work again, and we still have a few sessions with Gina.'

I smiled back at him and felt a surge of affection. 'Cup of tea and a biscuit?'

'Please.'

*

Later that night, some devilish part of me couldn't resist a quick look on Tom's Facebook page. There were some new posts showing photos of him. I looked at the date. Yesterday. Hmm. Who'd tagged him in? I clicked through. A woman called Cici Williams. Hmm. My age, dark, attractive. They'd clearly had a day out at Regent's Park Zoo. I was pretty sure he'd sold the location to her as an adventure. Hmm. He hadn't wasted any time.

40

Matt

W e were making progress, Cait and I, I reflected as I got ready to go to the gym for a morning workout, and I was beginning to think we would make it through this rough patch. Much to my surprise, the counselling was helping. We were talking more and I wanted to make it work because I couldn't imagine life without her, even when she was being psycho-woman though she seemed to have calmed down lately.

I opened the front door to leave at the same time as Debs rang the doorbell.

'Oh hi. Cait's not here at the moment. She's gone to the supermarket.' Debs looked uncomfortable and didn't make eye contact. 'Is something the matter?'

She shifted on her feet. 'Possibly, er . . . could I come in?'

'Yes. Of course.' I held the door open for her and we went through to the kitchen.

'So what is it, Debs? Has something happened? Cait will be back in about an hour if you need to see her.'

'Actually, I know she's not here. It's you I want to talk to.'

'Me?'

Debs nodded.

'Is it about the spa brochure?'

'No. Nothing like that. It's . . .'

I waited for her to get out whatever it was.

'It's about you and Cait.'

'Me and Cait? What about us?'

'I . . . this is really difficult for me, Matt.'

'I can see that, but now you've got me worried. Has something happened to Cait?'

'No, I mean yes, not bad, or at least it might be—'

'Debs, whatever it is, please just come out with it. Is Cait all right?'

'Yes, she's fine, but there's something I feel you ought to know. I . . . I've been agonizing over this for ages, but last night I thought, no, Debs, you just have to go and tell Matt.'

'Tell Matt what?'

'Do you know a man called Tom Lewis?'

I felt a prickle of anxiety. 'I can't say I do. Why? Who is he?'

'He's someone Cait used to know when she was at university.'

'OK. And?'

'He got in touch with her recently.'

'OK. When recently?'

'A few months back.'

Warning bells were beginning to sound. 'And you're telling me this why?'

Debs squirmed. 'I . . . I thought you should know. I am sorry.'

'And why should I know? What's this old acquaintance got to do with anything?'

'He was more than an acquaintance, Matt. He was her boyfriend for a year.'

I cast my mind back. I knew Cait had had lovers before me, of course she had, but none that she was still in touch with, to my knowledge. 'I don't understand why you're here telling me this, Debs. An old boyfriend has been in touch with my wife. And what has that got to do with you precisely?' *And why hadn't Cait mentioned this to me herself?* I wondered.

She looked directly at me. 'Because I believe you deserve better, Matt. I know you're a good and kind man and I don't think Cait appreciates you.' She stepped forward and put her hand on my arm. I took a step back. I didn't like the way this was going and I wanted her to go.

'I think you need to think very carefully about what you're saying, Debs. Cait is supposed to be one of your best friends. Does she know you're here?'

'Of course not.'

'And what are you hoping to achieve by coming here behind her back?'

'I wanted to let you know that *I* am here for you, Matt. As I said, I don't think she appreciates what she might be losing.'

'Losing? Who said anything about anyone losing anything? Is she seeing this bloke? Is that what you're trying to tell me?'

Debs nodded. 'She is. Personally I think she's making a big mistake.'

'Mistake? What's been going on, for heaven's sake? Has she been having an affair?'

'I . . . I'm not sure what's gone on, but I know she's been seeing him.'

I felt a hot flicker of rage ignite deep within. I wanted to know more, but not from Debs, not like this. 'Debs, I don't know what your motives were for coming and telling me this, but it really is none of your business. It's between Cait and me.'

'Please don't tell her that I told you.'

'But you did and, just out of curiosity, how did you find out about this?'

'She told me. He's on her Facebook page. At first she said he was living abroad, but then she told Lorna and me that he was currently in the UK and that she'd seen him.'

I was finding it hard to take in. 'On her Facebook page? And she said she'd seen him?'

Debs nodded. 'I know. It's not fair on you.'

I felt sick. I wanted Debs to go but also needed to know what she knew. 'She might just have been seeing him as one would any old friend.' *Though that doesn't explain why she didn't tell me*, I thought.

Debs said nothing. Her silence spoke volumes.

'Cait confided in you?' Debs nodded again. 'And you've completely betrayed that trust.'

Debs looked shocked. 'Only because I thought you deserved to know.'

'It's for Cait to tell me, not someone who calls themselves a friend but who clearly isn't.' *Did she sleep with him? How far had it gone?* I wanted to know, desperately wanted to know, but wouldn't humiliate myself by asking.

'Hey. No need to be like that, Matt. I knew you'd be angry but I was trying to help.'

'I would say you've done more damage than given help. I think you should go. Now.'

Debs stepped closer to me and looked into my eyes. 'But, Matt, I see who you are. I see . . . I've felt . . . and I know you felt something too.'

I moved away. Oh god, one drink in a bar, a bit of careless flirting, and she'd got completely the wrong idea. 'No. *No*. It wasn't like that. I think you ought to leave, now, before you say or do anything you regret. Debs, out, now.' I went back into the hall and opened the front door for her.

She looked shocked by my reaction but began to leave. 'Please don't tell Cait.'

'Just shut the door behind you, will you?'

When she'd gone, I stood for a moment to steady myself, took a few deep breaths to calm the anger that had erupted deep inside. *Cait, what the hell have you done?* I asked myself.

I went up to her study and opened her laptop. I knew she kept all her passwords in a book in the right-hand drawer in her desk. They were easy to find and there were the log-in details for everything. A moment later, I'd got into her Facebook page. I scrolled down to find friends. She had 179. I scrolled down again and there he was. Tom Lewis. I clicked on his profile. A good-looking man. I wanted to smash his smiling face in. Bastard. I read a few of his posts but saw nothing from or to Cait. I pressed on messages and ah . . . there they were. I wasn't sure I wanted to read them. This was Cait's private business after all, and it might be completely innocent, might be a harmless flirtation with the past, just as mine had been with Debs. I cursed myself for that. But why else would Cait have been working and pressing so hard to get our relationship to work? One last attempt to revive our relationship? Or was it all a lead-up to her telling me it was over between us? No. I had to give her the benefit of the doubt. I owed her that much at least, and not to go prying into her messages like a jealous lover. Trouble was, I was a jealous lover, and what Deb had said had thrown me. In all the time we'd been together, I had never doubted Cait's fidelity – never had any cause to until now – and I felt furious.

By the time Cait returned home about an hour later, I'd marginally calmed down. I'd skipped going to the gym and given what Debs had told me a lot of thought. Although part of me wanted to confront Cait the moment she walked through the door, I wanted to check the facts. Debs might have got the wrong end of the stick, just as she had here today in thinking there was something between her and me. *So why hadn't Cait told me about this Tom?* I asked myself over and over again. Was that because there was or wasn't something to know? I had an idea of how to approach it.

'Cait?'

She dumped the shopping bags on the island. 'Yes, Matt.'

'I thought I'd join Facebook. Could you show me how to do it?'

She turned away and started putting away groceries. I couldn't see her face, gauge her reaction. 'Yes, course. It's easy. But why?'

'I never had time before but, as we've been discussing, in this chapter of our lives, it's important to keep up friendships. I thought it would be a way to stay in touch with old friends and maybe make some new.' As she turned back to me, I studied her face for any sign of panic. Cait had never been good at hiding what she was feeling, but she didn't appear flustered. I decided to push it a bit more. 'How do you find friends?'

'They find you mainly, and I can pass some of our mutual friends over to you. Not everyone uses it, though. You soon get used to who does and who doesn't.'

'And do you ever get people wanting to be your friend who you don't want?'

Cait laughed. 'All the time. God knows where they appear from, but there are ways round it. You can put privacy settings on so that not everyone can see your posts, or you can accept some people so as not to hurt their feelings then put them on a restricted list so that they don't see everything. It can really take you back to the playground – especially if someone unfriends you.'

'Maybe I won't bother.'

'No, you should. It's fun. People post all sorts of weird and wonderful things. I'll show you. Give me ten minutes to set it all up.'

'OK.'

She disappeared upstairs. A short time later, she called me. 'I can show you now if you like.'

I went up to find her in her study and sat next to her at her desk, where she proceeded to show me how her Facebook page worked. I didn't tell her I already knew because I'd registered a few years ago then deleted my profile because I never used it.

'And, once you've registered, if you scroll down my friends, you can click on their profile then click "Add Friend" if you want them on your list.'

'Sounds simple enough. I'll go and give it a try. Who are your friends?'

'All sorts of people, Debs, Lorna, a lot of our local friends.'

'Anyone from the past? School? University?'

'A couple,' said Cait as she turned her face away slightly and began to fiddle with some bits of paper. She was as cool as a cucumber. Who'd have thought it? Had she been lying about other things? Other people? Was this Tom fellow one of many? How would I know without confronting her?

'OK, I'll go and join on my computer. Thanks.'

'You're welcome,' said Cait. 'Jed and Sam are on there and post sometimes too. I bet they'd love to see that you've joined.'

I went to my den and to my computer. I'd made a note of her password, so I opened her page and scrolled through her list of friends until I got to the bottom. There was no sign of Tom Lewis. She'd clearly just deleted him from her list so that I wouldn't see him and question her. *Oh, Cait, no*, I thought, *no*.

41

Matt

'A familiar complaint in a relationship is that one is always the first to initiate sex and the other has to be persuaded,' said Gina in our session with her a few days after the Facebook saga.

'Or in our case, neither initiates or has to be persuaded,' said Cait. 'We both gave up a while back.'

'Ah . . . And does that work for both of you? Some couples do opt for a celibate marriage and are perfectly happy to have companionship, but it has to be mutually agreed or it can lead to resentment on the part of the one whose needs aren't being met. Matt, how do you feel about it?'

I shrugged.

'Are you interested in her sexually?' Gina persisted.

'I still find her attractive, but my sexual battery has gone flat lately.'

'Cait?' asked Gina. 'Do you still find Matt attractive?'

'I do but, if I'm honest, I haven't thought about him sexually for a long time.'

'After the initial years of early passion, sexual attraction can fade,' said Gina. 'When you've seen each other hung over, grumpy, stressed; when you've done each other's laundry, put away each other's socks, seen each other unwell and so on, it can all get comfortable. The familiarity we seek works as the ultimate passion-killer.'

'Exactly,' said Cait. 'So what do we do about it?'

'It's not going to come back overnight. I'd like you to continue with your non-sexual massage—'

'Neither of us is very good at that,' said Cait.

'Then learn,' said Gina. 'Buy a DVD, do a course. How do you think the people who do massage got good at it?'

'Right,' said Cait.

That's her told, I thought. Gina could be very direct when she wanted to be.

'But also take turns in giving each other pleasurable non-sexual things. Think about things you'd like to do with each other. For example – cook together, go for a walk, run a bath for the other and put candles in the bathroom. Whatever works to make you closer and make you each feel more cherished. I want you to think of ten things you could do that you would enjoy doing together or do for each other. Write them down, then fold up the pieces and put them in a hat and pick one out when you have time.'

'Ten?' asked Cait.

'Ten,' Gina confirmed. 'Is that OK with you, Matt? You seem very quiet today.'

I shrugged again. I wasn't in the mood for therapy. What Debs had told me had shaken me to the core and I wasn't sure what was real any more.

'Is something bothering you?' Gina asked.

I shrugged again then looked at Cait. 'What are we really doing here, Cait?'

She looked surprised by my question. 'You know why we're here. To improve our relationship and go forward in a more positive way.'

'And do you *really* want to do that?'

'Of course. Why else would I be here?'

'You tell me.'

'Has something happened since our last session?' Gina asked. 'I felt we were making such good progress but, Matt, you seem to have shut down.'

'He has. He's hardly said a word all weekend,' said Cait.

'Have you anything you want to say?' asked Gina.

I shook my head. 'Nope. Let's just do the exercise.'

I began writing, though I could feel Gina watching me.

Theatre.

Walk in the country.

Lunch in town.

Mooch around the antique markets. *We used to like doing things like that.*

Cinema in the afternoon.

Cocktails somewhere glamorous. Cait likes a bit of glitz. I wonder if she had cocktails with this Tom fellow? I felt a surge of jealousy, and with it a wave of panic followed by acute sadness. Could it be true that she had another man and all this was a sham? I glanced over at Cait to see how she was getting on. She was chewing the end of her pen and looking out of the window. Part of me wanted to confront her, but not here, not now. Another part didn't want to know.

'Finding it difficult?' asked Gina.

We both nodded.

'So open it up a bit. Maybe put in pampering treatments. Things you've never done before.'

'Like what?'

'Well it's your list not mine, but mindfulness or meditation class, a Thai massage, go on an archaeological dig, volunteer as dog walkers at the local rescue centre, go to an author talk at a local bookshop, a concert – something you can talk about afterwards but whatever interests and appeals to you both.'

'Those are great ideas,' said Cait. 'I'm going to write all those down. Matt, do you agree?'

'Whatever,' I said.

Cait sighed as if exasperated. I knew I was behaving like a truculent teenager but I couldn't help myself. It was either that or strangle her.

42

Cait

I drove home from visiting Dad at Lorna's. He'd settled in well there and he and Lorna seemed very comfortable with each other, chatting companionably out in the garden with cups of tea, the dogs at their feet. I was glad to see him happy, a little jealous too. He was my dad, not Lorna's. I brushed that aside. It was a great resolution to what had been a year of worry about him, and her too, and he was only fifteen minutes away. I could visit any time. I hadn't had a chance to get Lorna alone to tell her that it was all over with Tom, nor Debs who hadn't replied to texts I'd sent in the last week. *No matter*, I thought, *I'd tell them next time I saw them both*.

As I drove, I thought about Matt. Just as I'd felt we were making progress, he'd turned into a misery again and retreated back behind his wall. I'd tried everything – researched material for his programme and come up with some good stuff, prepared his favourite meal, bought a good bottle of wine, but all he had to say was 'umph', as though he was a hormonal teenager. Luckily we had more sessions booked with Gina and I hoped that she might be able to get him to talk about whatever was bothering him.

I got home to a quiet house and no sign of Matt. *Must be out at the gym*, I thought as I spied a note on the island. 'Gone to stay with Duncan for a few days, maybe longer. I think you know why. Matt.'

My blood ran cold and I sank onto a stool at the island. *Oh god, he knows about Tom*, I thought immediately. How did he find out? What did he know? I had to talk to him. I had to explain that nothing had happened. I reached for my mobile and called his number. My call went straight to message service.

I went to the fridge and poured a large glass of wine, then went and sat in the sitting room. I felt sick and anxious. I tried Matt's mobile again. It was still on message service. I texted. 'Matt, please call.'

I have been a fool, I thought as I tried his number a third time – *an utter, complete fool*. What should I do now? Talk to Debs? Or Lorna? No. What can they say? Both had warned me that seeing Tom would be playing with fire. Or . . . was it one of them who'd told him? They were the only people who knew. I couldn't bear to think that either of them had gone to Matt – surely not. It couldn't be. I trusted them both, my oldest friends and confidantes. I had to speak to Matt. I glanced over at a wedding photo on the bookshelf and my eyes welled up with tears. 'I am so sorry, Matt, so very sorry.'

I drank my wine and sat staring out at the back garden. I felt numb with shock, unsure what to do next. I must have sat there in a stupor for hours because I eventually became aware that the light had faded and it was late evening. I went upstairs, got into bed and tried to sleep. I longed for a few hours oblivion but that relief wouldn't come and I spent a troubled night, tossing and turning until I eventually got up and went down to make tea and feed Yoda.

The house felt so quiet, and I understood Lorna when she'd described hearing the ticking of the clock and hum of the fridge-freezer. I had no desire to do anything – not to watch TV, read a book, not even to look at animal rescue clips or do quizzes on Facebook.

I went into Matt's den. I wanted to feel his presence. I sat at his desk and noticed piles of papers, notes for his TV series. On the right, he had an in-tray. In it was a blue paper file. I reached over and opened it. On the top sheet, it said, For Cait. A Book of Lists to let you know that I do speak your language and have been listening all along.

I began to flick through the pages.

On the second page, he'd written: Things I love about you. He'd listed:

Your eyes.
Your quirky sense of humour.
Your patience.
Kind heart.
Your endless curiosity.
The way you move.
Your zest for life.
You've put up with me all these years.
You're a great wife, social secretary, cook, friend.
You're a great mother to our boys.
A great daughter to your dad.

I groaned inwardly as I read what he'd written. He'd been working on this secretly and, as I flicked further through, I saw that there were pages and pages of lists, some complete, others unfinished.

On page three, he'd written. Things that I know annoy you about me and I will change. I smiled as I read:

I don't talk things through with you.
I snore.
I'm in your way.
I keep forgetting to turn the gas off when I've cooked.
I wear my dressing gown past 9 a.m. (not lately).
I make a mess in the kitchen.
I can be grumpy.

Another page listed ideas for date nights.

Another showed a list of things to do in our retirement. I smiled when I read 'learn how to tango' then 'keep chickens' and 'get a dog for long country walks'.

He'd clearly put a lot of thought into it and even compiled an A–Z of activities. *When did he think we were going to get time to do all this?* I asked myself as I glanced down through archaeology, bird watching, cookery classes . . . on it went.

On a page midway through was a list of options of where we could live, though it appeared he was still working on this page. He'd scribbled notes in the margin: downsize, get a cottage in Devon or Somerset, a houseboat on the canal; as long as we're together it will be home. That brought a tear to my eyes.

On the last page, he'd written: it's never too late, and he'd begun a list of writers and artists who didn't start until they were older. Pablo Picasso, J. R. R. Tolkien, Frank McCourt, Mary Wesley; the list went on for three pages.

I felt moved by the thought and effort he'd put into compiling the lists. All the time I'd been ranting and raving like a harridan about him not communicating, he'd been here in his den, trying to do just that. And now he'd left home. *Oh god, what have I done?* I asked myself for the umpteenth time. I tried Matt's mobile but, once again, it went to message service. For lack of anything else to do, I decided to clean. In an attempt to bring some order back into my life where I could, I swept and dusted until every surface was gleaming. I cleared out cupboards, wiped shelves, I polished tables, washed windows until they sparkled, scoured the bathrooms, changed sheets on all the beds but still no call from Matt.

Early evening, I poured a glass of wine and went into the sitting room. I glanced over at the bookshelves on the left wall. One shelf at the bottom held all our photo albums. I hadn't looked at them in years and had deliberately avoided them since Mum and Eve died. I got up and heaved them over onto the coffee table.

I sat back on the sofa and began to turn the pages of the first one. There were photos of Mum when she was young, and seeing her kind, familiar face made me catch my breath. Bittersweet though it was, I wanted to look, see more, remember her. There she was with my brother, Mike and me, as toddlers in the garden at the old family house where she and Dad had lived for over forty years before they down-sized to their bungalow. There was a great shot of her sitting in a train somewhere on a holiday with Dad. She was great looking: high cheek-boned, beautifully dressed in a tailored suit, like one of those Christian Dior models from the 1950s with the pinched-in waists.

I turned the page and saw Mum and Dad at my wedding – in fact, all the photos from that day. Matt, Eve and I, we all looked so young. Further pages showed Matt and me with Sam and Jed when they were young. In those pictures, Mum was older, her hair grown silver, but still the twinkle there that she always had in her eyes. It was a joy being reminded what a presence she had been in our lives, in my life, but unbearable to know that she'd gone. I'd had a good relationship with her and, after my boys were born, she'd been supportive but never intrusive, and had always been there either in person when I was at the end of my tether with exhaustion or on the phone with endless advice on how best to cope.

'Today of all days, more than ever, I want to talk to you,' I said as I sipped the wine. 'I've made a mess, Mum, been an idiot, and I don't know what to do or who to turn to.' But the room remained quiet and I felt a stab to the heart, knowing that I couldn't pick up the phone and hear her voice at the other end, comforting and reassuring that, in the words of her favourite saying, 'this too will pass.'

I got up to go to the fridge for another glass of wine; once there I took out the bottle and returned with it to the sofa.

In a second album, there were photos of Eve and me. Brownie camera shots from our school days, gawky teenagers in our grey and mauve uniforms, our skirts worn too short for school but hoicked up for the photos; later, in college days, in flared jeans and cheesecloth shirts. I smiled at seeing her. 'Bloody miss you too,' I said to the album. More photos showed us at Glastonbury, in our hippie gear, velvet and lace, my hair long, plaited, Eve's feather-cut around her elfin face.

As I pored over the pages, looking at the people I'd loved best in the world and lost, I felt a quaking deep inside, then a wave beginning to build. I took a deep breath to try and contain the intensity of it, but it was coming, rising, surging its way up, unstoppable, overpowering, erupting up through my chest, my throat, destroying anything in its way, and I heard a sound come out of me like a wounded animal. I leant back on the cushions on the sofa and let the tsunami of grief do its worst. I had no strength to resist so surrendered and let it pour out. 'When you're ready,' I heard Gina say in my head as the torrent inside spilled out in ice-hot tears.

I had no idea how long I was there on the sofa but, after a while, the waves subsided, leaving my head aching and my eyes sore and swollen.

There was one more album to look at. When I opened it, there were half a lifetime's photos of Matt and me. The bright, eager man I'd met so long ago; it pained me to look at him and think he really might have gone for good. One shot showed Matt with a tiny Sam in his arms, his astonished yet overjoyed face at his first son's birth; another showed the same delight when Jed came along. As I turned the pages, I recalled sleepless nights we'd spent when the boys were unwell or frightened, Matt always there to comfort them. A photo showed him playing football with the boys out in the back garden, another with his head bent over their homework as he tried to help and guide. Anger and frustration, distance when they grew and pushed the boundaries, then the proud father at their graduation. I remembered the sagging of his shoulders and posture at the death of his father, again when his mother passed, his strong and reassuring arm around me when my mother died, and again after Eve had gone.

He'd always been there, sometimes in the background, but constantly there, watching over me, trying to gauge how best to be or what to say to make things right. How could I have thought about leaving him? He'd been my rock, my safe place, and I'd shut him out. He hadn't deserved it.

Oh god, here comes another one, I thought as I felt another tidal wave gathering deep inside. I'd thought I had no more tears but I was wrong and, in the end, I didn't even know who I was weeping for – Mum, Eve or Matt. *No wonder I kept this all in*, I thought, *it hurts like hell*. It also occurred to me that the wall I'd built to keep the pain inside, had also kept Matt out.

As the light faded in the evening, I curled up on the sofa, empty and exhausted. Yoda jumped up beside me, nestled into my chest and started purring like an old bus. It was a comfort having him there and I soon fell into a deep, dreamless sleep.

43

Cait

I woke the next morning with a throbbing head and dry mouth. I went straight to my mobile. There was still no word from Matt but there was a text from Lorna. *Tried you last night, you OK?*

I didn't want to speak to anyone; instead I found a throw and went back to the sofa and slept. When I awoke late afternoon, there were four more texts from Lorna. *Are you OK? Call me. Am worried.*

I went upstairs, showered, made a cafetiere of coffee then heard the doorbell. *Matt? No, he has his keys.* I had no desire to see anyone but, after a few minutes, I heard Lorna calling through the letterbox.

'*Cait,* it's me.'

I went to the door and let her in.

'You look awful,' she said as soon as she saw me and took in the dressing gown. 'Are you ill?'

I shook my head. 'Matt's left me.'

'Oh god, no,' she said and hugged me. 'Let's make some tea and you can tell me what's happened.'

She led me through into the kitchen and made tea and toast while I filled her in on what had happened.

'There were only two people who knew about Tom—'

'It was Debs,' said Lorna.

'Debs? How do you know? Are you sure?'

Lorna nodded. 'She called me last night. She's in pieces, very upset.'

'*She's* upset? Why did she do it? Why would she do that?'

'I think you need to ask her that.'

'Do you know what she told him?'

'Only that you'd been seeing Tom.'

I felt a sudden panic. 'Matt's not with her, is he?'

'No, of course not, Cait. He loves you, but that's why I've been trying to reach you, to warn you that Debs had told Matt. I didn't know he'd gone.'

'Do you know when she told him? Was it yesterday?'

'I think it was a week ago. She's been agonizing ever since.'

'I'll kill her, though that explains why I haven't heard from her lately, and why Matt had shut down. I couldn't understand what had happened because we'd been getting on so much better, then he suddenly became uncommunicative and moody so it's beginning to make sense. God, what a mess. I know I've been a complete idiot, but it was never real with Tom. I know that now.'

'It's always been obvious to me that you love Matt. You've just been going through a sticky patch. Tom was just a—'

'A distraction, a stupid fantasy, an escape.'

'I never for a moment thought you were going to act on it.'

'Well, Debs did, and apparently enough to go and warn Matt.'

'I know. That was bad. It wasn't her place to tell him and, believe me, she does know that. She really regrets it.'

'Why would she tell him unless she thought Matt might be up for grabs? I thought she was my friend but, not only did she betray me, I reckon she was after my husband.'

'No, surely not? She wouldn't do that.'

'Wouldn't she? You know how desperate she's been to find a man, and she's often said she'd like an older man, someone like Matt. Or do you think telling him was revenge because I didn't put her in touch with Tom?'

'Don't think about it today, Cait. Drink your tea. It's not the time; nobody's thinking straight and you don't know what was said or why. What you have to concentrate on is getting Matt to come home.'

'I know, but he won't answer my calls.'

'So go round there. Talk to him. Camp on the doorstep.'

I sank my head into my hands. I felt utterly exhausted and just wanted to sleep.

Lorna came over and rubbed my shoulders. 'Come on, Cait, you can make it right again.'

'Can I? Or is it too late?'

'It's never too late; just let him know that you do love him. I don't think we need to even question if he loves you.'

Her words made my eyes well up again and I sobbed into her shoulder. 'How do you cope with the loss of Alistair?'

'I don't,' she replied. 'The pain doesn't lessen, but somehow you get used to it and learn to live with it. Never forget, the depth of what you feel after the loss of someone is directly related to how much you loved them. The deeper the love, the deeper the pain.'

'I understand that,' I said, and told her about going through the albums yesterday.

She hugged me again and her eyes were also full of tears, but I felt comforted and hoped that she did too.

*

I set off for Duncan's a couple of hours later. *What will I say?* I asked myself as I found his flat and parked the car. Apologize? Beg? Lie on the pavement and refuse to get up until Matt agrees to come back?

I got out of the car, went over to the block where Duncan had a first-floor flat and rang the bell. Duncan appeared a few minutes later, looking bleary eyed.

'Is Matt here?'

Duncan shook his head. 'No, he's out. What's going on with you two? He won't tell me anything but he's like a bear with a sore head.'

'Do you know where he is?'

Duncan shook his head again. 'Want to come in?'

'No. Thanks. Could you ask Matt to call me?'

'Sure, but what's going on?' he asked again as I headed back to my car.

Back at home, I sat and pondered what to do next. I tried calling Matt's phone again and, the third time, he picked up. 'Matt, thank god, where are you?'

'Down by the canal.'

'What are you doing there?'

'Walking.'

'Will you come home, *please*?'

'No, Cait. I need some time alone and I think you do too.'

'I don't. I really don't. I don't know what Debs told you, but this Tom guy, he was nothing, is nothing, nothing happened.'

'So why didn't you tell me about him yourself?'

'Because . . .'

'Exactly. You may say that nothing happened, but just the fact you didn't mention him was a betrayal of sorts.'

'I didn't sleep with him, Matt.'

There was a silence at the other end. 'It's not just that, Cait. You've been saying for months now that things haven't been right between us, so it's not just Tom. I think you need to think about what you want, what you *really* want, and I'll do the same. We need to decide whether the next part of the journey is to be together or not—'

'Matt, I already know. I want to be with you. Please come home.'

'Not yet. I need some space, Cait, to think things over.'

'I found your book of lists—'

'*No.* That wasn't finished.'

'I loved it.'

'Well, things have changed a bit since I started working on that, haven't they?' I could hear the anger in his voice.

'Matt, I'm sorry.'

There was a pause then he said, 'I'm sorry too.'

The phone clicked off.

He'd sounded weary and sad. I needed to do something to bring him home, something that would let him know how much I cared, how much I knew him and what he needed and liked. Book a weekend away? A case of his favourite wine? A gym membership? No. All these things could be done later. I needed something better, a grand gesture. As I thought, I flicked through the albums that were still lying on the coffee table. Matt with Sam and Jed. An early one of Matt from before he went to college, standing proudly, a black Alsatian at his side. Rex, his dog. An idea popped into my head. *That could work*, I thought. It would bring Matt home, I had no doubt about it.

44

Cait

I spent the next few days on websites searching. I gave Matt his space and, in turn, he didn't contact me. On the Friday morning, I found what I'd been looking for. A black Alsatian. Bertie. Four years old. I picked up the phone to talk to the animal centre and set off half an hour later.

After an interview and filling in applications at the rescue centre, Sally, the chubby redhead at the desk, asked which dog I was interested in.

'Bertie, the Alsatian,' I said.

Sally's face fell. 'Oh, but he's gone. I am so sorry. His details mustn't have been updated on the website.'

I felt so disappointed and got up to leave.

'If it's definitely an Alsatian you're after, we have had a new fellow come in yesterday,' said Sally. 'His owner died and there was no one to take him. He's not a black one, he's gold and brown. Would you like to take a look?'

No harm in looking, I thought, though I'd had my heart set on getting one that looked as close to Rex as I could find. I followed Sally through to the kennels at the back of the centre. Some of the dogs barked in greeting as we walked past, others sat at the back of their area on a blanket staring out at us.

Sally stopped at a kennel on the corner. 'Here he is,' she said. 'Come on, Charlie.'

I looked in to glimpse the saddest face I'd ever seen. He was curled up at the back on a blanket and raised his head to see who'd come to look at him, then sank his head back between his paws.

'How old is he?' I asked.

'He's three, and not taking too well to being in kennels, but then none of them like being locked up.'

She opened the cage and we stepped in. 'Just go easy with him,' said Sally. 'He's a friendly boy, just a bit puzzled and sad about where he is at the moment.'

I put down my bag and sat on the floor next to him. He looked up at me then slumped down again, so I gave his head a stroke. He reached out a paw up onto my leg and his tail wagged a millimetre.

'I think he likes you,' said Sally. 'I'll leave you to get to know each other and be back in a while.'

She left me with Charlie and I leant up against the back wall of the kennel and just let Charlie be. After a few moments, he looked up at me and I stroked his head again. 'You had a rough time lately, Charlie? Me too, but we could be friends, look after each other.'

He continued to regard me with serious brown eyes and nudged a bit closer so that his body was slumped against the length of my legs. I reached down and put my arm around him, and there we stayed until Sally came back.

'I think he's the one,' I said as she came into the kennel.

Her face lit up. 'That's fantastic; he's got a very gentle nature and all any of our dogs want is to be loved. We'd have to come out to your home to check out accessibility and so on.'

'That's fine,' I said. 'We have a garden, our kids have gone, we're on a quiet street, and both my husband and I will have time to walk him. He's away at the moment, but he's a true animal lover. I know he'll adore Charlie when he meets him.'

'Sounds ideal,' said Sally.

When we got outside the cage, I looked back inside, then suddenly Charlie stood up. I'd left my handbag in there, and Charlie trotted over to it, picked it up in his mouth and brought it to the door.

Sally opened the kennel and took the bag from him. 'Good boy,' she said, and Charlie wagged his tail and looked at me imploringly as if to say, *hey, where are you going? Get me out of here.*

'I will, Charlie, don't you worry,' I said. As I walked away, I heard a small yelp as if to say, *come back.* 'I won't be long. I promise.'

*

A week later, the animal centre had done the checks and Charlie was in the passenger seat in my car. I opened the window and he put his head out, as if to breathe in his freedom. When he turned to look at me, I could have sworn that he was smiling.

I drove straight to Duncan's flat and, once there, I sent Matt a text from the car. *Am at the front door, please come down.*

Luckily, he was in, and appeared a few minutes later. I felt overwhelmingly pleased to see him and, despite what had happened, he looked happy to see me too and . . . there was something else too, a frisson of attraction, the old chemistry we'd had but hadn't felt for so long.

'How are you?' I asked.

He shrugged a shoulder. 'OK. You?'

'You look well, trim.' He did. He'd lost even more weight and it had taken years off him as well as pounds.

'And you look . . . what is it?' He searched my face. 'Rested.'

I smiled. 'I've managed to get some sleep at last. Some days I haven't even got out of my dressing gown until past eleven.'

Matt smiled back at me. 'Good, I'm glad.'

'I miss you,' I said. One day I'd tell him about finally grieving for Mum and Eve, how it had felt, the fear of it, the eventual giving in to it, the utter exhaustion of it . . . but not today.

He nodded. 'Me too, Cait—'

'Before you say anything else, I have a confession to make.'

'Another?'

I nodded and couldn't help grinning. 'I have someone else in my life now.'

'*What?*' Matt was about to step back inside and close the door, but I stopped him. 'He's in the car. Let me get him.'

'Oh Cait, *no*—' Matt called after me.

'Back in a minute. It's not what you think.'

A few moments later, I was back at the door with Charlie at my side.

Matt looked bewildered. 'Who's this?' He looked down at Charlie, who was gazing back up at him. Matt bent over to stroke him and Charlie put up a paw and wagged his tail.

'This is Charlie. He's for you. You said you wanted a dog. Don't worry, I won't push you, and if you don't want him, I'll have him. I've already fallen in love with him.'

Matt looked up at the building behind him. 'But I can't have a dog in a flat . . .' he said, then he smiled slowly as he realized.

'Exactly,' I said.

45

Cait

'Thanks again for having Dad,' I said as Lorna and I walked the three dogs, Otis, Angus and Charlie, in Victoria Park.

'No need. I really like having him around,' she said, 'and he's great with the dogs. They both adore him already, and it's good that he's on site because he can direct the workers as to exactly what he wants in his part of the house. I think the arrangement's going to work well. What about you? Now that Matt's back, are you going to stay in the house?'

I shook my head. 'We're selling up and going to move a short distance out of town – not far, we love Bath but we'll get somewhere smaller and release some money at the same time. And what about the tip man?'

'Patrick? We've been out for a drink. I like him, and it'll work for the occasional outing to the theatre or whatever. I don't want any more than that and I don't think he does either, but it's early days. Have you heard from Debs?'

'She's texted, called and emailed but I haven't replied. I'm not ready. A card came from her with the word "sorry" written about fifty times. Have you?'

Lorna nodded. 'I have. She's gone travelling. A few days ago, she packed her bags and she's gone to visit Ollie in America.'

'For how long?'

'She didn't say. She said she was mortified about what had happened and couldn't face us for a while, so she's going to go away and try and make peace with herself and the world.'

'Sounds like Debs and I'm glad she's gone. I can't face her either. Not yet, maybe never. What about the spa?'

'She has a good manager there who can look after it. Maybe when she gets back you'll feel differently.'

'Maybe. I doubt it. We could never be friends as we were.'

'She recognizes that she could have been more supportive and sensitive to what you were going through. People make mistakes, Cait. I think she knows she did.'

'I know.' Debs wasn't the only one who'd made mistakes. I thought about all the stupidity in my head over Tom. 'I won't rule her out.'

Lorna raised her glass. 'Good. Just as marriages go through rough patches, so do friendships. And what about Tom? Have you heard from him?'

'Not a dickie bird, and that's fine by me. I doubt if I'll ever hear from him again.'

'And Matt?'

'He's doing great. He has a meeting this afternoon about the TV series he was working on.'

'Back to work?'

'Maybe. In the meantime, he and Charlie have become firm friends.'

'What about Yoda?'

'He wasn't too pleased at first, but they're working it out. Every time Charlie goes near him, he biffs him on the nose, so he's soon learnt who's boss in the house.'

Lorna put her arm around me and gave me a squeeze. 'And the river flows on,' she said.

I nodded. 'And the river flows on.'

46

Matt

'Matt,' said Bruce Patterson as we took our seats in a pub near his office. 'I've read the proposal for the retirement series and shown it to the team. It's had a unanimous thumbs-up.'

'That's great news.'

'More than that, I've shown it to my contact at the network. They love it and want to commission the series so we can pay you for your time and work so far. Of course, we'll need you to oversee to ensure it's exactly how you've envisaged.'

'Me?'

'Of course, it was always the deal that you got the gig if we got a commission. It will be full on, but you're used to that.'

'I'm sorry, Bruce, but this is as far as I go. I'm happy for you to use the material, more than happy, and could act as consultant in the background if you like, but the rest of it, not for me.'

'Not for you? But I'm saying the job's yours.'

'A few months ago I'd have done anything to hear the words you just said, but things have changed.'

'This could be big, Matt. There's potential for all sorts of follow-ups, maybe a book to accompany the series.'

'I hope it will be big, but not for me.'

'Why ever not?'

'New chapter in my life.'

'Ah. Another project?'

'Nope.'

'What then?'

I laughed. 'I never thought I'd say these words voluntarily: thanks for the job offer, but I've retired.'

*

After supper that evening, I'd just settled down to watch the news with my new faithful companion Charlie at my feet and Yoda curled up on the sofa arm, keeping a watchful eye, when Cait appeared at the door. She was wearing a figure-hugging, black lace nightdress. Very tasteful, very nice. She put her right arm above her head and seductively pressed herself along one side of the doorframe.

''Allo sexy monsieur. You fancy early night?' she asked, in an appalling attempt at a French accent. I sat up immediately and noticed that she was also wearing Jed's old pair of flippers from his snorkelling days. I remembered her telling me that she'd found them under his bed a while ago. *Interesting combo*, I thought as I burst out laughing, but that was Cait; she turned me on, she made me laugh, and I never knew what she was going to do next.

'An early night. Hmm? I think I do.'

Reverting back to her normal accent, she asked, 'Or we've got a new box set if you're not in the mood.'

'Oh no, no box set. See you up there in five minutes.'

'Great, and bring the blood-pressure machine. With what I've got in mind for you, we're probably going to need it.'

I laughed again. We were going to be OK.

Acknowledgements

With many thanks to:

My agents Chris Little and Emma Schlesinger for their constant support, encouragement and making me laugh a lot.

To my editor Kate Bradley for coming all the way to Bath to discuss books, for her incisive feedback and comments through the various drafts and for being the best of company.

To Claire Ward for coming up with another fabulous cover.

To all the team at Harper for getting behind the book with such enthusiasm.

Lastly to my husband Steve for his constant willingness to brainstorm ideas and characters and for being a great sounding board, it's much appreciated.

Matt's A – Z of Activities for Retirement

A: art, aerobics, amateur dramatics (acting), archery, kite flying, abseiling, archeology, architecture, athletics, allotment.

B: book club, bird-watching, baking, badminton, ballooning, ballet, batik, bead work, boxing, brass band, basket ball, bowls, bridge.

C: cinema, cycling, cookery classes, choir, croquet, climbing, canoeing, clay pigeon shooting, cartooning, cake decorating, calligraphy, circus arts, crochet, candle making, computer skills, cricket, card games.

D: dancing, dog walking, dress making, darts, diving.

E: exploring new places, embroidery, etching, Egyptian dance.

F: feng shui, flower arranging, friends, fencing, film club, fashion, folk dance.

G: golf, gardening, gym, gliding, guided walks.

H: holidays, hand-gliding, horse riding, hiking, hip hop, history, hockey.

I: illustrating, interior design.

J: jiu jitsu, judo, jewelry making, jazz.

K: knitting, karate, kayaking, kite flying, kazoo.

L: languages, learning a new skill, life drawing, lace making, landscape design, literature, lacrosse.

M: music, mountain biking, Morris dancing, murals, mosaics, martial arts, meditation, mindfulness.

N: National Trust, narrow boating, needlework, netball.

O: opera, origami, Open University.

P: photography, pottery, pub crawls, paint-balling, pony trekking, painting, playwriting, poetry, printmaking, puppetry, philosophy.

Q: Quoits, quiz nights, quilt making, quad biking.

R: running, reading groups, rambling, rowing, rounders, rugby.

S: salsa, sculpture, sailing, swimming, sewing, studying, school governor, snorkeling, surfing, snowboarding, skiing, sledging, scuba diving, soap making, spinning, storytelling, singing, song writing, skating, snooker, swing dance.

T: theatre, travel, tennis, table tennis, tap dancing, Tai Chi, tango.

U: University of the Third Age, ukulele.

V: volunteer work, video games, vegetable growing.

W: walking, writing, water skiing, white water rafting, windsurfing, watercolour painting, weaving, woodcarving, wrestling, wine making, wine tasting.

X: xylopyrography (the art or technique of producing a picture or design on a piece of wood by burning it with a heated, pointed instrument).

Y: yoga, yachting.

Z: zzzzzing, Zorbing (rolling down hill inside an orb), zithering (a zither is a musical instrument).

It's never too late!

Matt's list of a small number of the people
who have achieved their dreams after 50

- Mary Wesley wrote ten bestsellers including *The Camomile Lawn* after she was 70.
- Cezanne had his first one-man exhibition when he was 56.
- Daniel Defoe wrote *Robinson Crusoe*, his first novel, at 60.
- Patrick O'Brian only hit his stride as a writer with his *Master and Commander* sea stories when he was 65.
- Colonel Harland Sanders established the Kentucky Fried Chicken restaurant chain in his sixties.
- James Parkinson identified Parkinson's disease at 62, and at 63 Polish countess, Rosa Branicka, helped to develop surgical techniques for breast cancer by operating on herself.
- Coco Chanel ruled a fashion empire at 85.
- Priscilla Sitienei, a great-great-grandmother and former midwife in Kenya, enrolled in primary school at the age of 90.
- At 92, Marjorie Liggins from Sheffield married her 86-year-old dancing partner, Norman Camm.
- Laura Ingalls Wilder began writing the popular *Little House on the Prairie* books at 65.
- Estelle Getty achieved fame in *The Golden Girls* at 63.

- Billy Hopkins wrote his best-selling novel, *Our Kid*, at the age of 70.
- Fauja Singh ran his first marathon at 89.
- Grandma Moses became a folk-artist and cultural icon at 78.
- Harry Bernstein became a successful author at the age of 96.
- Hardinge Giffard, 1st Earl of Halsbury, sat down to pen a twenty-volume encyclopaedia of English law when he was 90.
- The oldest male and female Oscar winners are Jessica Tandy, at the age of 80, and Christopher Plummer, aged 82.
- The oldest person to become Prime Minister was Lord Palmerston at the age of 71.
- Singer Dame Vera Lynn made British chart history by becoming the oldest living artist to reach the Top 20. At the age of 97, The Forces' Sweetheart entered the UK's Official Album Chart at number 13.
- The oldest woman to complete a marathon was Gladys Burrill from Hawaii, who was 92 years old.
- Retired Lt Col James C Warren became the world's oldest person to receive his pilot's licence at the age of 87.
- Bertha Wood, born in 1905, had her first book, *Fresh Air and Fun: The Story of a Blackpool Holiday Camp* published on her 100th birthday on 20th June 2005. The book is based on her memoirs, which she began writing at the age of 90.
- John Glenn made history when, at the age of 77, he became the oldest person to travel in space.
- Frank McCourt, author of *Angela's Ashes*, became a best-selling author at 66.

- Actor Ronald Reagan became the 40th American President at the age of 70.
- Peter Roget invented the Thesaurus at age 73.
- In 1979, at age 69, Mother Teresa received the Nobel Peace Prize for her work.

Discover more gloriously funny and uplifting fiction from Cathy Hopkins

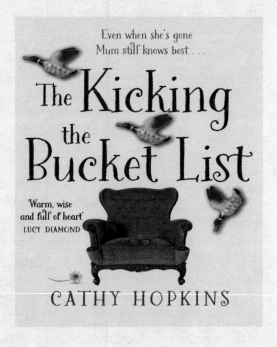

Warm, wise and full of heart . . .
I absolutely loved this book' Lucy Diamond